THE WILD GIRL

Also by Kate Forsyth

Bitter Greens

THE WILD GIRL

Kate Forsyth

Thomas Dunne Books
St. Martin's Press
New York

THOMAS DUNNE BOOKS.
An imprint of St. Martin's Press.

THE WILD GIRL. Copyright © 2013 by Kate Forsyth. All rights reserved. Printed in the United States of America. For information, address St. Martin's Press, 175 Fifth Avenue, New York, N.Y. 10010.

www.thomasdunnebooks.com
www.stmartins.com

Library of Congress Cataloging-in-Publication Data

Forsyth, Kate, 1966–
    The wild girl : a novel / Kate Forsyth. — First U.S edition.
        p. cm.
    ISBN 978-1-250-04754-0 (hardcover)
    ISBN 978-1-4668-4784-2 (e-book)
1. Romance fiction. I. Title.
    PR9619.3.F59W55 2015
823'.914—dc23

2015011780

St. Martin's Press books may be purchased for educational, business, or promotional use. For information on bulk purchases, please contact the Macmillan Corporate and Premium Sales Department at 1-800-221-7945, extension 5442, or write to specialmarkets@macmillan.com.

First published in Australia by Vintage, an imprint of Random House Pty Ltd

Previously published in Great Britain by Allison & Busby Limited

First U.S Edition: July 2015

10   9   8   7   6   5   4   3   2   1

For my darling husband, Greg,
the Amen of my Universe

'Every fairy tale had a bloody lining. Every one had teeth and claws.'

– Alice Hoffman

FOREWORD

The fairy tales collected and rewritten by the Grimm brothers in the early part of the nineteenth century have spread far and wide in the past two hundred years, inspiring many novels, poems, operas, ballets, films, cartoons and advertisements.

Most people imagine the brothers as elderly men in medieval costume, travelling around the countryside asking for tales from old women bent over their spinning wheels, or wizened shepherds tending their flocks. The truth is that they were young men in their twenties, living at the same time as Jane Austen and Lord Byron.

It was a time of war and tyranny and terror. Napoléon Bonaparte was seeking to rule as much of the world as he could, and the small German kingdom in which the brothers lived was one of the first to fall. Poverty-stricken, and filled with nationalistic zeal, Jakob and Wilhelm Grimm – the elder brothers of a family of six – decided to collect and save the old tales of princesses and goose girls, lucky fools and unlucky princes, poisonous apples and dangerous rose-briars, hungry witches and murderous sausages that had once been told and retold in houses both small and grand all over the land.

The Grimms were too poor to travel far from home; besides, the countryside was wracked by repeated waves of fighting as the great powers struggled back and forth over the German landscape. Luckily, Jakob and Wilhelm were to find a rich source of storytelling among the young women of their acquaintance. One of them, Dortchen Wild, grew up right next door.

This is her story.

CONTENTS

PROLOGUE

Briar Hedge

CASSEL

The Electorate of Hessen-Cassel, December 1814

And the maiden changed herself into a rose which stood in the midst of a briar hedge, and her sweetheart Roland into a fiddler. It was not long before the witch came striding up towards them, and said: 'Dear musician, may I pluck that flower for myself?' 'Oh, yes,' he replied, 'I will play to you while you do it.' As the witch crept into the hedge and reached to pluck the flower, he began to play, and she was forced to dance. The faster he played, the faster she danced, and the thorns tore her clothes from her body, pricking and wounding her till she bled. As he did not stop playing, the witch had to dance till she lay dead on the ground.

From 'Sweetheart Roland', a tale told by Dortchen Wild to Wilhelm Grimm on 19th January 1812

'Wild by name and wild by nature,' Dortchen's father used to say of her. He did not mean it as a compliment. He thought her headstrong, and so he set himself to tame her.

The day Dortchen Wild's father died, she went to the forest, winter-bare and snow-frosted, so no one could see her dancing with joy. She went to the place where she had last been truly happy, the grove of old linden trees in the palace garden. Tearing off her black bonnet, she flung it into the tangled twigs, and drew off her gloves, shoving them in her coat pocket. Holding out her bare hands, embracing the cold winter wind, Dortchen spun alone among the linden trees, her black skirts swaying.

Snow lay thick upon the ground. The lake's edges were slurred with ice. The only colour was the red rosehips in the briar hedge, and the golden windows of the palace. Violin music lilted into the air, and shadows twirled past the glass panes.

It was Christmas Day. All through Cassel, people were dancing and feasting. Dortchen remembered the Christmas balls Jérôme Bonaparte had held during his seven-year reign as king. A thousand guests had waltzed till dawn, their faces hidden behind masks. Wilhelm I, the Kurfürst of Hessen, had won back his throne from the French only a little over a year ago. He would not celebrate Christmas so extravagantly. Soon the lights would be doused and the music would fade away, and he and his court would go sensibly to bed, to save on the cost of lamp oil.

Dortchen must dance while she could.

She lifted her black skirts and twirled in the snow. *He's dead*, she sang to herself. *I'm free!*

Three ravens flew through the darkening forest, wings ebony-black against the white snow. Their haunting call chilled her. She came to a standstill, surprised to find she was shaking with tears as much as with cold. She caught hold of a thorny branch to steady herself. Snow showered over her.

I will never be free . . .

Dortchen was so cold that she felt as if she were made of ice. Looking down, she realised she had cut herself on the rose thorns. Blood dripped into the snow. She sucked the cut, and the taste of her blood filled her mouth, metallic as biting a bullet.

The sun was sinking away behind the palace, and the violin music came to an end. Dortchen did not want to go home, but it was not safe in the forest at night. She picked up her bonnet and began trudging back home, to the rambling old house above her father's apothecary shop, where his corpse lay in his bedroom, swollen and stinking, waiting for her to wash it and lay it out.

The town was full of revellers. It was the first Christmas since Napoléon had been defeated and banished. Carol-singers in long red gowns stood on street corners, singing harmonies. A chestnut-seller was selling paper cones of hot chestnuts to the crowd clustered about his little fire, while potmen sold mugs of hot cider and mulled wine. All the young women were dressed in British red and Russian green and Prussian blue, trimmed with military frogging and golden braid – a vast change from the previous year, when all had worn the high-waisted white favoured by the Empress Joséphine. Dortchen's severe black dress and bonnet made her look like a hooded crow among a vast flock of gaudy parrots.

At last she came to the Marktgasse, lit up with dancing light from a huge bonfire. Not one building matched another, crowded together all higgledy-piggledy around the cobblestoned square with its old pump and drinking trough outside the inn.

Only the apothecary's shop was dark and shuttered, with no welcoming light above its door. Dortchen made her way through crowds buying sugar-roasted almonds, gingerbread hearts, wooden toys and small gilded angels at the market stalls. She slipped into the alley that ran down the side of the shop to its garden, locked away behind high walls.

'Dortchen,' a low voice called from the shadowy doorway opposite the garden gate.

She turned, hands clasped painfully tight together.

A tall, lean figure in black stepped out of the doorway. The light from the square flickered over the strong, spare bones of his face, making hollows of his eyes and cheeks.

'I've been waiting for you,' Wilhelm said. 'No one knew where you had gone.'

'I went to the forest,' she answered.

Wilhelm nodded. 'I thought you would.' He put his arms about her, drawing her close.

For a moment Dortchen resisted, but she was so cold and tired that she could not withstand the comfort of his touch. She rested her cheek on his chest and heard the thunder of his heart.

A ragged breath escaped her. 'He's dead,' she said. 'I can hardly believe it.'

'I know, I heard the news. I'm sorry.'

'I'm not.'

He did not answer. She knew she had grieved him. The death of Wilhelm's father had been the first great sorrow of his life; he and his brother Jakob had worked hard ever since to be all their father would have wanted. It was different for Dortchen, though. She had not loved her father.

'You're free now,' he said, his voice so low it could scarcely be heard over the laughter and singing of the crowd in the square.

Dortchen had to look away. 'It doesn't change anything. There's nothing left for me, not a single thaler.'

'Wouldn't Rudolf—'

15

Dortchen made a restless movement at the mention of her brother. 'There's not much left for him either. All the wars . . . and then my father's illness . . . Well, Rudolf's close to ruin as it is.'

There was a long silence. In the space between them were all the words Wilhelm could not say. *I am too poor to take a wife . . . I earn so little at my job at the library . . . I cannot ask Jakob to feed another mouth when he has to support all six of us . . .*

The failure of their fairy tale collection was a disappointment to him, Dortchen knew. Wilhelm had worked so hard, pinning all his hopes to it. If only it had been better received . . . If only it had sold more . . .

'I'm so sorry.' He bent his head and kissed her.

Dortchen drew away and shook her head. 'I can't . . . We mustn't . . .' He gave a murmur deep in his throat and tried to kiss her again. She wrenched herself out of his arms. 'Wilhelm, I can't . . . It hurts too much.'

He caught her and drew her back, and she did not have the strength to resist him. Once again his mouth found hers, and she succumbed to the old magic. Desire quickened between them. Her arms were about his neck, their cold lips opening hungrily to each other. His hand slid down to find the curve of her waist, and she drew herself up against him. His breath caught. He turned and pressed her against the stone wall, his hands trying to find the shape of her within her heavy black gown.

Dortchen let herself forget the dark years that gaped between them, pretending that she was once more just a girl, madly in love with the boy next door.

The church bells rang out, marking the hour. She remembered she was frozen to the bone, and that her father's dead body lay on the far side of the wall.

'It's no use,' she whispered, pulling herself out of Wilhelm's arms. It felt like she was tearing away living flesh. 'Please, Wilhelm . . . don't make it harder.'

He held her steady, bending his head so his forehead met hers. 'Our time will come.'

She shook her head. 'It's too late.'

'Don't say that. I cannot bear it, Dortchen. It'll never be too late. I love you – you know that I do. Someday, somehow, we'll be together.'

She sighed and tried once more to draw away. He gripped her forearms and said, in a low, intense voice, 'I've been reading Novalis. Do you remember? He said the most beautiful thing about love. It's given me new faith, Dortchen.'

'What did he say?' she asked, wanting to believe, if only for a minute.

'Love works magic,' Wilhelm said. 'It is the final purpose of the world story, the "Amen" of the universe.'

She caught her breath in a sob and reached up to kiss him. For a long moment, the world stilled around them. Dortchen thought of nothing but the feel of his arms about her, his mouth on hers. But then the bonfire in the square flared up, sending the shadows racing away, and a great drunken cheer sounded out. Dortchen stepped back. 'I must go.'

'Must you?' He tried to hold her still so he could kiss her again.

She turned her face away. 'Wilhelm, we can't do this any more,' she said to the stones in the wall. 'I . . . I need to make some kind of life for myself.'

He took a deep, unhappy breath. 'What will you do?'

'I'll keep house for Rudolf, I suppose. And help my sisters. There's always work for Aunty Dortchen.' Her voice was bitter. At twenty-one years of age, she was an old maid, all her hopes of love and romance turned to ashes.

'There must be a way. If the fairy tales would sell just a few more copies . . .' His voice died away. They both knew that he would need to sell many thousands more before they could ever dream of being together.

'One day people will recognise how wonderful the stories are,' she said.

He took her hand and bent before her, pressing his mouth into her palm. She drew away from him, turning to the gate in the wall. She was shivering so hard she could scarcely lift the latch. She glanced back and saw him watching her, a tall, still shadow among shadows.

Happy endings are only for fairy tales, Dortchen thought, stepping through to her father's walled garden. She raised her hand to dash away her tears. *These days, there's no use in wishing.*

PART ONE

Into the Dark Forest

CASSEL

The Holy Roman Empire of the German Nation, 1805–1806

So they walked for a long time and finally came to the middle of the great forest. There the father made a big fire and the mother says: 'Sleep for a while, children, we want to go into the forest and look for wood, wait till we come back.' The children sat down next to the fire, and each one ate its little piece of bread. They wait a long time until night falls, but the parents don't come back.

From 'Hänsel and Gretel', a tale thought to have been told by Dortchen Wild to Wilhelm Grimm before 1810

LANTERN IN THE NIGHT

October 1805

Dortchen Wild fell in love with Wilhelm Grimm the first time she saw him.

She was only twelve years old, but love has never been something that can be constrained by age. It happened in the way of old tales, in an instant, changing everything forever. It was a fork in the path, the turn of a key, the kindling of a lantern.

That afternoon, Dortchen had gone with her friend Lotte to visit Lotte's aunt, Henriette Zimmer, who was a lady-in-waiting to the Princess Wilhelmine. They had been accompanied by Lotte's mother, Frau Grimm, and three of her brothers, Karl, Ferdinand and Ludwig. It was a long walk back to the Marktgasse from the vast green park of the palace, but no one suggested hiring a carriage. The Grimms were poor, and Dortchen certainly had no money in her purse. It was both scary and wonderful to walk through the forest at twilight, imagining wolves and witches and bears and other wild beasts lurking in the shadows.

'Look at Herkules,' Lotte said. 'He's all lit up by the sun.'

Dortchen turned and walked backward, staring back up at the palace, square and grand on its low hill, with six heavy columns holding up a great stone pediment. On the crest of the mountain behind was an octagonal building of turreted stone, surmounted by a pyramid on which stood the immense statue of Herkules, symbol of the Kurfürst's power. As the sun

21

slid down behind the western horizon, Herkules sank back into shadow. Light drained away from the sky.

'Hurry up, girls!' Frau Grimm called. 'It'll be dark soon.'

Supper, Dortchen thought. She turned forward again and quickened her steps. 'I mustn't be late or Father will be angry.'

'He won't mind once he knows you've been with us, surely,' Lotte said.

Dortchen did not like to say that her father did not approve of the Grimm family. There were far too many boys for his comfort, and, besides, they were as poor as church mice. Herr Wild had six girls to settle comfortably.

The shadowy forest gave way to parkland, then the long, straight road ran between wide plots of gardens, each confined behind stone walls, the gateposts carved with the initials of the owners' long-dead ancestors. They approached Dortchen's family's garden plot, where she had been meant to spend all afternoon, weeding and hoeing. She ran in and caught up her basket and gardening gloves, then hurried to catch up with Lotte, who turned to wait for her, one hand clamped to her bonnet.

The road led inside the medieval walls, the cobbles bruising Dortchen's feet. The jutting eaves and chimneys and turrets of the buildings were dark against a luminous sky. The first star shone out, and Dortchen thought, *I wish . . .*

She hardly knew how to frame the words. She longed to have someone of her own to love – a friend, a twin, a soulmate. She glanced at Lotte, at her thin face and the curly dark hair so unlike Dortchen's, which was thick and fair and straight. Lotte was only thirteen days older than Dortchen. Almost close enough to be twins. They had both been born in May 1793, the year that the King and Queen of France had their heads chopped off and the people of Paris had danced in streets puddled with blood.

Dortchen had always been fascinated by the story of Maria Antonia of Austria, who had become Marie Antoinette of France. She sometimes imagined herself as a beautiful young queen, dressed in white, dragged to the guillotine through a jeering crowd. In her daydream, Dortchen was rescued at the last moment by a daring band of masked heroes, led by a handsome stranger with a flashing sword. He threw her over the saddle of his horse and galloped away through the crowd, and the guillotine was left thirsty.

She wondered if Lotte ever imagined herself a condemned queen, a girl in a story.

Warm light spilt from the upper windows. The smell of cooking made Dortchen's stomach growl and her pulse quicken in anxiety. 'Let's hurry – I'm hungry.'

'I'm always hungry,' Lotte said. 'And all we have to eat is sausages. Sausages, sausages, every day.'

'It's better than stone soup, which is what I'll get if I'm home late.'

The small party reached the Königsplatz, its six avenues radiating out like the spokes of a wheel. In the centre of the square was a marble statue of the Kurfürst's father, the Landgrave Frederick, famous for having sent hundreds of Hessian soldiers to die fighting for Great Britain in the American Revolution.

'Did you know that there's an echo here?' Dortchen told Lotte. 'If you shout, you'll hear your voice bounce back six times.' She stood in the centre and demonstrated, much to the amazement of Lotte's three brothers, who at once came to stand beside her to test the echo too.

'*Ja!*' they shouted.

Back came the faint echo: *Ja, ja, ja, ja, ja, ja.*

'*Ja! Ja!*'

Ja, ja, ja, ja, ja, ja . . .

The church bells rang out and Dortchen remembered the time. 'Come on, I'm late. Father will skin me alive!' Catching Lotte's hand, she ran down the cobblestoned avenue that led through the crooked houses towards the Marktgasse. The gables shut out the last of the light, so they ran through shadows, with only the occasional gleam of candlelight through a shutter showing the way.

They burst out into the Marktgasse, the three Grimm boys racing past them, Lotte's stout mother panting behind. Dortchen saw at once that the windows of her father's shop were dark, and he had hung the quail's cage out the upstairs window. Her spirits sank.

A lantern bobbed across the square towards them. Behind it were two young men, dark shapes in long coats and tall hats. They strode up to Frau Grimm, arms spread in greeting. 'Mother, where have you been?' the younger one asked in mock reproof. 'We got home to a dark, cold house and an empty larder.'

'Jakob, Wilhelm, you're here at last.' Frau Grimm embraced them warmly.

'It's my other brothers.' Lotte ran forward to greet them, and Dortchen followed shyly. In the glow of the lamp, she saw two young men, both thin and dark and shabbily dressed. The elder of the two had a serious face, with straight hair hanging past his ears. The younger was the more handsome, with pale skin, hollow cheeks and wavy dark curls. He laughed at Lotte and swung her around by the hands.

Dortchen forgot about her father, forgot about being late, forgot to breathe. The world tilted, then righted itself.

'Lotte, not so wild! You're not a little girl any more,' the elder brother reproved her. Dortchen knew that he was named Jakob and that he was twenty years old, for Lotte had spoken often about her clever brothers.

'Don't scold, Jakob,' Lotte protested. 'I haven't seen you in such an age.'

Frau Grimm patted his shoulder. 'Look at you, so tall and manly. We've been so worried. What took you so long?'

'Professor von Savigny and I had to come the long way, through Metz,' Jakob replied. 'Strasbourg is full of French soldiers.'

'The Grand Army is on the move again? I thought Napoléon was all set to invade England,' Ferdinand said. He was the fourth of the five Grimm sons, seventeen years old, with the family's dark hair and thin, sensitive face.

'I guess he's changed his mind,' Jakob replied drily.

'Do they march against Austria?' eighteen-year-old Karl demanded.

'I suppose it was to be expected,' nineteen-year-old Wilhelm said. 'Austria did invade Bavaria, after all.'

'The French move so swiftly,' Jakob said. 'Napoléon left Paris after us, yet overtook us on the road. They say he drove for fifty-eight hours, only stopping to change his horses. The ostlers had to throw water over the carriage wheels to stop them from melting.'

'You saw the Emperor? What is he like? Is it true he's a dwarf?' Ludwig asked. At fifteen, he was the youngest Grimm brother and three years older than Lotte.

'He's not tall by any means, but one hardly notices. There's such a presence about him. His eyes, they're full of fire . . .' Jakob's voice trailed off.

'What about the Empress? Was she very beautiful? Are her dresses as shocking as they say?' Lotte wanted to know.

'Indeed, I'd be sorry to see you emulating her clothes, as half of Europe seems to do. If you can call a few wisps of muslin "clothes". As for beautiful – she wears so much rouge you cannot see her skin at all!'

'I wish I could have gone with you to Paris,' Wilhelm interjected. 'It was lonely at university without you.'

'I'm glad to be back with you all again,' Jakob said. 'Stimulating as Paris was.'

'We're glad to have you back too,' Ludwig said. 'Although you'll miss the house at Steinau. We're all very cramped here in Cassel.'

'We were cramped in Marburg too, I assure you,' Wilhelm said. 'At least it's not so hilly here. At Marburg, we had to climb hundreds of steps every day just to get around. And sometimes you'd walk in through the front door of a house and find yourself on the top floor!'

Dortchen waited for a chance to say her farewells. She was eager to get to the safety of the kitchen before her father noticed her absence, yet she found their talk of the outside world fascinating.

Wilhelm sensed Dortchen's eyes on him and glanced her way. 'But who is this? A friend of yours, Lottechen?'

'Oh, that's one of the Wild girls,' Karl said. 'There's a whole horde of them across the way.'

'It's Dortchen,' Lotte said. 'Dortchen Wild. She lives above the apothecary's there.' She waved her hand at the dark shop, with its mortar and pestle sign hanging outside.

'It's a pleasure to meet you, Dortchen. Is that a love name for Dorothea?' When Dortchen nodded shyly, Wilhelm went on. 'One of my favourite names. My mother's name, you know.'

'It's really Henriette Dorothea,' Dortchen said. 'But no one calls me that.'

'It's a very pretty name, both the long and the short versions,' he answered, smiling.

'What about Charlotte?' his sister demanded. 'Isn't that your favourite?'

'I like them both. Two very pretty names.'

Dortchen felt heat rising in her cheeks. 'I have to go. Thank you for taking me to afternoon tea, Frau Grimm. Bye, Lotte.' She hurried down the alley that divided her father's shop from the building in which the Grimms rented an apartment. Within seconds she was hidden in darkness, but she could hear the conversation of the Grimm family behind her.

'She seems very nice,' Wilhelm said. 'How lovely to have some girls living right next door, Lotte.'

'I hope they are sensible, hard-working girls, not like those silly friends of yours in Steinau,' Jakob added.

'Their father is very strict and keeps them close,' Frau Grimm said.

'She's very pretty,' Wilhelm said.

Dortchen smiled and clasped his words to her like something small and precious.

OLD MARIE

October 1805

Dortchen hurried through the gate in the wall and into the garden. A cobbled path led between wide beds overflowing with herbs. An old holly tree filled one corner, its branches weighed down with berries. Their servant, Old Marie, always picked holly at Christmas-time and put it on the mantelpiece in the kitchen, though if Herr Wild had known he would have ordered her to throw it on the fire. Dortchen's father thought such things pagan nonsense. The only reason holly grew in his garden was because it was a useful herb in winter, when most others were dead. Holly leaves relieved fever and rheumatism, and the powdered berries would purge a blocked bowel.

At the back of the garden were the stables and sheds. Apple trees were espaliered against the south-facing wall. As Dortchen hurried up the path, her boots bruised the thyme and hyssop and sage that spilt over the cobbles, releasing their scents into the night air.

Light illuminated a narrow window on one side of the kitchen door. Dortchen peeked through. Inside, Old Marie was busy at the fireplace. She was called that by everyone, to differentiate her from Dortchen's youngest sister, who was called Little Marie, or Mia. Old Marie was a stout woman in her late fifties, with round cheeks rosy and wrinkled as a winter apple. She wore a coarse calico apron over her brown stuff dress, and a white cap that covered most of her grey-streaked hair. Dortchen opened the door and slipped into the kitchen, a blast of hot air hitting her chilled cheeks. Mozart the starling swooped down to land on her shoulder, trilling a welcome. His dark wings were all starred with white, like snowflakes.

'Good boy,' Dortchen said and stroked his head with her knuckle.

'Good boy,' Mozart repeated. He was named after the composer, who had had a pet starling who'd learnt to whistle the last movement of his Piano Concerto in G. Although Old Marie's starling had never mastered a concerto, he had many words and sounds and songs, and chattered away all day long in a most endearing way.

'Dortchen, sweetling, where've you been?' Old Marie cried.

'Pretty sweetling, pretty sweetling,' the starling chirped.

'I've been that worried,' Old Marie went on. 'It's past the hour already. You know how your father hates to be kept waiting. Röse has come down once already to see where supper is. Quickly, take off your shawl and wash your hands, then you can ring the bell for me.'

'Does Father know I've been out?' Dortchen asked, putting down her basket and lifting Mozart down so he could hop onto his perch.

'I don't think so – he only went up from the shop ten minutes ago. He and your brother have been going at it hammer and tongs ever since. The whole house was shaking.'

As Dortchen took off her shawl and bonnet and hung them up, she said, 'Sometimes I think Father doesn't like us very much.'

'Bite your tongue,' Old Marie responded at once. 'How can you say such a thing, when you live in this fine big house, with all this good food to eat? Yes, he's a little gruff, your father, but he works hard and looks after you, which is more than can be said for many fathers.'

'He never buys us any treats or lets us do anything fun,' Dortchen pointed out.

'Better than taking you out into the forest and abandoning you, like the father of the little boy and girl in that story,' Old Marie said.

'I suppose so,' Dortchen replied. 'Though at least they got to have an adventure. We never go anywhere or do anything.'

'You call almost being eaten by a witch an adventure? Be glad for small mercies, Dortchen, my love, and pass me the salt.'

Dortchen did as she was asked, her mind wandering away into a deep, dark, thorn-tangled forest. She imagined leaving a trail of white stones to help find her way home. She imagined tricking the witch.

Still daydreaming, she began to get down plates for their dinner from the oak dresser. The kitchen was a long, low room, lit by smoky tallow candles and the orange roar of the fire. Heavy beams supported the brown-stained ceiling, with washing lines strung between them flapping with the week's laundry. Iron ladles and pots hung from hooks from a long oak shelf above the fireplace. The shelf itself held pewter bowls and tankards, and heavy ceramic jars of salt and sugar and oil.

A roasting jack, made of cast iron, stood before the fireplace. A complex set of wheels and pulleys kept the roast turning evenly, its juices dripping down into a pan. Old Marie heaved the roast beef off the jack and onto a platter, her round face red and damp with perspiration, then swung the boiling pot of potato dumplings off the fire. Dortchen hurried to help her, ladling boiled red cabbage into a tureen.

The kitchen door swung open and Mia rushed in. 'Old Marie, Mother's having a spasm. Where's supper? It's nearly quarter past.'

'I had trouble with the fire,' Old Marie said. 'The wind's in the wrong quarter.'

'Father's furious.' Mia jumped up and down on one foot, her loops of red-gold hair bouncing. She was eleven years old, the youngest of the six Wild sisters. Everything about her seemed round, from her soft, plump figure to her protuberant blue eyes.

'Tell your father to try cooking when the wind keeps blowing out the fire,' Old Marie answered, heaving up the tray with her rough red hands.

Mia gave a snort of incredulous laughter. 'You tell him! If you dare.'

'Mia, if you ring the bell, I'll help carry the food up,' Dortchen said.

The little girl seized the handbell and rang it vigorously, while Old Marie pushed the door open with her foot and carried out the platter of beef.

'Where've you been?' Mia caught up the potato dumplings.

'I've been to the palace,' Dortchen said. 'Lotte's aunt works there. We had coffee and cakes.'

'Did you see the Kurfürst?'

Dortchen shook her head, leading the way down the cold corridor, the tureen of cabbage in her hands. 'I met Lotte's big brothers. They've come home from university. At least, the second one has: Wilhelm. The other one was in Paris.' She pushed open the dining-room door with her hip and put the tureen down on the sideboard. Old Marie was laying out the plates on the table.

'Paris! Did he see the Ogre?' Mia demanded.

Dortchen nodded. 'He said that it's true that he's short as a dwarf, but he's so full of fire you hardly notice.'

'I'd like to see Napoléon one day,' Mia said.

'Pray to God you don't get the chance,' Old Marie said.

THE WILD ONE

October 1805

Dortchen's elder sisters came into the room in a swirl of skirts, talking over the top of one another.

'Supper at last!' Gretchen cried. 'I am near ready to faint with hunger.' The pretty one, she wore her flaxen hair in ringlets, a feat only achieved by the very uncomfortable practice of wearing rags in her hair to bed.

'Father will not be pleased,' Röse said with a certain amount of pleasure. 'It is a sign of a disordered mind to be so unpunctual.' Thirteen-year-old Röse was the clever one, and seemed to take pleasure in being positively dowdy. Her fair hair was scraped back in a thin plait, and a small book of sermons protruded from her pocket.

'Why so late?' Lisette asked. The eldest, and her mother's prop, she was also the tallest, with a long face and nose and beautiful, long-fingered hands.

'He's almost popped all his buttons already tonight,' Hanne said. She was the musical one, always getting into trouble for singing at the top of her voice around the house.

Dortchen would have liked to have been the clever one, and Mia would have liked to have been the musical one, but with six girls in the family, those roles were already taken by the time they were born. They had become the wild one and the baby, with absolutely no choice in the matter at all.

Dortchen was called the wild one because one day, when she was

31

seven years old, she had got lost in the forest. She had wandered off to a far-distant glade where a willow tree trailed its branches in a pool of water. Dortchen crept within the shadowy tent of its branches and found a green palace. She wove herself a crown of willow tendrils and collected pebbles and flowers to be her jewels. At last, worn out, she lay down on a velvet bed of moss and fell asleep.

She did not hear her family calling for her. She did not see the sun slipping away and the shadows growing longer. Waking in the dusk, she had gone skipping to find her sisters, her hair in a tangle, a wreath of leaves on her head. Ever since then, no matter how hard she tried to be good, Frau Wild would always say, with a long-suffering sigh, 'And this is Dortchen, my wild one, always running off into the forest.'

'You're too soft with her, Katharina,' Herr Wild would growl. 'You should've mastered her will by now.'

It was true Dortchen loved to be outdoors. With so many siblings, it was hard to find time to be alone, and the old house was always full of people shouting, arguing, singing, crying, slamming doors, ringing bells or running up and down the stairs. Out in the forest, it was just Dortchen, free as the wind in the leaves and the birds in the sky. Whenever she could, Dortchen would take a basket and go to the forest in search of fallen chestnuts or mushrooms. She would come home in the evening with her cheeks flushed, her lips stained with berry juice, and her head full of dreams.

'What do we have?' Gretchen lifted the lid of the tureen and wrinkled her nose. 'Not red cabbage again.'

Frau Wild drifted into the room, a shawl trailing from her elbows. 'Girls. The time. Your father.' She collapsed into a chair.

'Bad weather ahead. Better batten down the hatches.' Hanne pretended to swoon into her own chair, her hand held to her temple in mockery of their mother.

'You couldn't possibly understand, Hannechen,' her mother said in a faint voice. 'Who will your father blame?'

'Never mind, Mother,' Lisette soothed her. 'Perhaps Father hasn't noticed the time.'

'He always notices the time,' Frau Wild replied, one hand pressed against her chest.

The door opened so abruptly that it thumped into the wall. Hanne at once scrambled up and took her place by her chair, head bowed and hands folded. Frau Wild rose to her feet, murmuring, 'Oh, dear, oh, dear.'

Herr Wild came into the room and stood looking around with frowning eyes. He was a heavyset man, dressed soberly in brown, with grey hair drawn back from his forehead and tied in a queue. In one hand he held a pocket watch.

'Twenty minutes past the hour,' he said. 'Not acceptable.'

Nobody spoke.

'Katharina, you must keep better order. That servant of yours has no business serving supper at such a late hour.'

Frau Wild hurried into speech. 'No, sir, of course not. Normally she's very good. I don't know what held her up today. Perhaps the roasting jack broke again—'

'I have no wish to hear excuses,' Herr Wild said. 'Where is Rudolf?'

No one answered.

'*Rudolf!*' he shouted.

Frau Wild covered her ears. 'My nerves,' she moaned.

A few minutes later a young man sauntered into the room. His golden locks were brushed forward in careful disarray onto his forehead, and he had a magnificent pair of gingery sideburns. His tall, athletic figure was squeezed into tight pantaloons and a cutaway coat with two rows of enormous brass buttons. Dortchen wondered where he had got the funds for such fine new clothes. Certainly not from his father.

'No need to bellow, Father,' he said. 'I'm not deaf.'

'Neither am I, you insolent dog, if that is what you mean to imply. Nor am I too old to tan your hide. How dare you keep us waiting!'

'I'm not in for supper tonight, Father, I told you.'

Herr Wild pointed to the vacant seat. 'While you live in my house, you will do as I say. Take your place, or I'll kick you there myself.'

Rudolf strolled to his spot. 'I suppose I may as well save my thalers and eat here.'

Herr Wild folded his hands and intoned, 'Come, Lord Jesus, be our guest, and let thy gifts to us be blessed. Amen.'

'Amen,' the girls echoed.

Rudolf sighed and repeated, in a voice of long suffering, 'Amen.'

'Sit,' Herr Wild said and everyone sat.

Herr Wild took a large slab of beef, piled cabbage and dumplings on top, then passed the platter to Rudolf, who served himself, then held the platter for his mother. Frau Wild dithered for a while, trying to choose the slice of meat with the least amount of fat. At last she took one, then added a tiny spoonful of cabbage. 'My poor stomach can scarcely tolerate it, you know. Such a day I've had! I've barely the strength to eat a mouthful.'

'Never mind, Mother,' Lisette said. 'Perhaps some orgeat will help.' She poured her mother a glass of the sweet almond cordial. Frau Wild sipped it with a sigh.

By the time the platter reached Dortchen and Mia at the far end of the table, there was very little beef left. Mia sighed ostentatiously, and Lisette smiled and passed her some of hers. They ate in silence. Rudolf slipped his hand into his pocket and drew out his watch. Surreptitiously, he flipped open the case and glanced at its face.

'It's no use thinking you can sneak out once my back is turned.' Herr Wild spoke without looking up from his meal. 'I meant what I said, Rudolf. I will not have you gadding about town with those wild friends of yours, drinking and gambling and fraternising with loose women. Going out indeed! You will stay here and study your pharmacology books.'

'But Father—'

'Do not argue with me. By all accounts, war is coming and there'll be money to be made. I need you to finish your apprenticeship and be ready to work by my side. You haven't time for fooling around, Rudolf. Your Latin is execrable and your knowledge of the pharmacopoeia is weak. Even Dortchen knows more about plant properties than you do.'

'That's because she's always grubbing around in the garden,' Rudolf said.

'Which is what you should be doing, not wasting your days going to cockfights and the races,' his father responded.

'Well, that's certainly not where your proper little miss was this afternoon. I saw her sneaking in at ten past the hour. It's her fault supper was late, so you can jaw at her for a change.'

Dortchen fixed her eyes on her plate.

Herr Wild laid down his knife and fork. 'Dortchen Wild, were you late coming in this evening?'

Dortchen nodded her head. 'Yes, Father.'

'Why? Where were you?'

Dortchen did not reply for a moment, wondering whether it was a greater sin to lie than it was to disobey one's father.

'Hobnobbing with that Grimm girl, I bet,' Rudolf said.

'I . . . I did visit with Lotte and Frau Grimm, Father. But I was only a little late, it wasn't ten past the hour.' She shot a look at her brother. 'I was held up. Lotte's elder brothers had arrived. From university, you know. The biggest one, he said Strasbourg is full of French soldiers. The Grand Army's on the march again.'

'Against Austria?' Rudolf exclaimed. 'Father's right, there will be war!'

'What are we to do?' Frau Wild lamented. 'Will the Ogre march on Cassel?'

'No need to fear,' Herr Wild replied. 'The Austrians will soon have the French running with their tail between their legs. Still, there's no doubt the Kurfürst will be calling up new conscripts. Lucky for you, Rudolf, I can arrange an exemption—'

'I don't want an exemption,' Rudolf burst out. 'I don't want to spend the whole war puking and purging and bloodletting and blistering. I want to fight! The best fun to ever happen around here and you want me to stay home swotting up on Latin!'

'You're a fool.' Herr Wild pushed away his plate and stood up. 'Your first day tending the wounded on a battlefield and you'll be on your knees thanking the Good Lord that your father is wiser than you are.'

Rudolf stood up too, pushing back his chair so violently it fell over. He left the room, banging the door behind him.

Frau Wild fell back in her chair, one hand groping outwards. 'My drops . . . where are my drops? All this noise, my nerves are shattered.'

Hanne hurried to find her mother's drops while Lisette knelt beside her chair, wetting a napkin to press against her brow.

Herr Wild strode to the door and opened it. Pausing there, he turned back to address Dortchen. 'As for you, Fraülein, you'll spend your free afternoons this week doing God's labour in the garden, and Sunday on your knees reciting your catechism.'

'But Father,' Dortchen cried before she could stop herself. As he turned to face her, she faltered. 'This Sunday is the harvest festival.' Even as she spoke, she knew it was no use.

'You may look instead to the sanctity of your soul,' Herr Wild said, and shut the door behind him.

That Sunday afternoon, when all Dortchen's sisters went off to enjoy the harvest festival, Dortchen stayed home alone with her father. She knelt before him in the chilly parlour while he tested her on her catechism. It went on for hours.

'What is repentance?' Herr Wild asked.

'Dissatisfaction with and a hatred of sin . . . and a love of righteousness . . . proceeding from the fear of God . . . which lead to self-denial and mortification of the flesh, so that we give ourselves up to the guidance of the Spirit of God . . .' Dortchen stopped, unable to go on.

'And frame . . .' her father prompted.

'And frame all the actions of our life to the obedience of the Divine Will.'

'You should have it by heart,' her father said. 'Study it and I'll return in an hour to test you again.' He rose and went out, and Dortchen went to sit in the window seat, drawing flowers and faces on the frosty glass and looking down to the street below. Dusk was dropping over Cassel, the sun just a red smear behind the turrets and chimney pots, even though it was not yet seven o'clock. Men and women in their Sunday best were strolling along, many with ears of wheat tucked into the brims of their hats or their buttonholes. A little girl in a frothy white dress and a hat with yellow ribbons was skipping beside her father, her small hand in his large one.

At last, Dortchen saw her sisters returning with the Grimm family, flowers tucked into their bodices. Lotte was dancing ahead with Mia, their baskets swinging, while Lisette and Hanne followed arm in arm. Frau Grimm and Frau Wild walked together, one stout, one skinny, their bonneted heads close together. Jakob strode beside them, lighting their way with a lantern. The three younger Grimm brothers, Karl, Ferdinand and Ludwig, jostled behind, while Röse walked sedately some distance away, peering at her book of sermons.

Wilhelm and Gretchen followed along last of all. Ethereal in white muslin, she walked close beside him, his dark head in its tall black hat bent close over hers. Gretchen's bonnet swung from her hand. On her fair head was the harvest crown, woven of asters and autumn leaves, always given to the prettiest girl.

Dortchen felt a sharp pang. All week she had been daydreaming about Lotte's handsome elder brother. As she watched, Wilhelm said something that made Gretchen look up at him and smile. Dortchen turned away.

A RAIN OF DEATH

October 1805

'Napoléon has won a great battle against the Austrians!' Aunt Zimmer cried, before the door had even shut behind her. She whirled in on a blast of wintry air, her silk skirts blowing up around her white-stockinged ankles.

'What?' Wilhelm came to his feet, almost knocking over his inkpot. Dortchen looked around from the fireplace, where she was trying to teach Lotte how to make bread soup.

'But that's impossible,' Frau Grimm said, dropping her sewing in her lap. She sat in a rocking chair as close to the fire as she could, her feet propped against the fender. It had been a nasty day, veering between snow and sleet, and the Grimms' lodgings were draughty. As a result, all the brothers were crammed in the kitchen, their books and papers spread out over the table, the only light coming from mismatched candles stuck in chipped saucers.

'It's all too true,' Aunt Zimmer said. 'A courier arrived at the palace not an hour ago. The Austrian general has laid down his arms.'

The boys stared blankly at one another.

'But he couldn't have!' Lotte said. 'It can't be all over so soon.'

'Ten thousand dead, thirty thousand taken prisoner.' Aunt Zimmer subsided onto a chair with a billow of her silken skirts. 'Napoléon lost not even half of that.'

38

'But Ulm is only a few days' ride from here,' Frau Grimm said. 'Whatever are we to do?'

'Hope that the Emperor marches elsewhere,' Wilhelm said. 'What of the Russians? Were they not marching to Austria's aid?'

'No one expected Napoléon to move so fast. It's like black magic, the way he appears days before it's humanly possible to arrive.'

'But didn't the Austrians have scouts?' Jakob asked. 'How could General Mack not know the Grand Army was marching up behind him?'

'Napoléon moved so fast,' Aunt Zimmer said again.

'But what of the Austrian army?' Ludwig asked. 'I thought it was meant to be the best in the world.' He was drawing soldiers fighting on the page before him, quick vigorous sketches that sprang to life under his quill.

'The dispatch courier said the cannon smoke was so thick the Austrians could not see to shoot,' Aunt Zimmer said. 'It was like a rain of death.'

'What happens now?' Karl asked.

Aunt Zimmer lifted her hands and let them drop in her lap.

'The Emperor will probably have the Austrian general shot,' Ferdinand said. 'He'd have been better dying with honour on the battlefield than giving up so easily.'

'I don't think it could have been easy for him,' Dortchen said.

Ferdinand glanced at her in sudden interest. 'No, I suppose not.'

'What does the Kurfürst say?' Wilhelm asked.

'He's not happy. With Prussia at our back, Bavaria at our front, and Austria and France glowering at each other from either side, we're like a sausage in a bread roll,' Aunt Zimmer said.

'Don't mention sausages,' Lotte said, pulling a face. 'I never want to see one again.'

Her comment relieved the atmosphere of gloom and anxiety. Wilhelm grinned at her and rumpled her hair, and Ludwig drew a picture of a girl with tangled dark curls chasing a giant sausage with a fork.

'Ah, Lottechen, if I'd not had the pig killed before we came to Cassel, we'd not have anything to eat at all,' Frau Grimm said, shaking a fat finger at her daughter.

'That's why Dortchen's here. She's come to show me how to make bread soup, so we can have something besides sausages for supper,' Lotte told her aunt. 'She had to bring all the other ingredients with her, as our pantry is bare.'

'You're a good girl,' Aunt Zimmer told Dortchen, and blew her a kiss.

'She is indeed,' Wilhelm said, smiling at her. 'The soup smells delicious.'

Embarrassed, Dortchen tried to deflect attention away from herself. 'Oh, bread soup is easy enough. At least I don't have to throw myself into the pot like the sausage in the story.'

'Don't say that word!' Lotte put both her hands over her ears.

'What story is that?' Wilhelm asked.

'You don't know it? The story about the little mouse, the little bird and the sausage?'

Wilhelm shook his head. 'Won't you tell it to us?'

Heat rushed up into her face as she realised that the whole family was now staring at her. She shook her head and stirred the soup.

'Dortchen knows ever so many stories,' Lotte said. 'Go on, tell us!'

But Dortchen shook her head again and, taking the pan off the trivet, said she had better be getting home. 'Just sprinkle the chives and the fried bread on top of the soup when you serve it,' she told Lotte. 'See you tomorrow.'

As she put on her cloak and gathered up her jug and bowls, Wilhelm said to her, 'I'd like to hear one of your stories some time. I'm interested in old stories and songs and such things. Friends of mine are collecting folk songs at the moment, for a book they are writing. Do you and your sisters know any songs?'

Shyly, Dortchen nodded. 'Hanne and Gretchen know ever so many.'

'Perhaps one day they could come to tea and sing them to me and Jakob,' he suggested, then he glanced around the tiny room. With five tall boys pushing back their chairs so they could stretch out their legs, and stout Frau Grimm in her rocking chair, there was barely room for Dortchen and Lotte to turn around. He frowned, then shrugged a little. 'Well, never mind. Goodnight, Dortchen, and thank you for cooking us supper.'

'It was nothing. Lotte cooked as much as me.'

He smiled briefly and turned away, asking Aunt Zimmer, 'Any news about a job at the palace?'

Aunt Zimmer shook her head. 'I'm sorry, Willi. You know the Kurfürst was impressed with the letter Jakob wrote for the ambassador from Paris. But all the jobs have been taken already.'

'By sons of barons,' Wilhelm said.

'I'm sorry,' she said again.

'Oh, sister, I just do not know how we're to manage,' Frau Grimm cried. 'If it wasn't for Dortchen coming by tonight with some eggs and cream, we'd not have had a bite to eat.'

'And bread soup is not much for hungry boys,' Aunt Zimmer said. She took out some coins from her reticule and laid them on the dresser. 'Buy some beef and a cabbage at market tomorrow. But you'd best make it last. With all this war about, it's going to be a lean winter.'

As Dortchen slipped out the door, she saw Wilhelm press his lips together in humiliation.

That evening, as they cleared the supper table together, Dortchen told her sisters about how poor the Grimms were since their father had died.

'What can we do?' Lisette asked. 'It's not as if we have much coin to spare. And Father would never permit us to give food out of our own pantry.'

Dortchen thought of the food she had smuggled over the road that very afternoon. 'They're hungry,' she said, sweeping crumbs from the table into her hand. 'We should invite them for supper.'

'Father would never permit it,' Hanne said. 'You know how he hates company.'

'What about for coffee and cakes?' Dortchen suggested. 'We could do it one Friday when Father has gone to his church meeting.' As her sisters hesitated, she added, 'Wilhelm, the second eldest, he said he'd like to hear you sing.'

'We can have some music, and maybe a reading. Father could not possibly object if Mother sits with us,' Gretchen said.

'They're interested in old stories too – perhaps I could tell them one,' Dortchen said.

Gretchen laughed. 'Dortchen, you're only twelve. Much too young to be entertaining gentlemen.'

'But—'

'You and Röse and Mia couldn't possibly come,' Lisette agreed. 'For one thing, we simply haven't room in the parlour. By the time we have us three, and the three eldest Grimm boys and Mother, well, we couldn't fit a mouse in there.'

Dortchen threw down the cloth and went out of the room. No one noticed she had gone.

The hall seemed very full of black-clad young men the following Friday. Dortchen sat with Mia and Röse on the steps, peering through the banisters, as the eldest three Grimm brothers unwound their scarves and gave their tall hats to Frau Wild, who dropped first a scarf, then a hat, then another scarf. Wilhelm politely gathered them all up and hung them for her on the hatstand.

'Thank you so much for having us,' Jakob said. 'You're very kind.' He looked tired; his dark hair was rumpled and his fingers were stained with ink.

'Yes, thank you.' Karl looked with admiration at the three young women in their best pale muslins.

'We thought, if you liked, we could do it every few weeks,' Gretchen said. 'We can invite a few of the other young people we know in town, so you can make some new friends.'

'We've brought a book to show you,' Wilhelm said, holding up a slim leather-bound volume. 'It's a collection of folk songs by some friends of ours that has only just this month been published. We even contributed a few poems.'

'Though I wouldn't have let my name be associated with it if I had known what an unscholarly production it was,' Jakob said.

'Clemens said that it wasn't about preserving a historical artefact,' Wilhelm answered him. 'What he and Achim wanted to do was renew and revitalise the old songs so that they regained meaning for us all today.'

'Yet didn't he also say they wanted to prove an enduring sense of folk spirit among the German people?' Jakob asked. 'Wouldn't that aim have been better met by actually collecting the songs and tales in their original form? As far as I can tell, they've rewritten many of the songs and even made up some of their own.'

'Well, they are poets in their own right,' Wilhelm argued.

'Then they should publish a book of their own poems, not one which claims to preserve old folk songs,' Jakob said.

'I guess you're right,' Wilhelm replied, though in a rather uncertain tone.

Lisette cast Hanne and Gretchen a look. 'Won't you come through to the sitting room? It's cold out here in the hall. Perhaps, Herr Grimm, you could read us one of your poems?'

'They're not mine,' Jakob said. '*I* didn't see fit to write my own composition for a book that was meant to be a collection of folk songs. All I did was send Herr Brentano and Herr von Arnim a few old counting rhymes I remembered from my childhood.'

'Oh,' Lisette answered. 'Well, perhaps you could share some other poems with us?'

'Perhaps we could sing some of the songs?' Hanne suggested, as Lisette led the way into the sitting room. As the Grimm brothers followed the girls in, Dortchen saw Jakob turn to Wilhelm and make a very similar grimace to Lisette's.

Karl, who went in last, did not shut the door behind him. A narrow wedge of lamplight was cast out into the hall, falling through the balustrades and onto Dortchen's face. She pressed her face against the wooden struts, unable to hear what was being said within.

'A book of folk songs,' Röse said in a voice of deep disgust. 'I thought you said that the elder Grimm brothers were of a sober cast of mind, Dorothea. Indeed, I am glad now that I am not to be part of this so-called reading circle. No doubt they will soon be reading *novels*.' She stood up. 'I am going to go and study Schwager's sermons.'

'That sounds like fun,' Mia said.

'Fun! Indeed, I should hope not,' Röse replied. 'I do find the frivolous turn of your mind quite distressing, Maria.'

'I find the way you prose on all the time more than *quite* distressing,' her younger sister retorted. 'In fact, it makes me feel sick to my stomach.'

'That's from gorging yourself all morning. Gluttony is a cardinal sin, you know.'

'So is vainglory,' Dortchen answered swiftly.

Röse sniffed and stomped upstairs.

'I'm going to see if Old Marie has made any more strudel,' Mia said, running down the steps. Dortchen stayed where she was, looking through the staircase at the half-open door, straining her ears to listen.

'What a shame no music has been provided with the songs,' Hanne was saying. 'Though I know some of them. The words do seem a little different. Shall I see if I can remember the tunes?' She began to play the old piano.

'It's called "The Boy's Magic Horn",' Wilhelm said. 'Isn't that beautiful? I do think they've done something rather fine, Jakob.'

A low rumble from Jakob in response, then Hanne's clear voice rang out, singing, '*Up there, in the high house, a lovely girl is peeping . . .*'

Dortchen tensed, ready to run, wondering if her sister knew she was hiding in the hall. But no footsteps came near, so she crept down the stairs and sat outside the door, her back against the wall, the skirts of her dress folded up beneath her to protect her legs from the cold of the stone floor.

By the time an hour had passed and the Grimm brothers rose to leave, Dortchen was so stiff and chilled that she could scarcely scramble to her feet. As the sitting-room door was flung open, the warm light flooded over her. 'I . . . I've just come to get the dirty plates,' she managed to say.

'You're a good girl,' Lisette told her.

Dortchen gathered together the used cups and plates as Gretchen and Lisette brought their neighbours' hats and scarves and coats and said their polite goodbyes. Outside, an early dusk was already falling. Father would soon be home. Hanne sat at the piano, plonking a key with one emphatic finger.

'Well, I don't think much of those Grimm boys,' she burst out, when Lisette and Gretchen came back in, rosy-cheeked and laughing. 'I swear the eldest one fell asleep while I was singing.'

'Wilhelm says Jakob's been working very hard,' Gretchen said. 'They have virtually no income at all, you know. He and Wilhelm are hoping to get something published, to bring in a little money.'

'Oh, it's *Wilhelm* now, is it?' Lisette teased. 'You have become friendly.'

'Not at all,' Gretchen returned. 'It's just . . . well, so many Herr Grimms and Fraülein Wilds, we just thought it was easier.'

'Soon it'll be Willi.' Lisette clasped her hands together and fluttered her eyelashes.

'Oh, stop it,' Gretchen said.

Hanne sat at the piano again, singing at the top of her voice, '*My heart is sore! Come, my little darling, make it well again. Your dark-brown eyes have wounded me . . .*'

Gretchen laughed and ran out of the room.

A BITTER BLOW

October 1805

'"English fleet annihilated. Lord Admiral Nelson killed",' Herr Wild read aloud from the morning newspaper.

'What? Can it be true?' the girls all exclaimed.

'It'll be French propaganda,' Rudolf said. 'Old Cyclops can't really be dead.'

'According to the papers, he is,' their father replied. 'Killed in a naval battle off Cape Trafalgar.'

Dortchen laid down her knife, a lump in her throat.

Frau Wild groped for her drops. 'Is the Ogre never to be stopped?'

Dortchen had heard many people call the French emperor an ogre. She imagined him like a troll out of a story, grinding children's bones for bread.

'It's a new world, Mother,' Hanne said. 'We have to change with it. It's no use clinging to old thoughts, old fashions.' She flicked a glance at her father. 'The Emperor means to drag us all into the modern world.'

'Do not call that upstart "Emperor"!'

'But he is Emperor now, like it or not,' Hanne replied, undaunted. 'Half the world saw him crown himself, and the other half is now being crushed under his boot. It surely can't be long before our little kingdom is swallowed up too. And then what shall we do?'

'We shall have to fight,' Rudolf cried.

Hanne looked at him with scorn. 'Fight Napoléon? He'd tread on us and not even notice, just like you don't notice treading on an ant. No, our only choice is to join him.'

'Join him!' Herr Wild and Rudolf bellowed.

Frau Wild put both hands over her ears. 'Little birds in their nest agree?'

'Well, Bavaria signed a treaty with him and look at all the land he gave them,' Hanne pointed out.

'What do you know of such matters?' her father asked, but Hanne said impatiently, 'Oh, Father, I'm not a child, I read the newspapers. We all do. Everyone knows what France was like before the Emperor came to power. The churches were all closed, the fields were barren, the people were rioting for bread. The government couldn't even pay its own soldiers. Now look at them.'

'That Corsican upstart stole and plundered his way through Italy and Egypt, and now he turns his greedy gaze to the Holy Roman Empire,' Herr Wild said.

'Exactly – which is why the Kurfürst should join him just as soon as he can.'

Dortchen thought of the Holy Roman Empire. So many tiny countries stitched together into a patchwork eiderdown, each with its own archduke or archbishop, prince or landgrave, squabbling over borders and taxes and rights of privilege, each with their own weights and measures, their own laws and curfews. Some of the princedoms were so small that they could fire at each other from their castle walls. Yet for over a millennium they had held together. What would happen now a few of those stitches were torn loose? Would the whole patchwork unravel?

'Do not presume to express opinions on matters which you cannot possibly understand,' her father said to Hanne. 'What is the fifth commandment?'

Hanne only just managed not to roll her eyes. 'Honour thy father and thy mother.'

'And what meaning do you give to the word "honour"?' Herr Wild asked.

'That children be, with modesty and humility, respectful and obedient to parents, serving them reverentially, helping them in necessity and exerting their labour for them.'

'Very well, you can exert yourself in labour in the stillroom all afternoon. There are many powders to be ground and essences to be distilled if we are to be ready for whatever the next few weeks bring us.'

'Yes, Father,' Hanne said and rose, folding her napkin and dropping it on her plate. At the doorway, she turned and said sweetly, 'Because I agree we'd best be prepared for the worst.'

There was silence once she had gone.

'Is the Ogre really going to invade us, Father?' Mia asked in a trembling voice.

'Nonsense,' Herr Wild said. 'It's England that Napoléon wants to invade.' He slapped his hand on the paper. 'It says here that Napoléon never intended to fight against Austria, that he was provoked into battle by the Austrians mobilising against him.'

'What if the Austrians lose another big battle like the one at Ulm?' Dortchen asked. 'Could they lose the war?'

'Of course the Austrians won't lose,' Herr Wild said. 'Do you think some upstart from Corsica could possibly bring Emperor Francis to his knees? Enough foolishness. Eat your breakfast, do your chores. Rudolf, get to your books.'

For once, Rudolf did not argue but rose and went out of the room.

Dortchen and Lotte walked to school, clutching their bonnets against the cold wind. People stood in knots, reading the newspaper together. The hurdy-gurdy man sat on the kerb, his monkey huddled in his arms, his instrument sitting silently beside him. Across the road, the rag-and-bone man was patting the well-padded shoulder of a housewife, who dabbed at her eyes with the corner of her apron, her front step still unscrubbed. No one could believe it was true. The famous English admiral dead? The French triumphant on the sea as well as on land? The future seemed as dark and uncertain as the sky.

'Surely it cannot be true,' Lotte said, dragging her satchel of books behind her.

'The newspapers say so.'

'The local papers are full of lies, my brother Jakob says. It's the English papers we should be reading.'

Dortchen shrugged. 'Well, that's not something we can do very easily.'

'The palace!' Lotte cried. 'They'd have the English papers there. Prince Wilhelm is half English, you know. Let's go to the palace and see if we can find out what they say.'

'But we can't read English,' Dortchen protested. 'And the palace is so far away – it'll take us an hour to walk there and an hour to get back.'

'We don't need to walk all the way out to Wilhelmshöhe – the Kurfürst and his family are at the Palais Bellevue. I know because Aunt Zimmer is here with the Kurfürstin. It'll only take us fifteen minutes. And one of the count's secretaries will have translated the papers already.'

'I can't miss school.'

'What does school matter when we may be invaded any day?'

Dortchen did not reply. It was different for Lotte. She had no father, and though Jakob did his best to play patriarch, he was only twenty and never made Lotte kneel before him for hours, praying. Nor did he beat her.

Lotte sighed. 'After school, then. When you're meant to be doing your chores.'

Dortchen nodded.

That afternoon, after school was let out, the two girls hurried down the street, their cloaks muffled to their chins against the icy air, their satchels banging on their backs. Autumn leaves whirled against them, damp and black. A carriage clopped past them, the horse lifting its tail to drop a steaming pile of greenish turds that were then squashed into the cobbles by the wheels.

At the Königsplatz, the girls cupped their hands and called. One by one, six faint echoes bounced back at them. Dortchen and Lotte smiled at each other and, holding hands, ran across the square, dodging carts and carriages of all sizes and shapes.

Soon they were outside the Bellevue Palace, which was built in the French style with little dormer windows set into the steep slate roof. The palace had a lovely view across to the gardens and parkland on Aue Island, and to the rolling countryside beyond the river.

Two guards stood outside the front door. Lotte smiled at them and said she had come to visit her aunt, Henriette Zimmer, and they allowed the two girls in without any further questioning. The great hall within was busy with court officials rushing this way and that, all dressed in old-fashioned frockcoats, the heels of their buckled black shoes clacking on the floor. Two soldiers stood waiting outside a set of carved double doors, each dressed in a forest-green jacket with silver epaulettes over white breeches, and a tall shako hat with a green plume. One carried a packet of letters in his gloved hand.

Dortchen and Lotte stood to one side, not knowing where to find Aunt Zimmer.

The double doors swung open, and out came a rotund man dressed in shabby riding clothes and a powdered wig with two fat rolls of hair above his ears. Around him clustered a great many men, some in black frockcoats, some in green military jackets. One man was in Prussian blue, with a red sash and a great many medals.

'It's the Kurfürst.' Dortchen darted forward and curtsied to the man in the shabby riding coat.

'Dear me, who's this?' the Kurfürst exclaimed. 'What a pretty child. You're not one of mine, are you?'

'No, sir,' Dortchen replied in some confusion.

He frowned. 'Wanting to borrow money, I suppose.'

'No, sir.'

His expression cleared. 'Well, then, what can I do for you?'

'We just want to know, sir . . . We're worried about the war . . . Is the Ogre going to march all over us too?'

'Ah, the question of the day,' he replied, glancing about at the crowd of men. 'I wish I knew, Fraülein. I certainly hope we're too small to interest him. At the rate he and his army move, they could march right through us in only a few days. If so, we'll lose a great many pigs and cows and have a few fields trampled. I fear, though . . . I very much fear . . .'

He seemed then to recollect that he was talking to a girl. 'But never you mind your pretty head about that. Plenty of old grey ones to do the worrying for you, eh? Run along home to your mother, and tell her the Kurfürst sends his regards.'

Dortchen stood back, allowing the party of men to pass by her. She heard the man in Prussian blue say in a deep, stern voice, 'Your Most Serene Highness, I must have an answer for my emperor. Do you mean to stand with us or against us?'

In an irritable voice, the Kurfürst answered, 'Why must I choose? Cannot I stay out of it? You'll tear Hessen-Cassel apart between you, and then what will happen to little girls like that one with the blue eyes?' He disappeared through another door, the men trailing behind him.

Lotte had the presence of mind to ask one where they might find her aunt, and they were directed through many crowded corridors to a cold and elegant room where the cold and elegant Kurfürstin presided. Born Princess Wilhelmine Karoline of Denmark, she was tall, with ash-blonde hair arranged in stiff curls all over her head. Sitting with her was her pale daughter-in-law, Princess Augusta of Prussia, and a great number of ladies working away at their embroidery, among them Aunt Zimmer. She rose at once and requested permission to retire, then took the two girls out into the corridor, scolding them all the way.

'We knew that you're the one person who would know what's really happening with the war,' Lotte said.

Her aunt smiled and smoothed her hair, then said, 'Well, yes, I am rather at the centre of things, aren't I?'

'All the newspapers say the English admiral is dead,' Dortchen explained. 'Please, tell us it's not true.'

'I suppose you are half in love with Nelson, like all the other ladies. Ah, to lose an eye and an arm, and keep on fighting. It is romantic, I know. Alas, my little ones. It is all too true. Nelson is dead.'

'And the battle lost?' Dortchen gripped her hands together.

'No, no, he won the battle first. He gave orders right up to the last minute, by all accounts. We read about it all in the English newspapers.'

She patted her bosom for her spectacles, which hung on a chain about her neck, then beckoned a nearby lackey to bring her the papers, strewn all over a table in the hall. 'Here we are. *The Times* says, "We do not know whether we should mourn . . . or rejoice. The country has gained . . . the most splendid and . . . decisive victory that has ever . . . graced the . . . naval annals of England; but it has been dearly purchased."' Aunt Zimmer translated slowly from the English, stopping often to think of the right words.

Dortchen's eyes felt hot. She could not rejoice that the Ogre had at last been defeated at sea, when Admiral Nelson – one of the only men who had seemed able to stop Napoléon in his tracks – was dead.

'It's bad news for us all,' Aunt Zimmer said. 'Napoléon will be angry at losing his navy and determined to prove his strength. I dread the next few months, my dears. We must pray that Prussia joins forces with the Russians and the Austrians to stop this madman from destroying us all.'

RED SUN OF AUSTERLITZ

December 1805

The Wild sisters sat by the fire in the upstairs drawing room. Dortchen was hemming small muslin bags for the shop, Röse was darning stockings, while Lisette and Gretchen mended sheets and pillowcases. Hanne was cutting up the newspaper to make paper twists, while Mia worked reluctantly on her sampler. Although all the furniture was old and shabby, it was a pleasant room, the chairs softened with cushions and shawls, and a jug filled with rosehips and willow twigs on the mantelpiece.

'I feel like I'm turning into one of those old maids with a squint and red hands from too much housework,' Gretchen said, shutting one eye to thread her needle. 'Why can't we send out our sewing like other people do?'

'Father's too flinty,' Hanne responded absent-mindedly, her attentions caught by an article in the newspaper.

'It's Lisette who's the old maid,' Gretchen said. 'She's twenty-three already, and no husband on the horizon.'

'Father hasn't had time to find me one yet,' Lisette replied, her face reddening.

'You're too useful to him in the stillroom,' Hanne said. 'Stop working so hard and he'll marry you off quick enough.'

'That's your strategy, is it, Hanne?' Lisette shot back.

Hanne laughed. 'I intend to never marry. Mother has put me off it forever.'

Lisette was horrified. 'Not marry? Are you mad? Do you wish to be an old maid and have everyone snigger at you, and think you're left on the shelf because no one wanted you?'

'Besides,' Gretchen said, 'if you don't marry you'll be stuck here forever, looking after Mother and Father till they die.'

'Heaven forbid,' Hanne said. 'Find me a husband as fast as you can.'

'I have no intention of ever marrying either,' Röse said. 'I intend to be a prop to our parents in their declining years.'

'Father's not here, there's no need to suck up,' Hanne said.

Röse put her nose in the air. 'You malign me. I have no desire to impress Father with a false sense of daughterly devotion. I am simply expressing my own humble opinion. The thought of marrying disgusts me. I do not understand how any of you can bear the thought.'

'Better than being an old maid,' Gretchen said. 'Which is what you've been since the day you were born.'

'Better old-maidish than silly and frivolous,' Röse responded.

'Personally, I'd much rather be frivolous,' Gretchen replied. 'If only I ever got the chance.'

Hanne had turned the newspaper over and was reading the headlines. 'Oh no!' she cried, starting to her feet. 'Napoléon has won another great victory. Thirty thousand Austrians have been killed.'

'It cannot be true,' Gretchen said, dropping her mending.

Hanne showed her sisters the newspaper, and they all crowded about her.

'It seems impossible,' Lisette cried. 'I had thought . . . I had heard people say the French were exhausted after their great march . . . that Napoléon didn't want to fight.'

'It was a trick,' Hanne said. 'He wanted to lure the Austrians into attacking him.'

'But thirty thousand dead . . . in one battle . . .' Gretchen laid a hand over her mouth.

'They say it was over in less than a day.' Hanne held the news-sheet above her head so that Röse – who was a good head shorter – could not snatch it from her. 'He did this clever manoeuvre, bringing his men up where they were least expected and attacking on the flank. The morning mist was so thick that the Austrians couldn't see how Napoléon had tricked them. You've got to admit it was devilishly clever of him.'

'Hanne,' Lisette cried, glancing towards the door.

'Oh, don't worry, Father's at the church elders' meeting. Besides, it's not cussing if you mean it literally.'

'What about the Russians? Didn't they fight too?' Röse asked.

Hanne nodded. 'They're calling it the Battle of the Three Emperors. The Tsar himself was there, but he's fled now. He said they were like babes in the hands of a giant.' Her voice was full of amazed wonder.

'You sound as if you're glad Napoléon has won,' Dortchen burst out.

'I'm not *glad*, exactly,' Hanne answered, at last letting the younger girls seize the paper so they could read the account for themselves. 'Although I have to admit to a sneaking admiration for the man. He was crowned emperor only a year ago, and he celebrated his first anniversary by bringing his arch-enemies to their knees.'

'He lost the Battle of Trafalgar,' Dortchen reminded her.

'Well, yes, but Admiral Nelson was killed. And Napoléon cannot be beaten on land. We all thought the Austrian army was one of the best in the world. Now look at it. Napoléon has taken Vienna with scarcely any resistance, and crossed the Danube, and driven back the Austrians and the Russians all the way to Austerlitz. Now he has Emperor Ferdinand on his knees, begging to be allowed to keep his throne.'

'Don't you realise what this means for us, Hanne?' Dortchen cried. 'Who is left to fight him? Will the Prussians protect us? We're so small he'll swallow us up.'

'Which is why we should make a peace treaty with him, like the Bavarians. Yes, it may mean the Kurfürst loses his throne, but on the other hand we'd have a law that wasn't positively medieval. Privileges of the nobles abolished, trial by jury – imagine it!'

'You cannot mean it,' Lisette cried. 'You want the Kurfürst to be deposed?'

'We'd finally be dragged into modern times,' Hanne retorted. 'The French are changing the whole world, while we Germans are stuck in our ways like a hog in a mud puddle.'

Dortchen stared at her sister in utter surprise.

A knock sounded on the door, and Old Marie put her round-cheeked face around it, her grey hair tucked under a mob cap. 'Fraülein Lotte and Herr Wilhelm Grimm here to see you,' she said. 'Will I show them up?'

Gretchen looked about her at the shabby room and shook her head. 'No, show them into the parlour.' Dortchen, following close on her heels to the door, thought that Lotte and Wilhelm would be far more comfortable here than in the stiff formality of the parlour, but she said nothing. Already her elder sisters were streaming out the door and down the stairs. Holding the news-sheet aloft in her hand like a banner, Mia came hurtling behind.

Lotte waited for them in the parlour, her curly head hatless, and only a thin shawl wrapped about her. Wilhelm stood before the empty grate of the fireplace, his tall hat in his hand. He looked even paler than usual, with dark circles under his eyes. 'Have you heard the news of the defeat at Austerlitz?' he cried as soon as the sisters came into the room. 'Twenty thousand Russians killed. Aunt Zimmer says they were driven back across the river – the ice broke beneath them and many of them drowned.'

'How terrible,' Lisette said in a low voice, sinking down onto a chair.

'Thirty thousand Austrians gone,' Hanne cried, not wanting him to think he had all the news.

'Almost half the entire Austro-Russian army,' Wilhelm said. 'It must be the bloodiest battle in history.'

'How many did the Ogre lose?' Dortchen's voice shook.

'Less than ten thousand,' Wilhelm answered. 'It's like he's protected by some diabolical force.'

'God forbid one should assume it's because he's the better military leader,' Hanne snapped back.

'They say the sun was blood-red and swollen like a blister when it rose,' Wilhelm said. 'It was an evil omen.'

'Can nobody stop him?' Lotte asked. 'Oh, Wilhelm, does he mean to take over all of Europe? Hessen-Cassel too?'

He drew her to him, smoothing down her curls. 'You know how good the Hessian soldiers are,' he told her. 'There may not be many of them, but they've fought as mercenaries all over the world – they're very experienced. And the English will stand by us. Their king is our Kurfürst's cousin, and they've always helped each other.'

'But the English king is completely mad,' Lotte wailed. 'He tried to shake hands with a tree, thinking it was the King of Prussia.'

'His prime minister is not mad,' Wilhelm said. 'He'll send help if we're threatened, I'm sure of it.'

'What will happen now?' Gretchen asked Wilhelm.

'I don't know. I heard that the Austrian emperor has met with Napoléon, to discuss terms.'

'There can only be room for one emperor,' Hanne said with certainty. 'Napoléon will dismantle the Holy Roman Empire and take as much power for himself and his family as he can. Soon we'll all be French.'

'I'll never be French,' Wilhelm said. 'They can plant a French flag on our soil, they can impose their so-called code on us – they can even force us to speak their language – but it won't make me French. I'm German to the core.'

'Well said,' Dortchen cried.

Wilhelm smiled at her, and the cold hollow of her chest was warmed.

'We need to trust in our old allies, the Prussians, to stop him,' Wilhelm said. 'Napoléon's men must be exhausted and footsore, and sick of constantly fighting. They're a thousand kilometres from Paris – surely they cannot keep marching at such a pace. The Prussians will trounce them, don't you fear.'

'Bet you a thaler the Ogre wins,' Hanne said.

Wilhelm smiled bleakly. 'I haven't a thaler to spare.'

BRAVELY GREEN

December 1805

On Christmas Eve, the six Wild girls went singing into the forest, arms linked, following the tall figure of their brother, Rudolf, who strode ahead of them, an axe over his shoulder, his boots leaving black holes in the thin crust of snow.

'O *Christmas Tree, O Christmas Tree,*
Forever true your colour.
Your boughs so green in summertime
Stay bravely green in wintertime.
O Christmas Tree, O Christmas Tree,
Forever true your colour,' Dortchen sang.

'It's getting dark,' Rudolf called back. 'I'll find us a tree so we can get in out of the cold.'

'Make sure you find one that's tall and straight,' Lisette said.

'Of course I will,' Rudolf responded impatiently. 'I'm not an idiot, Lisette.'

'Sometimes I'm not so sure,' she answered, but he had crashed through the trees and did not hear. His sisters followed him, laughing.

The landscape was all white and black and grey, the interlacing pine branches dusted with frost flowers. Snow crunched under their feet, and their breath plumed white.

'I'm so glad to be out.' Dortchen spun in a circle, arms held wide.

'We'll need to be quick – it's getting very cold,' Hanne said, clapping her mittened hands together.

'How I wish I had a muff,' Lisette cried. 'And new fur-lined boots. These are practically worn through and my feet are frozen solid.'

'I'd rather have some new dancing slippers,' Gretchen said. 'Canary yellow, with silk rosettes and high heels.'

'As if,' Hanne scoffed.

'Where would you wear them?' Lisette asked. 'Father never lets us go dancing.'

'When I am married, I shall have a dozen pairs of dancing slippers, in every colour of the rainbow,' Gretchen said. 'And fur-lined winter boots.'

'Maybe we'll get some new boots for Christmas,' Mia said.

'I showed Father my boots last week and told him it was a scandal that we should be seen on the streets with holes in our shoes. You know how Father hates not to look respectable. I'm sure that I, at least, will get new boots,' Gretchen said.

'Here's a fine sturdy tree,' Rudolf called.

'Let me see,' Lisette cried, rushing forward, but Rudolf was already hacking at the tree trunk with his axe. Chips of wood flew up and the air was filled with the fresh, resinous scent of pine.

'You should've waited – we would have found a better tree further in,' Lisette said.

'I haven't got all evening to waste – I'm going to a cockfight tonight,' Rudolf answered. 'This one is just dandy. Besides, a big tree would just annoy Father. You know he only lets us have one under sufferance.'

Dortchen wandered away into the forest. The sky was a curious colour, like light shining through pale-green glass. Near the horizon a star was just trembling into being. She breathed deeply, the air hurting her lungs. Behind her she heard the smashing of branches as the pine tree hurtled to the ground, and the crash of its impact. She winced and lay down in a bank of snow, spreading out her arms and waving them up and down as though she were flying.

'Dortchen,' Lisette called. 'Where have you got to?'

Dortchen did not reply, looking up at the sky again through the white-furred pine branches.

'Dortchen!'

Lisette followed her footsteps through the snow and found her, still lying in the snow. 'Aren't you cold, little love?' She held out a mittened hand and pulled Dortchen to her feet.

'It looks like an angel was lying there – see?' Dortchen pointed to the shape her body had left in the snow, with outstretched wings made from the motion of her arms.

'You are an angel,' Lisette told her, hugging her. 'A very cold little angel. Look, you've snow all down the back of your dress. You'll be freezing by the time we get home.' She brushed the snow away.

Rudolf hoisted the tree into the buggy, tying it to the rail with rope. He then climbed up and unhitched their horse, Trudi, smacking her ample rump with the reins. Trudi huffed out a great blast of frosty air and began to clip-clop her way along the white road. The girls walked behind in the wheel tracks, singing once more.

Some way down the road, they came up behind a group of dark-clad figures, wrestling a tree along the wintry track. One stopped to bend over and cough, a wet hacking noise in the bell-clear air, and another rubbed his back. As the buggy came up behind them, they pulled their tree off to the side of the road to let the horse and its cargo pass. Dortchen glanced at them curiously and recognised Lotte's unruly dark hair curling from under her knitted cap.

'Lottechen!' she cried.

'Dortchen!' Lotte called back, and the two girls ran together and hugged as if they had not seen each other only that morning.

'What are you doing?' Dortchen asked.

'We wanted to cut ourselves a tree but we didn't realise it'd be so heavy. It feels like we've been dragging it along for hours. My arms are about to fall off.'

'Why don't you tie it to our buggy? There's plenty of room.'

'Could we really? That would be such a help.' Lotte skipped back to her brothers, calling the news to them, and Dortchen followed close behind.

'Good evening, Dortchen,' Wilhelm said, pausing to cough again. 'It's a lovely clear night.' His voice was hoarse and his face very pale, with a sheen of sweat on his brow.

'So you've been cutting yourself a tree too?' Karl asked. 'May we really tie it to your buggy?'

'Thank you for your kind offer, but there are six of us – we'll manage,' Jakob said.

'It's no problem, we have room,' Dortchen responded. 'And we're going straight past your door, so it's not as if we'd have to go out of our way.'

Dortchen's sisters came hurrying up, warmly seconding her suggestion and calling out to Rudolf to stop. Rudolf jumped down and helped hoist the Grimm family's tree onto the buggy. The light from the buggy lantern cast a golden radiance over his hair. Although he was only two years older, Rudolf was a head taller and considerably broader in the shoulder and chest than Jakob. Jakob scarcely looked at him, only muttering his thanks and moving away.

Jakob is proud, Dortchen thought. *He must find it hard to accept help.*

'Would you like to ride up here with me?' Rudolf asked him as he vaulted back up onto the driving seat.

'Oh, no, thank you,' Jakob said. 'Maybe Lotte . . .'

'I'd rather walk with Dortchen,' his sister said.

'Then perhaps Wilhelm could ride,' Jakob said. 'He's not well.'

'I'm fine, really I am,' Wilhelm said, but his brother insisted and gave him a boost up to the driving seat, next to Rudolf. Even that small exertion made Wilhelm catch his breath and cough. 'It's the cold,' he said, seeing Dortchen's anxious eyes upon him. 'It makes my asthma worse.'

She wanted to tell him to drink tea made from rosehips and elderflowers, but Rudolf had clicked his tongue and the buggy had moved on, leaving Dortchen to slog along in its wheel ruts.

The other Grimm brothers fell into place behind the buggy, walking along with the Wild sisters. After a moment, Hanne began to sing again.

To Dortchen's surprise, Jakob joined in. He had a fine, deep voice. Wilhelm turned about so he could join in too. Even Rudolf sang. Overhead, the sky was one vast spread of stars, rimmed with dark spires of trees.

Many other families had gone to the forest to cut Christmas trees, this being the only time of year that the law against cutting wood was relaxed. Many carts and buggies and wheelbarrows laden with snow-spangled trees lined the road, but everyone sang or chatted companionably, and so nobody minded the slow progress in the cold.

Inevitably, the talk turned to the war.

'So there will be peace? Austria will sign the treaty?' Rudolf asked Jakob, who now worked in the War Office and so had all the news first-hand.

Jakob nodded. 'They'll sign this week. The terms are so harsh, though, that the Kurfürst thinks the Austrians will be unable to endure for long. He believes it is Napoléon's intention to force Emperor Francis to abdicate.'

'To abdicate,' Rudolf said slowly. 'You mean . . .'

Jakob nodded. 'Yes. It'll be the death knell for the Holy Roman Empire.'

'But the Empire has been in place since Charlemagne . . .' Rudolf said.

'A thousand years,' Wilhelm said.

Jakob looked tired. 'France wants forty million francs in compensation. Emperor Francis will be beggared. France and her allies have taken Württemberg, Baden, the Tyrol, Venetia, Istria, Dalmatia . . .'

Nobody spoke. It seemed impossible to believe.

'What about Russia? Is no one to stand up to Napoléon?' Rudolf demanded.

Jakob said, 'The Tsar has retreated to Russia—'

'His tail between his legs,' Karl interjected.

'—and though England still fights the French on the seas, they've made no move to send an army to Austria's defence,' Jakob concluded.

'Our only hope is Prussia,' Wilhelm said.

'Yet Prussia and Austria have always been enemies,' Hanne said. The men shot her a look of surprise, but she forged on eagerly. 'Surely the King of Prussia would be glad to see Emperor Francis so humbled?'

'But surely not glad to see Napoléon ruling half of Europe,' Wilhelm pointed out. 'It won't be long before Napoléon seeks to conquer Prussia too.'

'Impossible,' Rudolf said. 'The Prussian army is the best in the world. They'll stop the French in their tracks.'

Jakob shook his head. 'Haven't you heard the news? The Prussian king has sent his warmest congratulations to Napoléon and signed a treaty with him. He's given him great swathes of land so that he will keep away; in return, Napoléon has said the Prussians can occupy Hanover.'

'But Hanover belongs to the British,' Wilhelm said.

'Yes – so the British have declared war against Prussia, too. They are now the only ones standing against Napoléon.'

'Can nothing stop him?' Gretchen cried.

Everyone was silent.

At last they made it back through the broken medieval walls, leaving the forest behind them. The streets of Cassel were lit with golden lanterns, and people in heavy coats and mufflers called 'Merry Christmas!' to each other as they hurried through the snow. A group of carollers stood on the church steps, singing to the crowds. The air smelt deliciously of woodsmoke and roasting chestnuts. As they walked towards the Old Town, the strip of stars overhead narrowed as the crooked, overhanging roofs and gables of the houses grew ever closer together, till it was almost like walking through a tunnel.

'I'm glad we ran into you,' Lotte whispered to Dortchen, pressing her arm between both hands.

'Me too,' Dortchen whispered back.

Rudolf pulled up the horse and buggy in the alley between the Grimm and Wild houses, and the young men began untying the Christmas trees. Dortchen hurried into the kitchen to ask Old Marie for some spiced wine. While Marie heated it by thrusting a hot poker into the jug, Dortchen ducked into the stillroom and scooped out some dried flowers from one jar and some dried leaves from another. She put them in a small muslin bag, thrust it in her pocket, then hurried to collect the tray of pewter tankards, which she carried out into the frosty night. Everyone was glad to accept a cup.

'What do you want the Christ child to bring you this year?' Wilhelm asked Dortchen, as she passed him a steaming tankard.

'Peace,' she said.

He smiled wearily. 'Apart from peace.'

She thought for a moment. 'I'd like a rocking horse,' she said. 'And a storybook with beautiful pictures. Oh, and a new doll to play with – one that is mine, all mine. All of our dolls are so old and battered, and Hanne chopped all their hair off. But Father thinks that we are too old for toys and must not waste our time playing.'

'I suppose there must be a lot of hand-me-downs, in a family of six sisters,' Wilhelm said.

She nodded. 'I've brought you something for your asthma.' Shyly, she showed him the small muslin bag. 'Put some honey in it and drink it before you go to bed. You'll feel much better in the morning.'

He gazed at her in surprise. 'Is that one of your father's remedies? I'm sorry, but I cannot pay you . . .'

'My father didn't make it, I did,' Dortchen said, which was true enough. She had indeed made it, but from her father's recipe. Wilhelm did not need to know that, however. 'It's a gift,' she went on quickly. 'It is Christmas, after all.'

'Well, then, thank you,' Wilhelm said, and stowed the muslin bag away in his coat pocket.

'I hope it helps,' Dortchen said. 'In summer, I will make you tea with linden blossoms. It helps with coughs, and reduces fever, and helps you sleep,' she added, afraid that he might know that the linden was called the tree of lovers, for its heart-shaped leaves and its intoxicating sweet smell.

'You're very kind,' he said.

Dortchen blushed.

Lotte ran up and grabbed her hand. 'What are you having for supper tonight?'

'Roast goose,' Dortchen replied.

'Mmm, that sounds good. Aunt Zimmer gave us a chicken, but it's rather scrawny.'

'There won't be much left of ours but a pile of bones,' Dortchen said apologetically, 'or I'd bring you some leftovers. We'll be making soup from the carcass, though. I could bring you some tomorrow.'

'Lottechen, do you ever think of anything but your stomach?' Wilhelm asked.

She hugged her thin belly. 'It won't let me stop thinking about it.'

Karl bent and scraped up a handful of snow, which he flung at Ferdinand. His brother retaliated, and Ludwig ran to join in. A moment later snowballs were flying everywhere. Lotte and Dortchen joined in enthusiastically, while Lisette and Gretchen squealed and ran for the gate to their back garden. Mia crouched down behind the buggy and waited till Röse took shelter there, then shoved a handful down the neck of her dress. Röse screeched. Her brother laughed and scooped up a snowball, which he threw with deadly aim straight at Jakob's face. Jakob wiped it away, his back stiff, and stalked inside. Wilhelm looked rueful. 'Come on, boys,' he called. 'Let's get the tree inside and decorated, or else we'll be late for church.'

'What a dull dog,' Rudolf said, and he sent a snowball whizzing towards Wilhelm. Wilhelm ducked and caught up a handful, which he flung back rather wildly. Rudolf laughed and sent a barrage of snowballs in return, each finding their mark. Ludwig and Karl ran to their brother's rescue, and soon Rudolf was seeking shelter behind the buggy, jeering and catcalling.

A window crashed open above them. 'Stop that noise,' Herr Wild's voice shouted, 'or I'll call the town watch.'

Everyone froze. Nobody spoke until the window was slammed shut again, then the Grimm brothers quickly dragged their tree inside, with Lotte giggling after them.

'Goodnight,' Wilhelm mouthed. 'Thank you for the wine.'

Rudolf made a face at his father's window, muttered something under his breath and took Trudi back to her stable. The girls gathered the tankards and, trying to keep them from clanking together, hurried back inside.

'I hope Father didn't realise it was us,' Dortchen said.

'It was fun, though,' Mia said. 'I can't remember the last time we had a snowball fight.'

Rudolf came in with the tree over his shoulder, and they set it up in the front parlour. Old Marie had kindled a fire, and with the lamps on the mantelpiece reflecting in the tall mirror, it looked as warm and welcoming as Dortchen had ever seen it. They decorated the tree with red ribbons and gold-painted pine cones, and Lisette and Hanne carefully affixed candles to the boughs. It was Dortchen and her little sister's job to hang the gilded tin angels, Rudolf lifting Mia to hang one at the very tip of the tree.

The church bells rang out, filling the night air with music. Out into the cold the family hurried, snow feathering their faces. They joined the procession of families making their way to the church, each with a lantern swinging brightly in the darkness.

Dortchen matched her steps to its rhythm, feeling her soul expand inside her body till it was pressing against the bones of her chest. *It's Christmas Eve*, she thought. *At midnight tonight, all the animals of the world will speak with human tongues. I wonder what they'll say . . .*

Old Marie knew an old tale about a man who crept out to eavesdrop on the animals in his barn. He heard one horse say to another, 'It'll not be long before we will drive our master to his grave.' Frightened, the man had turned to flee; he slipped on the ice and broke his leg, and had to lie all night in the barnyard. He caught pneumonia and died the next day. With black plumes on their heads, the horses had taken his corpse to the graveyard, just as they had prophesied.

I'll not try to listen tonight, Dortchen decided. *I'm afraid to hear what the beasts will say.*

THE BLUE FLOWER

May 1806

On her thirteenth birthday, Dortchen was released from the duty of the weekly wash and allowed to spend the day in the market garden. This made her happy, and she swung her basket and hummed under her breath as she went down the alleyway.

Overhead, the family's eiderdowns were hung on the washing line to catch the early-morning sun. It was a beautiful spring morning and Dortchen felt sorry for her sisters, who had to spend the day struggling with boilers and wringers and mangles, helping their mother and Old Marie with the week's wash. Already the scullery was full of steam, and Lisette and Hanne's faces and hands were the colour of boiled lobsters.

As Dortchen passed by the house where the Grimms had their apartment, she heard a low whistle and looked up. Wilhelm was standing at a window, smiling down at her. Heat rushed up her face. She had not seen Wilhelm in months – he had been at the university in Marburg, studying for his final exams. He was more handsome than ever, his dark curls hanging over his brow, his shirt unbuttoned to show his throat.

'Dortchen,' he called, 'you're the very vision of springtime. How are you?'

'I'm well, thank you. And you?'

'Glad to be home. I've passed all my exams, you'll be glad to know, and am now a fully accredited lawyer. Isn't it awful?'

'Are you home to stay?' she asked.

'For now. I must get a job. I'm hoping to find one here in Cassel.'

'That's good,' she answered, then bit her lip, thinking she sounded like a fool. She dipped her head and gave a small wave of her hand, knowing she should not be seen talking in the street to a young man who was still in his shirtsleeves.

'Wait,' he called. 'I have something for you.' He disappeared from the window. Dortchen waited, casting a quick look at her father's shop. No one seemed to be watching her. She took a few steps back into the shadow of the alley.

Wilhelm reappeared at the window. 'Look, I found it for you in Marburg.' He lifted up a small doll, dressed all in white frills, and showed it to her. 'Is it not your birthday today?'

Dortchen flushed pink. *He remembered my birthday*, she thought. 'Thank you,' she managed to say. 'She's beautiful.'

'I'll lower her down to you,' Wilhelm said, and disappeared again. In a moment he was back; he opened the casement wider and lowered the doll down to Dortchen on a string. Dortchen received her into her arms as tenderly as if it were a real baby. 'I'll call her Wilhelmine, after you and the Kurfürstin,' she said.

'I remember you hoped for a doll for Christmas,' Wilhelm said. 'I gave one to Lotte for her birthday too. You'll be able to play together.'

'Thank you,' she said again, and looked down at the doll in her arms. She had never seen such a lifelike doll. Its face was white and smooth, and skilfully moulded to look just like a baby's face, while its blue eyes and black curls had been artistically painted. Its body was soft and well-stuffed, much nicer than the stiff bodies of the old wooden dolls.

'It's made from papier-mâché,' Wilhelm said.

She nodded, although she did not understand what he meant, and turned to go back inside and put the doll safely away.

'Happy birthday,' Wilhelm called after her.

Spring turned into summer, and Dortchen was kept so busy in the garden and the stillroom that she scarcely had time to play with her new doll, or to go wandering in the woods with Lotte.

She only saw Wilhelm at a distance, usually at church on Sunday, or when the reading circle met at the Wild house. The circle had widened to include a few other friends, including Johann von Dalwigk, the son of a local baron, and Karoline and Gotthelf Engelhard, the daughter and son of the Grimm family's landlord.

Wilhelm always had a smile and a kind word for Dortchen, but this only made her heart ache more. She longed to be near him, but his presence made her hot-cheeked and tongue-tied, so that she felt she was always making a fool of herself. Her greatest fear was that someone would realise how she felt, and would mock her or tell Wilhelm. Yet she longed for him to realise, and to return her feelings.

One Friday afternoon, on the first day of August, Dortchen went to the big garden outside the town walls to cut cornflowers for her father. Their colour was as bright as the hot blue sky overhead. Her father would boil the blossoms to make eyewash. It seemed a shame, Dortchen thought. She would have liked to fill a vase with them and have them by her bed, to bring a little of the meadow into the house. Her father would think it a waste of good eyewash material, however.

She heard the garden gate open and turned. Wilhelm came towards her, a sombre figure in his black suit. Dortchen rose to her feet, very aware of her muddy apron and dirt-streaked face. She hoped he would think the red in her cheeks was from the sun.

'Good morning, Dortchen,' he said, taking off his tall hat. 'Have you seen Lotte?'

She shook her head. 'Not today.'

'Mother needs her help but she's run off again.'

Dortchen made a face. 'I don't blame her. It's such a beautiful day, it's a shame to be indoors.'

'She's not a little girl any more – she has to realise that. Mother cannot manage it all on her own. I wish Lotte was good and quiet like you.'

Dortchen was surprised. She wasn't used to being called good and quiet. 'No, you don't. Lottechen wouldn't be Lottechen if she was good and quiet.'

'True,' Wilhelm admitted. He looked at the basket of flowers, then picked one up. 'Such a lovely colour. Almost as blue as your eyes.' Dortchen blushed. Wilhelm slipped the flower into his buttonhole.

'You know they're called bachelor's buttons?' she asked. 'If you go home wearing one, people will think you're courting.'

'Oh, no, I can't have that.' Wilhelm took the flower out of his buttonhole at once. 'I can't afford to go courting. We can scarcely afford to feed ourselves as it is, without adding another mouth to the family.'

'Times are hard,' Dortchen said, wishing she had better comfort to offer.

At least there had been peace of a kind. After the Austrians had signed the peace treaty with France, Napoléon had been kept busy making his brothers kings of Holland and Italy, and marrying off his stepdaughter. Everyone hoped he would be happy with what he had won, and would not turn his rapacious gaze on the rest of Europe.

'I was about to make some tea,' Dortchen said, seeing Wilhelm move to put his hat on. 'Would you like to join me?' He hesitated, and she went on: 'You study too hard – some fresh air and sunshine would do you good. And I could make us a nice, fresh salad. I keep oil and vinegar in the summer house. And I have bread and cheese and sour pickles.'

'I am rather hungry,' he said, still hesitating.

'The bread and cheese is very good,' she tempted.

He smiled at her. 'It does sound lovely,' he replied, taking his hat off again. 'Though I don't want to eat all your food.'

'I have plenty,' she said, throwing her hands wide.

Wilhelm smiled. 'You are lucky to have such a big garden.'

'Father doesn't like to spend money on food when we can grow our own. And we need the land for medicinal herbs as well, of course. I wish this garden was closer. It's my job to look after it, most of the time, but it can be wearisome having to walk all this way.' As she spoke, Dortchen gathered salad leaves.

When her basket was full, she led the way to the summer house. This was a small wooden building, rather dilapidated, with a stove in one corner, and a cupboard in which Dortchen kept a few chipped cups and plates. Wilhelm sat down, toying with the blue flower he still carried.

Within a few minutes, Dortchen had a kettle singing on the stove, and bread and cheese and salad laid out on the rickety old table.

'You're very deft,' Wilhelm said admiringly. 'I do wish you'd teach Lotte. She shows no liking for domestic tasks at all.'

'You think any of us do?' Dortchen replied. 'The floors don't scrub themselves, though.'

'I guess not,' Wilhelm responded, smiling.

When he smiled, his eyes crinkled in a most attractive way. It made Dortchen want to make him smile again, but she could think of nothing witty or amusing to say. A silence fell. She made the tea, putting extra milk and sugar in it – she knew sugar was a luxury the Grimms could not afford. Wilhelm drank it thirstily, then fell upon the food.

Dortchen sipped at her own tea, then said, rather shyly, 'What work would you like to do, if you could do anything at all?'

Wilhelm shrugged one thin shoulder. 'I'd like to be able to study old poems and stories, and maybe write some of my own. I've been reading the work of Novalis. He's a poet, you know, a most tragic figure. He died when he was only twenty-eight. He said this thing about language and words . . . I find it very beautiful.'

'What did he say?' Dortchen asked.

'He said that words have a remarkable power. The word "God" is only three letters – yet how much meaning is in those three letters? It's vast, unimaginable. Think of the word "liberty". Only seven letters, yet it changed a whole country and looks like it might change the world.'

'That's true,' Dortchen replied.

'He said, too, that poetry heals the wounds of reason. I often think of that. Does reason wound us?'

'Sometimes,' Dortchen answered, thinking of her father.

Wilhelm looked at her with interest. She looked away, not wanting him to read her face. No one had ever spoken to her like this, as if she were an adult with a mind and a will of her own. 'If poetry is medicine for the world, then it would be rather a fine thing to write it, don't you think? You'd be like a doctor of the soul,' she said.

'I think so,' he replied. 'I'd rather be able to write than practise law. Not that that seems likely, anyway. It's three months since I completed my last exam, and still no job. I don't know what I'm meant to do.'

'You should write something,' she suggested.

Wilhelm shredded the bread between his long, thin fingers. 'I don't know . . . I doubt I've the talent for it.'

'You'll never know unless you try,' she answered.

He smiled. 'True. You're wise beyond your years, Dortchen.'

'What else did this poet say? What was his name again?'

'Novalis. It's not his true name – that was Georg von Hardenberg. I don't know where he got the name Novalis from, but you must admit it sounds much more poetic. He was one of the Romantics, you know. He said, "To romanticise the world is to make us aware of the magic, mystery and wonder of the world; it is to educate the senses to see the ordinary as extraordinary, the familiar as strange, the mundane as sacred, the finite as infinite."'

'That's beautiful,' Dortchen said.

'He was a great writer,' Wilhelm said. 'It's so sad he died so young – just think of what he might have achieved, had he lived longer. He wrote a book about a young man who dreams about a blue flower. It was your bachelor's button that made me think of him.' He gestured towards the cornflower lying on the table next to his plate. 'No one knows what the blue flower means. Death. Love. Beauty. Perhaps the yearning to express the inexpressible. The mystery of the blue flower is its power.'

Silence fell between them. Dortchen was entranced by all he had told her. She hugged her knees, thinking over his words. *To see the ordinary as extraordinary.*

Wilhelm put down his cup. 'But I'm keeping you from your work. I should go.'

'Oh, please don't,' she blurted, then added in a rush, 'I want to hear more. I'd much rather talk about poetry than weed the garden beds.'

'You're as bad as Lotte,' he teased. 'All right. What more do you want to know?'

'What did he die from?'

'Tuberculosis,' Wilhelm replied. 'It was very sad. He fell in love at first sight with a young girl called Sophie. They were engaged when she was only thirteen.'

'That's how old I am.'

'Yes, I know, and Lottechen too. Much too young to be married. They were told they had to wait until she was older, but she got sick with tuberculosis and died when she was only fifteen. He caught it from her, and four years later he was dead too.'

'That is sad,' Dortchen said. Her thoughts were busy with the poet who fell in love with a young girl. She wanted to ask Wilhelm what he thought about that but did not dare.

'She must have been an extraordinary girl,' Wilhelm said. He stood up. 'Now I really must go. Jakob will get home from work tonight and want to know what I've been doing all day, and I can't say I've been sitting around and chatting in the garden.' He bowed to her gravely. 'Thank you for the tea and the delicious lunch. If you see that wicked Lottechen of mine, will you send her home?'

Dortchen nodded. He smiled at her and, on a sudden impulse, picked up the cornflower and tucked it behind Dortchen's ear. 'There. It suits you.'

Once he had gone, she took the blue flower from her hair and kissed it, then she hid it safely in her bodice. Old Marie said that if you wore a cornflower next to your heart, it would bring love to you, whether a new love or a lost love. Dortchen thought she would keep this small blue flower forever.

As Dortchen walked back towards the town, she heard shouting. A crowd of people were huddled around a proclamation nailed to the wall. 'What is it?' Dortchen asked a woman sobbing into her apron. 'What's happened?'

'The Austrian emperor has abdicated,' the woman answered, her voice rough with tears. 'The . . . The Holy Roman Empire is to be disbanded.'

For a moment Dortchen's vision swam. 'What does it mean?'

'More war,' the woman answered, and tears welled up in her eyes again. She sank down into the gutter, her face in her hands. 'My boy! My boy!'

Dortchen walked away, her movements as jerky as those of a marionette. Her steps quickened, then she began to run for home, her bonnet flapping on her back and her basket swinging. She left a trail of small blue flowers behind her, crushed beneath the feet of the jostling crowd.

HOLLY THORNS

November 1806

Dortchen lay in her bed, listening to the skirl of pipes, the drum of tabors, the rhythmic beat of marching feet. The sound was thunderous, filling the night.

She sat up and pressed her face to the window, but all she could see was dark rooftops and church spires, for her room faced the back of the house. She slipped from the bed, putting her feet into her slippers and catching up her shawl. Quietly she made her way down the stairs and through the house. She went into the parlour, but could see nothing through the windows for her father had locked the shutters. The sound of marching feet was very loud in here. '*Aux armes, citoyens, formez vos bataillons, marchons, marchons . . .*' the French soldiers sang.

What will happen now? Dortchen wondered. *Will the soldiers break into our homes, and rob us and beat us and kill us?*

It had all happened so fast.

Prussia had declared war against France on 9th October. Supremely confident, they bragged that clubs would be all they needed to thrash Napoléon's 'cobblers'.

On 14th October, the French smashed the Prussian army at the twin battles of Jena and Auerstadt.

On 27th October, Napoléon and his army had entered Berlin, his soldiers singing 'La Marseillaise'. The Prussian king and queen had fled.

On 31st October, Napoléon's brother Louis had reached Cassel, bivouacking outside the town walls. Dortchen and her sisters had seen the innumerable red eyes of the French army's campfires from the window of their sitting room.

The Kurfürst escaped Cassel the next day, taking with him his family and a long train of baggage carts piled high with treasures. Weeping, Aunt Zimmer went with them. The Hessian troops had laid down their arms. Now Napoléon's soldiers were marching into Cassel itself.

I need to see it happen, Dortchen thought. *I need to mark the moment we stopped being German and became French.*

For once, the kitchen was chilly. Old Marie had banked the fire, fearing that the French might use it to burn down the house. There was no sound from Mozart, whose cage was muffled by an old eiderdown.

Dortchen lifted the latch of the back door and eased herself outside. She could see clearly, for a lurid red light filled the night sky, and the smell of smoke stung her nostrils. Her spirit quailed within her, but she could not bear to go back to her bed. She went down the step and into the kitchen garden, huddling her woolly brown shawl about her against the cold.

Little grew at this time of year, and the wide garden beds stretched empty on either side, sleeping under their thick blankets of straw. The fruit trees were pale and spindly, the bean stakes lonely pyramids of bare sticks. Only the holly tree was still bushy and green, its black jagged leaves sharp against the starlit sky.

An apple tree was espaliered nearby, and Dortchen tucked up her nightgown and climbed it nimbly, its horizontal branches thick and strong under her feet. She could hear the *beat, beat, beat* of the marching boots more clearly now, echoing down the main street. Her stomach jangled with nerves.

She heaved herself up so that she was lying on her stomach on the top of the stone wall, and stared down into the alley. Craning her neck, Dortchen could see the market square, in which marched rows of soldiers in the famous blue, white and red uniforms of the French Grand Army. All were wearing tall cockaded hats and carrying bayonets over their shoulders. Dortchen's eyes stung and she swallowed. It was hard to see the colours of France filling the Marktgasse, instead of the familiar green uniforms of the Hessian army.

A row of drummers marched past, and Dortchen leant so far forward to see them that she overbalanced and toppled down. It was a sharp drop and she fell heavily on her hands and knees on the cobblestones, crying aloud in pain as a holly thorn drove into the soft flesh at the base of her thumb. A few soldiers turned their heads and stared suspiciously down the dark alley, unhitching their bayonets.

Dortchen crouched still, clutching the dark shawl around her. She felt sick with fear. Had her father not warned all his daughters of the dangers of a town under French occupation? Had he not forbidden them all to set foot outside the walled garden? And here she was, naked under her nightgown, out in the street.

The soldiers were coming towards her, bayonets at the ready. In an agony of terror, Dortchen could not move, or even breathe. Suddenly the door across the alleyway swung open, letting out a faint gleam of candlelight. Someone came forward in a few swift steps, lifted her up and swung her through the door. Quietly the door was shut and latched. Dortchen and her saviour limped as quietly as they could up the three flights of steps and into the Grimms' apartment.

'Shh . . .' her rescuer said, holding a finger to his lips. It was Wilhelm. He looked pale and dishevelled, a lock of dark hair hanging over his brow. He took her into the kitchen and lifted her up onto the kitchen table, amidst a mess of dirty crockery, baskets of muddy vegetables and piles of thick, leather-bound books.

Dortchen stared at him with wide eyes. He smiled at her reassuringly and stood by the window, listening. Someone rapped against the door downstairs, then rattled it. When no one responded, the soldiers moved away after a few moments, but Wilhelm and Dortchen stayed silent a good while longer, straining to listen.

At last Wilhelm turned to smile at her. 'That was close,' he said. 'What were you doing – watching over the wall?'

She nodded shyly. 'Father said he would beat us black and blue if we even peeked out the window, but I wanted to see . . .'

'Well, how can I scold you when I was watching too?' His smile faded away, replaced by an expression of angry misery. 'Jakob told us all to keep to our beds, but I refuse to cower under the bedclothes as they take over our town without even a shot being fired. I felt . . . I felt I had to at least stand witness.'

'That's what I thought,' Dortchen said.

'But look – you're bleeding! Did you hurt yourself?'

Dortchen saw that blood was trickling down her wrist, and that her palms were grazed.

'Let me wash that for you,' Wilhelm said.

Dortchen watched as he moved awkwardly around the room, searching for salves and bandages. It was obvious he knew where nothing was, and she hid a little smile. As he bathed her hand and bound it with his own handkerchief, Dortchen burst out, 'I'm so glad the soldiers didn't find me.'

'Yes, indeed. I hate to think what might have happened. A pretty girl like you! Napoléon's soldiers are not known for their kind hearts.'

Dortchen looked away, trying to hide her pleasure and confusion. He poured some milk into a little beaker and brought it to her. 'Here, drink this – it'll warm you. Then I'd best take you home. I hate to think what my mother would say if she knew I was entertaining you alone, at this time of night, in the kitchen.'

'Or my father.' Dortchen gave a little shudder.

'Exactly. So let's get you home.'

Dortchen drank the milk and hopped down from the table, smoothing down her mud-stained nightgown. 'Thank you for the milk,' she said. 'And your hanky. And for coming to my rescue.'

He made a courtly bow, waving his hand and bending till his nose almost touched his knee. 'My pleasure, my lady.'

Dortchen laughed.

'I think I had better help you back over the wall,' Wilhelm said. 'I would not want to wake the household by ringing the bell.'

'Oh, no, please don't do that – my father would kill me!'

'Well, we don't want that. Though I pity him. It can't be easy having six pretty daughters and the Grand Army marching into town. Poor man.'

'There's six of you, too,' Dortchen pointed out. 'Should I call your mother "poor woman"?'

'Not at all, because most of us are sons and can make our own way in the world,' Wilhelm said. 'She has only one daughter to provide for.'

'Well, why can't we make our own way in the world too?' Dortchen complained. 'It's so unfair. Just because we're girls, we have to stay at home and sew and learn to cook and wait for someone to want to marry us. While boys get to work, and travel, and have adventures. My father never lets us go anywhere or do anything.'

'Well, it's his job to keep you safe in these dangerous times,' Wilhelm answered gently, his hand on the latch.

Dortchen huffed out her breath impatiently. 'If I was a boy, I'd run away and join the army and fight against the Ogre and make my fortune and marry a princess, just like the boys in all the stories.'

'I wish it were that easy.'

He opened the door. It was cold and dark and quiet outside. The sound of marching feet had died away. Wilhelm's breath puffed white as he bent to whisper in Dortchen's ear: 'I'll give you a leg-up over the wall. Will you be able to get down on the far side?'

She nodded, huddling her shawl about her, frightened to be out in the night again. She was very conscious of her bare legs under the nightgown.

'Very well, then. Here you go.' Wilhelm cupped his hands together, and she set a hand on the wall and a foot in the cradle of his hands. Swiftly, easily, he launched her up. Dortchen caught the top of the wall and managed to swing her leg over the top, tucking her nightgown down to preserve her modesty. She waved to Wilhelm, now a dark figure in the alleyway, then swung herself down into the apple tree.

The bare branches were silvered with frost. The berries of the holly tree looked white with rime. Old Marie said that all holly berries had once been white, but that the crown of thorns had been made of holly, and the berries had turned red when touched with Jesus's blood. She had a story to explain everything, Old Marie.

Dortchen's slipper touched the ground, and she clambered down and turned. The house loomed against the starry sky. To Dortchen's dismay, a light shone dimly in one window. She stood for a moment, swallowing hard, wanting to flee back to the messy warmth of the Grimms' kitchen. But there was no escape.

Slowly, she moved forward, hoping it was Old Marie, unable to sleep because of her rheumatism, or one of her sisters, looking for a chamber pot. Or even her mother, searching for her drops.

But it was Dortchen's father. He was waiting in the hallway outside the kitchen. The light from the candle he held shook all over his face, making the shadows around his mouth leap and grimace.

He looked her over, his eyes lingering on her tousled hair and mud-stained knees. 'Where have you been?'

'Father, I . . .' Dortchen tried desperately to think of a reason, an excuse, for being out of her bed, out of the house, after midnight, on the very night Napoléon's Grand Army marched into town. 'I just wanted to see.'

'You were outside! Look at you. Filthy slut. Into the study.'

'Please, Father, no . . . I didn't do any harm . . . I'm back again, safe and sound . . .'

He seized her arm and began to haul her down the hall.

'No, Father, please. I'm sorry!'

Her sisters hung over the balustrade, clutching shawls over their nightgowns. No one said a word as Herr Wild dragged Dortchen into his study and slammed the door.

In a wooden frame nailed to the wall were switches of various sizes and thicknesses. Herr Wild muttered, 'Disobeying me, dishonouring me. Does the Bible not say "Children, be obedient to your parents in all things, for this is well-pleasing to the Lord"?'

'Father, please . . .'

It was no use. When Dortchen would not lift her nightgown and lay her back bare, her father pushed her face down against the desk and ripped the nightgown away. When she would not lie still, turning and twisting and fighting him, he slapped her face hard, held her down with one great hand and reached for his heaviest switch. Then he proceeded to beat her, hard and long, till the blood was flowing down her back.

After a while, Dortchen tried not to cry and grunt and moan, but it made no difference. Herr Wild beat her till he was no longer angry.

Then he let go of her neck, wiped the blood from the switch, put it back neatly in its slot, muttered a prayer and went from the room, leaving his thirteen-year-old daughter lying face-down on his desk, unable to move for the white flame of agony that possessed her.

It was Old Marie who came. Frau Wild would be up in the bedroom with her husband, praying with him, trying to avoid bringing his rage down upon her own head. It was always Old Marie who came. She took Dortchen, limping and weeping, into the kitchen, bathed her back with cool water that stung like acid, and gently soothed her wounds with a salve made from willow bark and comfrey. She gave Dortchen some of her father's precious and closely guarded laudanum to drink, then helped her stumble up the stairs to her room.

Mia was sitting up in bed, her arms wrapped around her knees, looking frightened. 'Go sleep with Lisette, sweetling,' Old Marie said. Obediently, Mia got up and tiptoed away. Once she reached the door, she turned, ran back and kissed Dortchen very gently on the cheek. Then she was gone, her nightgown fluttering behind her.

Old Marie helped Dortchen lie down on her stomach. It hurt so much that Dortchen gasped and wept.

'Hush, my darling, hush, don't weep,' Old Marie murmured, stroking Dortchen's hair away from her forehead.

'But why? Why does he do it?'

'Not everyone shows their love in the best of ways.'

'He doesn't love me. He doesn't love anyone!'

'He does,' Old Marie whispered. 'He fears for you. He wants to keep you safe. Oh, I admit he can be cruel, my sweet. But love . . . love is not always easy.'

'I just wanted to see. He keeps us locked up like prisoners.'

Old Marie bent her mouth to Dortchen's ear. 'Do not anger him, sweetling. There was such darkness in his face tonight. I fear for you. Try to be good and quiet. He does not like it when you talk back to him. Try not to say a word.'

Dortchen thought of the old tale about the girl who could not speak or laugh for six years, who tore her hands to pieces weaving six shirts from nettles for her six swan-brothers. Her throat closed.

PART TWO

Weaving Nettles

CASSEL

The Kingdom of Westphalia, 1807–1808

'We can only be free of our swan-skins for one quarter-hour each evening. If you want to save us, you must weave us six shirts from nettles in six years and not once may you speak and not once may you laugh, otherwise all will be in vain.' As her brother spoke, the quarter-hour came to its end, and they were once again transformed into swans.

From 'Six Swans', a tale told by Dortchen Wild to Wilhelm Grimm on 19th January 1812

GREEN SAUCE

October 1807

'Dortchen, we need you. You must come straight away!' Lotte ran into the Wild family's kitchen without bothering to knock or say good evening.

'What is it? What's wrong?' Dortchen turned from the fireplace, where she was stirring a pot of soup. She was alone in the kitchen; Old Marie was busy turning out the linen cupboard with Frau Wild. The starling was perched on her shoulder.

'We have visitors come, noblemen, and not a thing in the house to cook for them.' Lotte clasped both her hands together imploringly. 'Please, can you help us? Please, please.'

'Please, please,' Mozart chirped in her ear.

Dortchen hesitated, glancing out the door. The light was fading. Her father would soon lock up his shop, and he would be expecting his supper. 'I can't,' she said. 'I'm sorry.'

'You don't understand – these are important people. They wrote that book of old songs and poems that Jakob and Wilhelm have been collecting for. Perhaps they can help us. Oh, please, Dortchen, please.'

'Please, please,' Mozart chirped.

Dortchen was torn. 'How many of them are there? What do you have in the pantry?'

'Nothing. Not a crumb. And there's a host of them. Herr Brentano and his mad wife and his mad sister, and Herr von Arnim. They know Herr von Goethe. They know publishers! Please, Dortchen.'

Dortchen looked in the pantry quickly. She dared not take much from their own shelves, for her father scrutinised the weekly accounts closely and was always scolding her mother and Old Marie for waste and improvidence. Besides, a cup of lentils and a jar of pickled onions would not be much use to Lotte.

'Here's a sack of potatoes. Take that – hurry, before anyone sees you – and start peeling. I'll be there as soon as I can.'

Lotte nodded and obeyed. The kitchen door banged behind her as she hurried away, the sack dangling from one hand.

Dortchen felt sick. Now there would be no potatoes for their supper tomorrow, and Herr Wild loved his fried potatoes.

I need something easy, she thought, *something that will feed a lot of people. Something cheap. Something quick. But what? Fish! I could do a green sauce . . . it's a Hessian speciality; they might like to try it.*

Pulling the pot of soup off the heat of the fire, she grabbed her shawl, her basket and her gardening knife and went out into the garden. Above the walls, the sky was streaked with sunset colour, catching the golden fruit of the apple trees. The garden glowed above and was soft with shadows below. She slipped out the gate and across the alley, running up the three flights of stairs to put her head into the Grimm family's kitchen. 'Lotte,' she called. 'Quick, run to the market and buy some fish. I'll make you some green sauce. All you need do is toss the fish in a little flour, then fry them in butter. Can you manage that?'

Lotte nodded, dropping her paring knife into the pile of dirty peelings.

'Put the potatoes on first,' Dortchen said. 'They take longer.'

No more was said. She ran back downstairs, across the alleyway and through the gate into her own garden, then dropped to her knees and began to cut handfuls of borage, sorrel, watercress, burnet, chervil, chives and parsley, placing the fresh green leaves into her basket.

A shadow fell across her.

'What are you doing?' Herr Wild asked. He must have seen her through the stillroom door, which opened out into the garden.

Dortchen's hands paused. 'I . . . I'm cutting herbs, Father.'

'I can see that. I'm not a fool. Why are you cutting herbs? Is supper not yet ready?'

She forced herself to look up. He stood over her, his hands on his hips, his legs planted wide. 'Yes, supper's ready. I'm just making a quick sauce. It won't be long.'

'Then what were you doing outside the garden gate? Were you meeting a boy out there?'

'No, Father, of course not. I . . . I was just making sure none of our apples had fallen over the wall.'

'Where are they, then?'

'What?'

'The apples. Where are they?'

'There was none out there. None had fallen.'

He grunted. 'More likely some thieving boy got to them first.'

She did not reply.

The church bells began to ring out, marking the hour. 'Excuse me,' she said, rising to her feet. 'I must finish.' Her skirts brushed against his leg as she passed him on the narrow path. He smelt of sweat, alcohol and tobacco smoke. Her father had drunk only rarely before the French invasion. Now he drank all day.

'See that supper is not late,' he said to her back.

It had been a year since the French army had marched into Hessen-Cassel. Many things had changed for Dortchen in that time. She was now fourteen and a half, and confined within stays that compressed her ribs and made her feel like she could not breathe. Her hair no longer swung free in a long plait but was curbed with a fistful of pins. She no longer went to school but stayed at home, helping her mother and sisters. Worst of all, she was no longer allowed to go out into the forest by herself, or even to the garden plot outside the town walls.

Hessen-Cassel itself had changed. It was no longer a free country with its own Kurfürst but part of the new Kingdom of Westphalia, which had been formed by mashing together the Duchy of Magdeburg, the Electorate of Hanover, the Principality of Brunswick-Wolfenbüttel and a few other small territories.

At first it seemed as if the new kingdom would be given to Napoléon's brother Louis, who was already King of Holland, but in April news had come that the youngest Bonaparte brother, Jérôme, had been named king instead. Jérôme was twenty-three years old, the same age as Dortchen's brother. Like Rudolf, Jérôme was more interested in gambling and hunting and cockfights than in matters of state. It was said that he had danced while Berlin was ransacked, and that he had already run up debts of millions of francs. Although so young, he had already caused a great deal of scandal. He had married an American heiress while visiting the New World, but had abandoned her and his newborn son at the command of his imperious older brother to marry instead a German princess, the daughter of one of the oldest ruling families in Europe. Jérôme and Catherine of Württemberg had been wed in Paris in April and were slowly wending their way towards Cassel.

In the meantime, the town was full of French soldiers. They drank and gambled and danced, taking what they wanted from the shops and houses, and paying with paper *assignants* that were virtually worthless. The palace had been plundered of its art treasures, and wagons filled with paintings and statues had trundled away from the town towards Paris. The arsenal had been taken over, the French taking all the guns and gunpowder and heavy cannons for their own use. Herr Wild's shop had been cleaned out of its drugs and medications, so the Wild sisters had all been kept busy in the garden and the stillroom, helping their father make new remedies to replace what had been taken. Although Herr Wild was promised reparation, he said he never expected to see a thaler of it.

The Grimm family was suffering even more. Jakob had quit his job at the War Office, exhausted by the demands upon him and unable to bear working for the French. He had applied for a job as the librarian at the palace, but had been passed over for someone with fewer credentials but nobler blood. Since Aunt Zimmer had fled with Princess Wilhelmine, she was no longer able to help them with gifts of food and money. It had been a hard summer, and Dortchen was not alone in dreading the coming of the winter months.

She flew about the kitchen, hurriedly putting eggs on to boil, and crushing the herbs with oil in her mortar. She would serve some with the boiled beef already prepared for their supper, then slip over to Lotte's with the rest as soon as she could.

Old Marie came hurrying in just as Dortchen was dunking the boiled eggs in cold water. 'Green sauce?' she asked, smelling the crushed herbs. 'Is there time?'

'There has to be time,' Dortchen answered.

Old Marie looked at her questioningly but said nothing. Together they peeled the eggs at top speed, then mashed them with vinegar and sour cream and herbs. Dortchen rang the bell and they whisked the meal onto trays and carried it to the dining room.

'Would you take the rest of the sauce over to Lotte?' Dortchen pleaded. 'Tell her I'll be there just as soon as I can.'

Old Marie nodded, though her wrinkled face was anxious.

At last the meal was done, and Dortchen was able to slip away under pretence of checking the livestock.

The Grimms' kitchen was hot and noisy. Frau Grimm and Lotte were juggling pots of boiling potatoes and pans of frying fish on the tiny fireplace, while Ludwig was sprawled at the table, drawing a caricature of Napoléon as a dwarf in military uniform with a dozen crowns on his head. He was trying to stack one more crown on but his arms were not long enough. At his feet lay a dozen toppled monarchs, looking dazed.

'Dortchen – thank heavens you're here.' Lotte's face was flushed, beads of sweat standing out on her brow. She tested the potatoes in the pot with a fork.

'Who's here?' Dortchen asked, hanging up her shawl. 'Do you think they can really help your brothers be published?'

'It's the authors of *The Magic Horn* – you know, that collection of old German songs,' Lotte answered. 'They've had other books published too.'

'One is Herr von Arnim,' Frau Grimm said, turning the fish in the frying pan. 'A very old noble family from Prussia.'

'His father is the director of the Royal Berlin Theatre,' Lotte put in. 'Or he was. I don't know if he still is, now that Berlin is occupied by the French.'

'They're Catholics!' Frau Grimm exclaimed. 'I never thought I'd see the day.'

'The other is the poet Clemens Brentano,' Ludwig said. 'He's here with his new wife. Apparently they eloped.'

'And his old wife in her grave only a few months, and her poor little baby with her,' Frau Grimm said, shaking her head in disbelief.

'She says he abducted her,' Lotte said, making a shocked face at Dortchen. 'The new wife, I mean.'

'It all seems rather irregular,' Frau Grimm said. 'I wasn't at all sure that I should receive them.'

'Except they might help the boys get jobs.' Lotte turned to Dortchen. 'Herr Brentano's sister Kunigunde is married to Professor von Savigny, who took Jakob to Paris last year, and his other sister, Ludovica, is married to the banker Herr Jordis, who employs Karl. So, you see, they are very well connected. Oh, if only they could help us some more. I don't know how we'll survive otherwise.'

Ludwig frowned at her. 'Lotte, you shouldn't say such things. Dortchen doesn't need to know all our problems.'

'I haven't any secrets from Dortchen,' Lotte replied impatiently. 'She's like a sister to me, isn't she, Mother?'

'Indeed, yes,' Frau Grimm said, poking at the fish in the pan with a fork. 'If I was ever to have another daughter, I'd like her to be just like Dortchen, the sweet girl that she is.'

Dortchen smiled at her. 'Well, if I was ever to have another mother, I'd like her to be just like you too.'

'Except hopefully a better cook,' Frau Grimm said. 'Oh, Dortchen, is the fish ready? I never can tell.'

Dortchen took her place at the fire. 'Only a little bit scorched,' she replied, skilfully turning the fish out onto a platter. 'I'm sure no one will mind.'

'I think my potatoes are overdone too,' Lotte said, prodding them doubtfully.

'Let's mash them,' Dortchen said. 'I brought some butter.'

'Bless you,' Lotte said.

OLD TALES

October 1807

The sitting room was full of people. Dortchen put the tray down on the big table in the middle of the room and looked around curiously.

Apart from the four eldest Grimm brothers, there were two men. One was thin and dark and serious-looking, very elegantly dressed in a starched cravat and a well-cut coat of dark-blue superfine over a snowy-white waistcoat. His hair was cut short à la Brutus, a few curls allowed to fall on his broad, pale forehead.

The other man could not have been more different. He was closer to thirty than twenty, and was broad-chested and heavy-jowled. Deep lines of dissipation ran from the corners of his loose-lipped mouth to his chin. His eyes were heavily pouched, his forehead marked with scowl lines. He did not wear the dark coat and intricate starched cravat of a man of fashion, but a loose emerald-green robe like a medieval scholar, with a bright-orange scarf wrapped loosely about his throat. His hair was short and messy, but – unlike the nonchalant disorder of his companion's – it looked as if he had not bothered to run a comb through it in some time.

The women were as strangely dressed as he was. One was little more than a girl, dressed all in black, from hem to collar to fingertip to bonnet. Her dress was made of muslin, however, not bombazine, and it looked as if it had been dyed in a hurry by an amateur, for the hue was patchy.

Her bonnet, too, had been inexpertly dyed, and Dortchen could see where flowers had been ripped away and replaced by swathes of black veiling. She sat by herself in a corner, though her eyes busily flicked from one person to another. Her face was a constant parade of emotions – anger, scornful disbelief, outrage, wistful longing – which crossed her face in moments as she listened to the ebb and flow of the conversation.

'She's wearing mourning for her lost innocence,' Lotte whispered to Dortchen. 'She and Herr Brentano' – she indicated the man in the orange scarf – 'were married this week. *She* says he abducted her. *He* says he came to Cassel to escape her, but found her in his carriage dressed in a wedding gown, and what else was he to do?'

'How old is she?' Dortchen whispered back.

'Sixteen.'

Only two years older than she was, and married to this world-weary man with the scowling eyes. Dortchen felt sorry for her. The girl in black must have seen her quick glance, for she stood up and pointed. 'Look, Clemens, there's a girl even younger and fresher than me. We've been married but a week. Time enough. Divorce me and you can carry her off in your carriage and ravish her like you ravished me.'

'Augusta,' her husband said warningly.

'Don't call me that any more,' she proclaimed in a trembling voice. 'Augusta Busmann is dead.'

'Oh, stop being so tiresome,' the other young woman said. 'You jump into Clemens's carriage and beg him to take you away. What did you expect him to do?'

'You have no heart, Bettina Brentano,' Augusta said, turning her face away.

'No, no, I am all heart,' Bettina cried. 'That's your problem, Augusta. You say you want to live a life of romance and danger and passion, but you're only pretending. If you truly want to be alive, you've got to feel it all – the pain, the guilt, the desire – all of it.'

Dortchen could not help staring at Bettina, who was the most extraordinary-looking creature she had ever seen. Aged in her early twenties, she was as small and delicate as a child, with large, dark eyes, pale skin and a riot of dark curls that hung all around her face in tight ringlets. She wore a white poet's shirt with billowing sleeves and a flowing collar, tied with a crimson sash over flowing purple silk. A bracelet of coins hung about one wrist. They chimed with every move she made.

'Supper's ready,' Lotte cried.

Karl and Ferdinand came and took up their plates, crowing with delight. 'It's a feast! Mother, you've done wonders.'

'Oh, it was Dortchen and Lotte.' Frau Grimm smiled comfortably.

Karl opened the wine and splashed it into pewter goblets, and Ferdinand passed them around.

'The poor fish,' Bettina said. 'I wish that I had been there when he was caught, so I could ransom him and set him free.'

'Do you not want yours?' Karl demanded. 'Because I'll take it gladly.'

'I suppose one must eat,' Bettina said, and she took a plate and fork back to the armchair by the fire, where she sat with her legs curled up under her. Dortchen, passing out forks and napkins, was surprised. That was Jakob's chair. The eldest Grimm brother seemed content to sit at the table and eat, however; he was deep in conversation with Wilhelm and the elegant young man in the white waistcoat, who must be Achim von Arnim.

'I have brought some stories to show you,' Achim was saying. 'They were collected by the painter Philipp Otto Runge. He heard them from some fishermen and did his best to write them down word for word. Oh, Jakob, they are real folk tales, free from artifice and preciousness.'

Achim put down his fork and pulled a sheaf of paper from his coat pocket. It was closely covered with beautiful handwriting. 'This one is very funny, about a fisherman and his wife. He catches a flounder that is really an enchanted prince, and so lets him go. The wife is angry and tells him he should have asked the enchanted prince to give them a cottage to live in instead of their filthy old shack. So the fisherman asks the fish and is given a lovely little cottage, but the wife is not satisfied. First she wants a palace, then she wants to be king, then emperor, then pope—'

'It sounds like Napoléon,' Wilhelm interjected. 'It wouldn't at all surprise me if *he* ends up wanting to be pope as well as emperor.'

'Is the Pope not his puppet anyway?' Jakob said, scooping up a mouthful of fish.

'Well, let us hope Napoléon ends up like the fisherman and his wife in this story, back in the filthy old shack where they belong,' Arnim said.

'Are you going to publish it in *The Boy's Wonder Horn*?' asked Jakob.

'We've decided to focus only on songs and poetry in *The Wonder Horn*,' Clemens said, bringing his plate over to join them.

'We've published the other story, "The Juniper Tree", in the magazine we've put together,' Arnim said. 'It's a sad, strange tale about a boy who is slaughtered by his mother and eaten by his father, but he comes back as a singing bird to take his revenge.'

'It sounds very old,' Wilhelm said. 'Like a Greek tragedy. May we make a copy of the stories? We're interested in old tales. Jakob is writing an article about Minnesingers, and I'm working on one about the Lay of the Nibelungs.'

'Why don't you send us your articles?' Arnim said. 'They sound just the sort of thing we're looking for.'

'We've called the magazine *Journal for Hermits*,' Clemens said with a laugh. 'Perfect for you two.'

'We've copied down quite a few old tales from manuscripts and books,' Wilhelm said. 'Would you be interested in publishing any of those as well?' He looked at Jakob with excitement gleaming in his dark eyes.

'Perhaps,' Clemens answered. 'Though maybe you should think of putting a book together, as we have done with *The Boy's Wonder Horn*.'

'We could write down any old stories that we hear,' Jakob said, his fork hovering above his plate. 'We could try to capture the simple, natural tone of the storyteller.'

'I'm sure such old stories have very deep roots,' Wilhelm said. 'They go far back into the past. It would be fascinating to collect them and save them from disappearing.'

Bettina had been sitting in her chair, gazing dreamily into the fire, her plate on her lap untouched.

'Aren't you hungry?' Dortchen asked shyly.

Bettina shrugged and took a mouthful. Suddenly, she cried out and thrust her plate away from her, and it crashed down onto the hearth rug. 'Green sauce,' she sobbed. Tears rose up in her great, dark eyes and flooded down her face. 'Oh, how cruel.'

At once people rushed to comfort her. Clemens sat on the arm of the chair and put his arm about her, and the Grimm brothers crowded close, asking questions. Wilhelm went down on his knees to scrape up the splattered meal. Achim passed her a snowy handkerchief, which she took, blowing her nose fiercely.

'But, my dear, whatever is wrong?' Frau Grimm said, sounding bewildered. 'Is the sauce too strong?'

'No, no,' Bettina sobbed. 'It is just . . . I have not eaten it since . . . we used to have it at the convent, you see, and it reminds me . . . my dear friend Karoline.'

'Ah,' Clemens said, drawing his sister's head against his sleeve. 'Her friend stabbed herself last July,' he explained. 'She was a poetess.'

'A great poetess,' Bettina declared, lifting her face from her brother's sleeve. 'She was broken on the wheel of life.'

'Had an affair with a married man,' Clemens said.

'We had planned to travel Europe together,' Bettina said. 'We were going to dress like men so that we were free to go wherever we pleased. Instead, Karoline is being eaten by worms and I am stuck with Kunigunde and her deadly boring husband.'

'You must not speak that way,' Jakob said. 'Professor von Savigny is a great man. You are lucky indeed to have been given a home with him.'

'Oh, I know,' Bettina replied. 'I should be grateful, shouldn't I? It is just that I cannot bear being surrounded by people who are happy in domesticity.'

'Come, come, my dear, that's no way to talk,' Frau Grimm said, putting the broken plate on the tray. 'A lovely young girl like you? Why, soon you'll be married yourself, no doubt, and dandling a little one on your knee.'

Bettina looked at her in horror. 'Oh, no – do you think so?'

'Of course, my dear.'

Bettina buried her face in her brother's sleeve again. 'Oh, Clemens, save me,' she said in a muffled voice. 'I'll end up all grey and moth-eaten, like an old coat.' She lifted her face, her eyes wide and flashing with emotion. 'You understand, don't you? Only the wild, the great and the glittering please me. I cannot bear an ordinary life.'

'Only ordinary people have ordinary lives,' her brother soothed her. 'Look at Augusta now. She'd like nothing more, would you, my dear? A nice little house with a nice little husband and a nice little baby. What a shame you decided to marry me.'

His wife turned and looked at him with scornful eyes. 'You are trying to drive me to despair, aren't you? You want me to put an end to myself so you'll be free again. But what would people say of you? Two wives dead in less than a year.'

'What on earth gives you the impression that I care what people say?' Clemens drawled. 'Altogether too bourgeois, my dear.'

'Oh, yes, you would think wanting to be happy is bourgeois, wouldn't you?' Augusta replied. 'Do you think agonies of the heart are only confined to poets? Well, I may not be a poet, but I feel just as deeply as you, Clemens. I hurt too!'

'No need for the histrionics, Augusta,' he answered in a bored tone.

His wife drew down the veiling so it hid her face. 'Augusta is dead. Call me that no more.'

'What, then, do you wish us to call you?' Achim asked, his face troubled.

'Call me Franz. I shall cast off these clothes of oppression, dress in the clothes of a man and travel the world as I please.'

'Oh, unfair,' Bettina said. 'You're just copying me now, trying to be interesting. Can't you think of your own wild scheme?'

Augusta pressed her hands to her breast and turned her face away again.

'You'll have to grow mutton-chop sideburns,' Bettina said with a giggle, 'or else no one will believe you're a man.'

Karl gave a snort of amusement. In a second, a roar of helpless laughter went around the room. Even Frau Grimm was laughing. There was such a contrast between the image of Augusta as she was now, draped head to foot in her black weeds and sitting in the pose of a tragic heroine, and the idea of her with thick sideburns, a walking stick and a tall hat.

'You're cruel. Cruel!' Gathering up her black skirts, Augusta fled from the room.

'Oh, dear, we shouldn't have laughed,' Frau Grimm said. 'Poor girl. She's overwrought.'

'Don't you worry about her, she's always overwrought,' Clemens replied, as Frau Grimm hurried after the weeping girl. 'You cannot imagine how I've suffered these past few weeks. But what was I to do? If I had not married her, she would've been ruined.'

'It's a difficult situation,' Achim said. 'Indeed, I wonder if you would not have been better off refusing to get into the carriage with her, Clemens. Surely you didn't need to drive off with her?'

'It was a whim, an impulse, a caprice,' Clemens replied. 'I gave in to the urge of a moment. Believe me, I had regretted it before the night was out.'

'Enough of such talk,' Bettina ordered. 'Don't you realise there are ladies present? Besides, who wants to talk about Augusta? That's just what she wants.'

'Not Augusta,' Karl said in a deep, lugubrious voice. 'Franz.'

They were all shaken with laughter again. Dortchen could not help herself, although she felt that she was being cruel.

'Bettina's right,' Achim said. 'Let us talk about your work, Jakob.'

Jakob and Wilhelm began at once to show Achim and Clemens some of the manuscripts they had been transcribing. Ludwig was busy with his charcoal and sketchbook, capturing the two male visitors in quick yet startlingly acute strokes on the page. Karl and Ferdinand hung close by, trying to join in the conversation, yet clearly out of their depth. Lotte and Dortchen hurried to clear away the dirty plates so Jakob could spread the pages of his manuscript out on the table. Bettina rose and brought them her own plate and goblet.

'I don't mean to be cruel,' she said confidingly to the other two girls, 'but I am all out of patience with her. Augusta is like that all day long, moaning and weeping and flinging herself about. She always wants to be the centre of attention.'

Dortchen thought that seemed true of Bettina herself. Yet somehow Clemens's sister was so full of charm and quicksilver wit that it was impossible to dislike her, while Augusta had been so odd and intense and melodramatic that no one could possibly be comfortable in her company.

'Well, it's much quieter with her gone, anyway,' Lotte said. 'We've never had so many people in our sitting room at once.'

'I do like eating like this, with our plates on our laps, and everyone sitting where they like,' Bettina said. 'So much nicer than having to worry about etiquette and precedence and all those boring things. That is how I shall have my dinner parties when I'm all grown-up.'

'Aren't you grown-up now?' Dortchen asked shyly.

'Heavens, no. Don't say so. I intend to remain a child just as long as I can. A poet should be like a child of solitude, Herr von Goethe says. And he is my hero, you know.'

'I love Herr von Goethe too,' Wilhelm said, turning around. 'Which do you prefer, Young Werther or William Meister?'

'Oh, Werther, of course, if we're talking about his men. But my favourite character is, of course, Mignon. Mignon, Mignon! If I was to change my name, that's what I'd like to be called. Don't you think I look a little like her?'

She capered around like a small child, and Dortchen realised, with amazement and fascination, that Bettina was wearing flowing silken trousers that were tied at the ankle, and not a skirt, as she had assumed. Dortchen had never seen a woman wearing trousers before.

'You do indeed,' Wilhelm assured her. 'Only I would never mistake you for a boy.'

'Is that a compliment?' Bettina cried. 'I believe it was. Clemens, you're right. Your friends the Grimm brothers are quite charming.'

'There is no charm in telling the truth,' Wilhelm replied.

'Oh, adroitly done. You're a courtier! Clemens, did you hear? I swear my head shall be turned.'

'Well said, sir.' Clemens clapped his hand on Wilhelm's shoulder. 'What you mean, of course, is that my hoydenish sister looks like she belongs with the raggle-taggle gypsies.'

'Well, that's a compliment too,' Bettina replied. 'I'd love to run away to the circus. Wouldn't you?' She turned appealingly to Dortchen and Lotte, who were once again standing and listening as if watching a play they didn't really understand. 'Wouldn't you much rather be like Mignon and living with the gypsies, than a stout *Hausfrau* counting your silver spoons?'

'Absolutely,' Lotte cried, though Dortchen was sure she had never heard of Mignon either.

Bettina smiled at Wilhelm. 'Did you know I've met Herr von Goethe?'

'No? Really?'

'Yes. I wrote to him and asked to meet him. He was in love with my mother, you know. So he invited me to tea. His house was just like you'd imagine, full of books and fine art and sycophantic people. He asked me, very politely, what interested me. "Nothing but you," I answered. So then he told me to make myself at home. So I went and sat in his lap and put my arms about his neck and my head on his shoulder and went to sleep.'

'You didn't?' Karl gasped.

'Yes, I did. I had a lovely little nap, and when I woke up he asked me to stay to dinner.'

No one could help staring at her. Bettina Brentano was such a strong and unusual personality, so full of life, so sure of herself, so determined to shock and enliven. At that moment Dortchen wished with all her heart to be like her, yet felt herself slipping deeper into the shadows. She could think of nothing at all to say, so quietly she packed up the plates and took them down to the kitchen. Lotte followed along behind her. They barely spoke as they did the washing-up together in the scullery.

Dortchen felt a lump in her throat, a quiver in her eyelids. 'Could I borrow some books?' she said at last. 'We don't have any, you know. Just the Bible and our psalm books and a few others that Father thinks are educational.'

'Of course, any time. We have more books than we know what to do with,' Lotte answered.

'Can I borrow that one they were talking about? The one with the girl called Mignon?'

Lotte nodded. 'I'll ask Wilhelm for it tomorrow and bring it over for you.'

Dortchen took up her shawl and wrapped it about her. 'All right. See you tomorrow, then.'

Lotte threw her arms about her. 'Thank you for helping us tonight,' she said, her voice muffled in Dortchen's neck. 'I couldn't have managed without you. I wish you really were my sister.'

'So do I,' Dortchen replied, her eyes growing hot. She drew away from Lotte, took up her basket and let herself out into the shadowy alleyway, then ran across to the safety of the gate opposite and the quiet, dark, frost-whitened garden.

From the upstairs window of the Grimms' sitting room came the sound of laughter.

THE THIRTEENTH DOOR

December 1807

The new King of Westphalia drove into Cassel on 7th December.

An hour before he was due to arrive, French soldiers banged on the doors with the butts of their bayonets, ordering the citizens of Cassel to line the main street and cheer the new king and queen.

'I can't believe Father is letting us go,' Mia said, catching up her bonnet. 'I haven't been anywhere but church or school for months.'

'He doesn't want any trouble,' Lisette said. 'Like it or not, we have a new king now, and only those who are seen to support him will prosper.'

'I wonder what he is like?' Dortchen asked. 'Do you think he'll be a good king?'

'Highly unlikely,' Gretchen said with a snort. 'They say he's quite decadent.'

'Maybe the coming of the new king will mean a turn in our fortunes,' Lisette said, putting on her bonnet.

'He's more likely to beggar us all,' Hanne said. 'I've heard he's already squandered a fortune.'

'Girls!' their father called. 'What's taking you so long? Hurry along now.'

They clattered down the stairs to the hall, where their parents waited for them, Frau Wild in a flutter of shawls, Herr Wild frowning and consulting his watch. Out they went into the grey afternoon, Herr Wild clearing a path through the crowd with his walking stick.

'So many people,' Frau Wild sighed. 'So noisy.'

'Let's go to the Königsplatz,' Lisette suggested. 'We'll get a better view there.'

'Stay close.' Herr Wild poked Dortchen with his walking stick. 'Don't you go running off anywhere, wild girl. It's not safe.'

'No, Father,' she answered.

It was not long before they recognised the Grimm family walking ahead of them. Jakob was supporting his mother, while Lotte danced beside Ludwig. The two parties soon joined together, Frau Wild and Frau Grimm each taking one of Herr Wild's arms, leaving Jakob free to walk with Rudolf and Wilhelm with Gretchen.

'Such a week we've had,' Lotte told Dortchen. 'Those writer friends of Jakob and Wilhelm's have been over every day, eating all our food and smoking cigars in the sitting room. Mother swears we'll never get the smell out of the curtains.'

'Do you think they'll help get something published?' Dortchen asked.

'I hope so. Jakob and Wilhelm are sure of it. Both Herr Brentano and Herr von Arnim have been full of praise for the work they've done. They said they might show it to Herr von Goethe. Wilhelm is in heaven at the thought of that.'

Dortchen did not reply. She had done her best to read Goethe's novel, late at night with the light of a stolen candle stub, but much of it had puzzled her. It had made her feel stupid. She did not understand many of the words, or why the characters said what they said and did what they did. A few lines had burnt themselves into her soul. The heroine talked about love as rapture. 'I will clasp him as if I could hold him forever,' she had cried. Dortchen had repeated those lines to herself many times. She had scanned the pages, looking for any other lines about love, but there seemed to be a lot about philosophy and not so many about romance.

They walked into the Königsplatz, which was already full of people, many of them wearing red, white and blue cockades in their hats. Soldiers were everywhere, keeping the crowds back from the street.

'Look.' Dortchen seized Lotte's arm and pointed. The marble statue of the Kurfürst's father, the Landgrave Frederick, had been knocked down and taken away from its plinth in the centre of the square. A bronze statue of Napoléon had been erected in its place, looking grim, his hand tucked inside his coat.

Lotte ran up the steps of the plinth and cupped her mouth with both hands, calling *'Ja!'* There was no answering echo.

'Maybe there's too many people here,' Dortchen said.

'There's always hundreds of people here, it's never stopped the echo before,' Lotte answered. 'No, it's because they've taken good old Freddie down. Who wants to look at that ugly dwarf?'

'Shh, Lotte,' Wilhelm said. 'It's not wise to call the Emperor names with so many French soldiers around.'

'And spies,' Ludwig said. 'He's got spies everywhere. That old beggar there could be one. Or that man selling hot pies. Or even that pretty girl with the violets.'

Lotte looked around warily and came down from the plinth. Her face was pale under her bonnet.

Herr Wild had found them a good vantage point near the street, and they huddled close, rubbing their gloved hands together. They heard the parade long before it arrived. First the rat-a-tat-tat of drums and the blowing of trumpets, then the marching of feet, the stamping of hooves and the rumble of wagons pulling heavy guns. Battalion after battalion of soldiers marched by in rigid formation, and then at last a gilded open carriage came into sight. It was pulled by four grey horses with red plumes on their heads.

The new king was young and handsome, with dark curly hair combed forward on to his forehead, laughing dark eyes and beautifully groomed sideburns. He wore military uniform, with very tight white pantaloons and a high cravat. Beside him sat his new wife, plump, plain and apprehensive, wearing a pale gauzy dress with a high waist and puffed sleeves. The inch of skin between her long gloves and the edge of her sleeve was purple with cold.

Behind the carriage ran small beggar children, hands held up pleadingly. Every now and again, one of the King's men threw out a handful of gold coins, causing fights to break out.

'He looks very dapper,' Rudolf said. 'I wonder if he ties his own cravat.'

'He looks like a fool,' his father replied.

The parade proceeded down the Königstrasse and out of sight. Everyone would have liked to have followed the cavalcade out to the palace, but dusk was already falling and it was cold. Reluctantly, they turned for home.

'I heard they've renamed the palace,' Wilhelm told Gretchen. 'It's not Wilhelmshöhe any more, but Napoléonshöhe.'

'Everything is changing,' Gretchen said. 'Mother says we must all try and speak French now but I just can't get my tongue around it.'

'French is really not that difficult,' Jakob said. 'You should try Old Norse.'

Gretchen flushed and dropped her eyes. She was very much in awe of the clever eldest Grimm brother.

'Lisette speaks French well,' Dortchen said. 'She's good at languages. Last night we heard the strangest sounds coming from her bedroom. It sounded like she was being strangled by a giant snake. We all rushed in and asked her, "Are you sick, Lisette?" But she just said, "No, you silly billies. I'm learning English."'

Both Jakob and Wilhelm laughed.

They were almost home when there was a distant bang, and a roar. Everyone screamed and ducked down, covering their ears, expecting a fusillade of shots. Instead, a shower of gaudy sparks shot up into the sky, then flowered into an enormous blossom of coloured lights.

'What is it?' Mia cried. 'Mama!'

'It's fireworks,' Jakob said. 'They must be setting them off at the palace.'

'We'll be able to see from the upstairs window,' Lisette cried. 'Come on!'

Everyone hurried towards the shop, craning to see as more fireworks were shot high into the sky. Herr Wild opened the front door and Rudolf led the stampede upstairs. Lotte and her brothers hesitated outside; they would not have such a good view from their window.

'Won't you come in?' Dortchen asked shyly, and she saw her father frown. But her mother, panting along in the rear, seconded the invitation, and so the Grimms accepted and followed Dortchen up to the drawing room. They all clustered at the window, watching as vibrant peonies and dahlias of fire flowered in the sky.

At last the fireworks faded away and farewells were made. Hovering near Wilhelm, Dortchen heard him say to Gretchen, 'Tomorrow, then?'

Gretchen blushed, smiled and nodded. Wilhelm put on his tall hat and followed his brothers down the stairs.

Standing by the window, Dortchen watched the Grimm family cross to their own house. Wilhelm turned and looked up, then gave a little wave. Gretchen, who was standing at the next window, waved back, then, smiling, went running out to help her sisters prepare supper.

Dortchen shut the window and stood standing by it, leaning her forehead against the cold pane. Her heart felt bruised.

The air stank of smoke and gunpowder.

'He wants you to tell him a story?' Lisette asked incredulously, the next morning at breakfast.

Gretchen nodded. 'He wants to know all the stories we know. He and his brother have decided to collect them.'

'How very odd,' Röse said.

'Surely it's just an excuse,' Hanne said. 'Really, he wants to sit and gaze into your beautiful blue eyes.' She clasped her hands near her ear and fluttered her eyelashes.

'He is handsome,' Frau Wild said. 'Such a shame.'

A little silence fell; all the girls knew what she meant. Herr Wild looked up from his newspaper and frowned. 'They're poor as church mice, Gretchen, without a prospect in the world. Not a family to be encouraging.'

'He's not courting me,' Gretchen said. 'He just wants me to tell him a story.'

'Faugh,' Herr Wild said.

'What story will you tell?' Dortchen asked. She was so jealous that she could scarcely frame the words.

'The one about Mary's child, I thought,' Gretchen said.

Frau Wild frowned. 'Should you? Do you think?'

'Why not? It's beautiful,' Gretchen said. 'I think he'll like it.'

'Lisette, you'd better sit with your sister.'

'No! I don't want to be the chaperone. It's humiliating. Besides, Father needs my help in the shop. I'm the only one who can understand all the soldiers.'

'Hanne . . .'

'I'm not going to chaperone her. Besides, it's Tuesday. I have to air all the bedding and dust the bedrooms.'

Frau Wild looked at Röse, but before she could speak, Dortchen said quickly, 'I'll sit with her, Mother. I can do the mending.'

Her mother nodded in relief.

'Gretchen had best darn all the stockings,' Hanne said. 'That'll dampen his ardour, if anything can.'

Gretchen laid a small fire in the parlour, hoping her father wouldn't mind too much, and Dortchen ran to the garden to pick a bunch of rosehips to brighten the room. It was not long before they saw the silhouette of Wilhelm in his tall hat passing the parlour window. Gretchen jumped up, smoothed her curls, straightened her dress and went to the door. She opened it before he could knock.

'Good morning,' he said, sounding flustered.

'Good morning,' she said, sounding the same.

She led him into the parlour, and the same round of greetings was repeated with Dortchen, who was sitting very straight in her chair by the fire, a basket of mending at her feet. Wilhelm was carrying his writing box, which he put down on the table.

'So, you have a story for me?' he asked Gretchen, getting out some paper and his inkpot.

'Yes. I thought I'd tell you a story about Mary's child,' Gretchen answered, blushing for no apparent reason. 'It's a tale Old Marie has often told us.'

Wilhelm dipped his quill into the inkpot and looked at her attentively. 'Yes?'

Gretchen cleared her throat and began. 'Near a great forest there lived a woodcutter and his wife. They had but one child, a three-year-old girl. They were so poor that they no longer had their daily bread, and they did not know how they were to feed her.'

'Not so fast – I cannot write that quickly,' Wilhelm said, dipping his pen in the inkpot again. Gretchen paused while he caught up, the scratching of the pen on the paper and the clicking of the nib in the inkpot the only sounds. 'Didn't know how to feed her,' he repeated.

On they went, Wilhelm constantly asking Gretchen to slow down, and Gretchen occasionally getting muddled and going back and inserting details she had forgotten. As she described how the little girl was adopted by the Virgin Mary and taken up to heaven, Dortchen listened critically, her needle flying faster and more smoothly than Wilhelm's pen.

'When the girl was fourteen years old . . .' Gretchen said.

The same age that I am now, Dortchen thought.

'. . . the Virgin Mary summoned the girl and gave her thirteen keys, saying, "I'm going on a long journey . . ."'

'Wait,' Wilhelm said. He turned the page round so that he could write across the existing lines. 'How many keys?'

'Thirteen,' Gretchen said. 'They were the keys to the thirteen doors of heaven. The Virgin Mary told the girl, "You may open twelve of the doors, but the thirteenth door is forbidden for you. Do not open it, whatever you do."'

'Interesting. A forbidden chamber motif. Let me guess – she opens it.'

'Yes,' said Gretchen, laughing. 'First she opens the other twelve doors and finds the Apostles behind them. Then she opens the thirteenth door and finds—'

'Hell?' Wilhelm asked.

'No! She finds God. Amazed, she reaches out to touch Him, then flinches back with pain. Her finger is all stained with gold.'

'And no matter how hard she washes it, she cannot get rid of the stain,' Wilhelm said.

'You know the story?' Gretchen asked.

'No, no, it's just like other tales I've read. Usually it's blood that can't be washed away.'

'Oh.' Gretchen looked away, blushing furiously.

Wilhelm flushed too. He straightened his parchment, cleared his throat and said, 'Give me a moment to catch up. She opened the door, found God, stained her finger with gold . . . Then what happened?'

Gretchen went on. 'Tackled with her disobedience, the girl denied it three times and was cast out of heaven. She found herself in a forest, with nothing to eat but nuts and berries.'

'You forgot to say she had lost her voice,' Dortchen said.

'Oh, yes. She had lost her voice and could not speak. Now I've forgotten where I was.'

'She wanted to cry out but couldn't make a sound,' Dortchen prompted. 'She wanted to run away but couldn't break through the thorns and brambles. Before long, all her clothes were ripped to shreds.'

'That's right. All her clothes were ripped to shreds and she had nothing to wear but her long golden hair.' Gretchen stopped again, embarrassed.

Dortchen realised why her mother had been concerned that Gretchen should tell Wilhelm this story. One did not talk about naked women with young men.

'Like St Agnes,' Wilhelm said.

Gretchen nodded gratefully. 'Anyway, one day a king found her and married her—'

'Even though she couldn't speak,' Dortchen put in.

'Yes. A year later they had a son, and the Virgin Mary appeared and demanded that she confess to opening the door.'

'The thirteenth door,' Dortchen said.

Gretchen cast her a look. 'Shh, Dortchen, you're muddling me.'

'I can't write down all the details anyway,' Wilhelm said. 'It's not humanly possible to write that fast. I'll have to remember them when I write the story out later.'

'Anyway, the girl wouldn't confess, so the Virgin Mary took her son away. This happened another two times, and each time the girl wouldn't confess and so the Virgin Mary took her child. The people of the land began to whisper that she had killed her children and eaten them, and called for her death. She was condemned to burn at the stake. Only then did the poor queen wish that she had confessed her sin.

'Up in Heaven, the Virgin Mary heard her prayer and gave her back the power of speech, so the queen cried out, "Yes, Mary, I did it!" Then rain fell from the sky and put out the flames, and the Virgin Mary appeared with the queen's three children, saying, "All is forgiven." And they were all happy together.'

Wilhelm's quill scratched quickly over the page, then he scattered sand to hasten the drying of the ink. 'I think I've got the gist of it, thank you,' he said. 'It's fascinating. I'm sure it must be old – there are echoes in there of other very old tales.'

'What will you do with the story?' Gretchen asked.

'For now, I'll just transcribe it and study it, looking to see how it compares with other stories of its type. Maybe, if we find a lot of old stories, we might publish them in a book. No one tells these old stories any more. If someone doesn't write them down, they might be lost forever.'

At that moment there was a banging on the window. Ludwig and Lotte were looking through, knocking and waving, their faces rosy from the cold. Gretchen hurried to the window and opened it wide.

'Wilhelm, come to the square,' Ludwig said. 'They've got a great bonfire going – they're burning all the Kurfürst's laws.'

'They're throwing in portraits of him, and copies of old decrees,' Lotte said. 'People are dancing and singing – it's like a party!'

Wilhelm stood up, his face grave. 'It's not something to celebrate, Lotte.'

'But you've got to hear what they're saying,' Ludwig insisted. 'The new king has declared a new constitution. Come and hear what he says.'

Wilhelm sighed and rolled his shoulders. 'All those years at university, learning the laws of the land, wasted. I will have to learn these new laws, I suppose, if I am ever to get a job under this new regime.' He packed up his writing box quickly, then turned and bowed his head to Gretchen. 'Thank you for the story.'

'We want to go too.' Dortchen jumped up, her mending falling unheeded to the floor. 'Gretchen, call Hanne and Lisette. You know they'll want to go too.'

Gretchen called to her sisters, and soon they were all in the hall, drawing on bonnets and gloves. Their father heard the commotion and put his head through the door from the shop. 'What are you doing? Where are you going?'

'They're proclaiming a new constitution,' Hanne explained. 'The King has thrown out the old laws and made new ones.'

'They're burning them all in the square,' Mia said. 'There's a great bonfire, and people are dancing around it.'

'We must go and hear what they're saying,' Lisette said quickly, as her father's expression darkened. 'Who knows what it means for us?'

Herr Wild looked back over his shoulder. There were customers in his shop. 'Where is that worthless son of mine?'

'Herr Grimm and his brothers will escort us,' Hanne said. 'There can be no harm in it, when we are all together, and Fraülein Lotte too.'

Herr Wild frowned, hesitating.

'They'll be announcing the new laws in French,' Lisette pointed out.

'Very well,' her father answered reluctantly. 'But you must be back before dark.'

'Thank you, Father.' Before he could say another word, Hanne opened the door and hurried out into the Marktgasse. Dortchen and Mia scrambled after her, with Lisette, Röse and Gretchen only steps behind. The five young men of the Grimm family were waiting for them impatiently, badly knitted scarves bundled about their throats. As soon as the Wild sisters had joined them, they began to hurry down the narrow street, Jakob leading the way.

They heard the roar of the bonfire and smelt the smoke long before they reached the Königsplatz. Soldiers were unloading a wagonload of scrolls and manuscripts, shouting, 'No more privileges for nobles! Equality for all! No more feudal dues! Liberty for all! Long live the Revolution!'

'Long live the Revolution!' shouted a young man with disordered chestnut hair and a faded red scarf loosely tied about his neck.

Hanne caught the young man by the sleeve. 'Is it true? A new constitution? What does it say?'

'All men are now free, regardless of their birth or their wealth,' the young man told her, his golden-brown eyes glowing with excitement. 'The serfs are all to be liberated.'

Hanne clapped her hands together.

Dortchen was amazed and thrilled and frightened all at once. She had always felt so sorry for the serfs working in the fields. They were often dressed in little more than smocks, their feet wrapped in rags. Sometimes, if one of their children was desperately sick, they would come begging to the apothecary's shop, offering turnips or a handful of eggs in return for medicine. Herr Wild would always take the exchange, even if the turnips were half-rotten.

What are the serfs to do now? she wondered. *Where will they go? How will they live? Will they own the land they have slaved on for so long?* It seemed impossible.

'People are free to worship as they choose – or even not worship at all,' the young man went on. 'Best of all, the nobles have lost all their privileges. They'll have to pay taxes like the rest of us.'

'Women too?' Hanne demanded. 'Are women to be given the same rights?'

A soldier nearby laughed and threw up his hands. 'Women? What need does a woman have of rights when she has a man to look after her?'

Hanne stamped her foot. 'Just as much need as a man.' But the soldier was busy throwing old title deeds onto the bonfire and paid her no heed.

The young man in the red scarf shook his head regretfully. 'I'm sorry, Fraülein. It is, as far as I can see, the one great flaw of the Emperor's vision. Women cannot vote, they cannot own property, they cannot be a guardian to their own children—'

'It's so wrong,' Hanne said. 'I swear I am twice as smart as those bone-brained French lawyers. If I were allowed to go to university and study law, I'd show them so, too.'

'I'm sure you would, Fraülein,' the young man said admiringly. 'Listen, he is reading the new constitution out now.'

A man in a white wig and gold-frogged coat stood on the steps, reading aloud from a scroll of paper. Dortchen listened carefully, but with the noise of the crowd, the roar of the bonfire and her own inadequate French, she caught only a few words. Jakob and Wilhelm were listening closely, both frowning.

'Well, at least we're casting off the chains of oppression,' Hanne said. 'We'll be the first country in any of the German states to have a constitution. This is a landmark day.'

Jakob turned on her angrily. 'Do you realise this so-called "constitution" was thrown together in Paris by a mob of half-drunk revolutionaries with blood on their hands? They fought and bickered over every single article, each pushing his own barrow, and paying no heed at all to centuries of tradition and custom. Not one of these articles has been tested in a court of law.'

'Fuddy-duddy,' Hanne said.

The young man in the red scarf laughed.

THE MERRY KIN

December 1807

Herr Wild was in a rage.

Glass shattered. Metal crashed. Pots smashed.

'What is it? What's wrong?' Dortchen whispered to Lisette, anxiety a cold stone in her gut.

'It's the new weights and measurements,' Lisette whispered back. 'The King has ordered all shopkeepers and tradesmen to adopt them. All of father's old jugs and scales and spoons are useless. He has to order in all new things, and it'll cost a lot. He still hasn't been paid for all the drugs the soldiers took when they first invaded. And, of course, it is the French who are selling the new measuring tools.'

'Confounded parasites,' Herr Wild shouted. 'Sucking my lifeblood away.'

'I don't think it's a good time to ask him about the ball,' Gretchen said.

'It's never a good time to ask him about anything,' Hanne said.

'Girls,' Frau Wild called in a low voice from the top of the stairs. 'Come away. Don't let him hear you.'

Disconsolately, the sisters trailed upstairs to the drawing room, where they took up their sewing and knitting. Outside, stray flurries of snow drifted down out of a pewter-grey sky, but it was warm and cosy inside. Frau Wild was lying on the couch, a small table crowded with drops and smelling salts and pillboxes at her elbow, and so Dortchen and Mia had to sit on the hearth rug with cushions behind them.

'Mother, won't you speak to him?' Gretchen wheedled. 'He'll listen to you.'

'I don't know why you think so,' Frau Wild said.

'But how are we supposed to meet any eligible gentlemen if we're never permitted to go anywhere?' Gretchen pleaded. 'Mother, you must appeal to him. I don't want to be left on the shelf like Lisette.'

'I'm only twenty-five,' Lisette protested.

'Only,' Gretchen shuddered.

'Please, girls, not so vulgar,' Frau Wild said.

'Tell him you fear Gretchen will form a *mésalliance* with that boy next door,' Hanne suggested, squinting as she rethreaded her needle.

'I am not so foolish,' Gretchen replied angrily. 'I admit that Wilhelm is very handsome, but have you seen his clothes? How could he afford to set up a house?'

'No prospects,' Frau Wild said.

'Exactly,' Hanne said. 'Father will be so horrified at the idea that he'll start looking around for alternatives at once. And what better place to meet suitable young men than at a ball at the King's palace?'

'I must say, it sounds so much nobler to talk of going to a ball at the King's palace instead of at a mere Kurfürst's palace,' Gretchen said.

'You shouldn't speak so,' Lisette chided her.

'The poor Kurfürst,' Dortchen said, remembering the stout man in the shabby clothes and powdered wig who had called her pretty.

'You should not be so lacking in taste,' Frau Wild said. 'It is most unbecoming.'

Gretchen tossed her head. 'Well, it's true. And you all must admit that the palace is a far merrier place now. It's been one ball after another. And we're invited to this one.'

'I can't believe Rudolf managed to secure us invitations,' Hanne said. 'Who would have thought any good would have come out of him going out carousing all night with those new cronies of his?'

'He's hardly showing up in the shop at all any more,' Lisette said. 'And when he does he's like a bear with a sore head.'

'Well, that's not surprising.' Gretchen giggled. 'Did you hear him trying to get up the stairs last night?'

'Last night? This morning, more like it,' Röse said. 'I thought we were being invaded by intoxicated soldiers. I was most discomposed.'

'Father is giving me more and more responsibility in the shop,' Lisette said.

'Who'd have thought?' Frau Wild said.

'I know! To think how reluctant he was to let me serve at all. He's always made me stay in the stillroom before. Yet with Rudolf always off at the theatre and the races . . .'

'And at gambling dens,' Hanne said with relish. 'I do wish we were allowed to go too. I'd love to see a gambling den. It sounds so decadent.'

'Not at all the thing,' Frau Wild said.

'Well, I'm glad Father doesn't let me serve in the shop,' Gretchen said. 'All those squalling babies and suppurating boils – I can't imagine anything more horrid.'

'You aren't allowed to serve in the shop because your French is so bad,' Mia pointed out.

'I don't think serving in a shop is at all ladylike,' Gretchen said, putting her nose in the air. 'Really, Lisette, I don't know how you stand it.'

'Father doesn't let me actually *serve* the soldiers,' Lisette said. 'I have to sit behind the counter and tell him in a low voice what they asked for and then fetch it from the stillroom for him. He handles all the weighing and wrapping, and the money. I'm supposed to pretend I'm invisible.'

'Pride is hard to swallow,' Frau Wild said.

Sometimes their mother's pronouncements were hard to decipher. Dortchen thought she must be trying to say that Herr Wild's pride was bruised by needing his eldest daughter's assistance, and that was why she had to pretend to be invisible. Hanne and Gretchen giggled and rolled their eyes, and Mia looked perplexed, but Lisette smiled gently at her mother. 'Yes, I know,' she answered.

'Anyway, what does it matter? All that matters is that Rudolf has got us invitations to the ball, and we have to convince Father to let us go,' Gretchen said. 'Surely he could not be so cruel and heartless as to forbid us?'

'Yes, he could,' Hanne said.

'Father won't like it,' Frau Wild agreed.

* * *

Frau Wild must have taken some opportunity to drop a hint in her husband's ear, because the next morning, at breakfast, he put down his coffee cup and said, 'What's this about a ball?'

The elder sisters exchanged nervous glances. 'King Jérôme is holding a Christmas ball, Father,' Lisette answered meekly. 'Many of the girls in town have been invited, including us.'

'Ridiculous,' he said. 'There's no reason for you all to go off hobnobbing with that Corsican tomfool.'

Gretchen and Hanne exchanged agonised glances.

'Not at all,' Rudolf said, looking up from his paper. He was looking rather rumpled, with his golden locks in disarray and his eyes bloodshot and heavy-lidded. 'It's good business practice, Father, to cultivate contacts at court.'

'Don't preach good business practice to me, you insolent pup,' his father roared. 'Is it good business practice to be out carousing instead of getting a decent night's sleep and being at work at a godly hour?'

'It is when you're carousing with the King's quartermaster,' Rudolf replied, pouring himself more coffee. 'He's promised to look into that debt you're still owed, Father.'

Herr Wild had begun to answer angrily, but at that he paused. 'What was that? My debt is to be repaid?'

'Perhaps,' Rudolf said. 'If we stay on the King's good side. King Jérôme is most generous to those he likes, and he certainly seems to have plenty of money to throw around. It's a great honour for the girls to be invited, and it would be short-sighted, not to say rude, to refuse his invitation.'

No one spoke, their eyes fixed on their plates. Herr Wild was scowling, but at least he was not yelling.

Frau Wild cleared her throat. 'A good chance for the girls, dear. To meet new people.'

Greatly daring, Hanne said, 'Yes, really, the only people we ever meet are those who go to church or those who live across the street.' She turned to Gretchen. 'Which reminds me, Gretchen, what about that handsome Grimm boy? Is he still pretending to write down any old tales you know, to have an excuse to spend an hour in your dazzling presence?'

Gretchen laughed and tossed her ringlets. 'Poor boy. He's so eager. Have you seen his coat, though? It's the shabbiest thing.'

Dortchen wanted to defend Wilhelm but did not dare.

Herr Wild's scowl deepened. 'Those Grimm fellows are a disgrace. Five of them, and only one has a job. Plenty of opportunities around for up-and-coming young fellows, but all they do all day is scribble, scribble, scribble, and go about looking like scarecrows.'

Dortchen could keep quiet no longer. 'But, Father, it is not their fault they are poor.'

'No? Then whose is it? Can't they get a job?'

'They're scholars,' she said. 'They're collecting old stories to make into a book.'

'Faugh,' Herr Wild said with the utmost contempt. 'Waste of paper.' He eyed Dortchen and she quickly looked down at her plate, biting her lip.

'It's a shame,' Frau Wild said.

'I'll not have it,' Herr Wild said. 'No more running over there at any time of day or night.' He stared hard at Dortchen, and she felt herself beginning to burn a fiery red.

'But what of our reading circle?' Lisette interjected.

'It will look very odd,' Hanne said. 'The Grimms are well connected, you know.'

'Their aunt is in exile with Princess Wilhelmine,' Gretchen said. 'And they know the von Arnims.'

Herr Wild frowned. 'Rackety lot they are too. Isn't he the fellow who eloped with that girl?'

'That was Herr Brentano,' Dortchen said.

'The poet,' Herr Wild said with the utmost disgust.

'Well, Father, if you let us go to the ball at the King's palace, we shall have a chance to meet someone apart from poets and impoverished scholars,' Hanne said with spirit. 'The King has collected many men of taste and influence around him.'

'Bankers,' Gretchen said. 'Noblemen.'

'I haven't the money to spend on new dresses and furbelows,' Herr Wild said. 'The coffers are empty.'

'That's the beauty of this ball,' Lisette cried. 'It's a fancy-dress party, Father. All the guests are to come in old-fashioned outfits.'

'You know Mother never throws anything out,' Hanne said. 'There are boxes and boxes of things up in the garret. I'm sure we'd be able to find something to wear.'

His frown deepened. 'I simply don't understand why you want to go gadding about all the time. Home is best.'

'Yes, Father,' the sisters replied obediently, but all were trying to keep smiles off their faces. He had not forbidden them to go.

After the morning chores had been finished, Frau Wild and her daughters went up to the garret, which was piled high with chests, broken chairs, cracked chamber pots, a cobwebbed spinning wheel, chipped ceramic jars and an old box-bed that smelt suspiciously of mice. Lisette and Hanne wrestled one of the chests out and flung open its lid, pulling out old gowns of gold brocade, blue flowered satin and crimson velvet stripes. 'How hideous!' Gretchen cried. 'Did you really wear all those petticoats, Mother? Look, it's hooped. What a scream!'

'Panniers were all the fashion,' her mother replied, sounding wistful. She took one of the gowns and held it against herself.

'You must've looked an absolute fright,' Gretchen said.

'I'm sure you were the prettiest girl in town,' Lisette said.

Frau Wild smiled tiredly at her. 'Not at all, I'm afraid.'

'I'm sure Father thought so when he met you.'

'Did you fall in love at first sight?' Dortchen asked.

Frau Wild folded the gown and put it down. 'Our marriage was arranged by our fathers. We did not meet until a week before our wedding.'

'Did you like him when you met him?' Mia wanted to know.

'My feelings were of no importance,' Frau Wild said. She sat down on a rickety old stool, one hand pressed to her chest. 'He has always been a good provider.'

Gretchen had not been listening, holding one dress against her, then throwing it down and trying another. She had pulled the hooped petticoat on over her own slim muslin dress, then swayed from side to side so the

116

stiff hoops – which extended a foot to either side of her body – rocked back and forth. 'How ever did you sit down?'

'We didn't, much of the time,' Frau Wild replied. 'Though it was possible, as long as you approached your chair backward and sat only on the very edge of it.'

'How did you get through the door?' Mia wanted to know.

Her mother smiled faintly. 'Well, we had to go sideways, of course.'

The girls shrieked with laughter. Mia seized a floppy straw hat with a wide satin ribbon and crammed it on her head, while Hanne held the crimson velvet against her and waltzed around, knocking over one of the old chamber pots. 'I can't believe you used to wear all this,' Lisette said, holding up a dress with waterfalls of yellowed lace from elbow to fingertip. 'Look at all the frills and ruffles. Wouldn't your sleeves trail in your soup?'

'We thought it very pretty back then,' Frau Wild sighed.

Röse had not joined the other girls rummaging through the chest. She liked to think she was above such worldly preoccupations. Instead, she was writing her name in the dust on a sideboard with her finger. 'Are there any books in that old chest?' she asked.

'No, I'm sorry,' her mother said. 'Your grandfather was not one for books.'

Röse sighed. 'I'm afflicted with illiterate forebears. Perhaps I'm adopted?'

Her mother shook her head. 'I'm afraid not, Rösechen. It was my poor old body that bore the brunt of your birth, and I suffer for it to this day.'

'I remember the day you were born very clearly,' Gretchen said. 'You bawled so loudly that all the windowpanes rattled and our neighbours thought we were slaughtering the pig.'

'You're the pig,' Röse said disdainfully, and began poking through the dresser's drawers.

Dortchen lifted a beautiful dress from out of the chest. Made of blue silk, it was sprigged with flowers and butterflies and worn over foaming white petticoats. She stepped into it and drew it over her own muslin. Lisette tied up the ribbons for her.

'How ever did you breathe?' Hanne asked, struggling to tie up the bodice of a brocade dress the colour of clementines.

'You got used to it,' her mother said. 'It did mean you couldn't walk too fast or dance too much.'

Another trunk was opened and riffled through. Hats were flung back and forth, and laughed over, and Gretchen and Hanne bickered over a faded silk shawl. Dortchen bent – as much as she could in the stiff bodice – and looked through the chest. She found, at the very bottom, a white wig resting upon a wooden head. Its hair was arranged high, with rolls of stiff curls over the ears. She lifted the wig out and put it upon her head. 'I look like Marie Antoinette,' she cried, whirling in front of an old spotted mirror. She looked quite unlike herself, like a princess out of an old tale, like a ghost.

'I want it! I'll wear that. I'll look like a queen.' Gretchen seized the wig and put it on.

'But I saw it first,' Dortchen protested.

'You won't be going to the ball anyway – you're too young,' Gretchen told her. 'Oh, look, it's perfect. I'll be the belle of the ball.' She spun in front of the mirror. With red spots of excitement burning high on her cheekbones and her large blue eyes sparkling, she looked very pretty indeed.

'Oh, but Mother—' Dortchen protested.

'There'll be other balls, my dear,' her mother told her.

'There's no need for Dortchen to go to a ball,' Herr Wild said from the doorway, startling them all.

'Oh . . . but why?' Dortchen blurted.

'No need for all of you to be married,' he said. 'Someone has to stay and look after your poor old parents.' Although he said it in a jocular way, his words still cut at Dortchen like a knife.

'But that's not fair,' she cried.

His brows began to lower. 'Come, now, that's no way to talk to your father. Six daughters are altogether too many to try to settle in these uncertain times. No one should expect it of me.'

'But . . . but what if I want to get married?'

He glared at her. 'You'll do as you're told, Dortchen, and that's the last I want to hear on the subject.' He then glared around at his other daughters. 'And keep your noise down. I have sick patients who expect some peace and quiet when they come to visit me.'

He clattered back down the bare wooden steps, leaving silence behind him. Mia took off the floppy shepherdess's hat and laid it back down on the chest. 'I suppose I'm not permitted to go either,' she said in a small voice.

'You're only twelve, Mia, of course you're not going,' Gretchen said.

'But we'll tell you all about it in the morning,' Lisette promised.

'And Mother's right, there'll be other balls, lots of them,' Hanne said. 'Aren't they calling him the "Merry King" already?'

'Well, I don't want to go,' Röse said. 'Really, I do think you girls think of nothing but your own frivolous pleasure. I shall stay home and study my prayer book and keep poor Father company.'

'I don't want to go either,' Mia said, not at all convincingly.

'You're just afraid no one will ask you to dance,' Gretchen said. 'And why would they, Mia? You'd stomp all over their toes and break them.'

'I would not! That's got nothing to do with it. I don't want to go because I have better things to do.'

'Like raid the pantry,' Gretchen said.

'Gretchen,' Frau Wild said.

'Well, I'm glad you're not coming,' Gretchen went on, ignoring her mother. 'Rudolf said that we were invited because they had heard we were the prettiest girls in Cassel. No one would think that if they saw us coming in with a dumpling like Mia.'

'No one would have invited you if they knew what a snake you were,' Mia shot back, her round cheeks turning red and her blue eyes more protuberant than ever. 'I hope no one asks you to dance and you spend the whole night standing against the wall with the other old maids.'

'I don't think that's very likely,' Gretchen replied smugly, twirling about so the long fringes of the shawl swung out. 'I shall wear this dress' – she pointed at the blue silk Dortchen was wearing – 'and this hat,' she said, pointing to the one Mia had taken off. 'I bet the King himself dances with me.'

Dortchen began to struggle out of the blue silk.

'Never mind,' Lisette whispered, helping her. But, of course, Dortchen did mind.

MIRROR, MIRROR

December 1807

All was dark and quiet in the house.

Dortchen's sisters had gone to the ball in high excitement, Frau Wild declaring she was quite worn out already and didn't know how she was to get through the evening.

Dinner had been a silent meal, and afterwards Röse, Dortchen and Mia had helped clear away and wash up. Old Marie had tried to cheer them, but it was hard not to feel low and depressed when their sisters were having fun at a ball and meeting the King, while they were left at home.

Once, Dortchen would have planned on sneaking out. She would have hung a green scarf on the washing line that hung between her and Lotte's bedroom windows, and put a note in the peg basket for her to find. Together, they would have crept through the dark town, muffling giggles and keeping to the shadows, all the way to the King's palace. They would have crouched in the shelter of the woods, watching people dance past the long windows, music spilling into the night. Perhaps they might even have danced together in the moonlight, two girls in long white nightgowns, hair flowing unbound down their backs.

Instead, she went to bed.

With Mia lying asleep beside her, breathing quietly, Dortchen lay under the heavy eiderdown and looked out over the snow-heaped rooftops. The moon was full, its face pockmarked with shadows, and the landscape of spires and chimneys and steep rooftops seemed strange and alien, embossed silver against black.

She heard footsteps on the stairs. Her body tensed. Heavy, slow footsteps, trying to be quiet. Those old wooden stairs creaked and groaned in protest with every step, however. Closer the sounds came, and then light probed under the door. The door handle turned and the door was eased open. Dortchen shut her eyes, pretending to be asleep.

The footsteps tiptoed across the room and Dortchen felt candlelight press against her eyelids. She did not move or even breathe. She could smell brandy and tobacco smoke. As her father bent over her, the fumes almost made her choke. She felt him pick up a tendril of her hair and tuck it behind her ear. For a moment his hand lingered on her, then he turned and went slowly away, the light receding with him.

The next morning the three eldest Wild sisters were full of news and importance.

'You should see the palace,' Gretchen cried, clasping her hands together. 'King Jérôme has thrown out all of the Kurfürst's ugly old stuff and ordered new furniture from Paris. It was exceedingly elegant.'

'No wonder Father's taxes are now so high,' Lisette said.

'You know what I heard? The King and his courtiers played leapfrog through the empty rooms before the furniture arrived. In their underwear!' Hanne laughed out loud.

'I was simply pestered with dance partners,' Gretchen said. 'My dance card is full. See? I've kept it. It'll be a souvenir of the night I met my husband.'

'I really do not think it was wise to dance the waltz twice with Herr von Eschwege,' Lisette said.

'Oh, pooh! He's by far the best catch,' Gretchen replied. 'They're a noble family, and besides, he's rich.'

'Gretchen, please, you should not speak so,' Lisette said.

'Why not? We all think it. I cannot bear all this hypocrisy. You're just jealous because Herr von Eschwege only danced with you once.'

'He asked me to dance again but I did not think it was wise,' Lisette answered, colour rising in her cheeks.

'So you say,' Gretchen mocked.

'Enough, Gretchen,' Frau Wild said. 'You must mind your tongue.'

Herr Grimm looked up from his newspaper. 'I should think so,' he said.

Gretchen pouted and looked sulky.

'Tell me, Gretchen, what is a girl's crown?' he asked.

'Modesty and gentility, skill, hard work and a love of labour,' Gretchen recited in a bored voice.

'No need to take that tone with me, young lady.'

'Sorry, Father.' Gretchen looked down at her plate.

Herr Wild looked around at his daughters, their heads bowed meekly. 'You all would do well to remember it.' He folded his paper, rose and went out of the room.

At once Gretchen revived. 'You should have seen me, Dortchen. I had men fighting to bow over my hand. Some of them were very handsome. I met Ferdy Schmerfeld. He begged me for one of my gloves but Lisette will be glad to know I refused. His cousin is very important in the cabinet. And I met . . .'

On she rattled, and all Dortchen could do was listen and pretend to smile.

It was a cold, hard winter, but the court of the Merry King was an endless whirl of balls, masquerades, hunts and sledge rides in the snowy forest. Lisette, Gretchen and Hanne were much in demand. 'So much coming, so much going,' Old Marie complained. 'No wonder your father is grumpy all the time.'

'Bad weather ahead,' Frau Wild moaned. 'Oh, girls, must you?'

'Yes, we must,' Gretchen sang. 'Though, Mother, I need a new muff. I must have a muff!'

One day, in mid-January, Wilhelm knocked on the door. Dortchen answered, having been in the kitchen stuffing a mattress tick with feathers plucked from the Christmas goose. She was wearing an old brown dress and a big apron, and small feathers clung to her coiled plaits and her hands.

Wilhelm was carrying his writing box. Even though it was mid-afternoon, the square outside was gloomy, the sky heavy with snow clouds.

'I'm sorry to interrupt,' he said. 'I was wondering if Gretchen might be willing to tell me another story?'

'I'll ask her,' Dortchen said. 'Come in, don't wait on the step.'

She left Wilhelm standing in the hallway and ran upstairs to the drawing room, where Lisette was ironing, Hanne was knitting a new winter shawl from some undyed wool given to their father in exchange for medicine, and Gretchen was standing before the mirror, pinching her cheeks and biting her lips. 'It's so unfair,' she was saying. 'All the women at court wear so much rouge but Father won't hear of us having any. I look so pale and uninteresting next to all those French *comtesses*.'

'Wilhelm is here,' Dortchen said. 'He wonders if you have time to tell him another story.'

Gretchen groaned. 'Oh, no – can't you tell him I'm busy?'

'There's no need to be rude to him,' Dortchen replied, colour rising in her cheeks. 'He is our neighbour. And his story collection is important to him. The least you could do is apologise.'

She went down to the front hall, where Wilhelm waited, looking ill at ease. 'I'm sorry if I've come at a bad time,' he said.

'You haven't,' Dortchen said. She heard Gretchen's impatient step coming down the stairs and turned to face her, trying to warn her with her eyes to be kind.

'Good afternoon,' Wilhelm said. 'I'm sorry to disturb you. It's just . . . well, I haven't had a story from you in a while.'

'I'm sorry, I don't know any other stories. I've told you all I can remember,' Gretchen replied, smiling.

Dortchen stepped forward. 'Wilhelm, won't you come in and have some tea? We could ask Old Marie to tell you a story – she knows lots of them.'

He hesitated. Gretchen looked over her shoulder and made a little face at Dortchen, but then said sweetly, 'Yes, why don't you?'

'A cup of tea would be welcome,' he admitted.

'Come into the kitchen – it's warm in there. It's cold, isn't it?' Dortchen took his hat and hung it on the hook, then held out her hands for his coat. Wilhelm shrugged it off and passed it to her. 'I know you won't mind us sitting in the kitchen,' she continued, leading the way down the hall. 'Old Marie will be busy but she's always happy to tell a story. She knows some very beautiful, strange ones – the sort you would like, I'm sure.'

Gretchen followed along behind, looking rather sulky. Dortchen said over her shoulder, 'Gretchen, why don't you call the others? Lisette's doing the ironing. She'd much rather have tea and hear a story, don't you think?'

'Very well,' Gretchen said. She moved slowly up the stairs, not liking being sent on an errand but not wanting to argue with Dortchen in front of a young man, no matter how poor and shabby.

Dortchen went quietly past the door to the shop, where she could hear the low rumble of voices. She hoped her father had not noticed Wilhelm passing by the window and knocking on the door. They reached the kitchen and Dortchen led Wilhelm inside.

'Come and sit by the fire, warm yourself,' she said. 'Old Marie, look, we have a guest for afternoon tea.'

Old Marie came out of the scullery, wiping her hands on her apron. She looked aghast. 'Dortchen, my sweet, you shouldn't be bringing Herr Grimm into the kitchen – it's not seemly. Take him to the parlour and I'll bring you a tray and lay a fire for you.'

'Wilhelm doesn't mind sitting in the kitchen,' Dortchen said. 'They sit in their own kitchen all the time. Besides, you know Father will be angry if you lay a fire in the parlour.'

Old Marie looked troubled. 'I don't think your father would like you entertaining a young man in the kitchen either.'

'I like it in here,' Wilhelm said, stretching his hands to the fire. 'Please don't mind me, Marie. It's very comfortable and cosy in here.'

'And no one in their right mind would ever call our parlour comfy and cosy,' Dortchen said, sitting down in the rocking chair.

'Very well. I'll make some tea.' Old Marie lifted the kettle, testing its weight, then hung it on its hook above the fire. 'Are you hungry? I have some damson plum cake, made from last year's preserves.'

'That sounds delicious, thank you,' Wilhelm said. As Old Marie went into the pantry, he turned to Dortchen. 'I must admit, I'm starving. It's been a long time since we've had plum cake.'

'You should come for tea more often,' Dortchen said. 'Old Marie loves people enjoying her cooking.'

Old Marie came out of the pantry, carrying the plum cake in one hand and the tin of tea leaves in the other. The pantry door banged shut behind her, and they heard quick footsteps coming down the hall.

'I'll warrant that's Mia – she can hear the pantry door opening from the attic, that girl,' Old Marie said.

Mia opened the kitchen door and came in, round and rosy as a plum cake herself, her loops of braids bobbing up and down. Gretchen and Hanne followed her, laughing together. Röse came reluctantly, holding a heavy atlas in her arms. 'Really, it is only the hope of sustenance that draws me here,' she said. 'You know I consider listening to old tales a most frivolous waste of time.' Lisette came last, her face red and hot.

'Just in time for tea,' Old Marie said.

'Wilhelm wants to hear a story,' Dortchen explained. 'Won't you tell one, Old Marie?'

'If Herr Grimm doesn't mind me peeling turnips while I talk,' Old Marie answered. 'You girls can help me. No sitting idle with your hands in your lap, thank you very much.'

This last remark was directed at Gretchen, who had sat down by the fire and was sulkily coiling one of her long blonde ringlets about her finger. She huffed out a sigh, rolled her eyes and came to sit at the table with her sisters, who pushed the basket of vegetables towards her. Old Marie sat down, with a little *ooof* of pleasure at taking the weight off her feet, and drew a bowl of turnips towards her.

'What tale shall I tell?'

'The one about the queen who thought she was the most beautiful of all,' Dortchen said, with a glance at Gretchen.

'A good winter tale,' Old Marie said.

'Shall I sharpen your quills for you?' Dortchen asked Wilhelm, who was unpacking his writing box at the far end of the table. He nodded in thanks, testing the end of one quill against his finger. Dortchen took up the remainder of the quills and his knife and began carefully whittling the end. Wilhelm drew a piece of paper towards him and looked expectantly at Old Marie.

'Once upon a time, in winter, a beautiful queen sat sewing by the window,' the old woman said, her gnarled fingers nimbly wielding her paring knife. 'As she sewed, she looked out at the snow. Ravens were flying through the winter-bare trees, their wings as black as the blackest ebony. The queen pricked her finger with her needle. Some drops of blood fell into the snow.'

Wilhelm looked up. 'I wonder if there were three drops of blood. If so, this story has echoes of Parzival. He was entranced by the sight of three red drops in the snow, recalling to him the memory of the woman he loved.'

'Maybe so,' Old Marie said. 'I don't rightly remember how many drops of blood there were, sir. Maybe it was three.'

Dortchen, sitting by Wilhelm's shoulder, saw him write 'Parzival – three drops of blood?' in the margin, before he again settled down to transcribe Old Marie's story.

'The red on the white looked so beautiful that the queen thought, "If only I had a child as white as snow, with lips as red as blood and hair as black as a raven's wing." Soon afterward, she had a little daughter who was as white as snow, as red as blood and as black as ravens, and therefore they called her Little Snow-White.'

'Really, I do not think she can have been very pretty, all black and white and red,' Gretchen said. 'She sounds like a magpie.'

'Magpies aren't red,' Hanne said, frowning. 'Do you mean a red-winged blackbird?'

'Can't she be fair?' Gretchen said. 'Everyone knows it is girls with golden hair who are the most beautiful.'

'Not necessarily,' Mia said, tossing her red-gold loops of braids.

'She can be golden-haired if you want her to be,' Old Marie said. 'Though the story I heard was that she was black-haired.'

'Write that she's got golden hair,' Gretchen said to Wilhelm, who smiled but did not write the words.

'Shh,' Dortchen said. 'Listen.'

Old Marie went on. 'Now, the queen had a mirror, which she stood in front of every morning, and asked, "Mirror, mirror, on the wall, who in this land is fairest of all?" And the mirror always said, "You, my queen, are fairest of all." And then she knew for certain that no one in the world was more beautiful than she.'

Dortchen knew the story well. In time, the little princess grew to be more beautiful even than her mother. The queen grew so jealous that she took her little girl into the forest and abandoned her there, hoping she would be devoured by wild beasts. Little Snow-White took refuge in the house of seven dwarfs, falling asleep at last in one of their beds.

'When night came, the seven dwarfs returned home from their work in the mines,' Old Marie continued. 'They lit their seven little candles and saw that someone had been in their house.'

Dortchen assumed a deep, gruff voice. 'The first one said, "Who's been sitting in my chair?"'

Wilhelm looked up, laughing in surprise.

'The second one said, "Who's been eating from my plate?"' Lisette put in, mimicking Dortchen's gruff tones.

'The third one said, "Who's been eating my bread?"' Hanne said.

'The fourth one said, "Who's been eating my vegetables?"' Mia growled, waving a turnip.

So it went around the room, each of the six sisters calling out one of the seven dwarfs' questions, till finally they reached the last one. 'Who's this lying in my bed?' Dortchen squeaked.

It was a long story. Wilhelm's fingers were cramped and stained liberally with ink by the time the queen had tried three times to kill her daughter – once lacing her so tight into her bodice she could not breathe, once with a poisoned comb, and finally by tricking her into tasting a poisoned apple. Little Snow-White died, but her body did not decay, and so the dwarfs put her into a glass coffin. A prince came past one day and fell in love with the beautiful dead girl. He convinced the dwarfs to let him have her. The prince would go nowhere without the dead girl, nor eat unless she was beside him. One day, his servant grew angry at having to carry the heavy glass coffin to and fro, and opened it up, sat up the corpse and slapped her hard across the back, saying, 'We are plagued by this dead girl all day long!' The terrible piece of apple she had eaten flew out of her throat and she woke from her enchanted sleep. The next day, the magical mirror told the cruel queen, 'You, my queen, are fair, it's true. But the young queen is a thousand times fairer than you.' Filled with jealousy, the queen went to see this fair young maiden be married to her prince. To her horror, she realised she was her own hated daughter, Little Snow-White.

'Then they put a pair of iron shoes into the fire until they glowed,' Old Marie said, 'and the queen had to put them on and dance in them. She could not stop until she had danced herself to death.'

'Which seems a most appropriate punishment for the cardinal sin of vanity,' Röse said with satisfaction.

'What a wonderful story,' Wilhelm said, scattering sand on the paper. 'I could not get all of it – you spoke too fast, Marie. But I think I got the gist of it. Look at my page, have you ever seen such a mess? I'll write it up again neatly when I get home, while it's still fresh in my mind.' He stood up, wiping his hands on a rag he kept in his writing box. 'May I come and show it to you when I'm finished, Marie, so you can see if I've missed anything important?'

'I haven't much book learning, I'm sorry, sir,' Marie said.

'I'll read it for you, Wilhelm,' Dortchen said eagerly.

A sudden draught of cold air gusted into the room. Dortchen turned her head and froze. Her sisters all fell silent, and Old Marie rose clumsily to her feet.

'I'm sorry, sir, were you wanting something?' she asked.

Herr Wild was standing in the doorway, his thick grey eyebrows drawn close down over his red-veined, bulbous nose. 'What's going on here?'

'We were having tea,' Lisette faltered.

'Old Marie was telling us a story,' Mia piped up.

'And we were peeling the vegetables for supper, Father,' Hanne hastened to add.

He ignored her. 'Have you nothing better to do than sit around and tell old wives' tales?' he said angrily to Old Marie. 'I don't pay you to gossip. Get on with your work.'

'I'm sorry, sir.' Wilhelm packed away his quills and penknife. 'You may not know that my brother and I have undertaken a scholarly collection of old tales. We hope to publish—'

'A waste of your time and my time, not to mention my servant's time. I'd appreciate it if you did not encourage her to fritter away valuable working hours again.'

'No, sir – I'm sorry, sir.' Wilhelm fumbled to shut the clasp on his writing box.

Dortchen longed to tell her father that they had all been helping prepare supper while Old Marie told her story but did not dare. His face was livid with temper.

'Lisette, I was looking for you,' he said abruptly. 'There's a Frenchman in the shop wanting something, the Lord himself only knows what – I can't understand a word he says. Come and decipher his gobbledegook.'

'Yes, Father,' Lisette replied and got up.

'You can show the young gentleman to the front door on your way,' he said.

Wilhelm bowed, said a subdued farewell and followed Lisette out.

Herr Wild stared at Hanne and Gretchen. 'Who invited that young man to sit in our *kitchen*? Do you think we should allow our standards to decline, just because the whole world is going to wrack and ruin?'

'Dortchen,' Gretchen said.

Herr Wild looked at his second-youngest daughter. 'Of course. Who else would it be?' He pointed one squat finger at her. 'You love telling stories so much. For one week, you must not speak unless it is in prayer. Do you understand me?'

'Yes, Father,' she began, but his large hand lashed out and caught her a ringing blow across the face.

'Not one word.'

She bent her head in understanding, her throat seizing up with unshed tears.

BROKEN AXLE

May 1808

Four days after Dortchen's fifteenth birthday, Frau Grimm died. It was as if the pin axle holding the Grimm family together had broken, so the whole machine fell apart.

Frau Grimm had been ailing all winter. It had been freezing, and the Grimms had not been able to afford much firewood or meat or winter vegetables. They all wore rags stuffed in their boots to stop the cold and damp from seeping through the holes in the soles, and their clothes were darned and patched and frayed at the cuffs. Lotte had had to cut up one of her old muslin dresses to make cravats for her brothers, and Ludwig's wrists hung out of his sleeves. What little money the elder two brothers made by publishing literary articles was swallowed up by the cost of the paper and ink and candles used to write them. Dortchen had smuggled them a cabbage or two, and some eggs and milk and feverfew tea, but nothing had helped Frau Grimm, who had taken to her bed in midwinter and not got up again.

'What are you going to do now?' Dortchen asked, pouring out tea from the big brown teapot into seven cracked and mismatched cups. The five Grimm brothers sat around the kitchen table, their hands lying idly before them. All were pale and wan, their dark hair uncombed, their chins unshaven. Lotte, meanwhile, was curled in her mother's rocking chair, with her mother's shawl clutched to her face, sobbing convulsively.

'Do?' Karl said, shrugging. 'What can we do?'

'I must get a job,' Jakob said. 'But doing what? I applied for a job in the royal library, but they passed me over for someone with half the learning and experience I have.'

'My law degree is useless,' Wilhelm said. 'I'd have to go back to university and study this confounded new code of Napoléon's before I could get a job even as a clerk.'

'And we have no money for anyone to go to university,' Ferdinand said. 'I'd have liked to have gone too, but no chance of that. So I'm even more useless than you two.'

'Aunt Zimmer cannot help any more,' Jakob said. 'She's in exile with Princess Wilhelmine and has her own struggle to survive.'

'She sends us food when she can, but it's never enough,' Ludwig said. 'We're hungry all the time.'

'Our only hope is to enlist,' Ferdinand said. 'But we don't want to fight for Napoléon. It'd be different if we could fight to save our own country, but he'd just send us off to Russia to die.'

'At least we'd get fed in the army,' Karl said.

Dortchen put two spoons of sugar into every cup and passed them along the table. She did not know what else to do. If she could have, she would have cooked them a feast, but her own family's pantry was almost bare too. The blockade against Great Britain and its colonies was taking a heavy toll, and the people of Hessen-Cassel were being cruelly taxed to pay for the King's endless round of parties, balls and fireworks displays.

'All we can do is pray,' Jakob said, with a new note of hopelessness in his voice.

Lotte looked up, her eyes wild. 'We've done nothing but pray for weeks. What good has it done us? Mother is dead and we're set to starve to death. God has forsaken us.'

'Do not speak so, Lottechen,' Wilhelm said gently, carrying a cup of tea to her. 'We must have faith—'

'Faith!' Lotte struck out at him, sending the cup crashing to the floor. 'What use is faith? What use is anything?'

Dortchen dropped to her knees to mop up the spilt tea, her heart aching for her friend. Wilhelm bent to pick up the broken cup. His dishevelled hair fell over his forehead. Dortchen yearned to reach up and brush it away, to smooth the lines of worry and despair etched on his face. What a burden it was for him and Jakob, to be responsible for this young family – and they were only in their early twenties themselves. How could they support them all?

'Is there no one else who can help?' she whispered.

Wilhelm shook his head. 'Don't you worry,' he said in a low voice. 'You have done so much for us already. We shall write to all our friends and ask them if they know of any work. It'll probably mean we shall need to go our separate ways, which we don't want to do . . . but there may be no other choice.'

'You mean . . . you'll move away?' Dismay filled her.

'What else can we do, if there's no work here? We cannot afford to pay the rent here or even our daily bread.'

Dortchen nodded, unable to speak. Misery choked her. She could not bear the idea of the Grimms moving away. Lotte was her dearest friend, while Wilhelm was her one true love, the other part of her soul. She knew that he would one day come to love her back. Right now, he thought of her as a child. But Dortchen was growing older. Sometimes, when the Wild sisters walked together to market, soldiers would hoot at them. Their eyes would linger on Dortchen's face and figure just as much as on Gretchen's or Hanne's. Dortchen was sure that Wilhelm would one day notice her in the same way. It was only this hope that gave Dortchen relief from her yearning to be with Wilhelm, to look after him, to bring him happiness.

'What . . . what can I do to help?' she managed to say.

'Could Lotte stay with you a day or two?' Wilhelm asked. 'We have so much to do to arrange the funeral, and Lotte cannot bear being under the same roof as . . .' His voice failed him.

Dortchen nodded, speechless. She knew Frau Grimm's body lay upstairs in her stuffy bedroom, the curtains drawn, sheets hung over the mirror, the clock stopped. Dortchen's mother was sitting with her, giving the Grimm brothers a break from their melancholy task.

'And . . . perhaps . . . do you know how to make black dye?' Wilhelm said. 'We shall have to go into mourning and we cannot afford to buy new clothes. Lotte will have to dye all her old dresses.'

'I'll make some for you this afternoon,' Dortchen said. 'Lotte and I can make it together.'

She took the weeping girl back to her own room and put her to bed, with a cup of chamomile tea and a cloth dampened with lavender water. Then she gathered together her courage and went down to her father's shop. Rudolf was busy chatting and making up packets of tobacco for a group of soldiers in French red, white and blue, while her father was putting together an elixir for a mother with a croupy baby. He scowled at the sight of her.

'Why are you interrupting me?' he demanded as soon as the customer was gone.

'I'm sorry, Father. May I go to the forest, to gather oak galls? Lotte needs to dye her clothes black.'

Her father grunted. 'Very well. Do not dawdle – you are needed here for your own chores.'

'Yes, Father.'

'Gather me some bark from a young oak tree, it makes an excellent gargle for sore throats. And bring me some fresh young leaves too. I have a customer with haemorrhoids and there's nothing better for them than a poultice of fresh oak leaves.'

She nodded and slipped away, keeping her face demure. She could not help a little bubble of happiness at the idea of an afternoon wandering free in the forest, far away from the desperate unhappiness and grief of the house next door, and the gloomy piousness of her own. It had been a long time since she had been allowed to go to the woods.

Dortchen went into the kitchen to get her basket and bonnet. The room was stiflingly hot, with the fire going on the hearth and a pot of soup bubbling away. Old Marie was busy polishing the silver, her old face rosier than ever.

'I'm going to the forest to gather oak galls,' Dortchen explained, taking down her basket from its hook. 'I'll look for mushrooms, too, while I'm there.'

'Can you bring me some acorns, too, if you can find any ready for picking?' Old Marie said. 'I'll grind them for flour and make us all some bread for our breakfast.'

'Really? You can make bread from acorns?'

'Indeed, of course you can. My grandmother always used to tell me that oaks were the first tree that God ever made, and acorns our first food.'

'I never realised it was such a useful tree. Father wants me to gather leaves and bark as well.'

'My grandmother used to grind up the bark to make snuff,' Old Marie said, smiling at the memory. 'My brother's nose only needed the smallest tap to start spouting blood, and she would make him sniff the oak snuff to stop the bleeding.'

Dortchen put on her bonnet and took up her shawl and gloves, listening with only half an ear, her thoughts still with the grief-wracked house across the street. She wished with all her heart that she could help them somehow.

'My grandmother would cut the bark on Midsummer's morning,' Old Marie went on. 'She'd gather up the oak moss as well, for good luck and good fortune.'

Dortchen's hands stilled halfway through drawing on her gloves. 'Good fortune?'

'Oh, yes. She always thought that oak moss gathered on Midsummer's morning was the best way to draw luck and prosperity towards you. She'd grind it up and mix it in oil, then rub it on a silver coin and put that in her pocket. She said a coin made in the year of your birth was best. Or else she'd bathe the coin in moonlight, light a candle rubbed with the oak-moss oil and pray to the lady of the moon to bring silver and gold.'

'Did you ever do it?' Dortchen asked.

'Would I be living under your family's roof if I was blessed with a fortune?' Old Marie asked.

'I suppose not,' Dortchen replied.

Old Marie gave her a hug and a kiss. 'I think myself lucky enough to have a warm bed and a roof over my head in these hard times, don't you worry, my sweetling.'

'What about your grandmother? Was she blessed with good fortune?'

'Indeed she was. We had our own farm back then, with an apple orchard and a whole flock of geese, and our own mill. And she lived to a great old age, my grandmother. But once she died, things turned sour. My father died and my brother was conscripted into the army and sent to fight in the New World, then my husband too, and we lost the farm.'

'Maybe it's because no one gathered the oak moss,' Dortchen said, pulling on the remainder of her glove.

'Oh, that's just an old superstition,' Old Marie said. 'What would your father say if he heard me filling your head with my grandmother's nonsense? They'd be calling me a witch and lopping off my head like that poor old woman in Switzerland. Shocking scandal, that was, and not so long ago.'

Dortchen smiled absently and went out the back door. That afternoon, in the shadowy green depths of the forest, she fingered the silvery filigree of oak moss growing on the north bole of the tree and began to make plans.

MIDSUMMER'S MORNING

June 1808

On the morning of Midsummer's Eve, Dortchen and her sisters and many other girls walked out into the woods that surrounded the palace, picking wildflowers to make midsummer wreaths for their hair.

They were accompanied by the young men of the town, singing and playing guitars and begging for buttonhole flowers, with stout matrons following behind in buggies to make sure no one was tempted to wander too far into the woods.

Jakob and Wilhelm and their brothers had set out with the Wild sisters, more 'to observe and record an intriguing remnant of our pagan past', as Jakob said, than with any idea of wooing.

It did not take long till their party mingled with others, however. Gretchen and Lisette walked with Herr Schmerfeld and Herr von Eschwege, two young men they had met at the King's ball, while Hanne argued about politics with a young chestnut-haired man who wore a loosely knotted red scarf instead of a cravat. Röse sat in the buggy with her mother, it being too hot for walking, she said, while Dortchen and Mia busied themselves plucking buttercups and clover and cow's parsley by the handful. Ferdinand and Karl walked with the Ramus sisters. Only Ludwig was not there. He had gone to Heidelberg to study art; his board and expenses had been paid for by the Grimms' good friends Karl von Savigny, Achim von Arnim and Clemens Brentano.

Lotte had refused to come. She was moping at home with Old Marie, helping her make midsummer cake from ground hazelnuts, fresh raspberries and crystallised rose petals. She had not left the Wilds' house since her mother had been buried. It was as if her black-dyed clothes had stained her spirit as well as her skin.

The last few weeks had not been easy for her brothers, either. Frau Grimm's pension, as the widow of a magistrate, had ceased with her death, and the endless worry and grief had brought on Wilhelm's cough again. He looked so pale and weary that Dortchen's heart ached.

Gradually, he began to fall behind the merry party of flower-pickers; Jakob strode impatiently on, not wanting to miss any pagan rituals that might persist. Dortchen fell back to walk with Wilhelm along the winding avenue that led away from the palace. The leaf litter below their feet hushed their footsteps. Sweet woodruff spread a carpet of starry white flowers under the shade of the trees.

'I haven't walked this far before,' he said. 'It's beautiful.'

'You haven't seen the Lion's Castle?' Dortchen asked in surprise. 'Oh, you'll love it. It looks like one of those remnants from the past you and Jakob love so much. Except that it was only finished five or six years ago.'

'Really? Then how—'

'It's a folly,' Dortchen told him. 'Apparently, it's the grandest folly in the world. The architect travelled to England to look at all their ruins and then came home and put everything he'd seen into this one glorious fake. Towers and drawbridges and arrow-slits – it has it all.'

'But it's all a fake?' Wilhelm asked.

Dortchen nodded. 'The Kurfürst built it for his favourite mistress, as a sort of private love nest. That's why the way there is hidden by the trees. He didn't want his wife seeing him going out there to meet her.'

Wilhelm laughed, but his breath caught in a wheeze. The wheeze turned into a cough and he had to stop, bending over at the waist, one hand resting on a tree for support.

Dortchen patted him on the back, wishing she knew what to do to help. 'It seems worse,' she said. 'Have you been drinking my linden blossom tea?'

'Yes, thank you,' he answered, his voice rasping. 'It seems to help a little.'

Dortchen looked up the road. It was empty of all but a few stragglers, a fat woman panting along with the help of a stick and a young boy, and a young couple wandering hand in hand. 'Do you want to go home?' she asked. 'I could beg for a lift for you in someone's buggy.'

'No. I'm fine. I want to see this Lion's Castle of yours. Let us just walk slowly for a while till I catch my breath.'

'All right,' Dortchen said, although she felt anxious about what her father would say if anyone mentioned she had fallen so far behind with a young man. They walked on through the jewel-bright leaves, through shafts of sunlight and cool shade.

Wilhelm looked about him with eager eyes. 'It's so beautiful,' he said. 'We've been so busy and anxious with Mother that I have not walked in the forest for a long time.'

'I'm very sorry about your mother,' Dortchen said awkwardly.

'I think all the endless worry about the wars, and our financial situation, was just too much for her,' Wilhelm said in a leaden tone. He began to cough again and had to stop once more, one hand on his heart, his breath wheezing.

'Your cough had seemed so much better,' Dortchen said. 'I thought the teas had been helping.'

'Mother's death brought it all on again. I find it hard to walk far, or to climb stairs. There's a constant piercing pain in my chest. And lately it's been getting much worse. I get these . . . attacks. My heart . . .' He looked away, embarrassed.

'Tell me about it – perhaps I know something that could help.'

'The doctor's given me some remedies. I take a large dose of mustard seeds in the morning, and then in the evening I have to breathe in the fumes of burning mercury.'

'Mercury?'

'Yes. It's that silver stuff they use in thermometers – have you ever seen it?'

'You mean quicksilver?'

He nodded.

'You breathe it in?'

'I burn it and breathe in the smoke. It makes me cough and cough, but afterwards my chest does seem clearer.'

Dortchen frowned. She had seen quicksilver once, when the thermometer at school had been broken by one of the boys. It had seemed wild, volatile, magical. 'But . . . your heart,' she ventured.

'My heart beats so fast that I can feel it pounding in my chest. Sometimes it lasts for hours. I cannot sleep, or hardly breathe . . . Oh, Dortchen, I'm afraid I'm going to die too. I feel as if my heart will simply burst. What am I to do?'

Her anxiety for him was acute but she tried to calm herself, thinking of what she could do to help him. 'Yarrow is said to be good at slowing down the heart. It's easy enough to find – you could gather some every day on your morning walk and then make a tea with it. Otherwise, there's monkshood . . . Father makes heart medicine with it but I'd be afraid to try. It's poisonous.'

'We might stick with yarrow then,' Wilhelm said.

'Motherwort and hawthorn are good for the heart too. I could try adding a few leaves to the linden blossom tea I make for you.' Dortchen hesitated. 'Are you sure it's a good idea to breathe in the quicksilver fumes?'

'Well, it's what the doctor told me to do, that time he came to bleed Mother just before she died. We used the last of our money to buy it from him.'

It occurred to Dortchen that putting leeches on Frau Grimm's breast had not helped her in any way, so it was possible that breathing mercury fumes was not of much use either. Many of the things the doctors and apothecaries did seemed strange and unhealthy to her. Dortchen thought that walking out in the fresh air and the sunshine, and eating and drinking the good things grown in the garden, was far more likely to heal illness than making people vomit, or cupping them, or giving them drops that made them sleep all day, like her mother did. She was only a girl, though, and not very well educated. The doctors had studied and had degrees, so surely they knew what they were doing. Uneasiness filled her, nevertheless, and she examined Wilhelm's face closely, noting the dark shadows under his eyes, the deepening hollows under his cheekbones.

'I don't have much mercury left and no money for any more,' Wilhelm said. His shoulders were slumped under his shabby black coat. 'So I guess I won't be able to carry on for much longer anyway.'

'Well, yarrow grows wild in the roadside ditches, so it will cost you nothing at all,' Dortchen comforted him. 'And I can give you a bag of lavender to put under your pillow. It might help you sleep.'

'I'm willing to try anything,' Wilhelm replied. His breath was short, and Dortchen could clearly hear his chest wheezing. She stopped, pretending to turn and gaze away into the forest, so that he might have a chance to catch his breath. Far away, on the horizon, she could see the twin spires of Martinskirche rising above the trees, and pointed them out to Wilhelm.

'Look how far we've come! With the spires to guide us home, we'd never need to leave a trail of breadcrumbs behind us.'

'Breadcrumbs?'

'Do you not know that story? It's about a little brother and sister who get lost in the forest, and find a witch's cottage made all of gingerbread. I'll tell it to you, if you like.'

She told him as much as she could remember of the story as they climbed the road through the trees, each bend bringing them higher up the hill. Wilhelm was able to save his breath for climbing, and Dortchen walked slowly, pretending to be absorbed in the tale. Wilhelm did not much like the parents, who so readily abandoned their children once times grew hard, but he very much liked the way the brother and sister outwitted the witch. 'If only I had some paper and my quill,' he lamented. 'I shall try to remember it all when I get home.'

'I can always tell it to you again,' she said.

The road levelled out into a wide, sunny clearing, with a view up to Herkules at the peak of the hill. Before them stood a tiny stone castle, lifting innumerable mismatched spires and turrets into the sky.

'There it is,' Dortchen said.

'It's like something out of a story,' Wilhelm said. 'I can imagine magical things happening there.'

He was looking flushed and his breath came too fast for Dortchen's liking. 'Come and sit down in the shade,' she said. 'Would you like some water?'

He nodded, and she led him to sit down on the grass in the shade of a sprawling elder bush. Dortchen drew a corked jug of water out of her basket, and gave it to him to drink. 'It's too late to gather any elderflowers and too early for elderberries,' Dortchen said, looking up into the tangle of grey branches overhead. Unripe berries were clustered on every twig. 'I'll come back in August and gather a basketful to make elderberry cordial for you. It'll help your cough.'

'You know so much about trees and flowers and herbs,' Wilhelm said in wonder. 'How ever did you learn?'

Dortchen shrugged her shoulders uncomfortably. 'It's about all I know. We learnt practically nothing at school, except how to recite our catechism and how to knit. I wish I had your book learning.'

'It's not much use to me, is it? I spend all day poring over old manuscripts and trying to ignore the ache in my fingers, while you make bread out of acorns and tea out of linden blossoms. What you do is at least helpful to people.'

'Stories are important too,' Dortchen said. 'Stories help make sense of things. They make you believe you can do things.' Once again she felt a sense of frustration at not knowing the right words to express what she meant. 'They help you imagine that things may be different, that if you just have enough courage . . . or enough faith . . . or *goodness* . . . you can change things for the better.'

Wilhelm turned and reached out his hand to her, clasping hers warmly. 'You're a good little soul, Dortchen. You always talk sense to me.'

She sat there motionless, her hand in his, unable to move or speak, unwilling to even breathe, in case it should break the spell of this moment. The Lion's Castle basked in the early-morning sunshine, a fine, smoky haze hung above the green woods, and a bird was singing in the tree above them. Then, with a rueful smile, Wilhelm let her hand go and turned back to the view.

Below them, small parties of people sat about on the hillside, sharing picnics, listening to the musicians or weaving daisy chains. Gretchen sat on an old tumbled stone, her white skirts arranged like a flower about her, her bonnet discarded so the sun shone on her golden head. Two young men sat beside her, and another lay on the grass at her feet. Hanne and Lisette sat nearby, but everyone's eyes were on Gretchen, for she was laughing and teasing the young men by trying to choose which one deserved the nosegay she had tucked in her bodice.

Nearby, Frau Wild was fussing over the picnic basket. Röse sat in the buggy, squinting over a book, and Mia was gathering wildflowers, though a wreath was already on her head and her basket was overflowing. Frau Wild kept stopping and looking around anxiously. Dortchen rose to her feet and stepped out of the shade, waving to her mother. Frau Wild's face brightened. She waved in response and turned back to her basket.

'My storytelling collection seems to have ground to a halt,' Wilhelm said, his eyes on the little group on the grass. 'Gretchen has given me a few stories, about cats and mice and dogs and sparrows. I really love one she gave me, about a golden bird and the youngest brother who must do all sorts of impossible tasks before he can win the hand of the princess.' He sighed.

'I know another story you might like,' Dortchen said. 'It's about three little men in a wood and the magical gifts they give a girl . . . a girl who is good and gentle and loving and kind.'

'Like you?' he teased, and she flushed bright red.

'I . . . I didn't mean—' she stammered.

'I know, I was only joking. What does this good, kind, gentle girl do?'

Dortchen could not look at him as she told the story, though it was one she had often told by the fire as she and her sisters sat sewing on wintry evenings. It was about a girl whose stepmother hated her and sent her out into the snow to find strawberries, dressed only in a paper frock. She came upon a cottage where three little men lived, and she was kind to them and shared her piece of old, hard bread with them. They then told her to sweep the back steps, and she obeyed.

'Under the snow were red, ripe strawberries,' Dortchen said, 'and what's more, the three little men decided to reward her for her kindness. One said she would grow more beautiful every day, the other that gold pieces would fall from her mouth every time she spoke, and the third that she would marry a king.'

When the girl went home, Dortchen continued, her stepmother was furious that it was her stepdaughter who had received all these gifts, and not her own daughter. She wrapped her daughter in furs and gave her cake and soft bread with butter, then sent her out to find the three little men. However, the stepsister was so rude and haughty that the three little men decided to punish her. The first wished that she would grow uglier every day, the second that a toad would leap out of her mouth at every word she said, and the third that she should die a miserable death.

'And so it was,' Dortchen finished. 'The stepsister grew uglier and meaner every day, and the house filled with hopping toads so that you squelched one underfoot at every step. At last the stepmother turned her out and she perished for cold in the forest. The kind girl married a king, and all her words were turned to gold coins so that everyone in the kingdom was well fed and prosperous, and everyone lived happily ever after.'

'It'd be a handy skill,' Wilhelm said. 'Spitting gold coins every time you spoke.'

'I should think it would be most uncomfortable,' Dortchen replied, thinking to herself, *Does he not understand?* His eyes turned to Gretchen again. Quickly she said, 'Though not as uncomfortable as coughing up toads.'

OAK MOSS

June 1808

The next morning, Dortchen rose well before dawn and dressed in the darkness.

She kept to the shadows as she crept through the sleeping town. The air still smelt of smoke from the midsummer bonfire that had been lit in the Königsplatz. Once she had to crouch in a doorway to avoid the patrolling night watch – one of Napoléon's innovations. The watchmen did not see her and she was able to hurry on, although her pulse was thudding so loudly in her ears that she was amazed they did not hear it.

By the time she reached the Schlosspark, light was fingering the top of the Herkules statue and painting the ruffled leaves of the trees with gold. The grass was silvered with dew. Dortchen put down her basket and brushed her fingers through the cool wetness, rubbing it all over her face. Midsummer dew made you beautiful, as everyone knew. And how Dortchen wished she was beautiful.

Refreshed, and laughing a little at herself, she hurried on, flitting from tree to tree, glad she was wearing her old green gown and brown shawl. She had to take care here. There would be soldiers patrolling the Schlosspark, guarding the sleep of their dissipated young king.

Every time she passed an oak tree, Dortchen gathered with trembling fingers the moss that grew on its rough grey bark. She plucked what acorns she could reach, and a handful of fresh green leaves, and went on.

The park had suffered under the French occupiers. Marble statues had been toppled and smashed, or used for bullet practice. The beautiful stone arches of the aqueduct were broken. Trees had been hacked down for firewood, and the meadows churned up by galloping hooves. Dortchen had always loved the beautiful park, with its sparkling cascades and fountains, and its stands of ancient trees. As a child, she had loved to run across the Devil's Bridge, hanging high above the mossy gorge, the waterfall foaming down to fall into Hell's Pond. She and her sisters had played hide and seek in the groves, and made daisy chains in the meadows. It hurt her to see the Schlosspark's wild beauty so damaged.

A small grove of linden trees grew on the far side of the lake, below the palace. Dortchen made her way there carefully, not wanting to be seen so close to the King's residence. The trees were in full blossom, bees reeling drunkenly from the pale-yellow flowers that hung down in clusters below the heart-shaped leaves. Dortchen harvested what she could reach, breathing the sweet scent deeply, then picked handfuls of the wild roses that grew in a tangled hedge along the path. She would crystallise the petals with sugar when she got home, or make rose water to sell in her father's shop.

She plucked some dandelions she found growing wild in a clearing, and then some meadowsweet, and at last reached the ancient old oak tree she knew from her last foray into the royal park. Here she found handfuls of the sparse grey moss, and she hid it deep within her basket, beneath the flowers and herbs and leaves.

By now, it was fully light. Old Marie would be awake, stoking up the fire, putting on the kettle to boil. Soon she'd be panting up the stairs, a heavy tray of tea things in her hands, to wake the girls of the house. 'Be quick, now, the cows are already out.'

'Is the goatherd out too?' Hanne would mutter, turning her cheek deeper into her pillow.

'Come, girls, up, up,' Old Marie would call, before taking the tea to Frau Wild, lying drowsily in her bed, while her husband was already up and calling for his shaving water. Dortchen knew the routine of her house so well that she knew the exact moment she would be missed, and what Old Marie would say to cover her absence.

Hurrying back towards the town, Dortchen tried to think of excuses. Would the herbs and acorns be enough?

She came in the back door and met Old Marie's worried eyes. Mozart chirped at her noisily. 'I have acorns,' she said.

'Plucked on Midsummer's morning,' Old Marie said in a resigned tone. 'Let me guess what else you have in there.'

'Dandelions and linden blossoms and wild roses.'

'All very useful. Your father wants to see you.'

'Where?'

'In his study.'

Dortchen went through to the pantry and unpacked her basket, hiding the oak moss in an old ceramic jar. Then, holding the bunch of leaves and flowers before her like an offering, she went through to the study. Her father was there, smoking a pipe, his teeth clamped about the stem.

He spoke not a word, but pointed his finger at the floor. Dortchen went and knelt before him, still holding the bunch of wild herbs. With a violent gesture, he dashed them from her hands. Dortchen flinched back and the flowers were scattered on the floor. He knocked out his pipe with a savage tap in the hearth and seized his switch, which had been lying ready across his knee.

In a low, shaking voice, her father began to speak. She heard only a phrase here and there, for terror was like a white sea roaring in her ears. 'We must kill sin at the root . . . We must know which are the master roots and mortify them . . .' All she could see was his long black boots, and the switch that he smacked continually against them, and his large hand with dark hairs springing out around white-clenched knuckles. He began to rock back and forth, swaying towards her. The switch flew out and struck her on the shoulder. She flinched, trying to bite back her cry, and he struck her again.

'Evil appetites . . . The worm that never dies, the gnawing worm . . .'

Unable to help herself, Dortchen bowed lower, protecting her face with her hands. He caught at the back of her neck, pushing her face-down against his thigh, striking at her back and buttocks while she was bent before him. Dortchen could not breathe. Small, sharp cries broke from her as the switch fell again and again.

Then there was the quick sound of boots on the floor, and Rudolf's voice. 'Enough,' he said. 'Father, there are customers who need you.'

Herr Wild froze, his switch raised high, and Dortchen's face still crushed into his thigh. She managed to gulp a breath, smelling old wool and tobacco smoke – and something else she could not identify, something dank and dark.

Her father pushed her away and she fell on her hands and knees before him. Pain roared in her ears. Her breath sobbed in her throat.

'It's a French soldier who wants a measure of mercury to treat syphilis, but for the life of me I cannot remember what the dose should be. Will you come?' Rudolf said in a bored tone.

'Ignorant fool,' Herr Wild said, adjusting his frockcoat. Once the door had banged behind him, Rudolf held down his hand for Dortchen.

'You shouldn't anger him,' he said. 'What a wild little thing you are, sneaking out in the dawn. What did you want to do, wash your face in the dew?'

Dortchen went scarlet.

'Well, you're a little idiot. You must have known Father would be furious. Go on, get out of here before he comes back. I have to go and spend the next few hours being lectured on correct dosages for syphilis. Just how I want to spend my day.'

Although his voice was rough, his hand was gentle in the small of her back as he guided her from the study. Dortchen kept her hand on the wall to steady herself as she sought the refuge of the kitchen. Old Marie was ready with a handkerchief soaked in lavender water and some healing salve.

Old Marie made tea for them and they drank it together in silence, Dortchen standing before the hearth as she could not sit down.

Frau Wild came down to the kitchen, her face drawn. 'Dortchen, darling, you must not enrage him so,' she said. 'He finds it hard . . . He does his best . . . And you're growing up now . . .'

'I know. I'm sorry.'

But Dortchen was not sorry. She had known what the penalty would be for creeping out of the house before dawn. It was worth it for those handfuls of spidery silver oak moss hidden in the pantry.

On the night of the next full moon, Dortchen waited till it was almost midnight before she crept from her bed. In her long white nightgown, she went barefoot across the room and lifted up the blanket on the little white cot in the corner. There, hidden beneath the lacy dress of her doll, Wilhelmine, was a small white candle, a vial of acorn oil infused with ground oak moss, and a small silver coin that had been minted in 1786.

Dortchen had ground the oak moss to powder with the same mortar and pestle that she had used to grind the gall nuts for the dye to stain Lotte's clothes black. No amount of scrubbing had turned the stone of the mortar and pestle white again. They were dyed indelibly black. Somehow this seemed right to Dortchen. There was darkness in this thing she was doing, no matter how she looked at it.

If her father caught her making spells, he would kill her.

The silver moonlight shone through her bedroom window, showing Lotte's dark hair spread out on the pillow. It had been more than a month since Frau Grimm had died but Lotte refused to go home. She never went walking in the park with the Wild girls, nor, most shockingly of all, would she go to church.

The spell was as much for Lotte as it was for Wilhelm.

Dortchen poured water into her washing bowl and set it on the windowsill so the moonlight gleamed upon it. She poured a small amount of the acorn oil into her palm. It smelt woody, like an ancient forest. Dortchen breathed it in deeply, thinking with a bitter sting in her eyes that it would be a long time before she would smell the forest again. She rubbed the oil on the coin, then dropped it into the water. She wiped her oily hands on her towel, then struck a spark with her flint. She put a twist of old paper to her tinder and lit the candle.

Golden candlelight glimmered on the water, mingling with the silver moonlight. Dortchen whispered the words that Old Marie had told her, the words that she had learnt from her grandmother long ago.

'*Lady of the moon,*
Bring him good fortune,
Fill his hands with silver and gold,
As much as he can hold.'

She sat watching the candle burn away, hoping with all her might that the spell would work, that her sacrifice had been worth it. At last the flame guttered away. She poured the water back into the jug and climbed into bed. It smelt as if she were lying on a bed of moss, under a ceiling of dark, shifting leaves, instead of in her own small bedroom.

Comforted, she slept.

A STROKE OF LUCK

July 1808

A week after Dortchen's moonlit spell, Jakob was offered a job as librarian at the palace.

It was not what Dortchen had been hoping for, but it did mean that Wilhelm and Lotte did not have to move away. There was now enough money for them to pay their rent and buy some food.

'I must admit, it was a stroke of luck, getting the job just when we were so desperate,' Jakob said. 'I only wish it had come before Mother died.'

There was a fraught silence.

'Are you enjoying the job, Jakob?' Dortchen said quickly.

'Surprisingly, yes,' he answered. 'All I've had to do so far is put a big sign on the door saying "Library of the King". He doesn't read and neither does the Queen, so I can do what I like, as long as I observe the etiquette of the court.'

They were sitting in the Grimms' kitchen. Lotte had reluctantly moved home again, and Dortchen had crept out to bring her some lentils and herbs to make soup. Dortchen had not seen Wilhelm all week, for her father had forbidden her to leave the house, except to go to church. Dortchen would have loved a chance to be alone with Wilhelm, to hear for herself how his breathing was, to measure his heartbeat with her hand, to smooth back the sweat-tousled curls from his brow. But that was impossible.

Dortchen's love for Wilhelm had long since ceased to be a source of secret joy for her. It was a leaden weight, a never-easing ache. He still thought of her as a child, perhaps even as another sister, but Dortchen knew her love was just as intense and true as that of any woman. There were times when she longed to be free of the fetters that bound her to him, just as she longed to burst free of the chains of duty to her family. Yet, as they were invisible and incorporeal, there was no hammer that could break those chains, no key that could unlock the shackles.

'Any news?' Ferdinand wanted to know.

'King Jérôme has borrowed more money from the Jews, and his first wife is causing trouble,' Jakob answered wearily. He loosened his stiff collar. 'Oh, and his spies have discovered that the Kurfürst hid many of his art treasures at the old castle at Sababurg. He has had them all fetched and is very smug to have them hanging on the palace walls again.'

'Spies everywhere,' Wilhelm said. 'You cannot have an innocent conversation in the street without someone eavesdropping on it, or throw away a bonbon wrapper without someone swooping to examine it for secret messages.'

'Napoléon fears an insurrection,' Jakob said. 'He has written to his brother, warning him to take care and not trust anyone, but Jérôme just laughs. He thinks he is loved because everyone comes to his parties. Well, I refuse to go, no matter how pressing the invitation. You know he has summoned his mistress to court, some painted actress who is to perform at this new theatre he is building? It's scandalous, the way he behaves.'

'Yet you work for him,' Ferdinand pointed out.

Jakob scowled. 'I work for him so you all don't starve, Ferdinand. Believe me, I'd much rather lounge around all day like you do.'

Ferdinand started up angrily, but Wilhelm dropped a hand on his shoulder and squeezed it. 'He hasn't lounged around *all* day, and neither have I, old man. I've been copying stories and Ferdinand has been transcribing songs for Herr von Arnim. Look what an elegant job he has made of it.' He passed a sheaf of papers to Jakob, whose face lightened.

'Well, that is good. Herr von Arnim will be pleased, I know.'

'What of the war, Jakob?' Ludwig asked.

Jakob laid down the papers and sighed. 'Only bad news. Or good, if you're a supporter of Napoléon. The eldest Bonaparte brother has given up his throne in Naples and gone to be king in Spain, but the Spanish rose up against him. Napoléon's generals have defeated them, though they had only fourteen thousand men and the Spanish forty thousand.'

'It is like he has conjured demons from hell to fight on his side,' Lotte said in a low voice. 'Soon he will rule the whole world.'

'He and his brothers,' Ludwig said.

'His brothers are just puppets,' Jakob said. 'Why, look at Jérôme. He gave up his wife and his little son to marry at his brother's bidding.'

'I think that's terrible,' Wilhelm said with vigour. 'A man shouldn't desert his family like that. That poor boy will grow up never knowing his father.'

Dortchen's lips twisted wryly but she said nothing, giving the soup one last stir and then putting on her bonnet and gloves. 'I must go,' she said. 'Old Marie will be serving up our supper now.'

Lotte got to her feet. 'I wish you'd stay a little longer. Have supper with us?'

Dortchen shook her head. 'I'm sorry, I cannot. I'll see you tomorrow maybe.'

Lotte hugged her and gave her a kiss. 'For five minutes, if I'm lucky.'

'I'm sorry,' Dortchen said again, and she let herself out. She went down the stairs and hurried across the alley, easing open the gate into the garden. All was quiet and she couldn't see anyone standing at the windows, so she slipped through the garden and into the kitchen, taking off her bonnet and hanging it on her hook.

'Is all well?' she asked Old Marie, who nodded, her round face creased with anxiety.

Dortchen let out her breath in a long sigh of relief. A feeling of compression about her ribs eased. 'Thank heavens,' she said. 'Shall I serve the soup?'

Mozart flew to her shoulder, running his beak lovingly through her

152

hair, which was tightly plaited about her head. 'Pretty girl, naughty girl,' he crooned.

'You are naughty,' Old Marie said. 'What if your father realises you've gone?'

Dortchen squared her shoulders. 'Lotte needs help. She's the only girl in a household of men and they expect her to do all the work we do here – and we have six girls, and Mother, and you. She's not been raised to it, and she's still crushed by grief. I can't not help her, I just can't.'

'You've a kind and loving heart, sweetling, but you're risking bringing trouble down on your own head.'

Dortchen nodded, beginning to ladle out the soup. She thought of the girl with six brothers turned into swans. She'd had to weave six shirts from nettles, without speaking or laughing, if she was to save her brothers. She had still been weaving the last one as she was sentenced to be burnt to death for witchcraft. One sleeve had been unfinished, and so when she flung the shirts to her swan-brothers, one was left with a wing in place of his arm.

Risking a beating was nothing compared to risking being burnt to death.

Sometimes you had to face danger if you were to help others.

A week later, all anyone could talk about was the Maid of Zaragoza.

A young Spanish woman, she had carried a basket of apples to feed the soldiers defending her home town of Zaragoza but saw them overcome by the relentless fire of the French. The French stormed the gateway, shooting down the fleeing soldiers, stabbing them with their bayonets. The Maid of Zaragoza had run forward, loaded one of the ancient cannons and lit the fuse with a match, crying, 'Zaragoza still has one defender!'

The cannonball tore the attacking French battalion to pieces. Undaunted, the Maid of Zaragoza had stayed at her post, loading and firing the cannon till the French had retreated. Although the small town later fell to the French, and most of its inhabitants were slaughtered, the story of the Maid of Zaragoza spread like wildfire.

Within weeks, one disaster after another had befallen the French army in

Spain. A squadron of French battleships in the harbour of Cadiz were fired upon till they surrendered. Another French battalion was defeated at Baylen in Andalusia; the new King of Spain, Joseph Bonaparte, had to flee Madrid, which was then occupied by the insurgents. It seemed as if the heroic action of one young woman had broken Napoléon's charm of invincibility.

'She was just a girl, an ordinary girl,' Lisette said in the drawing room, adding an extra frill of muslin to Mia's dress to accommodate her growing length.

'But to load a cannon, to shoot people down – how ever did she dare?' Gretchen cried.

'She was so brave,' Dortchen said. She felt ashamed. No one in Hessen-Cassel had tried to stop the French taking over. Once the Kurfürst had fled, everyone had just cowered behind their closed shutters while the French marched through the streets, singing 'La Marseillaise'. She had crept out to watch them, it was true, but it had never occurred to her to take up arms against them.

'The Emperor has gone to Erfurt to meet with the Tsar again,' Hanne cried. 'That's only a day's march from here, if he should travel at his usual lightning speed. Oh, do you think he will come here to Cassel? Wouldn't he like to see his brother? Imagine if the Emperor came here – we'd see him!'

'I don't want to see him,' Gretchen said with a theatrical shudder. 'I think I'd swoon with fright.'

'Only if there was a handsome soldier standing nearby to catch you,' Hanne responded.

The Emperor had no time to visit his feckless younger brother. He was too busy raising an army to march into Spain. Battalions of soldiers marched through Cassel on their way south, demanding food, ammunition and medical supplies. Dortchen and her sisters worked from dawn till midnight in the garden and the stillroom, harvesting plants and grinding them to powder, distilling essences, making up cordials, and cutting and rolling bandages. Dortchen had no time even to think of slipping across the road to the Grimms, nor was she ever left alone.

Wilhelm knocked on the door once or twice, hoping Dortchen could spare the time to tell him some more stories, but she did not dare. The third time he came, Frau Wild took pity on him and told him a tale about a straw, a coal and a broad bean that explained how beans got the black seam down their middle.

Dortchen came into the parlour to collect the newspapers and tear them into strips, which she then twisted tightly, ready to be used to light the fire, or candles, or her father's pipe, just so she could listen to the scratch of Wilhelm's quill on the paper, and his occasional soft phrases: 'Could you repeat that, please . . . Just a moment . . .' He smiled at the sight of her but did not pause in his hurried scribbling, and soon she had no excuse to linger and had to go away again.

At the end of July, Wilhelm went to stay with his Aunt Zimmer in Gotha. The knowledge of his absence was a cold hollow inside Dortchen. She was wretched, and unable to confess her misery to anyone.

It did not help when he came back excited by the discovery of some old manuscripts in the library there. His dark eyes glowed and his thin cheeks were hectic with colour; all his talk was of the poetic beauty and darkness and grandeur of the works he had found. Although he smiled at Dortchen and asked her how she had been, his concern seemed to be motivated more by politeness than any real interest.

Nor did he seek her out after church but stayed talking with Jakob, their dark heads bent close together, their speech filled with strange words that had no meaning to Dortchen. Indeed, it was as if they were speaking another language entirely.

That night, in bed, Dortchen wept, her chest shuddering with the need to keep her despair secret.

In late October, on a cold, blustery day, Lotte came rushing into the garden, calling Dortchen's name. 'Dortchen, it's so terrible . . .' she sobbed.

'What? What is it?' Dortchen straightened from the bed of herbs, her back aching and her gloves thick with dirt.

'It's Jakob . . .'

'What's happened? Is he ill, hurt?' Dortchen scanned her friend's face

155

anxiously. Lotte was thin and pale, and her dark hair was in a mess, straggling away from its hasty braid.

Lotte shook her head and tried to catch her breath, tears spilling down her cheeks. 'He's been called up for the conscription lottery. Oh, Dortchen, it's so unfair. What shall we do if he gets a low number? He'll be sent to Spain, he'll have to fight, he might die. He's the gentlest soul – how can they even think of making him a soldier? And what shall we do if he goes away? How shall we survive?'

Dortchen bit her lip. The conscription lottery was the very worst of Napoléon's harsh rules, she thought. Young men had no choice in the matter at all. If they were aged between eighteen and twenty-five, and over five-foot-one in height, their names would be put into a barrel and pulled out, one by one, till the army's quota was reached. Hundreds and thousands of men had been sent to fight in Napoléon's never-ending war. Hundreds and thousands had died. And still Napoléon's hunger for conquest had not been satisfied.

'Is there nothing we can do?' Lotte sobbed.

Dortchen hesitated. Only a medical certificate from a doctor allowed conscripts to escape their fate. Those rich enough paid doctors for the exemption. Those influential enough called upon favours, as Herr Wild had done for Rudolf. The Grimms were neither rich nor influential.

She took hold of both of Lotte's hands. 'All you can do is hope for the best,' she said. 'But Lotte . . .'

Her friend raised a tear-streaked face. 'Yes?'

'I'm sure all will be well. I feel it in my heart. But if he draws a low number, come to me. I'll give you some holly berries for him to eat, which will purge his bowels. They won't take him into the army if they think he has dysentery.'

Lotte squeezed both Dortchen's hands. 'Thank you,' she wept. 'Oh, thank you. What would I do without you?'

'It'll be fine,' Dortchen said.

And it was. When Napoléon and his Grand Army marched for Spain in late October, Jakob did not march with them.

His luck had held.

PART THREE

The Forbidden Chamber

CASSEL

The Kingdom of Westphalia, 1808–1810

Then the sorcerer also wanted the third daughter. He captured her in his pack basket, carried her home, and then, before he left, gave her the egg and the key. However, the third sister was crafty and cunning. She hid the egg first, and then she went into the forbidden chamber. When she saw her sisters all cut up in the basin of blood, she found all of their parts and put them back in their right place: head, body, arms, and legs. The parts started to move, and then they joined together, and the two sisters were alive again.

From 'Fitcher's Bird', a tale told to Wilhelm Grimm by Dortchen Wild before 1812

SPANISH LACE

November 1808

In late November, Achim von Arnim wrote, asking if he might come and stay with the Grimms.

Lotte told Dortchen the news while they walked to church that Sunday. It was a nasty cold day and the girls huddled together, sharing Dortchen's old shawl.

'What are we to do?' Lotte asked, her breath hanging white before her. 'It's a great honour . . . and of course he's been such a help to us already, paying for Ludwig to go to art school and publishing so many of Jakob and Wilhelm's articles in his magazine. Yet our house is so shabby and poor . . . where is he to sleep?'

'What about your mother's bedroom?' Dortchen knew that Frau Grimm's room had remained unchanged since the day she had died. Once her body had been carried out, Jakob had shut the door and no one had been in since.

'But we couldn't! Mother died in there.'

'All the best houses have beds that people have died in,' Dortchen said. 'Herr von Arnim needn't be afraid. It's not as if your mother would come back and haunt him. She was far too well behaved.'

Lotte couldn't help giggling. 'Can you imagine it? Mother in her old nightgown and cap, asking him what he was doing in her bed!'

Dortchen was glad that she had made Lotte laugh. Her friend had

159

hardly smiled in months. 'Do you think Herr von Arnim would shriek and run down the stairs in his nightgown?'

Lotte smiled faintly. After a long moment, she said, 'I suppose there's no harm in giving him Mother's bedroom. We can't let him sleep in the kitchen. But it will need to be cleaned out. And all our sheets are almost worn through.'

'I'll see if I can get away for an hour or two,' Dortchen said. 'You must ask Jakob for some real help, though, Lottechen. Get a woman to come in for the afternoon and do all the heavy work. You want Herr von Arnim to think well of you all, and you must admit the house has run to wrack and ruin lately.'

'I'm just so tired all the time,' Lotte said. 'I work from dawn till dusk, with scarcely a bite to eat, yet the house just seems to get dirtier and messier. At least I don't have Karl to pick up after any more.' Dortchen nodded. Karl had moved to Hamburg to try to find work. 'I could scarcely bear to get out of bed this morning,' Lotte went on. 'I knew there was nothing to get up for but housework.'

'It's hard in winter,' Dortchen sympathised. 'I had to crack the crust of ice on the water in my jug this morning, it was so cold.'

'I'm just so tired of it all,' Lotte continued. 'They expect me to cook and clean and iron and sew. I never get any fun.'

'Me neither,' Dortchen replied. Both girls sighed and said no more. There was no use in complaining. Housework was a woman's lot.

Achim von Arnim arrived in early December, bringing gifts of wine and muslin-wrapped fruitcake and a parcel of books tied up with twine. Dortchen watched from the drawing-room window as he stepped down out of his well-sprung travelling coach, elegantly dressed as always in a snow-white cravat and a greatcoat with a multitude of capes on the shoulder. Jakob, Wilhelm and Ferdinand were waiting to greet him. They shook his hand warmly, took his gifts and led him inside the tall, narrow house.

Dortchen leant her forehead against the cold windowpane. She would have loved to have packed a basket with some goodies and gone over to visit. She knew her father would be watching and listening, however, and she dared not take the risk.

Dortchen felt a shadow come over her spirit at the thought of her father. For months, she had kept out of his way, keeping her eyes lowered and her voice silent, working diligently in the kitchen and garden, places he never went. He watched her, though. She could feel the heavy weight of his eyes at mealtimes and on the way to church. She had no way to know why he regarded her with such frowning intensity. Was he sorry for beating her? Did he miss the old, light-hearted Dortchen, who sang and skipped and pretended to be a knight or a princess or a bird? Or was he pleased that she was growing into the silent, meek girl he seemed to want?

She could not lift her eyes to examine his face, to try to understand the forces that moved him. Dortchen was frightened of her father now.

After a long moment, she turned away from the window and went down to the kitchen to help begin supper.

The next day, at breakfast, Herr Wild was going through the mail when he gave a grunt of surprise. 'It's something for Dortchen,' he said, and opened it with his butter knife. 'From that Grimm family. They've asked her to go to the theatre. Apparently, that nobleman is taking them all, as a Christmas gift.'

'Dortchen has been asked to go to the theatre?' Gretchen cried. 'With Herr von Arnim? But Father, that's not fair . . .'

'Oh, Father, may I go? Please?' Dortchen pressed both her hands together and gazed at him pleadingly.

'Impossible,' Herr Wild said. 'Go to the theatre with those rackety young men? If their mother were still alive . . .'

'But Lotte will be there,' Dortchen protested.

'Dortchen will need a chaperone, of course,' Hanne said. 'I'll go with her.'

Gretchen stared, her mouth hanging open, then shut it with a snap. 'If Hanne's going, I'm going.'

'Dortchen doesn't need two chaperones,' Hanne responded. 'But it will be quite unexceptional for her to be accompanied by her elder sister.'

'Surely they're still all in mourning?' Gretchen laid one hand on her chest in exaggerated astonishment. 'How shocking that they should wish to go to the theatre.'

'It's been more than six months,' Dortchen said.

'What shall we wear?' Hanne said. 'We haven't an evening frock between us.'

'Absolutely not,' Herr Wild said, looking up from his newspaper. 'I do not think you are at all suitable as a chaperone, Hanne. Dortchen will decline the invitation.'

There was a long, depressed silence.

'I'll go with Dortchen,' Frau Wild said.

Everyone stared at her in utter stupefaction. No one could remember their mother ever going out in the evening.

She smiled faintly. 'I used to love the theatre.'

Dortchen wanted to fling her arms about her mother's neck and dance for joy. Instead, she merely whispered, 'Thank you, Mother.'

Herr Wild frowned, tossed the invitation towards Dortchen and got up from his chair. 'It'll be cold out,' he said to Frau Wild. 'You'd better wrap up warm.'

'Yes, sir.'

It felt strange to be the centre of attention for a change. Lisette lent Dortchen her best gown, in pale-blue flowered cotton, with the waist high up under the arms in the very latest fashion. Hanne lent her a pair of long white evening gloves, and Gretchen did her hair in a mass of tight ringlets, caught into a knot at the back of her head and allowed to tumble down onto her neck. Dortchen could scarcely wait for Wilhelm to see her. He had been away, looking for tellers of old tales at Allendorf, a town not far from Marburg, so she had not seen him in some weeks.

That evening, however, she was shocked at the sight of him. He was white-faced, with feverish eyes set in dark hollows. He smiled when he saw her, though with an obvious effort, and said, 'What a pretty dress. The colour suits you.'

Dortchen smiled and thanked him. 'Are you not well?' she asked him in an undertone, as they walked along the lantern-lit streets towards the theatre.

He shrugged, not looking at her. 'I'm having trouble sleeping.'

'Still?'

He nodded his head. 'I mean, I drift in and out, but often I'm awake well before dawn. I cannot tell you how much I hate the sound of your quail crying in the dawn. I cannot hear it without shuddering.'

'It does make a large noise for such a small creature,' Dortchen said. 'Father hangs it outside the shop's window so it will cry an alarm if anyone tries to break in during the night. People do try, you know, to steal medicines.'

'Has he not heard of a watchdog?'

Dortchen smiled. 'Another mouth to feed. A quail eats spilt seeds and insects, and provides eggs and meat for the table. Far more practical.'

Wilhelm smiled in genuine amusement. 'I think we need some of your family's good sense. That would never have occurred to me.'

'Why didn't you tell me you've been in such pain? Father might have a draught that could help.'

'Nothing helps. Besides, you've done far too much for us already.'

'I've done nothing.'

He cast her an amused look. 'You've been a good friend, Dortchen. Believe me, we know it.'

She cast her eyes down in sudden confusion. Did he somehow know about the lucky spell, and how she had risked her father's anger to do it? *He couldn't possibly*, she told herself. *He means the herbal teas and the gifts of food.*

'We can never thank you enough,' he went on. 'Without you, I think Lotte could well have gone half-mad with grief.'

She shook her head. 'Asking me to the theatre is thanks enough. I've never been before.'

'Well, I hope you enjoy it,' he answered with a faint smile.

At that moment, Herr von Arnim turned and asked him a question, and he moved away from her side. Dortchen tried not to follow him with her eyes, aware that both her mother's and Lotte's gazes were fixed on her face.

Instead, she looked about her. The streets seemed so different at night. Lanterns hung before each shop, illuminating the wares inside. Dortchen had never seen so many beautiful and luxurious things. Cassel had changed greatly in the year that Napoléon's little brother had been their king. The shops along Königstrasse had once been simple – chandlers and barrel-makers and sellers of vegetables – but now all sorts of new shops had opened up, milliners and corsetières and makers of boots, sellers of Oriental porcelain, hand-woven rugs from Bruges, and spices from the

Levant. Where once there had been the occasional tavern, now there were dance halls and gambling dens and a barouche manufacturer.

A group of bearded Jewish men in long black coats and white prayer shawls walked past on their way to Friday-night worship, long ringlets hanging down beside their ears. They stopped at the kerb to wait for a sedan chair, in which reclined a voluptuous woman dressed in an almost transparent dress, her bare chest and upper arms glittering with jewels.

'That's the King's actress,' Lotte whispered to Dortchen. 'She's in the play tonight.'

Frau Wild drew her shawl tighter about her shoulders and looked away. 'What is the world coming to?' she murmured.

'Did you know,' Jakob was saying to Herr von Arnim, 'that Polish Jews believe that they can bring a figure made of mud to life if they speak the divine name over it? They call it a golem and use it as a servant in the house. Is that not fascinating?'

'Indeed it is,' Herr von Arnim said. 'Is that what you're working on now, Jakob? You must write an article on the subject and send it to me.'

'I shall,' Jakob replied, and went on to tell their visitor more of what he had discovered. Wilhelm walked beside them, listening quietly, his shoulders stooped with weariness.

After a while, Herr von Arnim turned and asked, 'What about you, Wilhelm – what have you been working on?'

'Almost all my work in recent times has been a translation of old Danish heroic ballads,' Wilhelm replied.

'Ah, like those ones you sent me for the *Journal for Hermits*. They were magnificent.'

'They have such poetic depth and grandeur, don't they? I feel convinced that Herr von Goethe must have been inspired by them. The rhythm and sense of menace in "The Erl-King", for example.' He quoted, with one hand flung out dramatically,

'"My son, why do you seek your face to hide?
Father, cannot you see the Erl-King rides by our side?
The Erl-King with his crown and train?

My son, it's just a wisp of rain."'

He sensed Dortchen's gaze on him and smiled at her, but she could not smile back. Goosebumps had risen on her arms. She felt a cold shiver down her spine.

The theatre was crowded. Women in pale satin gowns with sweeping trains moved past, jewels glittering on their bare necks and gloved arms. Men in white waistcoats and dark coats escorted them, their chins resting on high starched cravats. Above, great oil lamps were suspended from the roof, casting a golden radiance over the lobby. Dortchen had never seen any light so bright and steady.

Frau Wild found the steps hard to climb, so Lotte and Dortchen fell behind the men as they climbed up to their box. Dortchen felt that her eyes were not large enough to take everything in. She heard the scrape of bows over violins and shivered with delight.

At the top of the stairs, Achim, Wilhelm and Ferdinand were clustered around a small, slight figure in an extraordinary gown of heavy crimson velvet, with dramatic long sleeves. The gown was trimmed with black lace, and the woman wore a matching mantilla on her head. She looked like some exotic bloom – a crimson dahlia – among a meadow filled with common white cow's parsley. All Dortchen's pleasure in her dress was lost.

'Is that Bettina?' Lotte asked incredulously.

'It is!' Dortchen cried, as the girl in the crimson velvet turned her head of thick dark ringlets to reveal a small, pointed face, laughing above a fan of black Spanish lace.

'I heard she was in Cassel,' Lotte said. 'Staying with her elder brother, who is now banker to the King.'

Dortchen whispered in Lotte's ear, 'I wonder if that is why Herr von Arnim has come to visit you? I'm sure he's in love with her.'

'Well, then, I feel very sorry for him,' Lotte said waspishly. At Dortchen's look, she said, 'I don't mean to be unkind. You must admit she would not make a very good wife.'

'She'd be an unusual one,' Dortchen admitted. 'But one is never bored when she's around.'

Bettina saw them approach and came forward with a few dancing steps, her crimson skirts swaying. 'How good to see you. You both look so pretty. Dortchen, you've grown so tall I'll get a crick in my neck looking up at you. Tell me, what do you think of my dress? Are you very shocked?'

'It's gorgeous,' Dortchen said. 'I'd love one just like it.'

'It's all the rage. The Maid of Zaragoza, you know. They call these long flowing sleeves à la Mameluke. It'd make Napoléon gnash his teeth to see me. He likes women to wear only white, you know. I wonder if his little brother is the same? Will he be here tonight? Shall I cause a great scandal? My sister-in-law tells me so.' She inclined her head towards a rather sour-faced woman in a slim white dress with tiny puffed sleeves and diamond bracelets clasped above her elbows.

'My brother is banker to the little King, you know,' Bettina went on, in the same laughing fashion, making no effort at all to lower her voice. 'She thinks it her duty to be as French as she possibly can. Hence the hideous dress. She's far too old to wear white.'

Her sister-in-law cast her a look of fury.

'But come, join us. Wilhelm was just telling us about poor Augusta. He saw her, in Allendorf, you know. Apparently, she's as mad as ever.'

Wilhelm cast her a look of laughing reproof. 'Bettina, I never said so. She was just . . . very dramatic. She wept and swooned when Clemens tried to leave her, and said she was sure they would never see each other again. Clemens had to run and jump the fence, for fear she would pursue him, wailing.'

Everyone laughed – even Frau Wild, who did not know who they were talking about.

Dortchen whispered to her quickly, 'Augusta is married to Bettina's brother Clemens, Mother. She is rather prone to melodramatics. Lotte thinks it won't be long before they're divorced.'

'Shocking,' Frau Wild said in a faint voice.

'You know Clemens wrote to me to join him in Allendorf, so I could meet the Mannels, the family with whom Augusta is staying?' Wilhelm said to Bettina, his eyes bright with fervour. 'He thought Friederike, the daughter there, could give me some stories for our collection. She was a very pleasant girl.'

'Friederike gave us quite a few songs for *The Boy's Wonder Horn*,' Herr von Arnim interjected. 'A most respectable family. Her father's a pastor, you know. They take in guests to try and raise a little money for her brothers' education. It's not a good time to be in the Church.'

'No, not at all,' Frau Wild said politely. 'Very sad.'

'I think she can help us,' Wilhelm said eagerly. 'She's promised to ask around and transcribe any old stories she can find.'

'That's wonderful news,' Bettina said warmly. 'Come on, admit it, you made her fall in love with you, Wilhelm.'

He flushed. 'Not at all. She's engaged to be married. I simply told her we're trying to save something of the true German folk spirit, and she was enthused with the importance of the task.'

'I'm sure she must be half in love with you,' Bettina teased. She looked towards Lotte and Dortchen for support, and his sister joined in teasing him. Dortchen stood stiffly by her mother's side, trying to keep her face from betraying her. She was sure everyone must guess the hot tumult of jealousy, anguish and despair that gripped her at the thought of this 'very pleasant girl', Friederike.

'Did you hear that Herr van Beethoven has been offered a post here in Cassel by the King?' Lotte said to Bettina.

'He won't take it,' Bettina said with authority. 'Beethoven despises Napoléon for making himself emperor.'

'Shh, Bettina,' Herr von Arnim said. 'Have some discretion.'

Bettina just dimpled at him. 'Do you not know Herr van Beethoven dedicated his *Eroica* symphony to Napoléon, but then when he heard the news that Napoléon had crowned himself, he crossed out the name with such vigour that he tore a hole in the sheet of music?'

'How can you know such a thing?' Lotte demanded.

'Oh, I know,' Bettina answered with utter certainty.

Dortchen and Lotte could only gaze back at her, convinced.

'I must tell you the funniest story about Herr van Beethoven,' Bettina went on. 'Did you know his younger brother was an apothecary?'

'Like my father,' Dortchen said in surprise.

Bettina paid her no mind. 'Well, his brother made a fortune selling drugs to the army and bought himself an estate. He wrote to tell his brother and signed himself most pretentiously "Johann van Beethoven, owner of land". Herr van Beethoven responded by signing "Ludwig van Beethoven, owner of brains".'

Everybody laughed.

A man in an ornately frogged coat and a white wig came out and began to ring a large brass bell. The crowd began to surge to their seats. 'Jakob,' Wilhelm called. His brother had been standing at the rail, his hands tucked under his coat-tails, observing the crowd. He turned at Wilhelm's voice and came towards them, a frown on his face.

'The King is here. That must mean news from Spain.' Jakob had a few quick words with one of the King's aides, then returned to their side, saying in a low voice, 'Napoléon has taken back Madrid. They say the Spanish rebellion has failed.'

'Ah, no,' Bettina cried. 'Those poor people! The Ogre will crush them like a flea.'

'Keep your voice down, you fool,' Jakob said. 'You may dress and act as you please, but do not bring danger down upon my family. We may not like what has happened to our country but we still must live here.'

Bettina pushed out her lip sulkily but said no more.

Dortchen stood back, watching wide-eyed as the young king made his way up the stairs to his box, dressed in white satin, medals glittering on his chest. He was laughing and waving to the crowd, who all bowed low or curtsied. Then he saw Bettina in her Spanish gown. His eyebrows shot up. He raised his quizzing-glass and swept her from the crest of her mantilla to the hem of her red velvet gown. Undaunted, Bettina dropped him a curtsey, smiling. He laughed and went on.

Dortchen wished she had Bettina's bravado.

UPRISING

April 1809

'I've come to say goodbye.' Wilhelm stood very straight in the doorway, holding his hat in both hands. His face and body were in shadow, as the square outside was bright with spring sunshine.

'Why? Where are you going?' Dortchen cried.

'I'm going to Halle. There's a doctor there who may be able to help me.'

'You're still not well?' she asked. 'The yarrow has not helped?'

'It's been a hard winter,' he said. 'I cough all the time. Sometimes I find it so hard to breathe.'

'What does the doctor say?'

'He's tried different remedies. The mercury fumes did not help at all – in fact, I'm sure they made me feel worse. But it's my heart he's most concerned about.'

Dortchen pressed her hand to her own heart, which had accelerated as if in sympathy. 'It is still giving you trouble?'

'It's like being stabbed with a red-hot arrow,' Wilhelm said. 'A few days ago my heart beat so fast and so erratically for so long – a good twenty hours – that I was sure I was going to die. Oh, Dortchen, I cannot tell you how sick and anxious it makes me feel. What if I was to die? I've done nothing I want to do in this world. I've not written a word worth reading, or made anything. I've never even . . .' Abruptly he stopped.

'What?' Dortchen asked.

'Nothing. It doesn't matter.'

'Does the doctor think you might die?'

'He shakes his head and pulls his beard and tells me to try sleeping sitting up – which is awful, if you've never tried it. Now he says it's beyond his ken and I must go to this heart specialist in Halle. It's going to cost a great deal of money, which of course we don't have.'

'I'm sorry,' she said. She wanted to reach out a hand to him but did not dare. They were standing right outside the shop window. 'I hope the doctor can help you.'

His mouth twisted. 'So do I.'

'When will you be back?'

'I don't know. Not for a while.'

Maybe not forever, her aching heart cried.

'Good luck, and God bless,' she said.

'Yes. Thank you.' He raised his hat to her, then turned and walked slowly away. She stood and watched him till he had climbed into the travelling carriage and the coachman had urged the horses into motion. By the time the coach had turned the corner towards the bridge, she could see nothing through the blur of her tears. She turned, dabbing at her eyes with the corner of her apron.

Her father stood in the doorway of his shop. 'He's not for you, Dortchen,' he said harshly. 'He's poor and improvident and, by the look of him, not long for this world. It's foolish to set your heart on him.'

'I know,' Dortchen said.

A few days later, war broke out again.

The entire front page of the newspaper was blackened out by the censors, so the townsfolk of Cassel had to rely on gossip and rumour. Dortchen, accompanying Old Marie to market, heard the same snippets over and over again.

'Have you heard? Austria has invaded Bavaria,' the grocer said, pouring lentils into his scales.

'The French are in utter disarray. They say soldiers are deserting by the thousands,' the fishmonger said, wrapping a spotted river trout in old newspaper.

'Balderdash! It's a trick,' the chandler said, tying up a dozen squat tallow candles in twine. 'You know the Emperor, he always likes to pretend he's weaker than he really is so as to take his enemies by surprise. Mark my words, he'll come down on the Austrians like a lightning bolt.'

'I heard he's galloping from Paris to take command. Three horses have died underneath him already,' the ribbon-seller whispered, receiving a small coin for a length of dark-blue satin.

That evening, all the talk was of the war. Only Lisette was quiet and distracted. She did not try to intervene when an argument broke out between Hanne and Rudolf, nor did she try to repress Gretchen, who was upset that the resumption of hostilities meant a ball at the palace had been cancelled.

The next morning, Herr von Eschwege called upon Herr Wild. They were closeted in the parlour for a good twenty minutes, then Herr Wild sent Dortchen running to find Lisette.

Lisette and Gretchen had both been sitting in the drawing room, too tense to sew. At the news Lisette was wanted, Gretchen turned first white, then red.

'Lisette?' she demanded. 'Surely not?'

Lisette blushed and got up, smoothing down her plain grey work dress. 'I wish I had something prettier to wear,' she said.

'Here.' Dortchen darted forward and seized the old silk shawl from where Gretchen had tossed it on the couch. She arranged it becomingly about Lisette's shoulders, then her eldest sister went hurrying down to the parlour, pinching her cheeks to bring colour into them.

'He was *my* beau,' Gretchen said angrily.

'Evidently not,' Dortchen answered.

Herr von Eschwege stayed for supper – the first time in the sisters' memory that anyone outside their immediate family had eaten under their roof. A tall, straight-backed young man with a monocle and a fine pair of blonde moustaches, he was most punctilious. He spoke only of the weather and hunting, and was assiduous in passing along the platters of food. Dortchen had almost decided she did not like him when she saw a spark of amusement in his eyes at how stiff and proper Mia was, sitting very straight in her chair and cutting her food into tiny pieces so she did not have to chew too obviously.

The house was thrown into a flurry of sewing, for Lisette had to take with her tablecloths and sheets and pillowcases, and the geese all had to be plucked to make a feather mattress for the couple. Lisette was radiantly happy, singing as she sewed and dancing as she carried a basket of wet washing to the line.

A week later, Herr Schmerfeld came – hat in hand, his cravat very starched – to ask Herr Wild for Gretchen's hand in marriage. It was to be a double wedding.

Gretchen was very pleased and spoke a great deal of Herr Schmerfeld's powerful connections in the cabinet and the fine house they were to inhabit in the elegant French quarter of the town. Lisette said very little, though the colour rose in her face every time Herr von Eschwege came to visit.

The night before the wedding, a rowdy party of young men gathered outside the apothecary's shop, banging pots and pans with metal ladles. Herr Wild stood at the window in his nightgown and nightcap, scowling, but he did not yell at them and shake his fist. 'I'll be glad when it's all over,' he said.

'How can you be glad when we're losing our dear, sweet daughters?' Frau Wild wept.

'Less mouths to feed,' Herr Wild said jokingly. 'If only we could marry Mia off, I'd be much plumper in the pocket.'

The next morning Dortchen was up early to cut dill from the garden for her mother to put in the daughters' right shoes, along with a pinch of salt.

It was a long, busy day, cooking and preparing for the wedding feast, and then walking with her family down to the town hall for the ceremony. Gretchen was most indignant that church weddings had been outlawed; Lisette said she didn't mind where she married her dear Herr von Eschwege.

'Hadn't you best start calling him Friedrich?' Hanne teased, and Lisette blushed and said it sounded so forward.

Afterwards, the house seemed quiet and empty. The depleted family sat down to supper with two chairs empty. Frau Wild kept her crumpled handkerchief by her plate, occasionally dabbing at her nose and eyes.

'Do stop weeping, Katharina,' Herr Wild said. 'They haven't died.'

'I'm just going to miss them so,' Frau Wild wept. 'What shall I do without my prop?'

'I shall be your prop, Mother,' Röse said most earnestly, taking off her spectacles to polish them with her skirt. 'You know I wish nothing more than to immolate myself upon the altar of daughterly duty.'

Frau Wild sighed. 'Thank you, dear,' she said, in a voice that was scarcely audible.

In the morning, the sisters had to renegotiate the chores. Hanne took on the work in the shop, Mia was deputised to dust and tidy the drawing room every day, Röse very unwillingly agreed to take on the ironing, while Dortchen was to take Lisette's place in the stillroom.

There was one unexpected benefit of having fewer sisters in the house. Ever since the French invasion of Cassel, Herr Wild had not permitted any of his daughters to walk out to the garden plot outside the town walls on her own. Now that the shop was so busy, there was not always someone free to go with Dortchen when her father needed something from the garden, and so one warm afternoon towards the end of April he begrudgingly gave her permission to go and gather daisy leaves, wood betony, lemon balm and hellebore, so he could make an infusion for a courtier with a bad case of gout.

'I am almost sixteen, Father,' she reminded him.

'All the more reason to keep you safe at home,' he grumbled, then waved an impatient hand. 'Go, go, I haven't all day.'

Dortchen walked through the busy streets, her basket on her arm, glad to be outside. Many of the tall, narrow houses had pots filled with flowers and herbs propped on their windowsills, and one had a basket on the front doorstep. The sky overhead was a brilliant blue, and sunshine dappled the cobblestones. It was impossible to believe that people were being blown to pieces only two days' march to the south. For days, the French and the Austrians had been hurling themselves at each other, their cannons and guns sending such clouds of smoke into the air that Dortchen had been able to see them from the window of her room.

Dortchen came to the garden and let herself in through the gate. Spring flowers danced within their hedges of box and hung in blossoming showers from the boughs of the fruit trees. She was glad to be alone and took her time walking down the paths and smelling the blooms, lifting first one, then another, to her nose. The garden was quiet of all but the faint humming of bees in the angelica flowers, and the distant twitter of birds. She pulled on her gloves and knelt down to weed the garden beds.

Bells rang out, sounding an alarm. Dortchen sat back on her heels, wiping away a strand of hair with her arm. Then came a rumbling noise that slowly but steadily grew louder. The pound of feet. Shouts and cries and screams of alarm. Dortchen's breath caught. She stood and ran to the gate.

A crowd was marching down the road towards the King's palace, most of them peasants in rough homespuns, waving scythes, forks, flails and axes in the air. Crudely made red-and-white flags fluttered above the crowd, tied as pennants to the bayonets of the soldiers riding down the road towards her.

Dortchen dropped to her knees behind the gatepost, her hands pressed over her mouth. A cannon boomed nearby and acrid smoke filled the air. People screamed. The rebels' horses broke into a gallop, men shouting, 'To the palace! Down with the usurper!' The cannon fired again and a house nearby imploded, dust and debris blasting out. A brick smashed down next to Dortchen and fragments rained on her head. Gunfire rang out.

For the next half-hour, all was chaos. Dortchen could only cover her eyes and ears with her arms as the palace soldiers slowly drove the rebels back. One poor man was blown right over the wall, falling to the ground next to where Dortchen was crouched. His rough work clothes were soaked with blood, and his unblinking eyes stared upwards into the sky.

At last, by the time the sun had slipped down behind the mountains, all had grown quiet and still. Dortchen gathered up her basket and tiptoed past the dead man. The street beyond was a ruin. Houses were smashed in, walls blown down, the blossoming branches broken and mangled. Corpses of people and horses lay everywhere. Dortchen's limbs trembled. She had never seen anyone die before and was acutely aware of her own vulnerability. The air stank of smoke. Hearing the galloping hooves of soldiers, she hid behind a wall until they had ridden past, then hurried on for home.

She was met in the square by her father and brother, both carrying lanterns and heavy cudgels.

'Where have you been?' Herr Wild demanded. 'You stupid fool! Did you not realise the town's in uproar?' He seized her arm in a bruising grip and shook her.

'I couldn't come any earlier – they marched right past me.' Dortchen stared up at him with imploring eyes. Surely he could not blame her for what had happened? 'I saw . . . Father, I saw people being shot! I hid behind the wall . . . but there's a dead man in our garden.' Tears ran down her cheeks.

Her father let her go with a noise of impatience. 'You should have come home at once!'

'I couldn't, Father, really, I couldn't. They were fighting right outside our garden. I'd have been killed.'

'We thought you were dead for sure,' Rudolf said. He put his arm around her and she leant against him, unable to stop herself from shaking.

'You're hurt . . . there's blood.' Rudolf dabbed at her face.

'No, I'm fine, I was just hit by debris . . . They blew up all the houses! Why? Why, Father? Who were they, all those people marching . . .'

'Damn fools,' her father said.

'Some kind of uprising,' Rudolf said. 'I heard they planned to storm the palace and take the King prisoner. They had a coach and six horses ready to race to the coast. They were going to hand him over to the English.'

'It was a mad plan,' Herr Wild said. 'It never would've worked.'

'I heard Baron von Dörnberg was at the back of it. He and some kind of secret society that had vowed to bring the French down.' Rudolf shook his head in disbelief. 'I saw him only yesterday, riding on the parade ground, overseeing the troops to march into Saxony. I never would have thought him a traitor.'

'A patriot, you mean,' Herr Wild growled.

Rudolf bit back a caustic comment.

'The rats will be leaving the ship now,' Herr Wild said.

Rudolf refused to argue with his father. 'Come, let's get Dortchen home,' he said. 'She's as white as a sheet.'

Slowly, they went home, Dortchen limping, finding all kinds of cuts and bruises she had not known were there. The streets were filled with angry French soldiers, knocking on doors, waylaying townsfolk, pushing bruised-faced prisoners towards the gaol. A cart trundled past, piled high with corpses. All the shops were shuttered and bolted, and houses had their curtains pulled tight.

Dortchen and her father and brother were stopped more than once by soldiers with suspicious faces; their papers were read, and questions hurled at them. At last they made it to the safety of the apothecary's shop, and Herr Wild locked and bolted the door behind them.

'Go and get cleaned up,' he ordered Dortchen. 'It's after suppertime. Eat if you can and then let me look at your cuts.'

Dortchen was sitting by the fire in the drawing room, her wounds washed with ivy water and bandaged with dock leaves, her weeping mother and sisters bringing her tea and healing possets and handkerchiefs soaked in lavender water, when the door knocker sounded long and hard. Frau Wild screeched and Hanne seized the poker. Dortchen started to her feet. 'Maybe it's the soldiers – maybe I was seen near the palace and they think I was involved.'

Her mother moaned and groped for her smelling salts.

'They'd not arrest a sixteen-year-old girl,' Mia asserted, though her face was pale. 'Would they?'

'I believe that age or gender would be of no account to authorities determined to thwart an act of rebellion,' Röse said, then she surprised Dortchen by taking her hand and squeezing it.

Together, the four sisters crept to the top of the main stairs, where they crouched, listening to the voices in the hallway.

To their surprise, they could hear Gretchen's voice, high-pitched and hysterical. 'I tell you, we have to flee. Ferdy's cousin, George, is suspected of being one of the conspirators. He has fled to Prague, and we must go too. What if Ferdy were implicated? What will become of me?'

A low rumble from her father, a quick question from Rudolf, then Gretchen continued. 'Yes, we go tonight, to Marburg. Ferdy has a house there. Hopefully that is far enough. I mean, we're guilty of nothing – we knew nothing about the uprising. I came only to tell you and to say goodbye.'

Herr Wild said something about 'your mother', then Gretchen's high-heeled slippers clattered up the stairs. She half-fell into her sisters' arms, sobbing, tears streaking through her rouge. She was very elegantly dressed, with a hat with two great curling feathers and a travelling coat of pale-blue cloth that made her eyes seem huge and luminous.

'Don't crush my hat,' she said, as a weeping Frau Wild reached two thin arms for her. 'There, there, it's all right. I'm only going to Marburg, not to the ends of the earth. Though I must say, I think it's quite disgusting. The house at Marburg is old. And has an outside privy. I hate to leave my water closet!'

Within five minutes she was gone, her husband having waited outside at the horses' heads.

The next morning Dortchen woke to the sound of drumming and rifle fire. The conspirators who had been caught had all been executed in the meadow outside the palace.

Dortchen felt she could never gather daisy chains there again.

FIREWORKS

August 1809

The pastor's voice droned on.

Dortchen fixed her eyes on her prayer book and allowed herself to drift away into a daydream.

Wilhelm had returned from his long stay in Halle looking strong and well. His eyes lit up at the sight of her. 'Dortchen,' he cried. 'Look at you! You're all grown-up.'

'I am,' she replied, smiling mysteriously behind her fan. 'I'm a woman now.'

'And a beautiful one,' he replied. 'I long to hold you against my heart. Will you dance?'

'Of course,' she replied, and held out her hand. He swept her into his arms . . .

The scraping of the wooden pews jerked her back to reality. Blushing, Dortchen scrambled to her feet. Her father and Röse frowned at her, and her mother looked anxious. But Ferdinand Grimm in the next row smiled at her in sympathy. She could not help smiling back, just a little.

Afterwards, when the congregation was standing on the church steps and chatting, Ferdinand came over to her. 'Infernally long sermon, wasn't it?'

Dortchen nodded. 'I'm afraid I'm prone to daydreaming in church. I'm always getting into trouble for it.'

'So am I,' he responded, then his expression darkened. 'At least, I used to be.'

She understood his meaning. 'You must miss your mother very much.'

'It's been fifteen months and yet the pain hasn't gone away,' he said. 'They say time heals all wounds. Well, how much time? When will I start to feel better?'

'I don't know. I'm sorry.' Dortchen felt ashamed at how inadequate her words sounded, but Ferdinand gave her a crooked smile.

'Have you heard from Lotte?' he asked.

Dortchen shook her head. To tell the truth, she was hurt by Lotte's silence. Lotte had gone to Marburg to stay with Gretchen, as everyone agreed she needed a change of scene to pull her from the doldrums. The visit had been extended, then extended again, and Dortchen had to fight her jealous fear that her dearest friend had transferred her affections to her elder sister.

'Me either,' Ferdinand said. 'I've written to her several times but she hasn't responded.'

'I'm sure she's having a lovely time.'

'I miss her,' Ferdinand said, sounding more like a lonely little boy than a man of twenty-one.

'Me too,' Dortchen said.

'Have you heard the King is throwing a grand fête tomorrow night to celebrate the latest French victory in Spain?'

'No,' Dortchen said. 'Though he hardly needs an excuse, does he?'

'If he throws a party to celebrate every new victory or conquest by his brother, it's no wonder he's hosting balls every night,' Ferdinand said.

'To our cost,' Dortchen replied.

'Yes, it seems as if there's a new tax every week.'

Dortchen nodded. Seeing her mother gather up her trailing shawl, she said, 'I'm sorry, I must go.'

'Wait,' Ferdinand cried.

She waited, looking up at him in surprise.

'Would you like to go tomorrow night, to watch the fireworks?' he asked.

'To the palace?' she asked, surprised.

'I thought we could watch from the hills,' Ferdinand said. 'There'd be a great view from Habichtswald.'

'I . . . Well, I'd love to see the fireworks, but . . .' She did not know how to explain to him that it simply was not permissible for a young woman to go into the forest at night with a young man, no matter how good friends they were. Ferdinand should have known.

He turned red. 'It's not just me,' he blurted. 'There's a whole party of people going. The Engelhards will be there. I think the Ramus sisters are going too.'

Dortchen bit her lip. 'If Julia and Charlotte should ask me, perhaps I may be permitted to go.'

'I'll ask them to ask you,' he said.

'They should ask their father to ask my father.'

Ferdinand nodded his head in understanding and hurried away to engage Julia Ramus in conversation. Soon her father, the pastor, came over to shake Herr Wild's hand, smiling. Dortchen kept her gaze down but she felt her father turn and rake her with his frown. Moments later, Charlotte Ramus approached her. She took Dortchen's hand and said, 'You're to come and watch the fireworks with us tomorrow night. Father's arranged it all.'

Charlotte was a plump girl, with mousy-brown hair and mousy-grey eyes. She radiated such cheerfulness and goodwill that it was impossible not to like her, and at sixteen, she was only a month or two older than Dortchen and Lotte, but the three had never become close friends. Perhaps it was because she was so good, or perhaps it was simply that there was no room for anyone else in Dortchen and Lotte's friendship.

'We've asked your sisters too,' Charlotte went on.

'Not Röse?' Dortchen asked, then pressed her hand to her mouth, ashamed to have spoken so unbecomingly about her own sister.

Charlotte only laughed. 'Oh, we asked her but I don't think she wants to come. She said something about the frivolity and foolishness of the minds of young women and then began to scribble in her notebook.'

'She's probably thinking of suggestions to give to your father for his next sermon.'

'Or reminding herself to look up the properties of gunpowder so she can lecture us on it tomorrow,' Charlotte replied.

'I'm sorry. She does like to think of herself as the clever one in the family.'

'Oh, that's all right,' Charlotte said. 'It must be useful to have a walking encyclopaedia as a sister.'

'More awful than useful,' Dortchen admitted.

'So we'll drive past tomorrow night and pick up you and Hanne and Mia,' Charlotte said. 'Mother is chaperoning us.'

'It's really so kind of you,' Dortchen said.

'Oh, it's a pleasure, really. We always feel so sorry for you Wild girls—' Then it was Charlotte's turn to clap her hand over her mouth. Her grey eyes looked into Dortchen's in consternation. 'Sorry,' she said in a muffled voice.

'We feel rather sorry for ourselves sometimes too,' Dortchen replied. 'But not now.'

Charlotte smiled. 'Well, see you tomorrow night, then.'

On the way home from church, Herr Wild lectured the girls on the necessity of finishing all their chores before they went out the next evening. He gave Dortchen a list of plants that he wanted plucked and processed from the garden – it was enough to keep her busy for most of the day.

The next morning, as Dortchen packed her basket, Hanne drew her aside. 'Dortchen, will you deliver a message for me?' She pressed a small piece of paper, folded over many times, into Dortchen's hand.

'A message? To whom?'

'His name and address is written there.' Hanne indicated the tiny scrawl on the face of the folded paper.

Even when she squinted, Dortchen could not read her sister's impatient scribble. 'But who is he? Where am I to go?'

'He's just a friend. He lives above the printer's shop behind the Königsplatz. Please, Dortchen, don't ask questions, just deliver it for me. And don't tell anyone.'

'Are you in love with him?' Dortchen asked.

Hanne laughed and shrugged. 'I don't know. Maybe. Yes!'

'That's wonderful,' Dortchen cried, embracing her surprised sister. 'Of course I'll help you. Does he love you too?'

'He says so,' Hanne answered, laughing. 'Though all we do is argue. But he's poor, Dortchen, and has no connections, and he's an anarchist to boot. Father would never allow it. You know what he's like.'

'I do,' Dortchen answered. 'Don't worry, I shan't betray you.'

So Dortchen delivered the note to the grimy printer's shop in the twisting alleys behind the Marktgasse, to a young man with ruffled chestnut hair and a faded red scarf loosely knotted about his throat. His face and striking golden-brown eyes seemed familiar; Dortchen thought she'd seen Hanne speaking to him before.

He caught up the note with a cry of delight and kissed it, then opened it and read it rapidly. He told Dortchen, 'Tell her I'll be there. And thank you, my little conspirator.'

Dortchen walked the rest of the way to the market garden with excitement and dread bubbling in her blood. She just hoped her father never found out.

It was a glorious warm summer's evening when the pastor's carriage pulled up in the Marktgasse.

Frau Ramus sat smiling with a big picnic basket on her lap, her two daughters perched either side of her. Ferdinand came out with a rolled rug and a dusty bottle, and handed up Hanne, Dortchen and Mia into the carriage; all were clutching a small contribution to the picnic. Herr Wild came out of the apothecary's shop to have a word with Frau Ramus, and to tell his daughters very sternly to behave and not put themselves to the blush. Ferdinand swung up next to the coachman and they rolled out of the square and towards the palace.

The sun slowly set behind the mountains, casting long shadows across the palace and the lake. The carriage drew into a clearing and the coachmen pulled the horses to a halt. Two other carriages were already there, with their occupants already stepping out, rugs and baskets in their hands. Dortchen recognised Karoline Engelhard and her brother, Gotthelf; they had shared their carriage with Jakob. The other was a party of four: three sisters, who ranged in age from nine to twenty-one, and their brother, a tall, slender boy with a high forehead and a strong Roman nose.

Karoline introduced them as the Hassenpflug family. Their father was the judge of the Court of Appeals and had been an important member of the Kurfürst's government. The eldest daughter, Marie, was a thin, delicate girl with large, lustrous black eyes and glossy ringlets. The second sister was called Jeanette and was two years older than Dortchen. She was of a much sturdier build, as was the youngest of the family, a tomboyish little girl with a slight squint, whom everyone called Malchen. The brother was named Louis; he was fifteen.

The party found a vantage point high on the hill and spread out their rugs. The valley below was filled with soft, misty light, and the lake glimmered below the palace. Half-hidden in trees, the towers of the Lion's Castle glowed golden.

A chair had been brought for Frau Ramus, who sat down gratefully, her daughters at her feet. At first, all anyone could speak of was the war and the recent French victories against the Austrians and the Spanish.

'It was not Napoléon's usual triumph, though,' Jakob said. 'In fact, the English are claiming it was a drawn battle.'

'He's fighting on too many fronts,' Louis Hassenpflug said.

'Yes, I think you're right,' Jakob replied, looking at the boy with new interest.

'So many poor young men killed or injured,' Frau Ramus said, shaking her head. 'The Ogre will have a lot to answer for when he finally meets his maker.'

'I don't think he's afraid,' Hanne said rather dryly. 'It seems to me Napoléon has very little belief in God.'

The Ramus sisters fluttered in distress.

'How else could he arrest the Pope? And annex all his lands?' Hanne went on.

'Well, the *Pope*,' Frau Ramus said. 'We do not care much for him, do we, girls? But our poor Father. Forbidden to hold wedding services, or to receive tithes . . .'

She would have gone on listing all that the pastor had lost under the new constitution, but Hanne cut in. 'I've heard that Napoléon said religion is the only thing that ever stopped the poor from murdering the rich.'

Frau Ramus threw up her plump hands in horror. 'What a thing to say. Wherever did you hear such a thing? Not that I'm surprised. A godless man, Napoléon, and we are all crushed under his heel.'

Her eyes sparkling, Hanne leant forward, as if about to say something else, but Dortchen intervened, not wanting her outspoken sister to shock their pious hostess any more than she already had. 'Tell me, Jakob, how does the storytelling collection go?'

'Slowly,' he answered. 'Both your sister Gretchen and Friederike Mannel have married now, and are too taken up with husbands and housekeeping to help us any more. We were hoping Gretchen could go and visit an old lady in the poorhouse in Marburg who Clemens says knows a great many wonderful stories, but she says her husband would not like her to go to such a place. We had all our hopes pinned on Lotte, but she's not written us a word since she's been there, so I must say I don't think she'll exert herself on our behalf.'

'I know Wilhelm and Ferdinand have been keeping busy copying stories from books and manuscripts,' Dortchen said. 'You must have quite a few by now.'

'Well, yes, a dozen or more, but what we really want is people to tell us old tales that were told to them as children. We want to preserve stories that would otherwise be lost.'

'Excuse me, what is this you are doing?' Marie Hassenpflug asked, leaning forward in interest. 'Collecting old tales?'

'Yes, it's a project that my brother Wilhelm and I are engaged in,' Jakob said, turning to her politely.

'And I,' Ferdinand said loudly. 'I've copied many stories for you.'

'Yes, that's true, you have helped us in the transcribing,' Jakob said.

'We know a few old tales, don't we, Marie?' Jeannette said, turning to her elder sister.

Marie nodded. 'Yes, we do. We could tell them to you, if you liked, Herr Grimm.'

'Thank you, that could be very useful,' Jakob replied.

'Would you like to visit us next week?' Marie said.

Jakob hesitated.

'He needs to wait till after he's been paid,' Ferdinand said. 'No money for paper and ink right now – nor for much else, I might add.'

A hot tide of colour flooded Jakob's neck and face. 'Thank you, Ferdinand, that's enough.' He bowed his head to Marie. 'I regret it may be a few weeks before it is convenient for me to call upon you.'

'We have plenty of paper and ink, Herr Grimm,' Jeanette said cheerfully. 'We'd be happy to put some at your disposal.'

'Thank you, Fraülein, but that is not necessary,' Jakob answered, shooting his brother an angry glance.

'Tell us some of the stories, Herr Grimm,' Malchen cried, but he shook his head.

'I'm sorry, I'm afraid that telling stories is not one of my strengths. You want my brother Wilhelm for that.' A shadow crossed over Jakob's face and he rose to his feet. 'Excuse me a moment,' he said, walking away.

Conversation moved on to other matters, but Dortchen sat quietly, looking after Jakob. After a while, she rose to her feet and followed him into the woods. Although the sun had set, it was still light enough to see her way through the mossy tree trunks.

She found him sitting on a fallen log, his face sunk in his hands. 'Jakob, what is it? What's wrong?' she asked. 'Is it Wilhelm?'

'I miss him,' Jakob said, the words torn out of him. 'You don't understand – it's as if a part of my own self is gone.'

'I do understand.' Dortchen sat on the log beside him. 'Believe me, I do.'

He looked at her intently. Dortchen felt heat rise in her cheeks but met his gaze steadily.

'I see,' he said.

They sat in silence for a long moment. Dortchen studied his expression. She saw the minute contraction of muscles between his brows, a flicker of something that looked like revulsion, the compression of the corners of his lips. Yet his eyes did not waver.

'We've hardly ever been apart,' Jakob said haltingly. 'Except for my trip to Paris . . . I hate this illness of his. I hate it.'

'Will he get better?' Dortchen asked.

'Of course he'll get better. It's nonsense, this illness – he brings it on himself.'

'The doctor doesn't think so.'

'Well, no, he wouldn't, would he? He's doing very well out of all his quack remedies.'

'Wilhelm looked ill before he went away,' Dortchen said.

'Yes,' Jakob agreed, 'but Willi takes everything too much to heart.'

'Will he come home soon, do you think?'

'I hope so,' Jakob said. 'Because I cannot afford all these medical bills.'

Jakob was only twenty-four years old and trying to provide for a family of six, Dortchen thought. 'It must be hard,' she said. 'Trying to look after them all.'

He glanced at her in surprise. 'You're a good little soul, Dortchen,' he said, rising to his feet. 'Come on, we had better join the others. We want no scandal attached to your fair name.'

They walked back to the clearing, where Frau Ramus was distributing chicken legs and sausages, and Ferdinand was offering around the dusty bottle of wine. When no one accepted, preferring apple cider, he poured himself a large cup and drank it down, then poured another. 'The fool,' Jakob uttered between his teeth.

Dortchen sat down on the rug next to Charlotte, spreading out her skirts and gazing down at the view. The light was fading from the sky. A few stars pricked through here and there. Ferdinand came and lay down at her feet, offering her the bottle.

Dortchen shook her head. 'My father would skin me alive if I came home smelling of alcohol,' she whispered, not wanting to tell him she hated the smell.

Ferdinand grinned. 'Just chew some peppermint leaves,' he whispered back. 'That's how I hide it from my brothers.'

Dortchen smiled and shook her head again.

It was a clear, moonless night. An owl hooted in the forest, then floated past on soundless wings. Frau Ramus asked Jakob to kindle her lantern and hang it from a tree branch. Mia and Malchen were making firm friends, weaving cat's cradles together with a length of old wool. Looking about her, Dortchen realised that Hanne had slipped away. She wondered where she had gone. She might have asked Frau Ramus if Ferdinand had not touched her arm.

'What did Jakob say to you?' Ferdinand asked her in an undertone. 'Did you talk about me?'

She glanced at him in surprise. 'No, we talked about Wilhelm.'

Ferdinand made a face of disgust. 'Of course you did. He's all Jakob ever worries about.'

'Oh, I don't think that's true.'

'Did you know I've had a poem published in a magazine in Switzerland? They didn't pay me, it's true, but it means something to be accepted, doesn't it?'

'Of course it does.'

'I knew you'd understand. Jakob says I won't make a living writing poems, but he doesn't understand. I want to be a writer, you see. My mind is above filthy lucre.'

Dortchen did not want to hurt his feelings so she murmured agreement, then listened quietly while he told her about the poems he had written, quoting his favourite lines to her and complaining about how stern his elder brothers were, and how lacking in understanding.

When the church bells tolled nine o'clock, the fireworks began. Dortchen cried out and flinched at the first loud bang, which brought back memories of the terrible day she had seen men shot down in the street. But the gorgeous fire-blossom that followed filled her with delight and she leant forward, eagerly watching the golden showers of light.

'So beautiful,' she said softly.

'Yes,' Ferdinand answered. Glancing at him, she realised he had his eyes fixed on her face. She looked away but was uncomfortably aware of his gaze for the rest of the evening.

Hanne slipped back to the party some time later. A white starburst high in the sky drenched the landscape with dazzling radiance. By its light, Dortchen saw that her sister's cheeks were flushed, her dress was crushed and her tumbling fair curls were tied back with a faded red scarf.

'Where have you been?' she whispered.

Hanne laughed and reddened further. 'Enjoying the fireworks.'

Later that night, Dortchen slipped down to Hanne's bedroom in her nightgown, her hairbrush in her hand. She knew that Lisette and Gretchen and Hanne had often sat together after going to bed, brushing each other's hair and talking, and that her sister must miss these late-night confidences.

Hanne was sitting up in bed, writing in a small book by the light of a candle. Her eyes widened at the sight of Dortchen, but then she smiled and patted her bed in welcome. 'You really are growing up, aren't you, little love?'

'I hope so,' Dortchen said, sitting down. 'Sometimes I feel like a woman grown, and other times—'

'Like a little girl again,' Hanne interjected, taking the brush and beginning to stroke it down Dortchen's long fair hair, which hung loose down her back.

'Yes.'

'Don't worry, I often feel the same way. At least, I did. I think I'm all woman now, though.'

Dortchen looked over her shoulder, trying to see Hanne's face. Her sister was flushed and triumphant. 'Do you mean . . . ?'

'Yes, I mean . . .' Hanne dragged out the pause mockingly. 'Johann and I made love tonight.'

'Hanne!' Dortchen's voice was sharp. 'No!'

'It was wonderful, Dortchen, even more than I had imagined. It was like a torrent, an earthquake, a flood. I could not help myself. And now everything has changed.'

'But Hanne – shouldn't you have waited? You're not married!' Dortchen twisted her hands together in sick anxiety. She heard her father's voice in her head. *We must kill sin at the root . . .*

'Why should I have waited? Love between two human beings is not a sin. It was the Church that said so, and the Church has lost all its power now, hasn't it? If it's not a sin to be married by the town mayor instead of by a pastor, then how can it be a sin to love someone without that piece of paper? Marriage is just a social institution now, Dortchen, and it has nothing to do with sin – or with love, for that matter.'

'Oh, but Hanne . . .'

Hanne reached for her restless hands and stilled them with her own. She was smiling, her eyes glowing. 'Don't you see, little love? All the old laws and customs have been demolished, and we need to remake the world the way we think it should be. And as far as I'm concerned, a woman shouldn't be just a chattel, a piece of moveable property owned by the men in her life, to be bartered and sold like a broodmare. Look at poor Mother. Married to a man she didn't even know, wearing out her body giving birth to child after child after child, forced to suffer his attentions when she fears and abhors him . . .'

Dortchen listened, her thoughts in a tumult. On the one hand, everything Hanne said had a clear ring of truth, so that Dortchen thought, *Yes!* On the other hand, though, she was worried. *Father will kill her!*

She said so at last, and Hanne sobered. 'He mustn't find out, Dortchen. Promise me you'll keep my secret.'

'I promise,' Dortchen said, hugging her sister close.

WINTER MELANCHOLY

August 1809

In late August, Lotte came home from Marburg surlier than ever, unhappy with her lot, her mouth full of Gretchen, Gretchen, Gretchen.

'Gretchen has two maids, a cook and a bootboy . . . Gretchen has the most perfectly beautiful clothes . . . Did you know Gretchen's husband buys her whatever she wants, as soon as she sees it? . . . Gretchen has so many friends, it was just such a whirl . . .'

I hate Gretchen, Dortchen thought.

'Did you do nothing but make morning calls and go to parties?' she asked Lotte. 'What about finding stories for Wilhelm and Jakob? Did you visit the old woman in the poorhouse in Marburg like they asked you to?'

Lotte wrinkled her nose. 'Well, I did, though it was perfectly awful. It was like going to a prison, Dortchen. The smell! I thought I was going to be sick. She gabbled away for a while, but she had hardly any teeth left and I could scarcely understand a word she said. And Gretchen was waiting for me.'

Gretchen, Gretchen, Gretchen, Dortchen thought.

Wilhelm came home from Berlin in December, paler than ever, his mouth full of Goethe, Goethe, Goethe.

'Herr von Goethe favoured me with an invitation to lunch . . . Herr von Goethe was most interested in my work on the ancient Norse sagas . . . Herr von Goethe was so kind, he allowed me to use his private box at the theatre . . . Herr von Goethe may write me an introduction to my translation of old Danish ballads, and if so it's bound to be published . . .'

I hate Goethe, Dortchen thought.

'I'm so glad you enjoyed Berlin,' she lied. 'But what of the sanatorium at Halle? Has it helped? Are you well?'

A shadow crossed his face. 'As well as I will ever be, I suppose. Dortchen, it was terrible. I had to sit chained to this machine while they ran an electrical charge through me. If anyone touched me, I'd get such a shock. Sparks would just fly out of me. I got blisters where the electrical connectors touched me. And the medicine they gave me made me so sick that I couldn't eat.'

'Oh, you poor thing.'

'None of it seemed to help,' Wilhelm continued. 'I had to wash my neck with mercury and bind my chest with a magnetic band, but my heart still pounds away at night, so hard that I cannot sleep.'

She had to touch his hand, her heart filled with sympathy.

'Well, I'm glad I'm free of the sanatorium,' Wilhelm said, trying to rally himself. 'I missed home so much.'

Did you miss me? she thought but did not say.

After leaving the sanatorium, Wilhelm had visited Achim von Arnim in Berlin with Clemens Brentano. The city was empty, he said. The Prussian king and queen had fled after the 1806 invasion, and the city had been stripped of many of its great treasures. 'Herr von Goethe himself almost died,' Wilhelm said. 'They invaded his house and there was gunpowder spilt all down the street, and soldiers running past with flaming torches. A single spark and we'd have lost one of the world's great writers. And Herr von Goethe met Napoléon, you know. The Emperor is a great fan of his work.'

Goethe, Goethe, Goethe, Dortchen thought.

Hurt and angry, Dortchen retreated behind the high walls of home, busying herself with the never-ending tasks of the kitchen and stillroom. She saw her friends only at church, and exchanged only polite, conventional words with them. It hurt her even more that they did not seem to mind.

It was a long, hard winter. All anyone could talk about was Napoléon and Joséphine's divorce. In March the following year, Napoléon married Princess Marie-Louise of Austria, daughter of his great enemy, the Archduke Francis, the former Emperor of the Holy Roman Empire.

'Poor girl,' Hanne said.

A few weeks later, Clemens Brentano followed the Emperor's example and divorced his wife, Augusta. Dortchen heard the news from Lotte, standing on the church step in the chill sleety breeze, her hands tucked inside her shawl.

'She's only nineteen,' Dortchen said. 'What is to happen to her?'

Lotte spread her hands and shrugged. 'I don't know. Surely it's better that they're apart, though? They made each other so unhappy.'

How can one human have so much power over another? Dortchen wondered. *Why are our spirits tied to another's whim? It's not fair.*

'I must go,' she said, her voice constricted.

As she hurried away to her mother's side, she felt Lotte's eyes on her, filled with misery.

At last, winter's grip on the weather began to loosen and the sun broke through the clouds. Taking advantage of the break in the rain, Dortchen took two heavy buckets of ashes to the ash hopper in the shed. She was hurrying down the slick, damp garden path when the gate creaked open and Ferdinand cautiously looked through.

His face lit up at the sight of her. 'Dortchen, at last. I've been looking out for you.'

'What's wrong?' she asked, looking back over her shoulder towards the house to make sure no one was watching.

'I was hoping you could help me.' Ferdinand stepped through into the garden and stood before her, twisting his hat in his hands. 'Wilhelm says he thinks your teas and ointments do more good than anything the doctor prescribes. I was hoping you could give me something too.'

'What is the matter?' Dortchen said. 'Are you not well?'

He shook his head. 'I have not felt well in months. I'm tired all the time,

I find it hard to get out of bed in the morning, my head aches and my chest hurts. I thought that if you could give me something to help . . . I cannot pay much . . . In fact, I can't really pay at all. I've written you a poem, though.' He held out a crumpled leaf of paper, covered in elegant, looping writing.

Dortchen looked anxiously back towards the house, biting her lip. 'Come into the shed. You can talk while I work.'

Quickly she led him into the shed, a small room on the side of the stable, where tools and buckets were kept, along with the ash hopper, a wooden contraption into which water was poured over ashes from the fire to make lye, one of the ingredients of soap. Trudi, the mare, turned her head and whickered in welcome, the cow whisked her tail and mooed, while the fat black-and-pink pig grunted in her sty, whuffling hopefully at the sight of the bucket.

'Not for you, sorry, Buttercup,' Dortchen told the pig, as she lifted the bucket to the hopper. Ferdinand hurried to help her. Their fingers brushed and Dortchen backed away, letting him empty the heavy bucket.

He put the bucket down, gazing at her with intense, dark eyes. 'What's wrong with me? Is it the same illness as Wilhelm's?'

'I've not heard you wheezing,' she said. 'May I feel you breathe?' Tentatively, she reached out a hand and laid it on his chest. She could detect no rattle. 'Will you cough for me?'

He did so, and she could tell his chest was clear.

'I don't think it's asthma,' she said. 'Though I'm no doctor.'

She began to take her hand away but Ferdinand reached up his own and covered hers. 'Dortchen . . .'

She slipped her hand away, realising that she was alone with him in a dim, shadowy shed, with no chaperone apart from a drowsy old mare, a cow and a pig. 'I have to get back.'

He caught her arm. 'Dortchen, please.'

Gently she pushed his hand away, stepping back. He let her go.

'Do you feel as if there is nothing good left in the world?' she asked. 'As if you've fallen into a deep, dark pit and there's no way out?'

He nodded.

'You're still grieving,' she told him. 'Only time will heal that.'

He heaved a sigh so deep it was almost a groan. 'Don't tell me that. Do you know how slowly the days drag past? Nothing to do but copy out endless old yarns while Lotte mopes around and complains about how much work she has to do and Jakob looks disapproving? Nothing helps. Nothing, that is, but—' He looked away, and she realised with dismay that his eyes were damp with tears.

'Winter always makes us melancholy,' she said after a moment. 'Now that it is spring, you can walk in the park and the woods, and soak up some sunshine. You'll soon feel better, I promise.'

'Sunshine,' he answered scornfully.

'I can make you up a tea that might help,' she said. 'Come into the stillroom, but please be quiet – it opens into the shop, and my father will hear us if we make any noise.'

They went quickly through the garden. To her pleasure, Dortchen noticed the chives had begun to sprout. Soon the lovage and bee balm and marjoram would follow.

She led Ferdinand through the back door and into the long, cool stillroom. Its shelves were laden with jars of all shapes and sizes, filled with dried leaves and flowers and black skinny leeches wriggling about in water. An apothecary's cabinet filled the wall beside the door into the shop, its many little drawers labelled with symbols in her father's neat script. A large still sat on the floor, which Herr Wild used to make his famous quince brandy.

'There was one thing that seemed to help me,' Ferdinand said, far too loudly.

Dortchen shushed him urgently and hurried across to the shelves. He came and stood very close behind her, whispering in her ear. 'The doctor left it for my mother. I've tried it and it makes me feel so much better. I know Jakob bought it here. I was wondering . . . I was hoping . . . May I have some more?'

Dortchen frowned. 'You shouldn't drink medicines left for your mother,

Ferdinand.' She moved away from him, feeling uncomfortable and worried. 'What was it?'

'Just some laudanum,' he said airily. 'Nothing too serious.'

Dortchen's frown deepened. Laudanum was the most popular of her father's drugs. When the French had first invaded Cassel and the soldiers had come to requisition medical supplies, it had been laudanum they had wanted most. Herr Wild had had to order in great quantities of opium to keep up his supply. He had spent many late nights cutting up the opium, dissolving it in boiling water, then mixing it with alcohol, honey and sweet herbs.

She looked over at the cupboard in which her father kept the more dangerous and expensive medicines – the opium, the powdered mandrake, the belladonna drops – and his precious silver-mounted bezoar stone, taken from the stomach of a gazelle and said to be the antidote to any poison. 'I cannot give you laudanum,' she whispered. 'It's expensive . . . and Father keeps a book where he writes down exactly how much he has sold and who bought it. Look, he keeps the cupboard locked.'

'I only need a little,' Ferdinand said.

'I can't give you any,' Dortchen said. 'It'd be wrong. Besides, I'm not at all sure it's the best thing for you.' She thought of her mother and her beloved drops, and how many afternoons Frau Wild spent dozing on her couch, the bottle of laudanum close beside her.

'Please, Dortchen . . . I thought you were my friend.'

Dortchen took his hands. Long-fingered, slim and stained with ink, they were so like Wilhelm's that she was filled with tenderness. 'I am your friend, Ferdinand, indeed I am. Believe me, I cannot give you any laudanum. My father would notice, he'd be angry and I'd get into dreadful trouble. But I can make you up a tea that might help. It's only flowers and leaves from the garden, but I grew them, I picked them and I hung them up to dry, and Father will not notice if a few are missing.'

Carefully, Dortchen weighed out some dried flowers of chase-devil and calendula, added some dried lemon balm leaves, then poured the mixture into a small muslin bag. Giving it to Ferdinand, she led him back out into the garden.

'Please don't come here like this again,' she whispered. 'I'll be in trouble if my father sees you here.'

He nodded, his face bleak, then he slouched down the garden path and out the gate.

These Grimm boys – if only they did not care so much about everything, Dortchen thought to herself.

It was advice she too could take, she realised, and she made up a measure of the same tea for herself. The dried yellow petals of St John's wort, which Old Marie called 'chase-devil' for the way it could drive the megrims away. Gaudy calendula, bright as the sun. Sweet-smelling lemon balm, guaranteed to lift the spirits with its aroma alone.

Looking about the stillroom, she remembered how she had loved coming here as a little girl. With an oversized apron tied over her dress, she would stand on a stool and crush fragrant herbs in a mortar, while her father told her what magical properties each plant had, and how he would mix it with this powder or that tincture to make sick people better. She had thought the stillroom one of the most wonderful places in the world.

Once again her eyes smarted and her throat closed over. She lifted the muslin bag of dried flowers and leaves to her face and inhaled deeply, hoping to bring some sunshine to her own winter-shadowed spirits.

MAY DAY

May 1810

On 1st May, there were bonfires lit in the park and the prettiest girls of the town danced about the maypole. The Wild girls were not permitted to do so, of course, but Herr Wild and Frau Wild did stroll down to Karlsaue Park to watch the spectacle with their daughters, leaving Rudolf in charge of the shop for a few hours.

Karlsaue was a beautiful tree-filled park built on the small island that lay between the Fulda River and a narrow stream that ran at the base of the hill on which the old town of Cassel was built. The Kurfürst had built an orangery at one end along classical lines, topped with a great many marble statues recollecting Roman mythology. These looked down over a long avenue of formal trees to a dainty, gold-topped temple on an artificial island in the centre of an artificial lake. Dortchen had often come here with her mother as a child, to roll her hoop along the path or play hopscotch on the smooth paving stones, which were so different from the small, uneven cobblestones in the Marktgasse.

With the weather so much warmer, Dortchen wore her new dress with the fashionable puffed sleeves and the bonnet that Lisette had sent her for Christmas. The bonnet was rose-pink with a matching satin ribbon that tied up under her ear, and it made Dortchen feel prettier than she ever had.

Strolling in the sunshine, listening to the music and breathing in the sweet scent of the spring flowers, it was impossible to feel depressed. Dortchen took a deep breath and squared her shoulders. *You must forget Wilhelm,* she told herself. *It's foolish to eat your heart out for a man who hardly notices you're alive.*

As if her thought had conjured him from air, she saw Wilhelm walking ahead of her, arm in arm with Lotte. Dortchen's face flamed and she fell back, overcome with confusion. But Wilhelm turned, and his face lit up at the sight of her. He bent and spoke a word to Lotte, and she turned to smile and wave. Dortchen could do nothing but try to compose her face and step forward to meet them.

Wilhelm took off his hat, smiling at her in genuine pleasure. 'Dortchen, how are you? It's so good to see you. We've seen nothing of you in months.'

'Helping my father in the shop takes up a great deal of my time,' Dortchen answered.

'I'm sorry to hear that,' he said. 'I was hoping to entice you to come to supper.'

'It's my birthday in a week or so,' Lotte said. 'But you know that – it's yours only two weeks later. We've had such a hard winter . . . Jakob has saved up some money and will buy me a new dress. Oh, I cannot wait to get rid of my blacks. I swear I'll burn them in the marketplace!'

'It's been almost two years since Mother died, and Lotte simply cannot let that dress out any more,' Wilhelm said. 'Besides, she'll be turning seventeen, so she should have a dress that befits her grand old age.'

'I know it'll be very expensive,' Lotte said, sounding anxious. 'Oh, Dortchen, we've been living on lentils and dried beans for months. No money even for salt.'

'I must admit, it's easier now the weather has started to warm,' Wilhelm said. 'We can buy fresh vegetables at the market, though meat is still a luxury.'

'Jakob says he'll buy us some for my birthday supper,' Lotte said.

'We're going to write to friends in Steinau to send us some butter – it's so much cheaper there – and to find some eggs and sugar, so Lotte can bake a cake.'

'Oh, please, say you'll come,' Lotte said. 'We all want you, even Jakob.'

Dortchen hesitated and looked at her parents. They were standing, very stiff and apart, on the shores of the lake, watching the ducks. When she was small, her father had brought his daughters down to the lake to feed the ducks stale bread. Now, any leftover bread was made into soup.

'We'll ask your mother and sisters too, if you like,' Wilhelm said. His understanding of her situation warmed her through.

'I'll ask my father if I may,' she said. 'If we tell him it is a joint birthday celebration, he cannot possibly refuse.'

That means we'll be able to bring some food too, she thought. *The poor Grimms should not have to feed us all.*

'I'll only come if you let me bake the cake, though,' she continued. 'I know what Lotte's cooking is like!'

'I'm getting much better,' Lotte boasted. 'It's hard to burn lentil soup.'

'You seemed to do it often enough,' Wilhelm teased.

'I'm so glad we'll celebrate our seventeenth birthdays together, Dortchen,' Lotte said. 'I could do with some fun. Such a dreary winter we've had. We ran out of firewood and couldn't afford any more, so we spent half the day huddled in our eiderdowns. Our hands were so cold we couldn't hold a pen or a needle or anything.'

Wilhelm went red. 'Taxes,' he said to Dortchen.

She nodded sympathetically. 'Oh, I know. Father fears the King will bankrupt us all.'

'Yet he still holds lavish parties every night, and he's always positively dripping with diamonds,' Lotte said.

'Jakob says the Emperor writes him furious letters and threatens to take his throne away from him,' Wilhelm said.

'Soon there'll be no pretence at independent kingdoms, and France shall stretch from the Mediterranean to the Baltic Sea,' Dortchen said.

'Cassel even looks French now,' Wilhelm said, nodding his head at all the women in their light high-waisted gowns, hair tied up in Psyche knots, their feet in flimsy satin slippers. 'Even you, Dortchen. I used to love to see you Wild girls in your gowns cut in the old way, with waists and a proper skirt.'

She gazed at him in surprise.

'You didn't have to wear them, though,' Lotte said. 'It was like dragging around a tonne of heavy material every day. So many layers, and so hot in summer. Dortchen looks so pretty and fresh in her light cotton.'

'She does indeed,' Wilhelm said. 'But Dortchen would look pretty in anything.'

There was no mistaking the look of admiration in his eyes. Dortchen felt heat rise in her cheeks and lowered her head so her bonnet hid her face. They walked in silence for a moment, then Wilhelm said, 'You see, that's why it's so important we preserve the old stories, before all of our ways are smothered by the customs of the French. Those who remember the old tales are getting fewer all the time. If we don't save them, they'll be lost forever, and that seems so sad to me.'

Dortchen nodded. 'Yes, it's important. There's so much wisdom and beauty in the old tales. It would be tragic to lose them.'

'Yes, exactly,' Wilhelm cried. 'That's why . . . Well, I know you're kept busy helping your father, but . . .'

'What?' she asked.

'I want to start up the reading circle again, though I want to make it more of a storytelling circle. You and your sisters know so many stories, and so do the Hassenpflug girls. And Julia and Charlotte Ramus know some too, and their father is the pastor and so is always visiting old people. Perhaps he will find some new tales for us too. We could meet every now and again and share the tales we've all found. Do you think you could come sometimes, you and your sisters? If your father could spare you?'

'We'd really love you to,' Lotte said. 'We've missed you so much.'

Dortchen felt a warm glow in her stomach. 'Really?'

'Absolutely,' Lotte said, giving her old wide smile.

'We plan to meet on Friday afternoons, when we can,' Wilhelm said. 'We cannot meet at our house, of course – it wouldn't be seemly – but Frau Ramus has offered to host the gathering at her house.'

He knows Father has his church meeting on Fridays, Dortchen thought, her pulse leaping with a sudden rush of joy. *He does want me!*

'Our collection is coming along well,' Wilhelm said, 'but sometimes there are so many different versions of a tale that it's hard to know which to keep and which to discard, or whether to blend them together to make a more complete whole. The stories are never fixed. They change from region to region, or from teller to teller.'

'I know I never manage to tell the same story the same way twice,' Dortchen said. 'If I'm telling a bedtime story to Mia, I might make it a little less scary. But if I'm telling the story sitting in darkness about the fire on All Hallow's Eve, well, then I make it as spooky as possible.'

'I was hoping you'd tell me some more stories,' Wilhelm said. 'Clemens has asked us to give him our collection to read, so we want to make it as good as we possibly can.'

'Jakob is afraid Clemens will lose it, or take the tales and retell them himself,' Lotte added, 'so he's made Wilhelm and Ferdinand copy out the whole collection in their very best script. It's taken forever, hasn't it, Willi?'

'It certainly has. By the end of every day my hand is cramped like a claw,' he said. 'But Jakob's right. It would be a tragedy to lose the collection, when it's taken us so long to find them all.'

'Dortchen,' Frau Wild called. 'Time to go.'

She nodded.

'So we'll see you on Friday?' Lotte asked.

Dortchen hesitated, glancing towards the dark bulk of her father, then quickly nodded again.

Wilhelm's face lit up. 'Oh, good. I'm so glad you'll come.'

It's just the stories he wants, Dortchen told herself. But still she went away down the path with the lightest heart she'd had in months.

SPINDLE

July 1810

'Mother, we're going to the pastor's house now,' Dortchen said, standing in the hot, gloomy bedroom, her hands clenched together. 'We won't be long.'

Her mother stared at her from beneath the heavy mound of eiderdown, a faint sheen of sweat on her skin, her eyes glazed and unfocused. 'But what if I need something . . .'

'Röse will stay,' Dortchen said. 'She'll be here if you need her.'

'I shall enjoy some hours of silent contemplation,' Röse said, settling herself in a chair by the window with a book in her hands.

'We'll be home in time to help with supper, as usual,' Dortchen said.

'Well, then, I suppose so.' Frau Wild turned her face away.

Dortchen, Hanne and Mia went downstairs.

'Do you think Mother is really ill?' Mia asked.

'Of course not,' Hanne said. 'It's just those drops of hers. She'd be much better if she gave them up.'

'She looks so pale and thin,' Dortchen said. 'She didn't touch the soup I took her at midday.'

'She should get up to eat,' Hanne said. 'No one feels hungry if they spend all day lying in bed.'

After putting on their bonnets and gloves, they went out the garden gate and down the Marktgasse towards the pastor's house. It was hot, and the streets smelt of horse dung, rotting cabbages and refuse. Many shops had closed, ruined by King Jérôme's profligacy, and there were beggars on every corner. The girls kept their heads down, their bonnets shading their faces. They had no coins to spare.

'I'll leave you here,' Hanne said, after a while.

'Be careful,' Dortchen said. She dreaded what would happen if their father ever found out that Hanne went wandering the streets alone, going who knew where, to do who knew what.

'I will,' Hanne responded, laughing. 'Give my respects to Frau Ramus.' She waved and turned to hurry down a little alleyway.

'Where does she go?' Mia asked. 'Does she have a lover?'

Dortchen nodded. Hanne's recklessness both frightened and electrified her. Was she kissing in a dark alleyway somewhere, her lover's hand rucking up her skirts? Or did the young man with the red scarf have a bed somewhere where they lay together in a tangle of hot, damp flesh? The thought made Dortchen feel rather hot and damp herself. She shook out the little fan she had made from folded paper and fanned herself, hoping Mia would not comment on her flushed face.

As always, the sick, fizzling feeling in Dortchen's stomach increased as she approached the pastor's house, knowing that her father was at the church for his weekly meeting of the elders. What if he saw her and Mia in the street? Perhaps the pastor would mention that his wife was expecting them for tea. Would her father be angry? They had been meeting now for several months, without Herr Wild being aware of it, and Dortchen was sure their luck must run out soon.

The door was opened by the pastor's housekeeper, a portly woman in an apron and cap. Dortchen and Mia gave her their bonnets and gloves and were shown into the parlour, a room with a great many little tables, lace mats, fringes and dried ferns. Frau Ramus greeted them warmly and led them towards the fireplace, where an arrangement of dried flowers filled the hearth. Her two daughters sat before it, talking eagerly with Lotte and the Hassenpflug sisters. Louis Hassenpflug stood with Jakob on the hearthrug, their backs to the fireplace. Wilhelm sat at the table, a sheaf of paper, an inkpot and quills before him. Dortchen and Mia came to sit beside him, smiling shyly.

Greetings were exchanged and coffee was poured. All the talk was of the Kingdom of Holland. Napoléon had thrown his younger brother Louis off the throne and annexed the country.

'It was only ever meant to be a puppet kingdom,' Jakob said. 'But I suppose Louis Bonaparte did not do his brother's bidding.'

'I've heard that Holland is practically bankrupt,' Dortchen said. 'Is that true, Jakob?'

'I believe so. The economy was ruined by the blockade, of course, as much as by Louis Bonaparte's ineptness. It's a country that relies on its trade.'

'Will we be annexed too?' Mia asked.

'Oh, I hope not,' Malchen cried. The youngest of the Hassenpflug sisters was perched on a low, cushioned stool, squinting around at everyone's faces.

Jakob shrugged his thin shoulders. 'King Jérôme is far more inept than even Louis was, so it's a possibility. You should see the letters Napoléon sends him. They're practically smoking with rage.'

'Father says Napoléon took Holland away from his brother because King Louis refused to introduce conscription,' Jeannette said. 'I wish King Jérôme had refused to do so here. I dread the day our Louis is called up and sent to fight.'

'I'm still too young,' her brother replied. 'And you mustn't call me Louis any more. I don't want to sound French. Call me Ludwig.'

'All our names are too French,' Jeannette said. 'I shall change my name to Johanna.'

'And I shall be Maria,' her older sister said, 'and not Marie.'

'Is your ancestry not French?' Frau Ramus asked. 'I had thought—'

'Not for a very long time,' Jeannette answered earnestly. 'Mother's ancestors fled France after the Sun King made martyrs of the Protestants. It must be a hundred and fifty years ago, or more.'

'We don't want to be French,' Malchen asserted robustly.

'Nor do I want to die fighting for them,' Louis said.

'We've been lucky,' Wilhelm said. 'All five of us Grimm brothers have escaped being called up so far. What are the odds? I dread Ludwig or Ferdinand having to fight. Or any of us, for that matter. I don't think I could kill a man.'

'Where is Ferdinand?' Dortchen asked. 'I thought he was to join us.'

A shadow crossed Wilhelm's face. 'He's not well.' He hesitated, then said in a low voice, 'I'm worried about him, Dortchen. He's not come out of his room in two days. He just sits there, with the shutters drawn, staring at nothing.'

'Has he a fever? Spots?'

'I can see nothing wrong with him,' Wilhelm said. 'I called the doctor and he said it was a preponderance of black bile. He bled him but that only made him worse.'

'The tea I made him has not helped?'

Wilhelm shook his head. 'I'm sorry. I don't think he drank it.'

Lotte drew a letter from her reticule. 'I must read you the latest letter from Bettina,' she said. 'She is so funny. She has no shame at all.'

'What has she done now?' Jakob asked in a tone of resignation.

'She went to call on Herr van Beethoven, without an introduction or anything. Simply because she thinks they should be friends.' Lotte unfolded the letter, written on fine pressed paper in violet ink. 'She says: "Herr van Beethoven and I are kindred spirits. Do you know how I know? I went to visit him, to sing to him. He did not hear me come in. He's almost deaf, you know. So I crept up behind him and put both my hands on his shoulders. He turned to me in rage, but I smiled at him and told him who I was. He knew my name, of course. He showed me the song he was composing. It was none other than Herr von Goethe's song for Mignon. Who else could he be writing that for but me? Even though he did not know me yet. It was Fate."'

'Only Bettina would do such a thing,' Dortchen said. 'If I crept up behind Herr van Beethoven and put my hands on his shoulders, he'd have me thrown into the street as an impertinent minx.'

'I wonder she dared,' Marie said, wide-eyed.

'Bettina Brentano would dare anything,' Wilhelm said, a note of admiration in his voice.

'She sounds like a most forward young lady,' Frau Ramus said in a disapproving tone.

'Perhaps we should hear some stories,' Jakob said. 'That is, I believe, the reason for this gathering, not to gossip about Bettina Brentano.'

'Can I tell the first story?' Malchen cried. She was sitting bolt-upright on her stool, her cheeks flushed with excitement. 'I know such a spooky tale, about a blood sausage.'

'It's a good story,' Jeannette said. 'If Malchen tells it wrong, Marie and I can correct her.'

'I won't tell it wrong,' Malchen protested. 'You two just shush and let me tell it.'

'Let's close the shutters so it's dark,' Louis said. 'It's much better when everything is all shadowy and scary.'

'I need the light to write by,' Wilhelm apologised.

'That's all right,' Malchen said. 'We'll pretend it's dark.'

Wilhelm dipped his quill in the ink, writing swiftly as Malchen told her story.

'A blood sausage and a liver sausage had been friends for some time, and the blood sausage invited the liver sausage for a meal at her home. At dinner time the liver sausage merrily set out for the blood sausage's house. But when she walked through the doorway, she saw all kinds of strange things. There were many steps, and on each one of them she found something different. There were a broom and shovel fighting with each other, a monkey with a big wound on his head, and more such things.'

Malchen spoke at breakneck speed, barely pausing for breath, and Wilhelm's quill scratched as he did his best to keep up.

'The liver sausage was very frightened and upset by this. Nevertheless, she took heart, entered the room and was welcomed in a friendly way by the blood sausage. The liver sausage began to enquire about the strange things on the stairs, but the blood sausage said it was nothing and shifted the topic to something else.'

Wilhelm held up his spare hand for her to pause; Malchen waited reluctantly, bouncing up and down in her impatience. When he nodded at her to continue, she again launched herself at the tale at full speed.

'Then the blood sausage said she had to leave the room to go into the kitchen. She wanted to check that everything was in order and nothing had fallen into the ashes. The liver sausage began walking back and forth in the room and kept wondering about the strange things until someone appeared – I don't know who it was – and said, "Let me warn you, liver sausage, you're in a bloody murderous trap. You'd better get out of here quickly if you value your life."'

Malchen spoke the words with immense relish, and her brother laughed. Charlotte and Julia Ramus pretended to be shocked at the word 'bloody'.

'The liver sausage did not have to think twice about this. She ran out the door as fast as she could. When she looked back, she saw the blood sausage standing high up in the attic window with a long, long knife, which was gleaming as though it had just been sharpened. The blood sausage cried out, "If I had caught you, I would have had you!"'

Frau Ramus looked shocked and said, 'Dear me, Malchen, what a bloodthirsty story.'

Louis laughed, and repeated, 'If I had caught you, I would have had you!'

Wilhelm waved his writing hand up and down, then made his hand into a fist and released it, while gently blowing on the page to quicken the drying of the ink.

Then Marie offered to tell a story. Jakob took Wilhelm's place at the table, picking up a freshly sharpened quill.

The story Marie told was one of the strangest and most beautiful that Dortchen had ever heard.

'A king and queen had no children at all,' she said. 'One day the queen was bathing, and a crab told her that she would soon have a daughter. And so it happened, and the king in his joy held a great celebration. But, because he had only twelve golden plates, he did not invite one of the thirteen fairies in the land. She cursed the baby princess, saying that on her fifteenth birthday she would prick herself on a spindle and die. The other fairies wanted to avert this curse, but the best they could do was make the princess fall asleep for a hundred years instead of dying.'

Jakob wrote steadily, his eyes on his page, his handwriting neat, firm and precise, as Marie told him that the king ordered all the spindles in the land to be burnt, but his daughter was pricked by a spindle on her fifteenth birthday and fell asleep.

'And this sleep spread throughout the entire castle,' Marie said. 'Even the flies on the wall fell asleep.'

Nobody stirred or spoke as Marie told her tale. It was as if she had cast a spell on them. She was so delicate and pretty, heavy dark ringlets falling down on either side of her face, and finely marked dark brows over black eyes that seemed full of sombre mystery.

'Roundabout the castle a thorn hedge began to grow, till it finally covered the entire castle. A legend circulated throughout the land about the beautiful sleeping Dornröschen, for so the princess was called.'

Little Thorn-Rose. Such a beautiful name, Dortchen thought. *It almost sounds like mine.*

She looked at Wilhelm, and saw his eyes were fixed on Marie. Jealousy stabbed her, as sharp as one of the thorns in the hedge. It was all she could do to keep still. Dortchen twisted her handkerchief in her hands, keeping her head bowed so no one could see her face.

'After a long, long time, a king's son came into the land,' Marie said. 'He heard the tale and went riding up to the thorn hedge. All the thorns parted before him and seemed to be flowers, and behind him they turned into thorns again. He kissed the sleeping princess and everything awoke from its sleep, and the two were married. And if they are not dead, they are still living.'

Marie had finished her tale. She smiled, her eyes downturned, while everyone congratulated her.

'It is a beautiful story,' Jakob said, wiping his quill on a rag. 'But it's French. We cannot include it in our collection.'

'Oh, no,' Marie cried out, distressed. 'But it's my favourite story. It's not French – my mother told it to me.'

'It's from Monsieur Perrault's collection,' Jakob said. 'Wilhelm, you must've read it – "La Belle au Bois Dormant".'

'Well, yes,' Wilhelm agreed. 'But there are significant differences too. In Monsieur Perrault's version, there are only eight fairies, not thirteen. And the princess bears him two children and the prince's mother tries to eat them. Surely Marie's tale has as many echoes of Brynhild and the Völsunga epic as it does of Perrault's story?'

'The maiden asleep in a remote castle, you mean?' Jakob said.

'Yes, until the right man comes just at the right time to awaken her. And surely the wall of thorns in Little Thorn-Rose's story is analogous to the wall of fire in Brynhild's story?'

'Perhaps,' Jakob said. 'I'll need to think on it.'

'It's too beautiful not to include,' Wilhelm said to Marie.

'Oh, I am glad,' she said, clasping her hands together and smiling up at him.

Dortchen stood up. 'It's time for us to go. Come on, Mia.'

As she gathered up her reticule, she was aware of Jakob's thoughtful gaze on her face. She made her farewells as politely as she could manage, drowning Mia's protests ruthlessly. As they went out into the hot, dusty street, Mia said, 'But why? What's wrong, Dortchen?'

'Nothing,' she answered, knowing that she lied.

I must stop loving him, she told herself. *But how?*

COMMON RUE

September 1810

One morning, in early September, Hanne leant over and vomited her morning coffee all over the floor.

Pandemonium erupted. Frau Wild wept and wrung her hands, Herr Wild shouted and stamped about and shook Hanne till she almost fainted, while Rudolf was disgusted. The three younger sisters all huddled together, frightened and alarmed.

'Why is everyone so angry?' Mia asked. 'It's not Hanne's fault if she's eaten something bad.'

Dortchen put her arm about Mia's shoulders. 'They think Hanne may be with child.'

'With child? You mean . . .'

Dortchen nodded.

'She has become a transgressor,' Röse said with dark satisfaction.

'Who is he?' Herr Wild yelled. 'I'll kill him!'

'I shan't tell you,' Hanne said, and he slapped her.

Hanne stumbled back, her hand covering her cheek. Herr Wild raised his hand again and Frau Wild tried to seize it. He smacked her instead, saying, 'What else could I expect, with a fool for a wife?'

He went out of the room, slamming the door behind him. Dortchen helped her mother and sister to the drawing room, then brought cool lavender water, smelling salts and her mother's drops. She was bathing her mother's head when the door banged open. Her father stood in the doorway, a beaker of dark-green liquid in his hand. Dortchen smelt the bitter scent of common rue. She stood up, her hands clenched. Rue was an old wives' way of ridding oneself of an unwanted child.

'Drink this,' Herr Wild told Hanne.

She pressed herself back against the couch. 'I won't.'

'You will,' he said, advancing upon her.

She closed her mouth obdurately. He seized her face, closing her nostrils with his large fingers. After a moment she had to gasp for air, and he poured the stinking liquid into her mouth. Hanne choked and spluttered, but he held her chin and nose tightly, forcing her to swallow. The next moment she vomited it up – all over her father's frockcoat. He snapped at her, cleaning himself with his handkerchief, and went back to the stillroom to make some more.

Hanne ran down the back stairs. Herr Wild caught her halfway across the garden and dragged her back to her room, where he locked her in, pocketing the key.

'You will stay in your room, with nothing to eat or drink, until you tell me the name of your lover,' he said through the wooden panels of the door.

'I'm not hungry anyway,' Hanne responded.

Herr Wild turned to go and saw Dortchen and Mia watching anxiously from the stairwell. He pointed a finger at them. 'You are not to leave this house – do you hear me?'

They nodded their heads, feeling sick and shaken.

Herr Wild went away, and soon Dortchen could hear the sound of sobbing. She knelt and put her mouth to the keyhole. 'Hanne,' she whispered.

After a moment her sister's voice replied shakily, 'Yes?'

'What do you want me to do? Shall I take a message to him?'

'Yes, please. Wait just a moment.' In a few minutes, a sheet of paper in her sister's untidy scrawl was pushed under the door. Dortchen folded it up small and hid it in her bodice, then went down the back stairs, trying to think what excuse she could make to go out.

Old Marie was up to her elbows in bread dough, looking very hot and bothered. Mozart hopped about the floor, pecking at a cockroach that scuttled by.

'He's locked all the doors and taken the keys,' Old Marie said.

'But . . . how am I to feed the birds? Or harvest vegetables for dinner?'

Old Marie shook her head. 'He said no one's to go out, else I'll lose my job. He says he will feed the animals himself tonight.'

Dortchen went to the window and stared out at the garden, which basked peacefully in the bright sunshine. She leant her head against the door.

'He's very angry,' Old Marie said.

Dortchen went upstairs to her bedroom. Mia had taken over Lisette's bedroom when her sister had married, so the little room with the sloping ceiling was now all her own. She opened the window wide, letting in a soft, warm breeze, then dropped her sister's folded note into the little basket where the pegs were kept, first scribbling a note to Lotte on the outside. Dortchen then tied her green sash to the basket and pulled on the washing line till the basket was hanging outside Lotte's window. It had been such a long time since she and Lotte had exchanged notes in this way that she could only hope her friend would notice the green sash and think to check the basket. A pang of nostalgia smote her, for the little girls she and Lotte had been.

'May I take Hanne some soup?' she asked her father that night at supper, after grace had been said and a silent meal half-consumed. 'She will need to keep up her strength.'

'She may have no food or drink till she does what she's told,' Herr Wild said. 'She will drink the rue and parsley mixture, that bastard will be expelled from her womb, and she will tell me the name of the man that ruined her so I may take a horsewhip to him and drive him out of town.'

'But, Father,' Dortchen protested. 'The baby's your grandchild. Surely—'

He stood up, pushing his chair back roughly, and pointed a finger at her. 'Do not speak another word, Dortchen, I warn you.'

She fell silent and he left the room, leaving his meal half-finished.

'Do you know who her lover is?' Rudolf demanded.

Dortchen did not answer.

When she and Röse and Mia had finished clearing away and washing up, she went up to her room. The basket had been returned to her side of the washing line. Hanne's note was gone.

The next morning, there was a knock at the front door. Dortchen could not open the door because it was locked, so she called out, 'Who's there?'

'Would you please present my compliments to your father and tell him that Herr Fulda is here to speak to him upon a matter of great importance,' the voice of a young man said.

'Yes, sir,' Dortchen replied, and she went with a racing pulse into the shop, where her father was serving a customer. He cast her an irritated look, so she went to the window and looked out into the street. Standing on their front doorstep was the young man in the red scarf, looking rather pale. He was accompanied by two friends, burly young men with coloured scarves about their necks and pugnacious expressions. Hanne had obviously warned him about her father's threat to kill him.

The customer paid Herr Wild and went out, and her father snapped, 'What do you want, Dortchen?'

'You have a visitor, Father. A young man named Herr Fulda presents you his compliments.'

Her father's expression darkened. 'Stay here. I'll be back soon.'

He went through the doorway into the house, leaving Dortchen alone in the shop. Such a thing had never happened before. She straightened a few jars on the shelves, then sat at the desk, looking at her father's neat ledgers. A name leapt out at her from the page. '*Herr F. Grimm*,' the entry read in her father's neat, precise handwriting. '*Tincture of opium, 10 mL.*'

Looking through the pages, she saw the same entry repeated every few days. Earlier in the ledger, it appeared less often, each entry being seven or eight days apart. *Where did Ferdinand get the money?* she wondered.

Shouting and a crash caught her attention. She got up and went to the door to the house, listening intently. A loud, angry voice boomed down the hallway. Her father. Then she heard quick footsteps. The front door opened and banged, and she saw Hanne's lover hurry past, his red scarf held to a bleeding nose. Dortchen's heart sank. She shut the ledger and returned it to its usual exact position on the desk, then sat on a stool behind the bench, trying not to wring her hands.

Her father came into the shop, breathing heavily, his face an unpleasant eggplant colour.

'No customers came,' she said.

Herr Wild walked to a shelf, took down a bottle of quince brandy, pulled out the cork with his teeth and drank straight from the bottle. 'That lecher says he wants to marry Hanne. I'll see them both fry in hell first.'

'Why won't you let them marry?'

'He's an unemployed land-loafer,' her father replied through his teeth. 'He has no money, no prospects. How is he to support a wife and child?'

'Surely there's something we can do to help,' Dortchen cried.

'I haven't the money to take on another mouth to feed, or to set them up in a house of their own. If a man cannot support his family, he should not get married.'

Dortchen thought of Wilhelm, and how he could not wear a cornflower in his buttonhole. She wondered how much money it would cost to rent a house, to furnish it, to buy all the mattresses and sheets and eiderdowns, the pillows and cushions and curtains, the rugs and towels and tea towels, the plates and bowls and cutlery, the pots and pans and skillets and ladles and knives. It would not be cheap. She tried to imagine Hanne and Herr Fulda setting up a life together without any money at all.

'But if they love each other . . .'

Her father scowled. 'Sentimental rubbish. Now, go and see if your sister has come to her senses.'

Dortchen called her sister's name through the door. 'Hanne, are you all right?'

'I feel sick,' her sister replied, her voice coming closer to the door. 'And so thirsty! Will Father not let me out?'

'Not until you drink his potion.'

'Well, I won't. I want this baby. And I know Johann will want it too.'

'He came, Hanne, and asked for your hand in marriage,' Dortchen told her sister.

'He what? Oh, the silly dear. What did Father do?'

'Punched him.'

'Oh, no! Was he hurt? Is he all right?'

'He had a bloody nose, but I don't think any lasting harm was done.'

'I hope Johann punched him back.'

Dortchen smiled. 'No, he just went away. What are you going to do?'

'Did Father give his consent?'

'No.'

'I didn't think he would. Well, we cannot marry without it. Not unless we run away and go somewhere miles from here, and I say I have no father. And even then I need a legal guardian to give permission. It's so unfair. I'm not Father's possession, to be sold like a cow or a duck.'

'It's the law.'

'The law should be changed. Bloody Napoléon talks of bloody liberty and bloody equality and bloody fraternity. Where are any bloody rights for women?' Hanne was crying again.

'Hanne, I'm going to lower you a jug of water on a string from my window. Put your head out the window and catch it.'

Dortchen ran down to the kitchen and filled a pewter jug with water from the scullery pump, grabbed half a loaf of bread from the table, then carried them swiftly up the back stairs, hoping not to run into Röse or her father. She opened her window wide and leant out. Hanne was at the window below, her face pale, her eyes red and swollen, her flaxen hair in disarray. Dortchen tied string to the jug handle as securely as she knew how, then lowered it to her. 'Thank you,' Hanne mouthed.

Dortchen showed her the bread, and she smiled gratefully. As soon as the bread had been lowered, Dortchen shut her window. She could not think of any other way to help her sister. Unless she stole her father's keys . . . The very idea filled her with terror.

That night Dortchen lay in her bed, trying to find courage. The hours passed, but she could not unlock her rigid muscles to creep downstairs to her parents' room. At last the darkness began to lighten. Soon the quail would cry. If she was going to do it, she must do it now.

Dortchen got up, walked barefoot across the room and went down the stairs, careful not to tread on the squeaky step. She put her hand on her parents' doorknob and turned it very slowly. The door creaked as it opened. Dortchen froze, listening, but her father's snoring did not falter. She slid one foot forward, then the other, her feet soundless on the thick rug, till she came to where her father's frockcoat hung on its wooden stand by the fireplace. There was just enough light seeping past the edge of the curtain for her to see its dark shape. She put her hand in one pocket, then the other.

The keys jangled. Her father snorted, muttered and rolled over. Dortchen stood motionless. His breathing seemed to steady. Dortchen waited another excruciating few minutes, then tiptoed out into the hall. As quietly as she could, she flew down the corridor to Hanne's room. In the dark, with her hands shaking, it was very difficult to find the right key. At last Dortchen found it and unlocked her sister's door.

Hanne sat up in her bed. 'Who is it?' she cried in alarm.

'Shh, it's me. I've got the keys. Hurry, it's almost dawn. Get up, get dressed – we need to get you out before Father wakes.' As she spoke, Dortchen was gathering together Hanne's dress and stockings and shawl. It was growing lighter by the second. She helped Hanne dress and swiftly pinned up her hair, then Hanne caught up a few treasures and pushed them into her reticule. The two sisters hurried down the back stairs to the kitchen.

As Dortchen struggled with the stiff lock of the back door, the quail called its loud, distinctive cry.

'Father will wake now,' Hanne said. 'Quick, Dortchen.'

At last they managed to get the back door open, and Hanne and Dortchen hurried through the dew-silver garden. The sky was clear overhead. It was going to be a beautiful day.

At the gate, the sisters embraced. 'Thank you,' Hanne whispered. 'Don't get caught putting the keys back.'

'I won't,' Dortchen said. 'Go, and God bless you.'

She went back into the kitchen and locked the door behind her. She stood with her back to it, listening. She heard a few faint noises. Her father would be getting up, and Old Marie too. The keys felt very heavy and dangerous. Dortchen must not be caught in the corridor in her nightgown, the keys in her hands.

She thought for a moment, her heart slamming in slow, heavy strokes against her ribs. Then she put the kettle on to boil. Very carefully, she crept up to her room, dressed rapidly and did her hair, and put the keys in the pocket of her gown. By the time she reached the kitchen again, the kettle was hissing and Old Marie was there, staring at it with worried eyes.

'I'll take Father up his shaving water,' Dortchen said. 'Since Hanne can't.'

She filled his porcelain jug with warm water and carried it up the stairs. It was hard to balance the jug and open the door, but she managed it. Her father was in his dressing room, in his socks and trousers and shirtsleeves. 'I have your water, Father,' she said, carrying it to him. He poured some into his bowl and lathered up the soap, his straight-edged razor lying on the cloth before him.

Dortchen went back into the dim bedroom. Her mother was a silent mound under the eiderdown. Dortchen went across the room and slipped the keys back into her father's coat pocket. The keys gave a betraying jangle and Dortchen looked around. Her father did not call out, though, so she turned to go with a quick rush of relief.

Her mother was watching her from the bed.

THE STORY WIFE

October 1810

Dortchen looked out the stagecoach window, hardly able to believe she was leaving Cassel.

They rattled over the bridge, the water of the river gleaming pewter grey in the early-morning light. The jumbled roofs of the Old Town were veiled with mist, and the whole valley before her was hidden. As the stagecoach began the descent, the mist swallowed up the view so that it was as if Dortchen were passing into another world.

She was going to Marburg, to assist at Hanne's wedding. The thought made her insides clench with excitement.

Hanne's disappearance had not been discovered till late in the evening of the day that Dortchen had released her. Dortchen had gone about her business all day with a twist in the pit of her stomach, dreading the moment when her father discovered Hanne was gone. He went up several times to speak to his daughter through her door, but had taken her silence as stubbornness. Just before supper, he took up another beaker full of the foul-smelling green mixture.

Dortchen and her mother had sat in silence in the drawing room, their hands idle on the sewing in their laps. Röse read on, oblivious, her hands busy with her knitting, while Mia sat in the big chair, pretending to sew. Dortchen listened to her father's heavy footsteps coming down the stairs and braced herself. He was furious, of course, but Dortchen kept her head, looked him in the eye and lied through her teeth.

'Perhaps she climbed down on a rope made of her sheets,' Mia cried.

'Then why are her sheets still on her bed, you stupid child?' her father replied.

Mia blushed. 'I . . . I didn't know.'

'Perhaps her lover brought a ladder and she climbed out the window,' Rudolf said.

'You think the quail wouldn't have woken and cried out?' his father replied. 'No, one of *you* let her out.'

'But you locked the doors yourself, sir,' Frau Wild said, twisting her handkerchief. 'You had the keys in your safekeeping.'

'She must've picked the lock with a hairpin,' Mia said, wide-eyed with amazement.

'Mmpf,' her father said, his scowling eyes on Dortchen. She turned away, trying to keep her face under control.

The next day a letter was delivered from Hanne.

'I want to be with Johann and nothing will stop me,' it read. 'Since I cannot marry without your permission, Father, I will simply live with him in sin. I do not believe in marriage anyway, and would only get married so people will not call my baby a bastard. Do not be concerned for your reputation. Johann and I plan to move far, far away. If you would prefer the respectability of a married daughter, then you may of course offer us your consent and we will be married as soon as we can. Please find enclosed the necessary documents. You may send them to us at the following address . . .'

In a rage, Herr Wild went to the address, only to find it a clearing-house for letters and documents. He tried to track down his errant daughter and her lover, but they had left town and he could not discover where they had gone. He checked with all the stagecoaches and posting-inns, but they had either walked away from Cassel or had friends with private means of transport. Herr Wild and Rudolf took turns waiting at the clearing-house, but no one turned up asking for a package addressed to Herr Johann Fulda. Eventually, after three long weeks, Herr Wild gave in and signed the forms to give consent for his daughter to marry.

Johann must have had a secret method for receiving messages, for a week later the Wilds received another letter from Hanne, saying the marriage banns had been posted in Marburg and asking whether Frau Wild and her daughters would attend the wedding.

'You may not go,' Herr Wild told his wife.

'No,' she said. 'I'm not well enough to travel to Marburg. But Dortchen and Mia must go, or else people will talk.'

'Rubbish! How are they to get to Marburg?'

'By stagecoach, of course,' Frau Wild replied.

'By themselves?'

'Old Marie can go with them. She'd like to see Hanne married. And it has been a long time since she last had a holiday.'

'And who is to pay for this little pleasure trip?' Herr Wild shouted.

'You, of course. We must pack up a dowry chest for Hanne. Dortchen can take it with her. Röse will not want to go, of course. She can stay and look after me.'

So Dortchen found herself with Old Marie and Mia on a bone-jarring, teeth-rattling, ten-hour stagecoach journey to Marburg, a small chest of linen and cutlery strapped to the roof. She had not been away from Cassel since she was a child, and looked with eagerness out the window at the smooth brown fields, dusted with frost, and the timber-framed cottages. The trees lining the road held their bare fretwork of twigs against a vast grey sky. Dortchen did not think she had ever seen so much sky. Rooks wheeled above their ragged nests in the treetops, calling sadly, and far away a grey shingled church spire lifted high above a huddle of small houses.

The roads were in such bad repair that the stagecoach was twice bogged in deep muddy mires and had to be dug out by the coachman, and it once buckled a wheel in a pothole. It took more than an hour to be fixed, with all the passengers sitting on their luggage on the side of the road, rubbing their hands together and stamping their feet in a vain effort to keep warm.

It was long past sunset when they finally reached Marburg. Dortchen was so stiff and bruised and exhausted that she caught only an impression of the great bulk of a church, and a string of lights so far above that it seemed like a constellation of bright stars, but must be the lantern-light shining out from the windows of the famous *Schloss*.

Gretchen's husband, Herr Schmerfeld, greeted them at the inn at which the stagecoach stopped for the night. He had sedan chairs waiting for them, one each for Dortchen, Mia, Old Marie and himself, and another for the luggage. Dortchen could not believe such luxury. She lifted the curtain and stared out into the cool night as she was lifted and carried up a steep cobbled road, a linkboy running before them with a lantern. She saw, crowded together, many timber-framed houses with heavy, protruding gables, their roofs almost touching overhead. Lots of young men in black gowns climbed the narrow streets, laughing. Marburg was a university town, she remembered; Jakob and Wilhelm had studied here. It gave her pleasure to know she was travelling a road that Wilhelm would have trodden.

The sedan chair reached a wide market square, and the carriers paused to catch their breath before attempting the next steep incline. Looking through the curtain, Dortchen saw a richly ornamented building with a clock on its parapet, and a statue of a soldier on a rearing horse, killing something that looked rather like a dog but was more likely a dragon. A man stood on the steps below it, selling hot chestnuts. Herr Schmerfeld bought them all some, in cones of paper made from old maps that warmed the hands beautifully. Dortchen ate them gratefully, for it had been a long time since their midday repast.

Herr Schmerfeld's house was at the very top of the cliff, right underneath the *Schloss,* and the poor sedan-carriers were panting by the time they set the chairs down in the cobbled courtyard. It was a large, whitewashed, gabled house with a pointed turret and black timber frames. The front door was huge and had forged iron vines twining across it.

Inside, all was modern, however. Rich carpets covered the floor from wall to wall, and gas-lit chandeliers hung in the hallway. Old Marie went up to get the girls' bedrooms ready and unpack their bags, while Herr Schmerfeld showed Dortchen and Mia into a large sitting room that was decorated with numerous golden statues of camels. Gretchen, Hanne and Johann Fulda were sitting by a roaring fire, drinking wine from crystal glasses. Hanne jumped to her feet at the sight of Mia and Dortchen and came forward with outstretched arms.

'It's so lovely to see you,' she cried. As she embraced Dortchen, she whispered, 'Is all well? Did you get into trouble?'

'Not really,' Dortchen replied, not liking to say that she and her sisters had not been permitted to leave the house since Hanne had run away. Except to go to church, of course. Each day they had to endure Herr Wild's suspicious rage and disapproval, while their mother had taken to her bed and stayed there.

It was a great relief to be away from Cassel.

The next morning, the four sisters went out to see Marburg, in the company of Gretchen's husband and Hanne's betrothed. French soldiers were everywhere, of course, but so too were young men in their black student's gowns, arguing loudly about law and philosophy. The Old Town itself was quaint, with the streets so steep that no horse and carriage could drive up them. This meant everyone walked, or rode in sedan chairs, or led about small donkeys loaded high with books and scrolls or panniers of vegetables – or even, Dortchen saw, two immense, carved chairs with red velvet seats and backs.

Away from the gloomy, repressive atmosphere of their father's house, Dortchen and her sisters became carefree, talking and laughing as they had not for years.

They visited the *Schloss* at the crest of the hill, which was half in ruins since Napoléon's troops had demolished the fortifications after an uprising earlier in the year. They then walked down the hills to the immense Gothic pile of the Elisabethkirche, the church built hundreds of years earlier to hold the tomb of St Elizabeth of Hungary. Nearby was a high wall with curving iron spikes and a heavy iron gate.

'That is the poorhouse,' Gretchen said. 'Can you believe the Grimms wanted Lotte to go there and write down stories from some old hag while she was here? They think of no one but themselves, those brothers.'

'I would like to visit there while I am here, if I may,' Dortchen said quietly.

Herr Schmerfeld looked at her with warm interest in his eyes. 'That is very commendable of you, Fraülein Dortchen. I shall arrange a visit for you, and ask my cook to prepare some soup for you to take.'

* * *

The next week was taken up with preparing for Hanne's wedding, exploring the town and visiting Gretchen's smart new friends. But once Hanne was safely transformed into Frau Fulda, and the new husband and wife had driven off to Nentershausen, where a new job and a home awaited them, Dortchen was at last free to visit the poorhouse. She hoped to coax a story or two from the woman Clemens Brentano had called 'the Marburg *Märchenfrau*'. The Story Wife.

Old Marie accompanied her, carrying a basket with soup and bread and cheese and a jar of sour pickles. They rang the bell outside the gate, and soon a small boy with shaggy hair and a makeshift grey uniform came to let them in.

The gate opened into a narrow courtyard that smelt unpleasantly damp. An arched door led Dortchen and Old Marie into a corridor, with steps leading upwards. Through an open door at the end of the corridor, they glimpsed thin, bowed figures in grey uniforms breaking rocks in the yard outside. The shaggy-haired boy led them down the corridor, past bare, cold rooms in which people lay on narrow pallets, or sat at long tables unravelling old rope or sewing cloth together. The smell was horrible. It was all Dortchen could do not to cover her mouth and nose with her gloved hands. Old Marie reached into her basket and took out a posy of dried lavender flowers, and Dortchen gratefully buried her nose in it.

At last they reached the office, a large, comfortable room with a fire burning in the hearth and a tray with the remains of a large meal on the table. Dortchen was greeted by a portly man in a grubby waistcoat and his even portlier wife in an even grubbier dress.

'Oh, what an honour, to have Herr Schmerfeld's sister-in-law visit us,' the warden's wife simpered. 'You're simply too good.'

Dortchen explained their mission, and the warden's wife shook her head doubtfully. 'Frau Creuzer is wandering in her wits, I'm afraid,' she said. 'I'm not sure you'll get much out of her. Mumbles away all day, she does, but it never makes much sense. And she's frightened of strangers.'

'She won't be frightened of us,' Old Marie said comfortably. 'An old biddy like me and a sweet young girl like Fraülein Wild? We've brought her some soup – I'm sure she'd like that. We'll sit with her a while and have a chat.'

'It'd cause bad feeling among the others, bringing her food,' the warden's wife said. 'Best give me the basket, and I'll share it among them all.'

Unwillingly, Dortchen did as she was asked. She saw the warden's wife's eyes light up as she rummaged through the basket; Dortchen was sure she would eat all the food herself.

'She won't say a word to you,' the warden's wife repeated, settling herself comfortably by the fire. 'Afraid of adults, she is.'

Dortchen had a sudden idea. 'Perhaps she would tell her tales to some children? Could some of the children from the workhouse come with us?'

Both the warden and his wife frowned. 'They've got work to do,' the warden's wife said.

'I'll pay for their time,' Dortchen said, drawing out her thin purse. Her mother had given her a few coins to spend in Marburg, but she had not yet had a chance to visit the shops.

'Very well, then,' the warden's wife said, heaving herself to her feet. 'Though I think it very odd.'

She rang a bell and a thin, stooped girl came to the door. 'Call some of the brats, and be smart about it,' the warden's wife told her. Soon a small group of grubby, anxious children were brought to meet Dortchen and Old Marie. Many had bruises on their thin arms and legs.

The warden's wife took them all upstairs to a long, gloomy room. Old ladies were lying on their pallets in rows, some still and silent, others rocking themselves and humming, or mumbling through toothless mouths. All were dressed in sack-like grey gowns and had bare feet. The warden's wife led them to a bed near a window, where an old woman sat hunched, knitting with grey wool.

'Frau Creuzer,' she said. 'Visitors for you. Be polite, now, and do as you're told. I'll be back soon.'

The old woman shrank away from the sound of her words, looking up with sunken eyes that were filmed over. Her thin grey hair hung in a plait down her neck, and she had barely a tooth left in her mouth. 'Who's there?' she asked in a trembling voice.

'Just another poor old woman like you,' Old Marie said soothingly. She brought a chair from the wall for Dortchen, then sat down on the bed, taking Frau Creuzer's thin, blue-veined hands in her own warm, comforting grip. 'My name's Marie Müller, and I've come as companion to Fraülein Wild, who is sitting just here.'

'We've heard that you tell the most wonderful stories,' Dortchen said gently. 'Would you tell us one?'

'Tell you a story?' the old woman said in disbelief. 'What for?'

'We have some children here from the workhouse,' Dortchen said. 'I know they'd love a story.'

'Poor mites, they're worn out from overwork. Won't you tell them a lovely old tale to make them feel better?' Old Marie said.

'Please,' one of the children said, settling down cross-legged on the floor.

'I haven't heard a story since my ma died,' another piped up.

'It's been ever so long since I've heard one,' another said.

The old woman hesitated, looking towards the sound of their voices.

'We love old stories,' Dortchen said gently. 'If you tell me a story, I'll write it down and then we'll put it in a book, to be preserved forever.'

'A story of mine, put into a book?'

'Yes, I promise.' Dortchen hoped she would not be wrong. Surely Jakob and Wilhelm would find a publisher for their book, even in these troubled times?

Old Marie reached into her pocket and drew out a small bag of sugarplums, which she pressed into the old woman's hands. 'A gift for you,' she whispered. 'Don't tell anyone.'

The woman squeezed the bag in her hand and heard the tinsel paper crackle. Her face lit up; she took out a sugarplum and popped it in her mouth, chewing quickly. Her whole face changed. 'I have not eaten a sugarplum since I was a child,' she whispered. 'Thank you.'

All the children were leaning forward, their eyes fixed imploringly on the bag of sugarplums. Old Marie smiled and pulled out another, which seemed to vanish among the dirty little hands in seconds.

'Well, then, maybe for the little ones,' Frau Creuzer said. Dortchen quietly opened up the small writing desk she had borrowed from Herr Schmerfeld and unscrewed the inkpot. As she dipped in one of the quills, the old woman began to speak.

GIRL IN ASHES

October 1810

'There's a story I always loved that my grandmother used to tell me,' Frau Creuzer said in a wavering voice. 'It was about a girl who was dressed in rags and had to work in the ashes, while her two stepsisters had everything that had once been hers.'

'It sounds wonderful.' Dortchen wrote swiftly, copying down what the old woman said. Frau Creuzer spoke so slowly, and stopped so many times, trying to remember what happened, that Dortchen was able to keep up quite well. On one or two occasions she had to look to Old Marie for help, unable to understand what the old woman had said, for her speech was greatly marred by her lack of teeth. Old Marie quickly translated for her, in a low voice.

'The poor child had to do the most difficult work,' the old woman said. 'She had to get up before sunrise, carry water, make the fire, cook and wash. To add to her misery, her stepsisters ridiculed her and then scattered peas and lentils into the ashes, and she had to spend the whole day sorting them out again. At night, when she was tired, there was no bed for her to sleep in, and she had to lie down next to the hearth. Because she was always dirty with ashes and dust, they gave her the name Aschenputtel.'

Dortchen wondered how to spell 'Aschenputtel'. It meant to wallow in ashes, she realised, and felt sorry for the girl in the story.

Aschenputtel's stepsisters were invited to go to a ball, but Aschenputtel had to stay home and do the chores. 'I know just how she felt,' Dortchen whispered to Old Marie, who smiled in sympathy but put her finger to her lips. The children were all listening intently, their eyes fixed on the old woman's wrinkled face.

Pigeons came and helped Aschenputtel sort the bad lentils from the good in a basin, but the stepsisters tore down their pigeon-roost when they realised Aschenputtel had watched the ball from its roof.

'They're so mean,' one girl cried.

'They were,' Frau Creuzer said, 'and they only got meaner.'

The next time the stepsisters went to the ball, they ordered Aschenputtel to sort out the bad seeds from the good in a sackful of seeds. Once again the pigeons came to help.

'The bad ones go into your crop, the good ones go into the pot,' the old woman chanted. 'Peck, peck, peck, peck, it went as fast as if twelve hands were at work. When they were finished, the pigeons said, "Aschenputtel, would you like to go dancing at the ball?"

'"Oh, my goodness," she said, "how could I go in these dirty clothes?"

'"Just go to the little tree on your mother's grave, shake it, and wish yourself some beautiful clothes. But come back before midnight."

'So Aschenputtel went and shook the little tree, and said, "Shake yourself, shake yourself, little tree. Throw some nice clothing down to me."

'She had scarcely spoken these words when a splendid silver dress fell down before her. With it were pearls, silk stockings with silver decorations, silver slippers and everything else she needed. Aschenputtel carried it all home. After she had washed herself and put on the clothing, she was as beautiful as a rose washed in dew.'

Dortchen could see the glittering silver dress and slippers in her mind's eye, and she imagined dancing in the arms of the prince under a thousand shining lanterns, till the clock struck the twelve notes of midnight. Her hand slowed as she imagined a prince with dark, curly hair and a thin, hungry face. Frau Creuzer was still talking, however, and she had to write quickly to catch up.

The same thing happened the next night, the old woman said, though this time the little tree on Aschenputtel's mother's grave shook down a golden dress and golden slippers. Again she danced all night in the prince's arms. But she did not know that he had commanded his servants to cover the steps with pitch to stop her from running away at midnight again. When she tried to escape, one of her golden slippers caught fast in the pitch and was lost.

The prince decided to find his lost love by searching for the girl whose foot fitted the tiny slipper. When he came to Aschenputtel's house, her stepmother gave her daughters a knife and told them to cut off parts of their feet so that they could wear the slipper and win the prince's hand. The eldest sister cut off her heel, but the pigeons called out and warned the prince.

'*Rook di goo, rook di goo!* There's blood in the shoe. The shoe is too tight, this bride is not right!' the old woman said, holding her hands up near her mouth to mimic a bird's beak.

The children all laughed.

The second stepsister cut off her toes to fit the slipper, but once again the pigeons revealed her trick to the prince.

'The prince looked down and saw that her white stockings were stained with blood,' the old woman continued. 'The prince took her back to her mother and said, "She is not the right bride either. Is there not another daughter here in this house?"

'"No," said the mother. "There is only a dirty cinder girl here. She is sitting down there in the ashes. The slipper would never fit her." But the prince insisted and so they called Aschenputtel, and when she heard that the prince was there, she quickly washed her hands and face. She stepped into the best room and bowed.

'The prince handed her the golden slipper, saying, "Try it on. If it fits you, you shall be my wife." She pulled the heavy shoe from her left foot, then put her foot into the slipper, pushing ever so slightly. It fitted as if it had been poured over her foot. As she straightened herself up, she looked into the prince's face and he recognised her as the beautiful princess. He cried out, "This is the right bride!"

'The stepmother and the two proud sisters turned pale with horror. The prince escorted Aschenputtel away. He helped her into his carriage, and as they rode through the gate, the pigeons called out, "*Rook di goo, rook di goo!* No blood's in the shoe, the shoe's not too tight, this bride is right!"'

The old woman dropped her hands and turned her blind eyes towards them, smiling toothlessly. The children clapped, as did the old ladies lying in beds nearby.

'Oh, what a lovely story,' Dortchen cried, scribbling down the last few lines. 'Wilhelm will love it.'

'Do you know any more?' Old Marie asked.

The old woman peered anxiously towards the door.

'No one's there,' Dortchen reassured her. 'No one's listening except us.'

The old woman allowed herself to be persuaded to tell another story, about a golden bird and three brothers. Both Old Marie and Dortchen were familiar with this tale, though the toothless old woman told it a little differently. Dortchen wrote down her version faithfully; by now her fingers were covered in ink and her hands ached.

The warden's wife came bustling in before the end of the story, and would have interrupted if Old Marie had not held her finger to her mouth warningly. The old woman must have heard her, though, for she began to gabble the story. Soon her words were incomprehensible.

'I told you she was useless,' the warden's wife said.

'She was not at all useless,' Dortchen cried. 'She told us a most beautiful story. Two beautiful stories. Herr Grimm will be so pleased.'

'Well, then,' the warden's wife said, not looking pleased. 'If you've finished . . . Frau Creuzer has work to do, and so do these worthless brats.'

Packing up her writing tools, Dortchen thanked the old woman as sweetly as she knew how. The old woman grinned at her and secretly popped another sugarplum into her mouth. The sound of her chewing followed Dortchen as the warden's wife led her to the door.

Dortchen had been dreading their return to Cassel, but with two new stories in her bag, the rickety wheels of the stagecoach could scarcely turn fast enough. As the road climbed away from Marburg, she gazed out the window at the pine-dark hills and wondered if Wilhelm would be pleased.

It was a few days before she could get away, but at last Old Marie asked her to go to the marketplace and wait in the line for bread, as their flour bins were empty. Dortchen did as she was asked, then climbed the stairs to the Grimms' apartment on her way home. Wilhelm was sitting at the kitchen table, frowning as he copied text from an immensely thick old book onto a fresh piece of paper.

'Wilhelm,' she said in a low voice. 'Is all well?'

He looked up and smiled wearily, rising to his feet. 'You're back. Welcome home. How was the wedding?'

'Beautiful, for a civil service. We all cried.'

'Of course you did,' he replied.

'I went to see the Story Wife of Marburg,' she said, unable to keep back her smile.

'You did? Dortchen, bless you. Did she tell you any stories?'

'Two,' Dortchen replied. 'One is the Golden Bird, which I know you know, but another is entirely new. I promise you'll love it.' She held out her sheaf of papers.

'Your timing could not be better,' Wilhelm said, looking over the first story quickly. 'We are about to send Clemens our manuscript – he might publish them in a third collection of *The Boy's Wonder Horn*. Wouldn't that be wonderful?'

He reached the end of the story, then turned to the second sheaf of papers. Dortchen watched him anxiously, hoping he would love it as much as she did. He looked up once or twice with glowing eyes, then continued to read. When he reached the end, he cast the papers down on the table and caught her in one arm, kissing her on the mouth. It lasted only a second but was indescribably sweet. Dortchen blushed crimson.

'I'm sorry!' he cried. 'I didn't mean to . . . It is just such a wonderful story. Thank you, Dortchen, thank you!'

'I'm glad you like it,' she answered shyly, then she went out, shutting the door behind her. In the dark stairwell she leant against the wall, pressing the back of her hand against her mouth, trying to stop the smile that insisted on growing there.

PART FOUR

The Singing Bone

CASSEL

The Kingdom of Westphalia, 1810 – 1811

A shepherd drove his herd across the bridge and saw a little snow-white bone lying in the sand below. Thinking that it would make a good mouthpiece for his horn, he climbed down, picked it up, and carved it. When he blew into it for the first time, to his great astonishment the bone began to sing by itself:

'Oh, my dear shepherd,
You are blowing on my little bone.
My brothers killed me,
And buried me beneath the bridge,
To get the wild boar
For the daughter of the king.'

'What a wonderful horn,' said the shepherd. 'It sings by itself. I must take it to the king.' When he brought it before the king, the horn again began to sing its little song. The king understood it well, and had the earth beneath the bridge dug up. Then the whole skeleton of the murdered man came to light.

From 'The Singing Bone', a tale told by Dortchen Wild to Wilhelm Grimm on 19th January 1812

THIEF IN THE NIGHT

January 1811

Dortchen woke from a deep sleep with a start.

She lay in her warm bed, listening. There was a muffled crash, then the quail in its cage began to call a warning. She heard her father's feet hit the floor and the sound of him running. Dortchen got up quickly, putting on her slippers and catching up her shawl. As she went out onto the landing, Old Marie opened her door and came out too, a candle in her hand.

'Is it burglars?' she asked in a quavering voice.

'I don't know,' Dortchen replied.

Together they went downstairs. Mia joined them on the way, her strawberry-blonde hair hanging down her back in a tousled plait, a shawl wrapped over her nightgown. Röse peered out of her door, her fair hair as neat as if she had just plaited it. 'Have you lost your senses?' she whispered. 'If some thief is below, do you wish to tempt him to violence? Stay safe in your room, sisters.'

A pistol shot rang out. Mia and Dortchen jumped and cried out, clutching at each other. With Old Marie huffing behind, they ran down the stairs and into the shop.

Their father stood at the far end of the stillroom, the door into the garden hanging open and letting in a blast of cold air. He held a smoking pistol in his hand and rammed another lead shot into it. Then he ran out into the snowy garden, his nightgown flapping under his frockcoat. A few seconds later they heard the garden gate bang open, then another pistol shot. The spray of sparks from the pistol lit up their father's face.

'No!' Dortchen cried, then bit her lip.

Her father locked the gate again, and stumped towards them. 'He's gone, the scoundrel,' he said. 'The gate was still locked – he must've come over the wall. I saw a shadow slipping away down the alley but must've missed him. My powder's damp, damn it.'

The girls stepped back to allow him back into the stillroom. Herr Wild looked around irritably. There was broken glass all over the floor, and a puddle of some strong-smelling brown liquid. 'He's knocked over a bottle of cordial. Get it cleaned up, will you, Marie?'

Old Marie nodded and went in search of a mop. Herr Wild put down the pistol on the benchtop and said, 'Look, the cupboard has been forced open. That scoundrel knew exactly what he was looking for.'

He went over and looked through the cupboard, its door swinging off one hinge. 'All the opium's gone, and the tincture I'd made up. Nothing else. The thief knew exactly what he was looking for and where to find it.'

A terrible thought occurred to Dortchen. Could Ferdinand Grimm be the thief? She had shown him where the opium was kept. She pushed the thought away, upset with herself for thinking such a thing. It had been months since he had asked her for laudanum. Surely he would not have broken into her father's shop in search of it?

Her father saw her face and his eyes narrowed. 'What do you know about this, Dortchen?'

'Nothing, Father,' she answered.

He took a hasty step towards her. 'You lie! You think I'm a fool? Did you tell some lover of yours how to get in over the back wall? Did you tell him where the opium was kept?'

'No, of course not! . . . How can you think such a thing?'

He rushed forward and seized her by the untidy mass of her braid, dragging on it so hard she stumbled and fell to her knees before him. 'Tell me the truth!'

'I am telling the truth. Father, stop, you're hurting me!'

'I paid a fortune for that opium,' he said in a chilly voice. 'It'll be the devil of a job replacing it. And how am I to pay for it? That opium would have kept us in food for months. Now it's gone. And you know who took it.' He shook her so hard she felt as if her hair was being torn out by its roots.

Tears sprang to her eyes. 'Father, I swear . . . on the Holy Bible . . . I know nothing.'

He let her go and she fell to the ground, her nightgown billowing up around her. Hastily she pulled it down, huddling her shawl about her. She was very conscious of her father looking down at her, his eyes glinting.

'Excuse me, sir, I need to sweep up,' Old Marie said, standing in the doorway with a mop and duster in her hand.

Herr Wild muttered a low curse and turned away, going to the sideboard. He poured himself a snifter of quince brandy and tossed it back. Dortchen scrambled to her feet and hurried away, feeling sick and shaky.

Mia followed behind her. As they went back into the cold, draughty house, she slipped her hand into Dortchen's.

'But I need my drops,' Frau Wild said. 'You know they are the only things that help me.'

'You'll have to manage without them for a while,' Herr Wild said.

'But I can't . . . I'm in pain . . .'

'There's nothing I can do about it, Katharina. The blockade means I cannot buy opium from India, which means it must come over the Alps from Turkey, with bandits and rebels and battlefields the whole way. I can make you up a tincture of willowbark and henbane. That's the best I can do.'

Frau Wild took to her bed and stayed there, keeping Dortchen and Mia busy carrying up trays with broth and hot flannels and healing teas. Röse offered to comfort her mother by reading to her from the psalm book, but Frau Wild put her hand to her head and begged her daughter to desist.

That night, while she lay awake in her bed, Dortchen could hear her parents arguing downstairs. She got up, went out and sat on the stairs, listening, her stomach twisting.

'Please, no, sir,' her mother whimpered. 'I'm not well.'

'A man has needs, Katharina, as you well know.' Herr Wild's voice was loud.

'Please, no . . .'

Then her mother fell silent, and all Dortchen could hear was a kind of low grunting, like a pig at the trough. Dortchen ran back to her bed, making a cave of her eiderdown, pressing her pillow over her ears. It was a long time before she slept. She felt uneasy and afraid, though she had no idea what to fear.

The next day – Sunday – was miserable and grey. Sleet gusted past the windows and rattled the chimneys. The Wild family prepared for church as usual. Frau Wild dragged herself from her bed, her thin face pale and sweaty, and dressed herself in an assortment of shawls and scarves. Dortchen knew she would have preferred to stay in bed, but Herr Wild would never let anyone miss church.

There was only Röse, Dortchen and Mia left at home, for Rudolf had gone off to do his final training in Berlin. They trailed after their parents through the slushy streets, the hems of their gowns growing sodden. The church seemed colder and gloomier than ever, and half the pews were empty.

One quick glance was enough to show Dortchen that Ferdinand was not present. Jakob and Wilhelm were there, in shabby coats and badly knitted scarves, their thin faces pale. Lotte looked tired and worried. Dortchen felt anxiety roiling in her stomach.

After the service, everyone met in the church porch to exchange pleasantries. Most of the talk was about the threat of war with Russia, for the Tsar had a month earlier declared that he would no longer support the Continental blockade, the means by which Napoléon hoped to break England.

'The blockade has failed, and the Ogre should admit it,' Lotte said. 'As long as England rules the waves, she ships anything she needs from her colonies. It is us who are suffering.'

'He's calling for more conscripts,' Frau Hassenpflug replied, one hand on her son Louis's arm. 'Please, let him not take our boys.'

'I'd rather blow my own leg off than march on Russia,' Louis said, tight-lipped and grim. 'Surely Napoléon cannot think to beat the Tsar?'

'He's beaten the rest of the world – why not Russia?' Frau Wild said in a faint voice.

'He's not beaten England yet,' Wilhelm said, 'and they say the war on the Peninsula is costing him dearly.'

'Yes, but the King of England is a raving lunatic,' Herr Wild said impatiently. 'They say the death of his youngest daughter tipped him over the edge, and they must keep him locked away. With a mad king at its helm, how can England possibly hold out against Napoléon?'

'Perhaps the English prince will be declared regent,' Jakob suggested. 'He's a grown man, and keen to take the crown, by all accounts.'

'By all accounts, he's a fat fool more interested in fashion and gambling than in affairs of state,' Herr Wild responded, barely able to contain his irritation at being spoken to by his two young and improvident neighbours.

'The English prime minister is of sound judgement, though, I believe,' Jakob replied stiffly. 'But you must excuse us. Our younger brother is unwell, and I do not wish to leave him alone too long.' He and Wilhelm bowed and put their tall hats on their heads, then turned to beckon Lotte, who was chatting to the Ramus sisters.

Dortchen caught Wilhelm's sleeve. 'What is wrong with Ferdinand?' she asked in a low voice.

Wilhelm shrugged. 'I don't know. He seems to want to sleep all day, and complains of a headache all the time. Certainly it's hard to coax him to eat. He just pushes it away and says he's not hungry, which upsets Lotte, who laboured to make it for him, and exasperates Jakob, who laboured to pay for it.'

Dortchen bit her lip. 'Has he grown thin and pale and listless?'

Wilhelm's gaze sharpened on her face. 'Yes, though he's been so for a while now. Why? What do you suspect?'

She shook her head. 'I'm sorry, I don't know. Have you called the doctor?'

Wilhelm nodded. 'He bled him and recommended he sniff some

smelling salts, and then charged us half a week's wages. Jakob said he's more than happy to bleed Ferdinand himself next time.'

'What about you? How does your work go on?'

Wilhelm's expression lightened. 'Slowly, but steadily. Jakob plans to write a pamphlet calling for contributions and send it out through the country. He has asked for old tales and legends, the sort that might be told for children at bedtime or in the spinning room in winter. We hope many people will respond.'

'What of Herr Brentano? Did he like the stories you sent?'

Wilhelm's face altered. 'We don't know – he didn't say. We've heard nothing from him in all these months.'

Dortchen could not believe it. 'He isn't helping you find a publisher?'

Wilhelm shook his head. 'I'm just glad we went to the trouble of copying all the stories before we sent them to him. It was not easy, you know, with paper so hard to come by now.'

Dortchen nodded her head. The rag-and-bone man was always knocking on the back gate, begging for any scraps of paper they might have; he sold what he could find to the fishmonger and the butcher and the baker, who would wrap their wares in them. The Wilds never had any paper to sell. Dortchen's father now wrapped his sugarplums and marchpane in old newspaper instead of the pretty gold paper he had once used.

'Come, Wilhelm,' Jakob called. Wilhelm lifted his hat, smiled at Dortchen and went on his way.

Dortchen turned back to her family, and realised, with a sudden lurch of her stomach, that her father was watching her.

'I tell you, he's not for you,' Herr Wild said in an undertone, grabbing her arm. 'I see the way you look at him, with those big doe eyes. He's nothing but a sickly wastrel with no income and no prospects. You're to stop seeing him, do you understand?'

'He's our neighbour,' Dortchen replied. 'Does the Holy Bible not tell us to be charitable to our neighbours?'

He squeezed her arm so hard that she gasped. 'Did I fail to make myself clear?'

'No, Father,' she answered, dropping her eyes, trying not to flinch as his grip tightened. He snorted and let her arm go.

THE OPIUM CHEST

January 1811

The next morning, Dortchen was washing the breakfast dishes in the scullery when she heard a frantic knocking at the garden gate. Drying her hands on her apron, she hurried out into the garden, which lay brown and bare under a thin dusting of snow.

Dortchen made a shushing noise as she neared the gate, looking back over her shoulder to be sure her father was not in his stillroom, from where he would hear the knocking and see her go to open the gate. The knocking ceased and Dortchen unlocked the gate, then cautiously eased it open.

Lotte stood on the other side, dressed in an old gown and apron. She had no bonnet or gloves on, and her face was contorted with tears. 'Dortchen, you must come,' she gabbled, catching at Dortchen's hands. 'It's Ferdinand. I cannot wake him. I don't know what to do. Please, Dortchen, help me!'

'What do you mean you can't wake him?'

'I called him and called him, then went in and shook him. I've shouted in his ear, I've slapped his cheeks. Dortchen, he will not wake.'

Dortchen pressed her hands over her eyes. 'I don't know . . . Have you thrown cold water over him?'

Lotte shook her head. 'No, but—'

'Try that. See if it helps.'

'You won't come?'

'I can't. Not now. If you really need me, hang your red shawl out your window – I'll come when I can.' Dortchen glanced at the house, then pushed Lotte out the gate, shutting it in her face. She hurried back to the scullery and her dirty dishes, hoping she had been unobserved.

When next she glanced out the window, Lotte's red shawl was hanging over the washing line, flapping wildly in the wind. It would be frozen solid soon. Dortchen stared at it unhappily. She took down her basket and put in it a small bag of coffee beans and her mother's smelling salts.

'If Father asks for me, I have gone to the market,' she said to Old Marie. 'What do you need?'

Old Marie looked at her in surprise. It was not wash day, the only day she had no time to do the shopping.

'I need to get out,' Dortchen said.

'Be careful,' Old Marie said. 'Don't anger him.'

'I'm just going to the market. Is there not some job you must do that will keep you busy here?'

Old Marie sighed. 'I suppose I could clean the silver.'

She told Dortchen what she needed, and Dortchen put her arms about Old Marie's plump form and kissed her. 'Thank you.' Then she put on her bonnet and gloves, wrapped a heavy cloak about her and went across the alley to the Grimms' house.

Dortchen was chilled through even after those few small steps, but Lotte was looking out for her and flung open the door and drew her in. 'Thank you so much,' she said. 'I hope I didn't get you into trouble?'

'No, no,' Dortchen said. 'How's Ferdinand?'

'The cold water roused him a little, but he's fallen asleep again now. He looks so strange . . . we're all so worried.'

'I brought some coffee,' Dortchen said. 'That may help. Let's put it on, then see if my mother's smelling salts do any good.'

Once the coffee pot was hanging over the fire, Dortchen went with Lotte into Ferdinand's bedroom, feeling very self-conscious. Jakob and Wilhelm were both trying to rouse their brother, shaking him and calling his name. Their faces were white and frightened. They had dragged the curtains open, so that the pale winter light struck in through the mullioned windows.

Ferdinand lay back against his pillows, his dark curls damp, his eyes shut. His head lolled, and his arms were as limp as empty coat-sleeves. His nightgown and pillow were stained with water, and a bucket sat on the floor. As Jakob shook him, Ferdinand's eyes opened a slit, showing the black edge of a greatly dilated pupil.

'Dortchen, you've come.' Wilhelm seized both her hands in his. 'Thank you.' He smiled down at her with such warmth in his eyes that Dortchen felt colour rise in her cheeks.

'I cannot stay long,' she said. 'I'm meant to be at the market. Let me look at him.'

Wilhelm stood back, and Dortchen bent over Ferdinand. She felt for his pulse, as she had seen her father do; it seemed sluggish and uneven. His skin was clammy and cold, though that may have been the effect of the icy water. She bent and smelt his breath. There was the distinctive whiff of laudanum, and she bit her lip in distress.

'I don't know . . . I'm not sure, but I think he may have drunk too much laudanum,' she said. 'It makes people sleepy. Perhaps, if you drink too much, it makes it hard to wake up.'

'Laudanum!' Jakob cried. 'But where would he get the stuff?'

'He's been buying it from my father for quite some time,' Dortchen said. 'I saw Ferdinand's name in his book.'

'But how could he afford it? It's not cheap,' Jakob said. 'It almost broke our backs buying some for our mother, when she was ill.' He straightened, looking at Wilhelm. 'The money tin.'

'Surely he wouldn't . . .' Wilhelm said.

'You blamed me,' Lotte said angrily. 'You said I was not keeping my housekeeping accounts well enough, and accused me of buying myself treats.'

'Yes, but . . .' Jakob began, then looked back at his brother. 'I cannot believe he would steal from us.'

'You believed it of me,' Lotte said in a resentful tone.

'No, no, we thought . . . Well, we simply thought it was a mistake.'

While they argued, Dortchen was waving her mother's smelling salts under Ferdinand's nose. At first, it had no effect, then Ferdinand coughed and his eyes opened, staring blankly before him.

'Ferdinand,' Dortchen called, bending towards him. 'You need to wake up.'

'Dortchen,' he whispered, his voice hoarse. 'You've come to me. Did you know I wanted you?' His eyes began to slide closed.

'Ferdinand, you mustn't go to sleep again. Sit up.' She nodded to Wilhelm, who lifted Ferdinand up. 'Lotte, go and make the coffee,' Dortchen said, and her friend flew out of the room, leaving Dortchen alone in the bedroom with three young men. Although this made her feel most uncomfortable, Dortchen focused all her attention on Ferdinand, again waving the smelling salts under his nose.

He smiled at her mistily. 'You look like an angel.'

'You need to wake up, Ferdinand. You need to get up and walk around.' She looked at Wilhelm, who folded back the bedclothes and pulled Ferdinand up. Jakob bent and freed his brother's bare legs, and drew them around till he was sitting on the end of the bed.

Dortchen looked away, never having seen a man's bare legs before. In deference to her embarrassment, Wilhelm caught up a long dressing gown and wrapped it around Ferdinand, doing his best to cover the naked skin. Lotte came back in, carrying a steaming hot cup.

'Coffee,' Wilhelm said. 'Dortchen, you shouldn't have.'

'It's the only thing I could think of,' Dortchen said. 'Father will have to drink ground acorns like the rest of us for a while.'

Wilhelm took the cup and held it to Ferdinand's lips, but his brother was growing agitated and almost knocked it out of his hand. 'Dortchen!' he cried.

Dortchen stepped back into his line of sight. 'I'm here, Ferdinand,' she said. 'Be still, all is well. You just need to wake up now. Drink your coffee, else we'll all gladly have it instead.'

'I haven't had coffee in months,' Lotte said.

Dortchen managed to coax Ferdinand to drink a few mouthfuls, then Wilhelm and Jakob together made him walk about the room. His legs were wobbly and his brothers bore most of his weight, but he was awake enough to grumble and to look about, calling for Dortchen.

'Why did you do it, Ferdinand?' Jakob asked. 'A healthy young man like you doesn't need laudanum. Where did you get the money?'

Ferdinand grew distressed. He struggled to get away from his brothers. 'You don't understand . . . You're so perfect all the time . . . I do my best, but it's never enough for you . . . I can't sleep without it . . . too many ghosts, too many failures . . .'

While his brothers struggled to calm him, Dortchen looked swiftly around the room. She saw a small brown bottle that had fallen to the ground – she recognised it as one that her father sold. It was empty but smelt of laudanum. That alone did not prove that Ferdinand had been the thief who had broken into the stillroom. She had to find the stolen opium.

Lotte was busy trying to persuade Ferdinand to drink more coffee, while his two brothers held him steady. Dortchen bent and looked under the bed, then opened Ferdinand's clothes chest. Under a few threadbare shirts and cravats, she found a small wooden chest stamped with a strange, exotic symbol. She quickly opened the chest and found, as she had expected, a number of large balls wrapped in dried leaves and petals. The smell was overpowering, sweet yet pungent. One of the balls had been broken open, revealing a lump of sticky brown substance with a hole gouged out of one side.

'What's that?' Wilhelm asked, coming to stand beside her.

Dortchen shut the chest and cradled it against her, turning to face him. 'My father's shop was robbed earlier this week,' she said. 'His opium was taken, plus all the laudanum he had made up.'

'Are you suggesting you think Ferdinand was the thief?' Wilhelm demanded. 'No, I don't believe it. He wouldn't break in to your house and steal laudanum. Why would he?'

Dortchen gazed at him unhappily. 'Laudanum . . . Some people come to like it too much, to rely on it.' She thought of her mother. 'My father is always complaining about how hard it is to keep up supplies to some of his customers, who come asking for it more and more often. That's what Ferdinand was doing. And . . .' She paused, upset by the look on Wilhelm's face. She took a deep breath and forged on. 'Wilhelm, he came to me last year, asking me to get some for him. I said that I couldn't, and showed him how the cupboard was kept locked.'

'He couldn't have stolen it – he's not a thief.'

'This is my father's opium,' Dortchen said. 'I have to return it to him. We cannot afford to replace it. There's hundreds of thalers' worth in this.'

Her heart quailed within her. Wilhelm was looking at her so angrily, and she could not think how to get the opium back to her father without him realising she'd had a hand in it.

Ferdinand saw what Dortchen was holding and came at her in a rush. 'No, you cannot take it back.'

Dortchen flinched as Ferdinand seized her arms, but Wilhelm caught him and pulled him away roughly. Ferdinand stumbled and almost fell.

'Don't you see?' he pleaded. 'I need it. I need it! It's the only thing that makes me happy. Dortchen, please.' Ferdinand came towards her again, hands held out, but his brother held him back.

Wilhelm was so distressed that he could scarcely speak. 'Dortchen says he stole the laudanum from Herr Wild's shop,' he said to Jakob. 'She says this chest is her father's.'

Silently, Dortchen showed Jakob the balls of raw opium.

He regarded them grimly. 'Well, clearly they aren't Ferdinand's.' He looked at his brother. 'Ferdinand must return them to your father and apologise.'

'Oh, no, please, don't,' Dortchen blurted in response. 'I'm sorry, it's just . . . he'd be so angry. He already thinks so badly of you all. I'm sorry, but he does. Couldn't we just return the chest, without him knowing who—'

'You mean, return it on the sly?' Jakob said. 'That would be dishonest.'

'Father would have Ferdinand hauled up before the court,' Dortchen said. 'Is the penalty for theft not hard labour? It would kill him.'

Ferdinand was half-swooning in Wilhelm's arms, his hands reaching towards the chest. 'I'm sorry . . . I must have it . . . Don't you understand? Give it back . . .'

Jakob and Wilhelm's eyes met. Wilhelm nodded slightly.

'We thank you, then,' Jakob said. 'If you can replace the opium without your father realising . . . I will give you some coins to cover the cost of what he has already taken.'

'It's too dangerous,' Wilhelm said. 'What if Herr Wild catches her putting it back? He will suspect her. Give the chest to me. I will leave it on the doorstep tomorrow at first light.'

Jakob nodded. 'Good idea.'

Dortchen's breath whooshed out in a great sigh of relief.

'Ferdinand can write a letter of apology and leave it with the chest,' Jakob continued.

'Unsigned,' Dortchen said. Jakob and Wilhelm nodded in agreement.

'Very well,' she said. 'I have to go. My father will kill me if he catches me here.'

'Thank you. I'm sorry.' Wilhelm spoke awkwardly, not meeting her eyes. 'It's difficult to believe my own brother would stoop so low.'

'He's dragged down by grief and melancholy,' Dortchen said. 'It's not easy for him to follow in your footsteps. He feels—' she struggled to find a word that would not be cruel to utter, 'unworthy.'

Ferdinand turned away, stumbling to his writing table, where he sank down on the stool, his face bent down, his fingers sunk into his hair. 'It's fine for you,' he said to Jakob. 'You and Wilhelm were given everything – the fine education, the years at university. Yet you blame me for not being able to get a job, or to settle down to study on my own. I'm sorry, all right? I'm sorry.'

He laid his head on his arms and shut his eyes.

'I'll leave you the smelling salts. Whatever you do, don't let him sleep.' Dortchen looked around at her friends. They were all mortified and angry. She felt they blamed her for finding the chest. Gently, she put it in Wilhelm's hands. 'Don't be caught putting it back,' she warned him. 'I don't want you being sentenced to hard labour either.'

He did not answer her.

MAIDEN WITH NO HANDS

March 1811

'How is he?' Dortchen asked.

Wilhelm shook his head. 'Not well at all. He must be getting hold of more somewhere. He goes out of the house raging, and comes home hours later dizzy and sick and smiling.'

Dortchen was distressed, but she had to school her countenance to composure. As usual, the only chance she ever got to speak to Wilhelm was in the church porch, in full view of their families and neighbours.

'I've been trying to keep an eye on the shop, to make sure he does not come in,' Dortchen said. 'But it's impossible. I'm so busy all the time.'

'Could you not ask your father?'

'No.' Realising how sharp her tone was, Dortchen said more gently, 'I'm sorry. But I dare not. He will guess who stole the opium.'

Wilhelm sighed. 'Jakob has locked away the household funds . . . I cannot imagine where Ferdinand is getting the money from.'

'It must be a great worry to you.'

He nodded. 'Jakob is at work all day, so he expects me to keep an eye on Ferdinand. But how can I, unless I lock him in his bedroom? I have work of my own to do.'

'Have you found any more new stories?'

'We have. An old soldier called Johann responded to Jakob's pamphlet and has given us a few stories in return for our old trousers. It shows you what desperate straits he's in if he's prepared to wear our threadbare cast-offs. He told us a very funny story about an old dog whose owner wanted to shoot him. The dog made a deal with a wolf, who agreed to pretend to steal his owner's child so the dog could rescue the baby and be spared.'

Dortchen smiled, but, conscious of her father's glare, said, 'I'm glad you're finding some new stories. I must go now.'

Wilhelm detained her with a quick hand on her arm. 'Perhaps I will see you this evening at the King's celebration? They're going to have fireworks and a cavalry charge and opera singers on barges. It should be a grand spectacle.'

'I cannot go,' Dortchen said. 'Father says I gaddy about too much as it is.'

'When do you ever gaddy about?' Wilhelm said. 'You hardly ever come to the storytelling circle any more.'

'I'm not allowed,' Dortchen said. 'Too much work to do.'

'What of your sisters? Are they allowed to go tonight?' Wilhelm was frowning, his mouth set sternly.

Dortchen nodded. 'Rose said she was more than happy to stay home and look after Mother, but Father says she must go. He wishes her to be on her best behaviour as he is going to introduce her to someone. She's to leave her spectacles at home.'

'That sounds ominous,' Wilhelm said.

Dortchen had to smile. 'It does, doesn't it? Röse says she is willing to immolate herself on the altar of parental authority, if she must, but why is she obliged to do without her spectacles?'

'He must be an ugly old man,' Wilhelm said.

'That's what I think too.' Dortchen would have liked to have told him that she suspected her father of arranging a marriage for Röse to salve his wounded pride over Hanne's defiance, but her father was scowling at her and so she only bent her head and went to talk commonplaces with the Ramus sisters.

Dortchen was not unhappy to be left alone with her mother and Old Marie that evening, while her father went out with Röse and Mia. She lit a fire in the drawing room, and the three of them settled down to sew more muslin bags for the shop and chat by the warmth of the flames. Darkness had fallen early outside, and Dortchen had drawn the curtains and brought up a tray of tea for them to share.

A knock sounded on the front door.

'Why, whoever could that be?' Frau Wild said sleepily from her couch, where she lay with a rug over her legs. She had been most relieved at the mysterious reappearance of the stolen opium and had been sipping from her bottle all afternoon.

Dortchen's heart was singing. 'It'll be Wilhelm and Lotte,' she said with utter certainty.

Both her mother and Old Marie looked concerned, but Dortchen hurried down the stairs. Old Marie huffed behind her, bleating, 'Dortchen, sweetling, it's not seemly – let me answer the door.'

To Dortchen's surprise, Jakob was with his brother and sister on the doorstep. 'You did not go to watch the spectacle?' she asked him, taking his coat and hat and scarf.

'Another French victory does not give me joy,' he answered gravely. 'I had hopes that this new English commander Wellington would prove Napoléon's undoing in Spain, but they've been in deadlock for months. Now the French have won back Badajoz, I think it cannot be long before the English are driven from the Peninsula.'

'But has not Wellington built massive earthworks and fortifications all along the Portuguese border?' Wilhelm said, smiling down at Dortchen as he relinquished his hat and coat to her. 'Surely that will stop the French.'

Jakob sighed. 'Let us hope so.'

They went up the stairs in melancholy silence. The newspapers were calling the war in the Peninsula 'the Spanish ulcer', since it was a wound that refused to heal. Hundreds of thousands of men had already died there, defending ruined towns and potholed roads, yet Napoléon refused to give up, sending thousands more to die for his determination to break the spirit of the Spanish and force them to be yet another puppet kingdom, ruled by one of his brothers.

Frau Wild sat up as the three visitors entered the room, looking worried and patting ineffectually at her hair, which was falling out of its pins as usual. 'Such a surprise,' she said. 'We were not expecting.'

'We heard you have been unwell,' Jakob said. 'We do hope you are felling better.'

Frau Wild pressed one hand against her breast. 'Well as can be expected,' she replied.

The two Grimm brothers sat down by the fire, looking about the room with interest. In the warm firelight, it seemed cosy and welcoming in a way that the formal parlour never did. A vase full of pussywillow and narcissus stood on the mantelpiece, and a large bowl of sugarplums sat on the table. Dortchen offered them around and everyone took one, even Jakob.

They talked of the war and the new tax on tea and sugar and pepper, and the difficulty of finding good wool since the blockades were keeping British products from their shore. Then Old Marie came back up the stairs with freshly made herbal tea, and little damp cakes made from chestnuts. She made to go back down to the kitchen but Dortchen cried, 'No, Marie, stay with us. Why don't you tell us all a story? I know Jakob and Wilhelm would be glad to hear one.'

Old Marie hesitated, then sat on the hardest chair in the room, smoothing down her skirts. 'If you don't mind, ma'am,' she said to Dortchen's mother, who waved her hand vaguely and murmured, 'Not at all.'

'I'll get paper and quills,' Dortchen said to Wilhelm, hurrying across to the writing desk against the wall. He smiled at her as she returned, her arms full.

'You're very kind,' he said to her in a low voice. 'How did you know I was longing to hear another of Old Marie's wonderful stories?'

'You must seize the chance when it's offered to you,' she replied. 'It's not often Father's out.'

'What story would you like, sir?' Old Marie asked, taking up her sewing again.

'One we haven't heard before,' Wilhelm answered.

'Do you know the one about Little Brother and Little Sister?' she asked.

'Do you mean the one about the witch and the house made of gingerbread? Yes, Dortchen has told me that one.'

'No, this is a different tale, about a brother who drinks enchanted water and is turned into a deer. His sister looks after him till one day she is discovered by a king, who falls in love with her and marries her.'

'No, I haven't heard that one,' Wilhelm said, unscrewing the inkpot and dipping in his quill. Excitement was gleaming in his dark eyes.

As Old Marie told the story, Dortchen took up a needle and thread and the basket of darning, and settled down to sew and listen. Smiling, Lotte did the same, while Jakob sat forward, his gaze intent on Old Marie's wrinkled face, his hands clasped loosely before him. Wilhelm's quill scratched on the paper. Frau Wild sighed, leant her head back against a cushion and closed her eyes.

When the story had finished, with the queen and her children saved from betrayal and death, Wilhelm laid down his quill with a sigh.

'We must put it in the collection,' he said to Jakob. 'Yet we'll need to rename it. We can't have two tales called "Little Brother and Little Sister" – it'd be confusing.'

'You could give the children names,' Dortchen suggested.

'Like what?'

'I don't know.' Dortchen thought for a moment. 'Names for two clever children. Names for two children who outsmart their elders.' She was reminded of a little rhyme Old Marie always used to say: 'What Hänschen doesn't learn, Hans never will.' She had often said it to Gretchen, to encourage her to learn how to bake bread and wash linen and tend the fires while she had the chance.

'Something that rhymes,' Wilhelm said. 'It always sounds better if it rhymes.'

'How about Hänschen and Gretch—' she began, but she did not want to give the brave little girl of the story the same name as her own vain and self-centred sister. 'What about Hänsel and Gretel?'

'Sounds good,' Wilhelm said. 'But we'll give those names to the other Little Brother and Little Sister tale – the one about the gingerbread house – since you were the one to tell it to us.'

Dortchen flushed with pleasure.

'Do we have time for another story?' Wilhelm asked. 'We never seem to be able to sit in quietness like this and share tales.'

'Talking about names, I know a tale you'll like,' Dortchen cried. 'If only I can remember it. It's about a girl who the king thinks can spin straw into gold, so he marries her, hoping for wealth and power. But it was all a lie of her father's, and if the king finds out he'll kill her.'

Wilhelm drew a fresh piece of paper towards him. 'Tell it to me.'

Dortchen told him eagerly, her eyes fixed on his face. The others in the quiet room seemed to fade away into the shadows, as if she and Wilhelm were alone in the circle of firelight, his quill recording her every word, his eyes continually rising to meet hers, to gaze at her face, her mouth, before looking away again as he hurried to catch up with the story. Dortchen found it hard to breathe – her stays felt too tight upon her ribs, her skin hot and flushed from the fire, her blood fizzing with some indescribable emotion. Joy and fear and longing, and something strange and eager and quick.

When she had finished the tale, with its grotesque villain and his secret name, there was silence for a long moment. Dortchen and Wilhelm sat smiling at each other, oblivious to anyone else.

'Thank you – it's a marvellous story,' Wilhelm said, his voice low and gruff. 'You tell it so beautifully. I can never hope to capture it half as well.'

Dortchen's flush deepened till she felt her whole body was on fire.

'I have another tale for you, if you like,' Old Marie said, breaking the spell.

Dortchen sat back, embarrassed, aware of everyone's curious eyes on her face. Wilhelm turned to Old Marie politely. 'Of course, that would be wonderful.'

'It's about a father who cuts off his daughter's hands,' Old Marie said. She was sitting forward in her chair, her hands tense and still upon her sewing.

'I don't think I've heard that one before,' Dortchen exclaimed.

Old Marie regarded her with sombre eyes. 'It's not a tale for children.'

'Jakob, you may need to write this one down,' Wilhelm said, shaking his ink-stained fingers. 'My hand is aching.'

Jakob came to sit at the table, taking up a fresh quill and sheaf of paper. Wilhelm sat on the hearthrug, so close to Dortchen that she could have reached out and run her fingers through his crisp, dark curls. She was very conscious of his warm body, leaning so close to her knee, and his pale, long-fingered hand, hanging down. If he had wanted to, he could have leant forward and cupped her calf through the thin material of her dress. The idea of it made her stomach twist and her loins clench.

Old Marie's story was about a poor miller who promised the Devil his daughter in return for wealth. When she proved too good for the Devil to take, he chopped off her hands and drove her out into the world.

As Old Marie told the story, Dortchen felt the blood drain from her face till she was afraid she might faint. She sat back in her chair, turning her cheek against the hard wood, her knees twisting away from where Wilhelm sat. She was conscious of his troubled gaze but would not meet his eyes. She could not have explained why Old Marie's story horrified her so much. Surely it was just a story?

No story was just a story, though. It was a suitcase stuffed with secrets.

Old Marie spoke on steadily. In her tale, the girl without hands sought refuge in a king's walled garden, and he took pity on her beauty and helplessness and married her. A pair of silver hands was forged for her. The king's mother was horrified by his choice, however, and plotted to discredit the handless maiden. She had to flee back into the forest, taking her young son with her. There she was helped by a mysterious old man, who told her to wrap her maimed arms about a tree. The girl did as she was told, and her hands magically grew back.

Dortchen heard the front door open. She started up, filled with terror. Old Marie darted a look at the sitting-room door, then stared at Wilhelm, her voice rising and quickening as she hurried to finish her tale. Wilhelm stared back at her, looking tense.

Frau Wild sat up too, her hand groping for her drops. 'Perhaps . . . another day?' she suggested.

Old Marie paid her no heed. 'The king, meanwhile, had been searching for his poor, maimed wife all through the vast, dark forest. He found his queen and his son by the spring, but could not believe the beautiful woman with the flawless white hands could be his wife. She showed him the silver-forged hands as proof, and he embraced her joyfully, crying, "Now a heavy stone has fallen from my heart."'

Jakob wrote swiftly, the scratch and dip of his quill drowned out by the stamp of feet on the steps, the sound of Mia's high voice and the low growl as her father replied.

'And so she was healed, and all was forgiven and forgotten, and the king and his queen celebrated a second wedding feast, for now at last they were equals,' Old Marie said rapidly. Jakob wrote the last few words, laying down his quill just as the door to the sitting room opened and Herr Wild stepped in.

He looked around the shadowy, firelit room with lowering brows. Wilhelm scrambled to his feet, stepping away from Dortchen's chair. Jakob rose more slowly, bowing his head in greeting, while Lotte jumped up, looking scared. Old Marie kept placidly sewing, her white-capped head bent over her hands.

'Oh, you're home,' Frau Wild said, twisting her handkerchief in her hands. 'Did you have a pleasant evening? Look, we've had company too. So kind. Enquiring after my health.'

'Is that so?' Herr Wild replied unpleasantly. 'How very officious. You do all look cosy. We, however, are chilled to the bone. Marie, do you think you could bestir yourself to warm us some soup?'

'Of course, sir,' she answered, rising to her feet.

Röse opened the door and stumbled in, windswept and woebegone. 'Mother?' she said. 'Mother, are you here?' Her eyes were red-rimmed, her nose pink at the tip.

'Of course, my little love,' Frau Wild said, sitting quite upright. 'Whatever is the matter?'

Röse went in a rush across to her mother's couch, collapsing in a welter of skirts beside it. A sob broke from her.

'Why, nothing at all is the matter,' Herr Wild said heartily. 'She is to be congratulated. Our little Röse is to be married.'

CLAMOUR OF BELLS

March 1811

On 20th March 1811, Napoléon Bonaparte's son was born in Paris. As soon as the news reached Cassel, a clamour of bells rang all through the town, continuing on and on all afternoon.

'I wish they would shut up,' Mia said crossly. 'It's giving me such a headache.'

'The Ogre will never be defeated now, will he?' Dortchen said. 'It's a dynasty. Napoléon and his descendants will rule us forever.'

Both girls were leaning on pitchforks in the herb garden, their hands muddy, their aprons smeared with dirt. A barrow of compost steamed nearby. With Rudolf gone to Berlin, the hard work of digging and cleaning out the sty and the stables was now done by his sisters, on top of all the extra work in the house and stillroom.

'I suppose we must just get used to it,' Mia said. 'After all, it's been five years now.'

'I'll never get used to it,' Dortchen said. 'Never.'

'We should be practising our French,' Mia said. 'I heard they plan to outlaw German altogether. Besides, Father needs us in the shop. He's too old a dog to learn new tricks.'

Dortchen said nothing. She was being stupid with her French on purpose, so her father would not call her to help him in the shop. That only made him angry and impatient with her, though, and he humiliated her by calling her in anyway and watching as she did her best to stutter through.

That night there was a ball at Napoléonshöhe. Many girls from the town were invited. If Rudolf had been home, he would have got tickets for his sisters. But Rudolf was not home. Lotte, who had just turned eighteen, was to go with her brother and the Hassenpflug family. Dortchen tried not to mind. It was her eighteenth birthday in three days, and while all the girls of the town dressed in their best and waltzed the night away, she had to stay at home, peeling turnips and feeding the pig.

Frau Wild was unwell again and kept to her bed, and so Herr Wild supped with his three youngest daughters, who sat in a row at the long, dark table, their heads bowed over their meagre meal.

'Soon you'll be sitting at the head of your own table,' he said to Röse, who bent her face closer to her plate to hide the tears in her eyes.

'Oh, for goodness' sake!' he cried. 'You'd think you would be glad at the prospect of marrying a well-established gentleman with his own business. But no, all I get is this weeping and whining. And I thought you the good, obedient child.'

Röse got up and ran from the room. Herr Wild turned his frown on his other daughters and poured himself another deep glass of quince brandy. By the time Mia and Dortchen were permitted to rise and clear the table, most of the bottle had gone.

As Mia and Dortchen washed up in the scullery, the younger sister turned to the elder sister and said, in a low, scared voice, 'He's really old, Dortchen. Older even than Father.'

'The man Röse is to marry?'

'Yes. He's old and fat and he smells of beer. And he didn't talk to Röse at all. He just asked Father if she was good and obedient, then said it was a shame she was so scrawny.'

Dortchen wiped the plate again and again, even though it shone with cleanliness.

'If it was me, I'd run away,' Mia said.

'Where?' Dortchen said. 'Where would you go?'

Mia shrugged and looked miserable.

'Where could you go?' Dortchen said in a low voice.

There was nowhere.

Dortchen and Mia put on their nightgowns and tiptoed through the cold, dark corridors to their rooms, Dortchen carrying Röse's flannel-wrapped bed-warmer in one hand and her own in the other. Röse was lying face-down and fully dressed on her bed. 'Get changed and hop into bed,' Dortchen said, her pity making it hard for her to speak. 'I'll warm your bed for you.'

Röse sat up and drearily began to undress, as Dortchen slid the pan full of hot coals between the icy sheets.

'I'm so sorry,' Dortchen said, knowing her words were no comfort.

Röse shrugged. 'We must do as Father tells us. Doesn't the Bible say so?' She pulled on her nightgown and climbed into bed, huddling into a ball, her back to Dortchen.

Dortchen stood, wanting to say more, wondering if she should pat her sister's shoulder or try to embrace her. Röse had never liked being touched, though. After a moment, she went out and climbed the steep steps to her own room.

Even with her feet on the hot bed-warmer and the eiderdown wrapped around her, Dortchen could not get warm. She sat up, wrapped her shawl about her and leant her head on her knees. She stared across at the dark windows of the Grimms' apartment. Would Wilhelm dance? she wondered. Would he dance with Marie Hassenpflug? Was she smiling up at him now, those glossy, dark ringlets hanging across her smooth shoulders? Was she twirling in his arms, his hand on her slim waist? The very thought of it was agony.

The church bells were striking the half-hour after midnight when lights flowered in the dark Grimm house. Pressing her forehead against the glass, Dortchen could see the revellers going inside, cloaked against the night chill. She heard distant laughter and the sound of the front door shutting. She followed the path of the lantern through the house, as first one window warmed into life and then another. She saw candlelight flicker up in Wilhelm and Jakob's bedroom, towards the front of the house, and then in Lotte's window, in the bedroom directly opposite. Dortchen watched, hoping her friend would open the curtain and look out, but the curtains hung motionless. After a few moments, the candle was blown out and darkness closed in again.

Dortchen slid down, pushing the bed-warmer down so it could warm the arctic regions at the foot of the bed. She began to drift towards sleep. Darkness swallowed her.

Sometime later – she did not know how long – something startled her. A faint cry, a flicker of light at the edge of her eye, some sixth sense that brought her upright, her pulse jumping.

In the Grimm house opposite, a light was moving quickly, erratically, from one window to another, as if someone was running with a candle in hand. More windows glared with light. Dortchen thought she could hear shouting, banging, crashing. She sat and watched, tense and anxious, till the sky began to fade to grey and the orange eyes of the windows opposite no longer seemed quite so ominous. Every sinew and nerve in her body wanted to run across the alleyway and see what was wrong, but she did not dare.

HELTER-SKELTER

March 1811

At last Herr Wild had shaved and breakfasted and gone to open the shop. Dortchen at once dropped the plates in the sink and raced across the alley and up the stairs, into the warm disorder of the Grimm family's kitchen.

Lotte sat weeping by the fire. She looked up as Dortchen opened the door, then flew across the room and into her arms. 'How did you know to come when I needed you so badly? Oh, it's terrible. Ferdinand's gone mad. We don't know what to do. Thank God you're here. We all wanted you. Oh, Dortchen, what can we do?'

'What's happened? What's wrong?'

'Jakob found out that Ferdinand's been stealing things to sell to get more laudanum – Mother's pearl ring, Father's gold cufflinks, a brass candleholder, a little glass vase that Mother always loved . . .' Lotte spoke so fast that all her words came out in a tumble.

'What did Jakob do?' Dortchen asked, her heart sinking.

'He was so furious. He locked Ferdinand in his room yesterday morning. Ferdinand's been in such a rage, banging on the door, shouting. It was unendurable. So we all went out last night – to the ball, you know. To give Ferdinand time to cool off. It was all quiet when we got home. We thought he must have recovered from his temper tantrum, so we went to bed. But, oh, Dortchen, in the middle of the night he began to scream and scream,

258

like imps were dragging him down into hell. Nothing we could do would calm him. He punched Wilhelm and knocked over his stool and threw his chamber pot at Jakob. The mess!'

Dortchen tried to think which of her father's remedies might help such madness and rage. Her father would prescribe laudanum, but Dortchen felt sure in her heart that it was Ferdinand's craving for the opium tincture that was at the root of his problems. She would have suggested chamomile tea, but she knew he would not drink it.

'He's been asking for you,' Lotte said. 'Dortchen, I . . . I think he's in love with you. He keeps yelling out your name, calling you his angel. We found this story . . .'

'What story?' Dortchen demanded.

'A story about a girl called Henriette.'

Her first name. Dortchen stared at Lotte in dismay.

'Dortchen . . . In the story it says that he loves this Henriette, but she is in love with another and all he can do is shoot his rival, or poison him.'

Dortchen sank down onto a chair, twisting the corner of her apron. She had a strange sensation, hot and cold at once, her limbs weakening in a rush. Lotte was staring at her but she could only avert her face.

'Ferdinand was beside himself,' Lotte went on. 'He leapt on Wilhelm and tried to strangle him. Jakob could barely drag him off.'

Dortchen tried to speak but her voice failed her. 'Is . . . is he hurt?' she managed to croak at last.

'Ferdinand or Wilhelm?' Lotte's eyes were intent on her face.

Dortchen felt a betraying flush spread up her chest and face, till it felt as if her cheeks must be scarlet. She would not meet Lotte's gaze. 'Both,' she answered.

'Wilhelm was hurt badly,' Lotte replied. 'Half-strangled to death.'

Dortchen was on her feet, hands pressed against her heart. 'No! Please, tell me he's all right.'

'I knew it!' Lotte crowed, clapping her hands. 'You love him, don't you? Oh, Dortchen, wouldn't it be wonderful? We'd be sisters.'

'How badly is he hurt? Where is he?' Dortchen demanded.

'He's fine, apart from a few scrapes and bruises.' Lotte was smiling in a way that seemed quite heartless to Dortchen. Realising how she had just revealed the most secret part of herself, she sank back into her chair and bent her head down on her arms, so mortified and ashamed that she could not look her friend in the face.

Lotte came and knelt beside her, trying to prise her fingers away. 'What's wrong? Are you crying? Why are you so upset?'

'You mustn't say anything,' Dortchen whispered into the darkness of her arms. 'Please, Lotte.'

'Surely Wilhelm loves you too?'

Dortchen shook her head violently. 'He thinks of me as another little sister.'

'But—'

'I am almost certain he is in love with Marie Hassenpflug.'

'Marie? You think so? I mean, we have been seeing them, because of the stories . . . but I'd swear that's all it is. It's you he asks about all the time.'

Dortchen lifted her face. 'Really?'

Lotte nodded. Her smile was gone and she had an anxious knot between her brows.

'Dortchen,' a grave voice came from behind them.

The two girls whipped round, flushed and startled. Jakob stood in the doorway, dressed only in his shirtsleeves, his jaw dark and rough.

'You've heard about Ferdinand?'

Dortchen nodded.

'He's been asking for you. Will you come and see if you can calm him? I can do nothing with him – it's like he's gone completely mad.'

Dortchen nodded again and stood up, smoothing down her skirt. She hoped there were no signs of tears on her face. Jakob led her along the corridor, with Lotte following behind, and she looked hesitantly into Ferdinand's bedroom.

Ferdinand crouched in the corner between his bed and the clothes chest. His skin was wet with sweat, and his eyes were strangely bright. Every now and again a shudder shook him. Wilhelm sat on the bed, trying to coax him out of the corner. 'You've always hated me,' Ferdinand said, his voice loud and aggressive. 'You want me gone.'

'Of course I don't hate you – how could you say such a thing?' Wilhelm said in distress. 'Please, Ferdinand, will you not get back into bed? You need to rest.'

'You think I can rest? My bones are being gnawed away, my blood is in a fever. Why are you so cruel? Why will you not help me?'

'I want to help you, you know that. What can I do?'

Ferdinand leant forward eagerly. 'Get me some more laudanum, Willi. Please. I have to have it. I'll die without it. Can't you see how much pain I'm in? Please, Willi. Please.'

Wilhelm shook his head.

Ferdinand began to rock back and forth, whimpering like a hurt animal. His hands shook, and sharp tremors jerked his limbs. He looked at his brother with hatred. 'Am I to have nothing? Always, everything was done for you and Jakob, and I was left with nothing. Nothing!' He struck out at Wilhelm, who tried to seize his hands and calm him. Ferdinand cried out at the contact and shrank away, covering his face with his hands.

Dortchen stepped into the room, holding her breath. The room stank – the carpet was stained with the spillage from the chamber pot.

Ferdinand's head whipped around at the sound of her step, then he was on his feet and rushing towards her. 'Dortchen! You've come. I thought they'd keep you away. Dortchen, you've got to help me. They're trying to kill me. Help me get away from here. You . . . you can help me. Dortchen, I need . . . I need more. Please. It's killing me. Won't you help me? Please, Dortchen.'

He shook her roughly. She cried out and tried to get free, but he would not let her go.

'Tell them,' he demanded. 'Tell them I need it. I must have it. Get me some. Dortchen, please, can't you see? It hurts . . . They're trying to kill me . . . Help me.'

Wilhelm and Jakob both raced forward, gripped their brother and struggled to pull him away, but Ferdinand would not let Dortchen go. His fingers dug deep into the soft flesh of her arms, and his eyes stared into hers, wild and strange. She looked at Wilhelm, begging for help.

'Let her go!' Wilhelm cried, wrenching at Ferdinand's arm.

Ferdinand turned and punched Wilhelm hard in the jaw, sending him sprawling. 'You!' he screamed. 'Why must you have everything and me nothing? It's not fair. She's mine, I tell you, mine.' He seized Dortchen in his arms and kissed her, violently and desperately, his hand writhing in her hair.

She tried to twist herself away but could not. She heard the muslin of her dress rip. She tried to cry out but her voice was stifled by his devouring mouth.

Vaguely, she was aware that Jakob was shouting at Ferdinand to stop. Hands pulled at Ferdinand but he would not let her go, his rough stubble searing her soft skin, her mouth mashed against his teeth. As she struggled against him, he caught her wrist in his hand, hurting her.

Finally, Wilhelm managed to hurl him away. Ferdinand fell and Dortchen staggered backward.

'Stop it, stop it!' Lotte screamed.

Panting and in tears, Dortchen pulled together her torn dress. The metallic taste of her own blood was in her mouth. She could still feel the hot brand of Ferdinand's body against her, the feel of his hand at her breast. Blinded by tears, she turned to flee.

Behind her, Ferdinand cried out. 'No, Dortchen, don't go, don't go! I need you. Can't you see how much I need you? Help me! . . .'

Casting a look back over her shoulder, Dortchen saw Ferdinand on the bed, held down by Wilhelm and Jakob, his dark hair in wild disarray. Wilhelm's eyes met hers, angry, disgusted, hurt, accusing. Tears spilt down her face. She ran from the room.

'Wait! Dortchen, wait!' Lotte cried.

But Dortchen did not stop. She ran down the stairs, out the side door and across the alleyway, barely noticing the blast of frigid air that met her. Helter-skelter, she went through the garden gate, wanting only home, safety, silence, seclusion.

Instead, she ran headlong into her father, who was waiting for her in the garden, his arms folded. He took note of the torn lace, her disordered hair, her swollen lip and flushed face.

'Wild by name and wild by nature,' he said coldly. 'I always knew it. Into my study, Dortchen. Now!'

'It's nothing, Father,' she said, holding her dress together. 'I slipped, I fell. Nothing's wrong.'

He cast her a look of scorn and she felt coldness settle down over her. Numbly, she followed him down the hallway. 'You do not need to beat me, Father. I've done nothing wrong.'

'Where have you been?' he demanded.

'Next door. Herr Ferdinand Grimm is unwell. They asked me to look at him.'

'You lie! You were in the arms of your lover. Do you think I don't know the signs? Who is he? This Herr Ferdinand of yours?'

Involuntarily, she shuddered. 'No,' she answered. 'I . . . I have no lover.'

He opened his study door and she hung back, not wanting to go inside. He yanked her in and shut the door behind her. 'We shall see. Bend over and lift your skirt.'

She backed against the desk. 'Father, please – I swear to you, I've done nothing wrong. Please—'

'Do you think I don't know how you deceive me? You are like your whore of a sister, always sneaking out and going behind my back. You think me a fool.'

'No, Father, I swear—'

He slapped her across her face. 'Do as I say!'

When she did not obey, he caught her by the arm and spun her around, forcing her face-down over the desk. He dragged up her skirts. She struggled against him, crying, 'Father, please, this is unseemly – I am not a child.'

'And no maiden either, I'd wager,' he answered her, panting with exertion. He twisted her arm up behind her, making her cry out in pain. He yanked down her drawers.

'Father!'

'Be quiet,' he panted.

She tensed, expecting the sting of the switch against her bare buttocks. Instead, she felt her father's thick fingers enter her from behind. She cried out and he jerked her arm back, forcing her to be still as he probed her.

For a moment, time slowed. She stood still, feeling his fingers thrusting deep, his body forcing her legs further apart.

Then his fingers slid out. He stepped away, fastidiously wiping his hand on his kerchief. 'So you are a maiden still. He has not yet got you on your back, then. Better keep it that way, I warn you. I'll be keeping my eye on you, Dortchen Wild.'

Shaking, she pulled up her drawers and dragged down her skirt. She backed away from him.

He cast her a look of angry impatience. 'Don't look at me with those wounded eyes, Dortchen. You think you're the first maiden I've checked? Go wash yourself and get ready for dinner. It had better not be late.'

Dortchen left the study and stumbled down the hall. She hardly knew where she was. The house was so cold and so dark and so strange. She bumped her hip trying to climb the stairs, then banged her shoulder on the wall. Her legs were trembling. By the time she reached her bedroom, her breath was short in her throat. She crawled into her bed and lay there, unable to stop the shudders that wracked her from head to toe.

Mia came looking for her later, shouting about supper and the time. When Dortchen did not answer her, Mia galloped back down the stairs. Then Old Marie came in, wiping her damp hands on her apron, her wrinkled face worried.

'What is it?' she asked. 'Are you ill?'

Dortchen did not answer.

'My sweetling, what's wrong?' Then Old Marie saw her torn bodice. Dismay filled her. 'My poor blessed girl – what's happened to you? Who was it? Are you hurt?'

'No!' Dortchen cried. 'I'm fine. Leave me be.'

Old Marie patted her shoulder. 'Now, now, let me help you change. Look at your dress, all torn. I'll have that mended for you in the morning. What happened? Your father is so angry – what have you done?'

'Nothing,' Dortchen whispered.

Old Marie clucked her tongue but said no more. She helped Dortchen into her nightgown, then tucked her in. 'The old tyrant threatened me with sacking if I came near you, but how could I leave you all alone and upset, my little love? You sleep now, and don't you mind your father. It's the world he's angry at, and he's taking it out on you.'

She tiptoed away and Dortchen shut her eyes. All she could see was Wilhelm's angry, accusing gaze, and Ferdinand's pleading eyes and outstretched hands. It seemed she could please no one, help no one, no matter what she did. She could not get rid of the sour taste of Ferdinand's mouth, or the feel of her father probing her.

Perhaps her father was right. Maybe she was wild by nature, and so destined to call such loathsome passions upon herself. At the thought, Dortchen began at last to cry, and once she began she could not stop.

The next day was her eighteenth birthday.

THE COMET

April 1811

Spring came, and with it Röse's wedding. She looked thin and white and sick, while her new husband was large and red and hearty. Afterwards, the house seemed emptier and quieter than ever.

Dortchen did her best to be a good daughter. She did not defy her father and sneak over to the Grimms' apartment, nor did she look for excuses to go walking in the springtime woods. She stayed at home, laboured in the house and garden, tended to her ailing mother and was obedient to her father's commands. When Mia complained that their days were so dreary now, she reprimanded her and told her to mind her manners.

From her occasional hurried conversations with Lotte, Dortchen knew that Ferdinand had continued to be wild and unpredictable for more than a week, but that he had gradually quietened and no longer sobbed for laudanum. Instead, he sat in his darkened room, staring at the wall, unwilling or unable to lift his hand to anything. Wilhelm, meanwhile, had suffered a relapse and had taken to his bed with sharp pains in his chest, erratic poundings of his heart, and difficulty breathing. Dortchen did not sneak into the stillroom to make him up some linden blossom tea, or to infuse honey with thyme for him to swallow. She simply studied her French books and darned her father's stockings.

There was much talk and worry over the increasing tension between

France and Russia. France was slowly taking over Poland and had seized the Duchy of Oldenburg, whose heir was married to the Tsar's beloved sister, Ekaterina. In May, Napoléon recalled his ambassador to St Petersburg. Jakob heard at the palace that the Tsar had told the French ambassador, before he left, 'I will not draw my sword first, but I shall sheathe it last.' In August, Napoléon harangued the Russian ambassador in Paris, telling him that the Tsar had no hope of winning if France moved against him.

In the summer, Ferdinand went to Munich to stay with Ludwig, who was studying art at the university there, and Wilhelm went to stay with Paul Wigand, an old friend from his university days. It was easier for Dortchen to have him gone. She no longer strained to hear his cough as she hung out the washing on the line between the two houses. Later, she heard from Lotte that he had made a visit to another old friend, Werner von Haxthausen, only to find that his friend had fled to Sweden in fear of reprisals for his activities undermining French rule. Wilhelm had found a house full of Werner's sisters, however, who had enthusiastically decided to help him find old stories for his collection.

'He says the youngest girl, Anna, told him a wonderful tale the very moment she first met him,' Lotte told her. 'Before they'd even reached the house. Wilhelm is very excited – he's sure they'll be a treasure trove of stories.'

Dortchen nodded and turned away, a familiar ache about her heart.

The summer turned into autumn, and Dortchen gathered baskets full of quinces, as golden as apples, to help her father make brandy. The smell of the fermenting fruit made her feel unwell, but she choked back her distaste and stirred in the sugar as her father bade her.

As the first chill turned the leaves of the apple trees red, Wilhelm came home. Dortchen saw him sitting with Jakob and Lotte in church, and felt her heart lurch unpleasantly. She lowered her eyes and followed her parents to their pew. She was conscious of his eyes on her many times during the service, but she did not return his look. Her father noticed him too, and glared at her warningly. Dortchen found it hard to see the words of her hymn book, her eyes swimming with tears.

After the service, her father shouldered his way through the crowd in the square. He did not pause to speak to anyone or to speculate about the war, and his wife and two remaining daughters followed obediently.

Dortchen suddenly ran back and caught Wilhelm's sleeve. 'I did not want him to kiss me,' she said, in a low, intense voice.

Something sparked in his eyes. She had no time to decipher it, or to hear the words that sprang to his lips. She turned and hurried back to join her family.

That evening, as Dortchen sat wearily on her bed and took off her shoes, she saw a green scarf hanging on the washing line. She started up, opened her window and pulled the peg basket towards her with fingers that trembled. Inside the peg basket was a note from Lotte: 'Coffee and storytelling this Friday afternoon at the Hassenpflugs?'

Dortchen did not know what to do. She did not reply to the note. As the days passed and Friday approached, she found herself in an agony of indecision. Should she ask her father for permission to go, or sneak away while he was at the church elders' meeting? What if she went and her father found out? Would Wilhelm and Lotte understand if she did not go?

After lunch on Friday, she went upstairs to collect her mother's tray. Frau Wild lay in her bed, one hand clenched against her left breast, a small table beside her cluttered with laudanum drops and smelling salts and lavender water.

'Mother,' Dortchen said hesitantly.

'Yes, dear?' her mother spoke faintly.

'I've been asked to the Hassenpflugs for coffee this afternoon. May I go?'

'I suppose so, dear. What does your father say?'

'I . . . I haven't asked him.'

'Well, then, no need to bother him. Your father's very busy. Please give my regards to Frau Hassenpflug.'

'Yes, Mother.'

'Perhaps . . . fish tonight? The market is on the way home.'

'Yes, Mother.'

Dortchen carried the tray out, her breath whooshing out with relief. She changed her dress and tidied her hair, and put on her best bonnet and her mother's old fringed shawl. Her heart was pounding as sharply and erratically as she imagined Wilhelm's did. Then she called Mia and whispered the news to her. In minutes, both girls were hurrying through the narrow streets towards the elegant boulevards and wide squares of the French quarter, where the Hassenpflugs lived. Dortchen could not help looking behind her every few steps, afraid to see her father. But they reached the Hassenpflugs' house safely and were shown into a large drawing room that had the tallest mirror Dortchen had ever seen, hanging over an elegantly carved marble fireplace in which a fire crackled cheerily.

Jakob, Wilhelm and Lotte were already there, drinking coffee from tiny porcelain cups. The two men rose as Dortchen and Mia shyly came in. The three Hassenpflug sisters were seated on wide couches with spindly gilded legs. All wore beautiful pale dresses, embroidered on the sleeves and hem with flowers. They smiled in welcome and beckoned the Wild sisters in. Their brother, Louis, stood on the hearthrug, a cup in one hand and a cake in the other. He waved the cake at them enthusiastically.

Frau Hassenpflug bustled forward to meet them. 'Fraüleins, we have not seen you in so long,' she said. 'Tell me, how is your mother? Ah, what a shame. Do please give her my regards. And your sister? Enjoying married life? And your dear father?' Frau Hassenpflug's conversation was like a river in full snowmelt, only occasionally smashing up against the boulder of a response.

Murmuring commonplaces, Dortchen came forward. Jakob surrendered her his seat so she could sit next to Wilhelm. Colour rose in her cheeks and she dared not look at him. She sank down on the couch and accepted a cup of coffee and a plate of sugar-dusted strudel.

Conversation resumed. After a while, she dared to glance up at Wilhelm. He was regarding her gravely. 'You are well?' he asked.

She nodded and tried to smile.

'I'm sorry we did not call on you, to enquire after you . . . after—'

'Much better not,' she replied swiftly, colour burning her cheeks.

'I do apologise . . . Ferdinand—'

'How is he?'

Wilhelm shrugged. 'Unhappy. Strange and withdrawn. We do not know what to do – he does not listen to a word we say.'

Dortchen looked up at him. 'He was . . . he was not himself.'

'No.'

Their stilted conversation ceased. Dortchen made an effort. 'I believe you've been to Höxter?'

Animation lit his face. 'Yes. It is so beautiful there. I do wish we could live in the country. I am always so much better away from town. And I have found so many new stories. Our collection is coming along so well. I do believe we may have enough for a book now.'

'That would be wonderful,' Dortchen said. 'Do you really think you might be able to get it published?'

'Times are hard,' Wilhelm said, 'and the French keep a close eye on publishers, to make sure they do not transgress the censorship laws. But a scholarly collection of old tales would surely not concern them. I must admit, I have high hopes of success.'

Dortchen was leaning forward to answer him when she was interrupted by Marie, who brought over the coffee pot. 'We have not heard from you in such a long time, Dorothea,' she said, her thick, dark ringlets falling over her shoulder as she poured another cup for Wilhelm. 'Do you have a tale for us today?'

'I always know a tale to tell,' Dortchen flashed back, not liking the slight tone of condescension in Marie's voice. 'What would you like to hear?'

'Something amusing,' Marie answered. 'Herr Grimm, do you wish to write it down? I have some paper and quills here for you, ready sharpened.' She indicated a small table nearby, on which writing materials lay ready.

'Yes, of course, thank you,' Wilhelm replied, rising and going to the table. Marie sat down beside him, unscrewing the inkpot and preparing a blotter and the sand tray. She said something in a low voice to him and he smiled.

Left alone on the couch, Dortchen told the story of Clever Elsie, a girl who thinks herself very smart but is in reality remarkably stupid. When she had finished, everyone laughed and clapped, though Marie's smile seemed rather forced.

'That was brilliant,' Wilhelm said, coming over to congratulate her. 'Do you have any more like that? We could do with some humorous stories in our collection.'

'I do,' she answered, then, acting on a wild whim, said, 'Come to the garden the day after tomorrow. I'll be harvesting pumpkins and winter squash, but I can talk as I work. You can sit in the summer house and write.'

So, two days later, on a glorious, crisp autumn afternoon, Dortchen told Wilhelm another tale, about a wishing-table, an ass that spat golden pieces from front and back, and a cudgel that beat your enemies senseless. It made Wilhelm laugh, and Dortchen did all she could to make the story droll and amusing, acting out the different voices and pretending to be the ass that farted gold coins. He lingered afterwards, helping her to harvest and talking as the shadows slowly lengthened over the garden.

He came again a few days later, and she told him another silly tale about a louse and a flea. Soon they were meeting in the garden whenever they could, Wilhelm always carrying his battered writing box, Dortchen making him tea on the summer house stove and giving him fresh beans to eat, or blackberries, or an apple. Those hours were increasingly precious to Dortchen. Whenever she told Wilhelm a story, all his attention was on her and only her. The intensity of his regard filled her with tingling light.

She told him the tale of Frau Holle, and how, when she shook out her featherbed, snow fell on the earth. She told him another story about three feathers, and yet another about a cobbler and some elves. Wilhelm loved this story so much that she told him two more about elves. Another day, she told him the story of a princess with a golden ball, and a frog that, when thrown against the wall, turned into a king. Wilhelm told her about other stories he had discovered and the books he was reading, and he recited poetry to her.

Of course, this enchanted time could not last.

One evening in early October, as darkness was falling, Dortchen was driving home from the garden in the pony trap when she noticed a strange star on the horizon. It was large and bright and had a peacock's tail of pale light trailing behind it. Yet it did not spark and fall, as a shooting star would, but seemed to glide almost imperceptibly along the horizon, its tail flaring as if blown by an invisible wind. The star was so striking that Dortchen pulled Trudi to a halt. All around her, people stared and pointed and muttered uneasily.

A few days later, the Great Comet was reported in the papers. Its tail stretched for thirty-three million kilometres, one said. Another said that because the comet had first been seen in France, it was a sign that the heavens were smiling on Napoléon. He would surely triumph against the English soon, the newspaper said, and all Europe would be at peace under his benevolent rule.

Old Marie was anxious, however, and muttered about evil omens. She closed the shutters early so she would not see the comet pulsing above the rooftops. In the marketplace, everyone agreed: dark times were ahead. Perhaps the comet even portended the end of the world.

FIRE AND FROST

November 1811

Late one Saturday night in November, Dortchen was woken by the sound of warning bells.

She sat up. The air smelt of smoke. She knelt in her bed and rubbed her hand on the icy pane of the window, making a peephole. She could see nothing but the familiar landscape of spires and gables and chimneys, glittering with frost under a sharp-edged moon. Icicles rimmed the window frame. She ran barefoot to the other window, which looked out across the marketplace. She could see the orange glare of fire diffused through the glaze of frost on the glass.

Cassel was on fire.

Her heart thumping, Dortchen shoved her feet into her slippers and dragged her shawl about her. She ran to pound on Old Marie's door. 'Fire!' she cried. 'Marie, the town's on fire.'

'Goodness gracious!' came the housekeeper's frightened voice. 'Have we been attacked?'

Dortchen ran downstairs. Her father was already up, his frockcoat thrown over his striped nightgown, and his feet in slippers. He held a candle in one hand and his pistol in the other. The bells continued to ring the warning. Frau Wild called out plaintively from her bed, 'What is it? What's wrong? Oh, my nerves! I'm having a spasm.'

'What's happened?' Mia cried, clutching at Dortchen. 'Have the Russians attacked?'

'I don't know but there's a fire,' Dortchen replied. 'A big one.'

Herr Wild caught up his pistol, stumped down the stairs and flung open the front door. His two youngest daughters ran after him. 'What's going on?' he shouted out into the square, where dark figures were hurrying about.

'The Palais Bellevue is on fire,' someone shouted back. Dortchen recognised Wilhelm's voice. He came towards them, carrying a lantern. He had dressed hastily, his coat thrown over his shirt, which was unbuttoned at the throat; a long knitted scarf was knotted loosely about his throat in place of a cravat.

'The palace is on fire? What is it?' Herr Wild demanded. 'An attack? Sabotage?'

'I don't know. It's fierce, though, and spreading fast. My brother Jakob has gone to try to save the books – he's the librarian there, you know. He sent word that we must be prepared – there are fears the whole town will burn. We're filling buckets with water.' Wilhelm nodded at the pump outside the inn.

A crowd of people was milling about the pump; many houses in the Marktgasse, including the Grimms' apartment, did not have their own water supply.

Wilhelm saw Dortchen and his eyes widened in sudden admiration. She realised she was dressed only in a nightgown and shawl; the heavy mass of her hair was tumbling out of its plait.

Her father saw the look on Wilhelm's face and pushed her back. 'Get inside. Mia, you too.'

Just then there was a shout, and two soldiers rushed up, carrying a man on a makeshift litter. Their faces and hands were stained black with soot, and their clothes stank of smoke. 'You must help us,' one cried. 'He's badly hurt. A flaming beam fell on him.'

'Who is it? Is it Jakob? The librarian at the palace?' With terror in his voice, Wilhelm flung himself down on his knees beside the litter and raised his lantern so he could see the injured man's face. It was not Jakob. The stranger moaned and turned his blistered face away from the light, lifting hands that looked like black claws.

'Bring him into the shop,' Herr Wild commanded.

As the soldiers carried the litter into the hallway, both men had time to notice Dortchen, pressed back against the wall, clutching her shawl close. They flickered warm glances of appreciation over her figure and face.

'Dortchen, get dressed,' Herr Wild snapped. He flung open the door to the shop and led the soldiers in. Mia ran after them. As the door swung shut behind her, the hallway was left in darkness, the only light coming from the lantern in Wilhelm's hand as he crouched outside the shop. 'Thank God it's not Jakob,' he said.

He got up, staggering a little, one hand to his heart. Dortchen rushed to help him. He put one arm about her and she felt the burn of his touch. He felt it too, and flinched away. 'I'm sorry,' he said, trying not to look at her but unable to look away. His face was all shadows and golden planes.

'You must get back inside,' Dortchen said. 'It's freezing out here – you'll get sick.'

'I must make sure we have some water, in case the fire spreads.'

'Hurry, then,' she said. 'If the queue for the pump is too long, send Lotte to our kitchen – she can fill her bucket there.'

'Thank you,' he said.

They stood together on the doorstep, staring at each other. The air between them seemed to fizz and spark. Slowly, Wilhelm raised the lantern so he could see her face. Dortchen's skin heated. 'I did not know your hair was so long,' he said.

Gently, he picked up the end of her plait, which formed a tiny curl. Her hair was a thick golden rope between them. He tugged on it ever so lightly, and she took a step towards him. Their eyes were steady on each other's faces.

An explosion rent the air, and fiery sparks shot up over the rooftops and lit up the square. Dortchen remembered where she was, and how she was dressed, and pulled away. 'I must go.'

'Yes,' he said, like a man awakening from a dream. He drew a deep breath and let the end of Dortchen's braid go.

Dortchen stepped back inside the house, leaving the door open just a crack. She peeked through. Wilhelm was still standing on the doorstep. Their eyes met, and involuntarily each smiled. With her lips still curved, Dortchen shut the door.

She ran back up to her room, shivering violently from the cold, and hurriedly dressed in her oldest gown.

In the shop, her father was tending the injured soldier's burns. Dortchen went to help him, silently preparing honey and healing herbs. Mia was rolling bandages swiftly, and Old Marie came in with cups of hot coffee. The two soldiers had gone back to fight the fire, which glared ever brighter through the shop windows.

'What shall we do if the fire spreads to us?' Mia cried.

'Fight to save the house,' Herr Wild replied, his gaze on the injured man. 'It is all that I own. Without it, we're destitute.'

The bells had not ceased their insistent clamour.

'Fill the buckets,' Herr Wild said. 'And get all our spare blankets and dampen them down. Dortchen, go and calm the animals. They'll be frightened by the smell of smoke.'

The sisters obeyed at once. As Dortchen hurried down the pathway, a lantern in her hand, she saw that the silvery mantle of frost on the garden was marred with black smuts. Trudi was restless in her stall, tossing her head and dancing about, trampling down her straw. The cow was mooing plaintively and the birds were awake and squawking.

Even with the smell of smoke thick in the air, and the air itself full of tiny black flakes, Dortchen smiled to herself as she went about her work.

Wilhelm wanted to kiss me.

By dawn, the danger had passed. The night had been so cold that the fiery sparks and embers had fallen onto frost and been extinguished. The Palais Bellevue was nothing but cinders and charred timbers. Jakob had managed to save most of the books, but now they sat piled in the courtyard, at the mercy of the weather.

'It's a symbol,' Herr Wild said. 'There's no palace for the Kurfürst to return to, no throneroom. Hessen-Cassel is gone. A thousand years of Hessian rule is over.'

The small family sat at the breakfast table, their bread tasting like ashes. Frau Wild drooped over her plate like a wilted flower. 'I knew that comet was a bad omen,' she said.

'Perhaps the fire is what it foretold?' Dortchen said, hoping to reassure her. 'Maybe we've had the worst of it and our luck will now turn.'

But that night, as she knelt in her bed and looked out at the skyline, the comet was brighter than ever.

THE SINGING BONE

January 1812

After Christmas, Frau Wild and her two unmarried daughters travelled to Nentershausen to visit Hanne and her husband, Johann. Hanne was expecting another baby, and Frau Wild wanted to see her grandson, who was already seven months old and toddling everywhere.

One morning in mid-January, the sun came out and the sky was brilliantly blue. The snow was so white that it hurt the eyes, and the icicles hanging from the bare branches of the trees glittered like magical swords. Dortchen and Mia both wrapped up warmly and went out to walk in the garden. Both felt so light-hearted and free that they romped like children, making snowballs and flinging them at each other.

Then Dortchen saw a tall, dark figure walking towards them, muffled up in a dark coat and with a tall hat on his head. Something about the slightly stooped posture, and the way the walker looked about him with eager interest, made her stomach flip. Her hand flew to her mouth. Surely not . . . How could Wilhelm be here, so far from Cassel? Unable to help herself, Dortchen ran towards him, crying his name.

He smiled at her. 'Good news,' he cried. 'My book is published! Look, here it is.' He pulled out a small leather-bound book and opened it to the title page, his fingers clumsy in his thick gloves. Dortchen took it eagerly, examining the drawing of a knight and a musician,

278

surrounded by twining vines, birds, butterflies and a plump, smiling angel.

'*Old Danish Epic Songs*,' she read. 'Translated by Wilhelm Grimm.' She looked up at him in delight. 'Wilhelm, that's wonderful! A book – a real book!'

'I know. I could not let myself believe it till the book actually arrived. I doubt it will make me much money. Who is interested in old Danish songs, apart from me? But at least it is something to show for all those months of hard work. There were times when I thought I'd be better going off and getting work as a stablehand or signing up as a soldier.'

'No, no,' Dortchen said, distressed at the idea. She cradled the little book as if it was the most precious treasure, then reluctantly passed it back to him. 'Do you think . . . If they want your translations of old Danish songs, perhaps might they want your collection of old German stories?'

'Oh, Dortchen, I hope so. Achim came to visit us for Christmas. He read our manuscript and loved it. He's going to show it to his publisher!'

He held out both his hands to her; she took them and he swung her about. She laughed for joy.

'We need more stories, though,' he continued, 'and who else should I come to for stories than the girl who knows them all?'

'All this way? Wilhelm, you really came all this way, just for some more stories?'

'I wanted to see you,' he admitted. 'And show you the book, of course. I knew *you'd* be happy for me.'

Dortchen blushed and smiled, then, realising he was still holding both her hands, drew them away gently. 'You had best come in and have some coffee. You must be chilled to the bone. Come and see Hanne and meet her little boy. He's a holy terror!'

'Just like Hanne herself,' Wilhelm responded, smiling. They walked together back towards the house, past a grinning Mia, who had been amusing herself by throwing snowballs at a tree. When Dortchen's boot slipped on a patch of ice, Wilhelm's hand shot out to steady her. Her heart sang with joy.

Hanne and Johann made Wilhelm welcome, although a quick, knowing glance passed between them. Frau Wild was troubled by his appearance and murmured a few incoherent phrases, which Dortchen hoped Wilhelm would not be able to decipher. They had coffee and strudel, and talked a great deal about his book and the fairy tale project. Wilhelm was both very hungry and very happy, and so the small, messy, crowded room rang with laughter and talk.

'Have you heard the news?' Wilhelm cried. 'Achim and Bettina are to be married at last.'

'She has decided to succumb to the evils of domesticity?' Dortchen teased.

'Achim has wanted to marry her as long as I have known him, but he could never persuade her that marriage is not a living death.'

Hanne snorted. 'She could have asked me. I have never been happier.'

'Ah, yes, but you were lucky to land a jewel of the first order,' her husband said. 'Once I was taken, what was this Bettina to do?'

Dortchen entertained them with a few of Bettina's exploits, and Hanne and her husband laughed till they almost cried.

Baby Hans, meanwhile, had been cruising around the room from one piece of furniture to another, holding on with both hands, laughing happily as the adults laughed. Whenever the gap between the furniture was too large, he would drop down on all fours and crawl, before pulling himself up again. The skirts of his white dress and the heels of his hands were quite grubby, and he was dribbling profusely, but he was such a chubby, merry little fellow, with a crest of fluffy yellow hair and one charming, protruding tooth, that when he pulled himself up by Wilhelm's trousers, Wilhelm smiled and picked him up, tossing him up in the air. Hans shrieked with laughter. '*Da-da-da-da*,' he said.

Dortchen was struck with a piercing longing for a baby of her own, one with ruffled dark curls like Wilhelm's. *He would be a wonderful father*, she thought. *He would not beat his children, or force them down to pray at his feet. He would play with them and sing them songs and tell them stories.* A vision rose up before her, of Wilhelm sitting by the fire with dark-haired, dark-eyed children clustered about his knee, reading from a book, while she sat opposite, darning his stockings and smiling. It was such a potent vision that it blew all the laughter and chatter away from her, and she fell silent.

'But you are here to listen to Dortchen's stories,' Hanne said, coming to whirl her son away from Wilhelm. 'Why don't you go out to the summer house? You can be quiet there. Mia can help me put this limb of Satan to bed.'

'Come, I'll light the stove for you,' her husband said, standing up. 'It's quite cosy out there. And certainly nice and quiet.' He gave Hanne a wicked look. She smiled back over her shoulder at him as she carried Hans away, drowsy against her shoulder. 'Mia, come with me,' she ordered, and reluctantly Mia followed, turning back to stare at Dortchen and Wilhelm as they stood, awkward and self-conscious, to follow Johann out into the glistening, snow-draped afternoon.

The summer house was a small round building made of stone and glass. A porcelain stove in one corner was soon roaring away, and Johann brought them thick fur rugs, hot mulled wine and a small writing desk. The room was so small that Dortchen's and Wilhelm's knees were practically touching once they settled down on the cushioned seats. Dortchen busied herself smoothing her dress, while Wilhelm sharpened a few quills. Then he looked at her expectantly.

'Once upon a time,' she said, and took a deep breath. For some reason her lungs felt unable to get enough air. She went on, faltering a little at first, then strengthening as she remembered the story.

'Once upon a time, in a certain country, there was great concern about a wild boar that was destroying the peasants' fields, killing the cattle and ripping people apart with its tusks. The king promised a large reward to anyone who could free the land from this plague, but the beast was so large and strong that no one dared to go near the woods where it lived. Finally, the king proclaimed that whoever could capture or kill the wild boar should have his only daughter in marriage.'

Three poor brothers decided to try their luck. The elder two were clever and shrewd and cruel. The youngest was innocent and kind. As Dortchen told Wilhelm this, she felt a sudden misgiving. Would he think she meant Ferdinand? But she had begun the story and so had to go on.

The two elder brothers stopped at an inn for some wine to embolden them. The youngest went on into the forest, where he met a dwarf who gave him an enchanted spear, as a reward for his kind heart. With the spear, the third brother was able to kill the boar. Having hoisted the huge beast onto his back, he travelled towards the palace to claim his prize. But on the way he met his brothers, who, furious and jealous, killed him as they crossed a bridge. The body of the youngest brother fell down into the stream, and the elder brothers went on with the boar to claim the reward.

'After many long years,' Dortchen continued, 'a shepherd was driving his herd across the bridge when he saw a little snow-white bone lying in the sand below. Thinking that it would make a good mouthpiece, he climbed down, picked it up and carved out of it a mouthpiece for his horn. When he blew into it for the first time, to his great astonishment the bone began to sing by itself:

Oh, my dear shepherd,
You are blowing on my little bone.
My brothers killed me,
And buried me beneath the bridge,
To get the wild boar
For the daughter of the king.

'"What a wonderful horn," said the shepherd. "I must take it to the king." When he brought it before the king, the horn again began to sing its little song. The king understood it well, and ordered the earth beneath the bridge to be dug up. Then the whole skeleton of the murdered man came to light. The singing bone sang and sang till his brothers could no longer deny their murderous deed. They were sewn into a sack and drowned alive. The murdered man's bones were laid to rest in a beautiful grave in the churchyard.'

Wilhelm laid down his quill and shook his aching hand. He looked pale and troubled. 'Do you think . . .' he began.

Dortchen could not bear it. 'No,' she cried, seizing his hands and drawing him closer. 'It was not your fault. It was the opium. You could have done nothing different . . . Oh, Wilhelm. Drinking laudanum is like dancing with the Devil. There's no happy outcome.'

Dortchen thought of her own weary, worn-down mother, whose only joy seemed to come when she drank down her drops, and tears sprang to her eyes.

Wilhelm's face softened. He drew Dortchen closer, and she subsided against his shoulder with a sigh. His arm was strong about her. Outside, a sudden wind shook snow against the frost-glazed windows, but inside, all was warm. She looked up at him. There was only an inch or so between them. It was natural that she lifted her face, and he lowered his. Their lips met.

It was the merest brush, yet it acted like a spark to tinder. He shifted and drew her closer. Again their mouths met, and this time the contact was closer, longer, harder. His hand crept up to cup the back of her neck. She uttered a soft sigh.

They kissed again, separated, then swayed back together. Involuntarily, their mouths opened. Dortchen felt like she might swoon. There was the lightest touch of tongue against tongue. Wilhelm groaned, and the sound made Dortchen press herself closer. Slowly, with absolute daring, his hand found her waist and traced its curve. They kissed again, drew away, then fell back against each other, hands finding skin at the nape of the neck, the modest dip of the neckline, the soft blue-veined wrist.

It was overwhelming. They had to fall apart, panting, staring at each other with wide eyes. Neither could speak.

'I did not want him to kiss me,' Dortchen said at last.

'I know . . . I'm sorry . . . If you could but know how it hurt me to see you in his arms.'

'I thought you were angry.'

'I was. But not with you.' He kissed her again, swift and hard, then fell back, flushing. 'That's not true. I was so angry with you. And I did not know why.'

She nestled against his shoulder. The stove roared and spat. It was so hot in the summer house now that the windows were running with condensation. He bent his head and kissed her behind her ear. She had never known how much the soft, sensitive skin there had longed to be kissed. He nuzzled lower, and she turned her head and kissed the corner of his mouth. For a moment there was absolute stillness between them. She felt dazed, drunk, exultant. He kissed her back and one finger grazed the curve of her breast. At once, both backed away, flushed and embarrassed.

Dortchen could not look at him. 'I know a beautiful love story,' she said.

He cleared his throat and turned away to fuss with his paper and ink and quills. 'Will you tell me?' he asked.

So she began the tale of the six brothers who were turned into swans, and their young sister who could not speak or laugh for six years, till she had woven shirts from nettles to save them from their enchantment.

'After she had already spent a long time there, it happened that the king of the land was hunting in these woods. His huntsmen came to the tree in which the girl was sitting. They called to her, "Who are you?" But she did not answer.

'"Come down to us," they said. "We will not harm you."

'She only shook her head. When they pressed her further with questions, she threw her golden necklace down to them, thinking that this would satisfy them. But they did not stop, so she then threw down her belt, then her garters, and then – one thing at a time – everything that she had on and could do without. Finally, she had nothing left but her shift.'

As she spoke, Dortchen loosened her collar, her skin flushed with heat. Wilhelm's gaze dwelt on the small triangle of skin she had exposed.

Dortchen cast down her eyes and continued. 'The huntsmen, however, not letting themselves be dissuaded, climbed the tree, lifted the girl down and took her to the king. The king asked, "Who are you? What were you doing in that tree?"

'But she did not answer. He asked her in every language that he knew, but she remained as speechless as a fish. Because she was so beautiful, the king's heart was touched, and he fell deeply in love with her. He put his cloak around her, lifted her onto his own horse and took her to his castle. There, he had her dressed in rich garments, and she glistened in her beauty like bright daylight, but no one could get a word from her. At the table he seated her by his side. Her modesty pleased him so much that he said, "My desire is to marry her, and no one else in the world."'

Dortchen's throat closed over and she could not speak a word. Flushing, she moved away from Wilhelm. There was a long, strained silence.

'What happened?' he asked.

'She had a cruel mother-in-law,' Dortchen said. 'The king's mother stole away all the queen's babies while she was sleeping, and smeared the queen's mouth with blood and proclaimed that she must have eaten them. At last the king could no longer protect his beloved. She was condemned to be burnt at the stake.'

'But couldn't he help her?' Wilhelm asked, incredulous. 'Surely he'd not let his beloved die so horribly?'

'He believed the lies against her,' Dortchen said. 'When the day came for the sentence to be carried out, it was also the last day of the six years during which she had not been permitted to speak or to laugh; she had thus delivered her dear brothers from the magic curse. The six shirts were all but finished – only the left sleeve of the last one was missing. When she was led to the stake, she laid the shirts on her arm.

'When the fire was about to be lit, she looked around and saw six swans flying through the air. Knowing that their redemption was near, her heart leapt with joy. The swans rushed towards her, swooping down so that she could throw the shirts over them. As soon as the shirts touched them, their swan-skins fell off and her brothers stood before her, vigorous and handsome. However, the youngest was missing his left arm. In its place he had a swan's wing.'

'What a beautiful, strange tale,' Wilhelm said. 'What about the queen? Was she saved?'

'Yes,' Dortchen said. 'The king realised that she had kept mute to break the curse on her brothers, and he forgave her and freed her and they lived happily ever after.'

Something in her heart cried out, *Can you not see that I too am kept mute?* But she could not speak.

Wilhelm wiped the end of his quill on a rag. 'That story was extraordinary,' he said. 'Dortchen . . .'

He leant forward and kissed her. She wound her arms about his neck and drew him down to her. Long moments passed. Each grew bolder, daring to touch, to creep their fingers across the other's bared skin, to undo a button here and a ribbon there. Dortchen's breath came faster and she moaned deep in her throat, shifting her hips. Wilhelm stilled, holding himself away from her.

'I must stop,' he said. 'We should not be doing this. What would your father say?'

She froze and sat up, buttoning up her bodice with trembling fingers, unable to look at him. He groaned and caught her hands. 'Dortchen, Dortchen,' he whispered, then bent to kiss her palms. 'Don't go. I'm sorry. This is wrong, I know, yet . . . Dortchen . . .' He tried to kiss her lips but she turned away.

'Don't go,' he said. 'If you go, the spell will be broken. We shall have to return to everyday life. Stay here, just for a while.'

'I could tell you another story,' she said, turning back to him, lifting one hand to stroke back the lock of hair falling over his forehead, as she had longed to do so many times. 'As long as I am telling stories, we are outside time.'

He sighed and bent to kiss her. Their lips met, their breath mingled, and they felt again the irresistible force that drew them to each other like magnetised iron.

'Dortchen, I . . . I wish . . .'

'Shh,' she said. 'Listen to my story.'

Wilhelm sighed, looking at her with a kind of wild longing in his eyes, but the duty and habit of work was too strong in him. He drew another ragged quill towards him, and a fresh piece of paper, and began to write as she spoke.

Dortchen told him the tale of Sweetheart Roland, who helped his beloved escape from a house of hatred and murder, but then forgot her and left her standing at a red boundary stone in a field.

By now the light was fading from the translucent sky outside. Darkness was closing in. Sweetheart Roland prepared to marry another, but the girl came heartsore to his wedding and sang. Hearing her voice, he remembered her and cast off the false bride, swearing his love to her again.

As Dortchen finished the tale, Wilhelm threw down his quill, caught her in his arms and kissed her. Despite herself, Dortchen fell back beneath him. Her mouth opened, her hands tangled in his hair and she welcomed his weight upon her. They kissed as if the world were about to end and this was all the chance of life left to them. They kissed as if they were starving and the other was all sustenance. Dortchen lost all sense of herself. There were only their mouths and their shy hands, and the brush of flesh against flesh.

It was Wilhelm who came back to himself. 'I must stop,' he whispered. 'Oh, Dortchen, I'm sorry, I'm all in a daze. I hardly know what I'm doing. We must stop.'

'No,' she groaned, pressing her mouth against his throat.

'No, no, we must. I . . . any moment now . . . Dortchen, I cannot.'

He lifted himself away from her, and she realised that her bodice was unbuttoned. She sat up, flushing, her hands flying to close her bodice. She looked up at him and at once he bent his mouth to hers, and the strange, sweet delirium swept over her again. She moaned. His hand swept up her skirts and found bare flesh. He groaned and pressed closer to her.

A knocking on the door drove them apart. Mia's voice called plaintively, 'Are you never coming in for dinner?'

Dortchen and Wilhelm could hardly breathe. Their eyes fell away from each other. He turned and pressed his forehead against the cold, foggy glass, trying to compose himself. Dortchen again did up her bodice, blushing and confused.

'Are you there?' Mia called.

'Coming, sweetling,' Dortchen replied. 'Just a moment.'

Mia opened the door and barged in, curious and bright-eyed. 'Dinner's been ready for ever so long,' she said. 'Whatever have you been doing?'

'Telling stories,' Dortchen replied, then rushed her sister out into the snowy night. Overhead were ten thousand stars, filling the arch of the night sky. She saw the faint trail of fire from the comet along the horizon and heard Wilhelm come out behind her, rustling his sheaf of pages. She risked a glance at him and he smiled at her; she could not help but smile back.

'Hanne says you must stay the night,' Mia said to him. 'It's late now.'

Wilhelm's eyes flashed towards Dortchen and she felt his surge of excitement as if it were a visible spray of light. But then he drew back and shook his head, saying, 'I should not. I'll stay at the inn.' And before Mia or Dortchen could protest, he had lurched away towards the gate, his arms full of white paper, his feet leaving dark holes in the snow.

MIDSUMMER SWOON

June 1812

Winter turned to spring, and spring to summer, but Dortchen and Wilhelm could only snatch occasional moments together.

They kissed behind a tree in Karlsaue Park while the citizens of Cassel picnicked only a few feet away.

They let the little fingers of their hands touch as they sat side by side, listening to a concert in the amphitheatre in the garden of Napoléonshöhe, with Frau Ramus and her daughters – the biggest gossips in Cassel – sitting right beside them.

They saw each other in church, and found it hard not to gaze at each other every second of the sermon.

One day they managed to walk the length of the central path of Karlsaue Park, exchanging hurried words. 'Oh, Dortchen,' Wilhelm said. 'I think of you night and day. This is torture. If only we could marry.'

'My father would never permit it.'

'If I had a job? If I could support you?'

'Surely then . . .' She spoke doubtfully.

'If our book of old tales was a success . . .'

'It is to be published? You've heard?'

'No. Not yet. I hope it will. Surely it will. Such wonderful stories.'

Dortchen cast a quick glance over her shoulder. Herr Wild was sitting on a park bench, staring at her, his thick brows lowered dangerously. 'We could run away,' she whispered.

Wilhelm looked at her in surprise. 'Where could we go? What could we do?'

'I can cook and clean and sew, and I can work with my hands as well as any farm labourer,' she said. 'Surely we could find work?'

He shrugged his thin shoulders and spread his hands. 'Who would hire me?' he said simply. 'I get out of breath just climbing the stairs to our apartment every day.'

'Then let us marry now. I can come and live with you all. You know I can cook and clean – I'd work hard.' She gazed at him pleadingly.

Wilhelm squeezed her hand surreptitiously. 'Oh, my little love, I wish that we could. But I cannot ask Jakob to feed another mouth.' His face was set and hard and unhappy. 'Surely you can understand that, Dortchen? Already he is supporting too many on his salary. We live on broth and dry bread as it is. If we can just be patient a little while longer, till I find a job . . . or a publisher for the fairy tale collection . . .'

'It'd be no use anyway – my father will never give us permission. Never.' Dortchen turned to face her father, who was now stumping angrily towards them. 'Coming, Father.'

'I'm sorry,' Wilhelm said. 'Dortchen . . .'

She did not answer, but submitted to her father's heavy hand on her arm. She felt Wilhelm's eyes on her back as they walked away.

Times were hard for them all. Shops everywhere were closing down, driven into bankruptcy by the inability of the King and his courtiers to pay their bills. Beggars slept in the alleys and accosted Dortchen in the market with desperate eyes and hollow cheeks. The queues for bread and meat began well before dawn and lasted till the last piece was gone.

Tea, coffee, sugar, pepper and opium were rare luxuries, their price unaffordable to anyone but the King and his courtiers. Dortchen's own family could only drink coffee made from acorns picked up off the grass in the park and laboriously ground by hand. Their tea leaves had been used so many times that they produced only the merest suggestion of colour and flavour. Nothing was wasted any more. Even the pig had grown lean, for Old Marie used every scrap to try to keep the family fed. They lived on cabbage soup and boiled potatoes, with rough bread made from rye and beans, and the occasional scrawny chicken.

It did not help that the house was full again. Rudolf had come home from Berlin, bringing with him a nineteen-year-old French wife and a young baby. Herr Wild had been furious.

'Get your French whore out of my house!' he had bellowed.

'Louise is my wife,' Rudolf had answered. 'Marianne is my daughter. If you throw her out, I'll go too.'

'How dare you marry without my permission?'

Rudolf had been unrepentant. 'Times have changed, Father. I'm twenty-nine years old. I don't need your permission to marry. You may not have noticed, but the Dark Ages are over.'

'I won't have that French whore in my house,' Herr Wild returned.

Rudolf stood. 'Very well, we'll go. But I warn you, we will never come back.'

Frau Wild had fallen to her knees, sobbing, begging her husband to reconsider. At length, when his delicate, dark-haired daughter-in-law had knelt and sobbed too, Herr Wild had allowed himself to be persuaded. But his face was heavy and dark with rage, and he would not look at his granddaughter.

Marianne was not easy to love. Thin and sallow, with a face like a barrel-grinder's monkey, she screamed all day and all night. Dortchen gave the little girl cool chamomile tea to drink, and rusks made of toasted acorn bread to chew on, and Marianne seemed to calm and grow easier. This meant that Louise thrust her into Dortchen's arms at the first sign of a wail, and retired to her bed with a headache. Louise seemed to have a lot of headaches.

Between the housework and the garden and the baby, Dortchen never seemed to have time to go next door, or to walk in the park, or go to the palace for concerts. Her days were consumed.

In mid-June, Jakob and Wilhelm heard from Achim's publisher in

Berlin. Despite the hard times, he was willing to publish their collection of children's and household tales. Wilhelm told Dortchen in the square outside church, keeping his hands shoved deep in his pockets to stop himself from reaching out to her.

She answered him gravely – 'That is good news indeed, Herr Grimm' – for she was aware how many eyes had begun to dwell on them, full of speculation. She smiled and moved away from him, but later that evening she dashed over to the Grimms' apartment with a bottle of dandelion wine, and they shared a small glass of the cloudy golden liquid, and then a quick but earth-shaking kiss behind the door as he walked her out.

It was not enough. It was not nearly enough.

On Midsummer's Day, when the people of Cassel went walking in the gardens and woods around Napoléonshöhe to make wreaths of wildflowers, Dortchen whispered to Wilhelm, 'Come, slip away with me. No one will notice we're gone. Come and meet the linden trees that I pluck to make your tea.'

His dark eyes kindled. He looked around swiftly; everyone was talking and singing and making chains from daisies and buttercups. Frau Wild was resting beneath a tree, with stout Frau Ramus to keep her company. Mia was playing hoops with Malchen. Lotte and the elder Hassenpflug sisters were feeding the swans that floated on the lake.

Dortchen ducked through a gap in the trees, following a winding path to a small grove of old linden trees, their branches hanging with heavy creamy-white flowers. A hedge of briar roses, with delicate pink-white flowers blooming among the thorns, shielded them from the eyes of anyone walking past.

The garden was alive with birdsong. A blackbird looked at her with a cheeky eye, then hopped away to search for worms. The scent of the linden blossoms was intoxicating. She sat on a low-hanging branch and waited. It was not long before Wilhelm stood before her, throwing down his hat and reaching out to slide his arm about her waist.

'Dortchen,' he whispered against her throat. 'If you only knew how I have longed for you.'

They kissed, deeply and hungrily. He undid the ribbons of her bonnet and cast it away. 'Why must you keep your hair in all these infernal braids?' he asked. 'Oh, I'd love to see your hair all loose and flowing, like it was on the night of the fire.' He twisted a tendril about his finger and kissed her tenderly.

She could not speak. She shaped the line of his cheekbones, so thin and hollow. She longed to cook for him, to make him a feast and feed him till he was not hungry any more. She would feed him suckling pig, and asparagus dripping with butter, and raspberries with sugared cream, and he would lick her fingers clean.

Her stomach twisted, desire sharp in her, and her limbs turned to honey. Wilhelm drew her close, his arm hard against her back, drawing her earlobe into his mouth. She almost swooned against him, and he smiled, turning her and pressing her against the linden tree.

'I'm weak at the knees,' he whispered. 'Oh, Dortchen, the power you have over me. I know I should not . . . but I cannot keep away.'

They kissed again, more slowly, taking the time to tease and entice each other, to taste the whole of each other's mouth. Dortchen delighted in the feel of him in her arms, warm, tall, his bones hard under his skin. They slid down to the ground, her head pillowed on his arm, their legs twining together.

Sun struck down through the linden blossoms. The air was sweet with their scent. Dortchen and Wilhelm lay in each other's arms, stroking and kissing the small expanses of skin available to them, the soft skin of the wrist, the nape of the neck, the pulse at the base of the throat.

They dared not explore deeper under each other's clothes, afraid that they might drown in the force of their passion. It was too dangerous here in the garden, with people promenading only a few feet away. All they could do was kiss, till Dortchen felt her soul had left her body.

'I love you,' she whispered, so afraid that she could scarcely shape the words.

Wilhelm lifted her palm to his mouth and kissed it lingeringly. 'I love you too,' he answered. 'Oh, Dortchen, I don't think I can wait much longer. I want you so much. If only we could be married now. If only the war would end! If only people buy our book and make our fortunes. Oh, Dortchen!'

He held her face in his hands, kissing her, his body pressing hers into the ground. She could feel his urgent desire, and something deep within her longed to open up to him, to have him even closer. Her body moved restlessly under his.

'I don't want to wait . . . Isn't there some way for us to be together?'

'Don't say it,' he cried. 'Don't tempt me. We have to wait. We just need to be patient. I know it's hard . . .' He kissed her, and she melted back into his arms.

Lying together in the sun-dappled grass, the scent of linden blossom all around them, Dortchen felt happier than she had ever felt before. All she and Wilhelm needed was love, and luck, and peace, and a little time. Surely that was not too much to ask?

The next day, Napoléon declared war on Russia.

PART FIVE

The Skin of Wild Beasts

CASSEL

The Kingdom of Westphalia, June 1812–January 1813

The wise princess said her father the king must first get her three dresses: one as golden as the sun; one as silver as the moon; and one as sparkling as the stars. Then she asked her father for a coat made from all kinds of fur, from every kind of animal in the kingdom. A thousand animals were caught and flayed to make the coat, and the three dresses were made, golden as the sun, silver as the moon, and as sparkling as the stars. The king said they would be married the next day.

From 'All-Kinds-of-Fur', told by Dortchen Wild to Wilhelm Grimm on 9th October 1812

THE MARCH AGAINST RUSSIA

August 1812

Half a million soldiers, marching against the inexhaustible resources of the Tsar.

Thirty thousand men taken from the war in the Peninsula.

Twenty thousand men from Prussia.

Thirty thousand men from Austria.

Twelve thousand from Switzerland.

Twelve thousand from Württemberg.

Eight thousand from Baden.

Eight thousand from Hesse.

'I don't think there are eight thousand young men left in the whole country,' Dortchen said, so sick with fear that she had to hunch over the cold hollow in the pit of her stomach. 'Oh, Marie, how are we to raise so many?'

'Don't you fret, sweetling,' Old Marie said, her sleeves rolled up to her elbows as she churned the butter. 'The Emperor Napoléon says the war will be over in twenty days – and if anyone knows warfare, it's him.'

'Sweetling, sweetling,' Mozart chirped as he hopped about on the floor.

Dortchen's fear for Wilhelm was acute, but she could not confess it. No one must realise. With eyes downcast, she asked for permission to go to the forest in search of fallen acorns and beechmast, and reluctantly her father allowed it. Dortchen plucked oak moss with trembling fingers and hid it deep in her basket, which was filled to the brim with every leaf and flower and lichen and mushroom that Dortchen could find. That night, she cast another spell for Wilhelm's protection, determined to do all she could to save him.

Napoléon ruled most of Europe already. Would he never be satisfied? Would he not stop till all the young men were dead?

There was no one left to stand against him.

The English king was mad, and their prime minister had been shot dead. Their parliament was in turmoil. Their troops struggled on in Spain, with hundreds dying to defend a donkey track, and thousands dying to take back a ruined village. It was madness. And the English were now at war with the United States as well. It was impossible for them to hold out against Napoléon.

Elsewhere in Europe, everyone lay quiescent under Napoléon's yoke, too afraid to try to throw it off. Only Russia remained unconquered, and Napoléon seemed determined to bring the Tsar to his knees, just as he had conquered all the other great rulers of Europe, from the Pope to the Austrian emperor.

Over the next few days, Dortchen felt such weariness in her spirit that she could scarcely find the strength to go about her chores. The day they held the conscription lottery, she found it hard to get out of bed. Her whole body ached, as if she were a hundred years old. Yet she got up and washed her face and neck and dressed and went downstairs, as she had done a thousand times before.

Everyone turned out to the Königsplatz, even Frau Wild, leaning heavily on her husband's arm. As one name after another was read out, people gasped and sobbed and cried out. Young men turned pale. Their mothers wept and clutched them close. Sweethearts and young wives screamed and swooned. Babies wailed. Through it all, Dortchen stood cold and still as a statue, all her senses attuned to one name, one brief collection of syllables: Wilhelm Grimm.

Let them not say his name . . . Let them not say his name . . . Let them not say his name.

So Dortchen did not notice when another brief sequence of syllables was read out. 'Rudolf Wild,' the corporal called.

Dortchen's mother staggered against her, clutching at her arm. 'No, not my boy, not Rudolf,' she moaned. It took a moment for Dortchen to understand. Her sister-in-law, Louise, was sobbing, the baby in her arms screaming. Rudolf stood silently, his lips white, his fists clenched. Herr Wild swayed, reaching blindly to the lamp post for support. 'I don't understand,' he said. 'The medical examiner promised me . . .'

Dortchen felt cold. All the way back to the shop, supporting her mother's tottering steps, she thought numbly how she had taken oak moss from the forest and made a spell to keep her lover safe. Not one thought had she spared for her own brother.

'I could mix powdered holly berries into some ale for you,' she said to Rudolf that night, as they began the weary business of preparing him for the long march to Russia. 'It'll make you vilely ill. Surely they won't make you march if you have dysentery?'

Rudolf smiled grimly. 'I'm not so sure about that. Father's doctor friend said there would be no exemptions; the Emperor must have his army, and anyone seeking to escape the conscription lottery would be thrown into gaol. I'd rather take my chances marching to Russia than rot in prison. Perhaps I'll make my fortune. They say that Napoléon's troops returned from Egypt absolutely laden down with loot.'

'Mind you bring me back some furs,' Louise said, bringing a pile of freshly laundered shirts and collars into the room. 'I'd like a mink stole and muff, and some sables.'

'Your wish is my command,' Rudolf said gallantly, clicking his heels together and bowing. 'I'll bring some back for you too, Dortchen.'

'Just bring yourself back safely,' she said, then she hurried out of the room so he would not see how close she was to tears.

The next few days were a whirl of washing, sewing, shopping and packing. It was awful to see Rudolf dressed in the white breeches, black gaiters and blue cutaway coat of a French soldier, a shako perched rakishly on his golden curls, though Louise clapped her hands in delight. 'You look so handsome.'

'I have to say, the uniform is darned uncomfortable,' Rudolf replied. 'These gaiters press so hard on the back of my knee that I can hardly walk, and the buttons dig in. And have you ever seen such ugly shoes?'

'You wouldn't want boots with heels and a pointed toe when you have to walk thousands of kilometres in them,' Dortchen said.

'They've been drilling us,' he said. 'We're meant to walk seventy-six steps a minute, unless the Emperor is in a hurry, in which case we have to walk a hundred steps a minute. And if he's in a real hurry, we have to do so for up to fifty kilometres a day.'

'I have a dreadful feeling the Emperor's in a hurry,' Dortchen said. 'I'll pack a spare pair of shoes for you. Surely you'll be wearing the leather thin with so much walking.'

'I wish I could be in the cavalry and have a horse to ride,' he grumbled.

'Father can't afford to buy you a commission,' Dortchen said. 'He says you're costing him a fortune as it is.'

Apart from the uniform, Rudolf had to purchase a heavy bayonet, which was taller than he was, a gun-cleaning kit and packets of cartridges. He was also given a sturdy pack made from cowhide to carry on his back. Dortchen filled it with spare clothes and shoes, a sewing kit, boot wax, a little saucepan, a flint-box, some warm underwear and a thick red muffler that she had knitted for him.

'But it's so hot,' Rudolf said irritably.

'It'll be cold in Russia,' Dortchen said.

'I'll be home before the weather turns,' he said, trying to smile.

She pressed it upon him earnestly. 'Please, Rudolf. Just in case.'

Dortchen went to market with a basket of cabbages and a jar of acorn coffee to barter for a bag of flour so she could cook some hard tack for him, a rather tasteless biscuit that would keep for months. When she came home, she saw the rag-and-bone man in the alley. He was buying sheaves of paper from Wilhelm, who smiled wearily at her.

'What are you doing?' she asked, her voice high and shrill as she recognised the scrawled and ink-blotted pages as Wilhelm and Jakob's manuscripts.

'He's offering good money for old paper,' Wilhelm said. 'We've transcribed all the stories neatly now. We don't need the original manuscripts – they're just piling up around our sitting room.'

'The army needs the paper to make cartridges,' the rag-and-bone man said, grinning toothlessly at Dortchen. He was a ragged old man, with black fingernails, and grime so deeply engrained in the pores of his skin that he looked like a Nubian. 'Paying good money for paper, they are.' He waved the manuscripts at her. 'Going to Russia, these papers are, to kill Cossacks.'

It made Dortchen feel ill, to think of those marvellous old stories being used to wrap gunpowder and iron shot to kill people. She gazed pleadingly at Wilhelm, but his mouth was set firm.

'We need to eat, Dortchen,' he said.

She nodded, though her heart was sore. The rag-and-bone man heaved the manuscripts into his handcart, tipped his battered hat at Wilhelm and went trundling away.

Wilhelm put his hand on Dortchen's arm. 'I'm sorry about Rudolf.'

Tears filled her eyes. 'I can't believe it. Father's begged for an exemption but the conscription board is adamant. The Emperor must have men to feed his filthy war machine.'

Wilhelm cast a quick glance around. They were hidden in the shadows of the alleyway. He bent his head and kissed her. 'He'll come back, Dortchen. They say the war will be over in a matter of weeks. You know the Emperor. He'll march in, trounce them and set up a new kingdom. I wonder who will be the new Tsar of Russia? Napoléon's running out of relatives.'

Dortchen did not smile. 'Maybe it will be over that quickly, Wilhelm, but at what cost? Rudolf is going to have to shoot people dead, or be court-martialled and executed himself. He could be wounded or killed. Oh, Wilhelm, I'm so afraid. I never thought he'd be chosen. I thought Father would make sure of that.'

'I'm sure he tried,' Wilhelm answered, but it was no comfort to her.

'I need to go in . . . There's much to do,' she said, stepping away. He kissed her again, quickly, surreptitiously, but for once she did not melt into his embrace and kiss him back. She hurried away, blinded by tears.

That night, at dinner, everyone sat around the table and tried to eat their soup, which seemed thinner and more tasteless than ever. Rudolf pretended to be excited. 'I've always wanted to travel the world,' he said.

'Fool,' his father replied.

Louise wept into her handkerchief. She was the kind of girl who looked pretty even when she cried. Rudolf put his arm about her and kissed her, and she turned her face into his shoulder and cried harder. Dortchen thought how awful it must be for her, to be foisted upon a stern and unwelcoming father-in-law and a sick mother-in-law, with a baby that screamed incessantly, and now her husband was marching off to war. She rose and went to the sideboard, where the lavender water was kept, and dribbled some onto her handkerchief. She pressed it into Louise's hand and was rewarded with a faint smile.

The next day, when the Hessian battalions marched out, the roads were lined with weeping women and stoic fathers. Dortchen and her family waved and called till Rudolf was out of sight, but they could not bear to leave till nothing was left of the Hessian battalions but a faint plume of dust on the horizon.

Twenty days passed without a letter from Rudolf. The newspapers were filled with the black squares of the censors' rule, and Dortchen could only wonder what bad news lay beneath. It was strange to pray with all one's might for the French forces to win, after so long wishing for their defeat.

In August the newspapers reported the French had won a great battle at Smolensk. Outside the church that Sunday, everyone rejoiced at the news, but Jakob said curtly, 'It's interesting that they report the victory at Smolensk but not the defeat at Polotsk.'

'What? What's that? A defeat?' Herr Wild caught Jakob's elbow.

Jakob removed himself from Herr Wild's grasp. 'Yes, a battle was fought and lost the same day. I've read the dispatches from the front.'

Herr Wild's shoulders drooped and he turned away. He gestured curtly to the women of his family and they all obediently hurried to his side. 'No time for gossiping,' he said sharply. 'Work to be done.'

A letter came a few days later, in Rudolf's untidy scrawl. 'All we do is march and march,' he wrote. 'You would not believe how poor and miserable the land is. The Russians are burning everything as they retreat, so that we march through blackened fields and burnt-out villages. It means we cannot scavenge for food, so we're all hungry. I never thought I'd be glad of all that hard tack Dortchen baked me. Love to all, and give baby Marianne a kiss from me.'

'What about a kiss for me?' Louise cried, tucking the letter away in her bosom. 'German men are so ungallant.'

By the end of August, the newspapers reported that one hundred and fifty thousand Grand Army soldiers had been lost – to sickness, hunger, exhaustion and desertion – without more than the occasional quick skirmish being fought. Some had shot themselves, it was said in the market, rather than keep on marching.

'I saw the Emperor,' Rudolf wrote. 'I was surprised how fat he was. Obviously some food must be getting through, not that I or any of my comrades have seen any.'

On 8th September, news came that a great battle had been fought at the small village of Borodino. Fighting had begun at dawn and had continued without respite all day. It was, people said, the bloodiest battle ever fought. More than seventy thousand men had died.

It was impossible to take in. So many deaths. More people than lived in all of Cassel.

'What of my boy?' Frau Wild wept. 'Oh, merciful God, please let him have survived.'

The newspaper was half-black, as if stained by smoke and blood, rather than the censors' ink. Dortchen's father folded it, laid it neatly by his breakfast plate and went to open a fresh bottle of quince brandy. For the first time Dortchen could remember, he did not open the shop. He sat in his gloomy study, the shutters drawn, and drank his way through the bottle. Dortchen had to do her best with any customers who came; she was unwilling to rouse her father from his stupor but did not want to turn away anyone who was in need of help.

Every day the family waited anxiously for the post to arrive, but there was never anything but bills. Louise and Dortchen went to the army barracks to beg for news, but got only a shrug from the man behind the desk. 'We do not have names yet,' he said. 'It'll be some time before all the dead are identified. With some, it's impossible.' He made an expressive gesture with his hands, like a bomb blowing up. 'We will never know.'

Frau Wild stayed in her bed, the shutters drawn, her eyes staring blankly before her. She ate very little, only the spoonfuls of soup that Dortchen brought to her mouth, and the occasional sip of tea. She rarely spoke.

Louise was far more voluble. She wept noisily, bewailed her fate, begged for news, then screamed with despair at the lack of it. She paced the floor, she complained, she demanded, and she gave contradictory orders. At times she squeezed her little girl so close to her breast that the baby screamed. At other times she thrust her into Dortchen's arms, sobbing, 'Ah, my little one. I cannot bear to see her! It hurts too much. Take her away, take her out of my sight. Let me have some peace.'

Dortchen, Mia and Old Marie did their best to keep everyone fed and the machinery of the big house grinding along, but all carried the weight of fear and uncertainty on their shoulders.

Herr Wild, meanwhile, drank alone in his study.

At last, a letter came from Rudolf. 'I have seen hell,' he wrote. 'The smoke from the cannon fire was so thick it looked like a volcano erupting. The ground was piled high with the dead and dying, as high as my waist. I did my best to help. We had to chop off many men's arms and legs. We didn't even have any brandy to give them, let alone laudanum. I was drenched in blood and gore by the end of it, and we had a great pile of severed limbs behind us, still wearing boots and gloves as we had no time to remove them. We had no food or water to give the injured, nor any medicines, and we had to rip up the shirts of the dead to make bandages. Surely the war must be won now. Surely we can come home.'

'At least he's alive,' Dortchen said, trying to comfort her weeping mother and sister-in-law. 'He's not hurt. And he's doing his best for the wounded. That has to mean something.'

Frau Wild wiped her eyes. 'When will this war end? Are we never to have peace?'

'France has been at war for as long as I've been alive,' Louise said. 'Why do people keep attacking us?'

'*You* keep attacking *us*!' Mia cried.

'Not at all,' Louise answered coolly. 'We are only defending our hard-won freedoms. Austria and Prussia and England all attacked us first, and Spain and Russia joined in. If they had left us alone, the Emperor would never have sought to subdue them.'

'Yes, he would have!' Mia's face was crimson with rage. 'He's a tyrant and a bully and a despot. He wants to be king of the world!'

'Not just a mere king,' Louise answered. 'Emperor of the world. And if Russia surrenders, he will be.'

'The newspaper says the Tsar has lost half his army at Borodino,' Dortchen said. 'Surely he must sue for peace now?'

But the Tsar did not surrender. The Russians continued to retreat, burning their land every step of the way, all the way back to Moscow. The French marched after them.

On 14th September, Napoléon and his army entered Moscow. *Surely now the Tsar must surrender*, Dortchen thought. *Please, let the Tsar surrender!* But the Tsar did not surrender.

'Moscow burns!' the headline read the next day.

Dortchen read the newspaper over her father's shoulder as she served breakfast. The retreating Russians had set their ancient city on fire, the article said. They had burnt shops, grain stores, factories, warehouses and arsenals – anything that might have been of use to the French. Russian soldiers had opened wide the doors of all their prisons and insane asylums, spilling criminals and madmen into the streets. The exhausted soldiers of the Grand Army had found themselves fighting desperate, violent men whose only chance of escape was to kill all who stood in their way.

'The whole city was soon on fire,' the newspaper said. 'The heavens were lit red from horizon to horizon. The Emperor was forced to flee Moscow in the middle of the night. Behind him, unfortunate soldiers and citizens screamed as they were caught in the flames. The ancient city of the Tsars has been reduced to ashes, and with it much of the Emperor's army.'

Herr Wild lurched out of the room, knocking over his chair.

'What is it?' Frau Wild cried, her hand at her throat. 'What's wrong?'

Dortchen could not answer her. It seemed to her that the end of the world truly had come. The omen of the comet had come true.

ALMIGHTY FATHER

October 1812

'Dortchen! Where is that dratted girl? Dortchen!' Herr Wild's bellow sounded down the hall.

Dortchen was in the kitchen, trying to put a meal together out of lentils, broad beans, and cabbage. She sighed, wiped her hands and took off her apron, then went reluctantly down the hall towards the study. There had been no letter from Rudolf, and the news in the morning paper was so bad that her father had once again spent the day in his study, drinking. She dreaded responding to his call, but knew that if she took too long he would suspect her of sneaking out.

'I'm here, Father. What is it?'

'I can't take off my dratted boots.'

Her father was sitting in his chair, an empty bottle and glass before him, the newspapers flung all over the floor. His frockcoat was unbuttoned and his cravat was askew, and he was doing his best to tug off his boots but failing in his drunken haze.

'Pull them off for me,' he demanded.

Dortchen bent and tugged at his boot. It was stiff over his swollen foot, and she had to exert all her strength. At last it pulled free, but her father tipped over backward and came crashing to the ground. 'Damn fool,' he cried. He picked up the boot and flung it at Dortchen, hitting her hard on the side of the head. She cried out in pain.

'Stupid girl,' he grumbled, sitting up. 'Pull off the other one.'

Dortchen wanted to throw the boot at his head and tell him to take his own boots off, but she did not dare. She bent, pulled off the other boot, dropped it on the floor beside him and walked out of the study.

'No need to be insolent,' her father called after her.

The day passed. Dortchen carried endless trays of soup and tea up and down the stairs to weeping women who would not eat. The chamber pots all needed to be emptied, the fireplaces cleaned and the ashes dragged out to the hopper. The horse, the cow, the pig and the chickens all had to be fed, and their stalls cleaned out. Dortchen was so exhausted that she could scarcely move.

That evening, as the family sat down to a silent meal, her father threw his soup bowl at her, telling her it was pigswill and not fit for a working man's dinner. The hot soup splashed her face, and the bowl clattered on the ground, spreading its contents all over the rug.

Frau Wild protested faintly, and Mia looked at Dortchen apologetically. Dortchen cleaned up the mess and said nothing.

The next morning, Herr Wild beat Mia for dropping the jug of breakfast ale. The jug was made of pewter and was not even dented, but he had punished his youngest daughter as if it had been the most precious crystal.

Mia was red-eyed and sniffling on the way to church, wincing with every step. Dortchen walked beside her like an automaton. Herr Wild walked ahead, with Frau Wild, Louise, Dortchen and Mia following along behind anxiously. Marianne's angry wail was muffled against her mother's shoulder.

The square outside the church was empty; they were late. As Herr Wild pushed open the heavy arched door, it scraped on the flagstones. Everyone in the church looked around.

Dortchen saw Wilhelm gazing at her anxiously. 'Is all well?' he mouthed.

She shook her head. Conscious of her father's suspicious glare, she looked down at the ground. She had never wanted more to shelter in the warmth and strength of her lover's arms, but she dared not even look at him again.

She heard nothing of the pastor's sermon. His voice was an endless drone. The scrape of boots on stone signalled to her when to stand and when to sit. She sang without knowing which was the hymn of the day, and turned the pages of her prayer book without glancing at the words.

Her father did not drink that day, it being Sunday, but that only made his temper worse. Instead of skulking in his study, he stormed about the house, kicking over a basket of darning Mia had left in the hallway, and yelling at Frau Wild till she wept and ran to her bedroom.

'Batten down the hatches, bad weather ahead,' Mia said forlornly, but Dortchen did not have the heart to smile.

She had to get away from the house. Gathering all her courage together the following morning, she went to the study and knocked tentatively on the floor.

'What do you want?' her father's slurred voice asked.

'Father, it's me, Dortchen. I need to go to the garden. The fruit has to be harvested. It'll drop and rot if I don't go and pick it.'

There was a long silence, then the door slowly opened. Her father peered at her through the gap with red, suspicious eyes. 'Yes,' he said. 'The fruit.'

Dortchen's breath gusted out in relief. 'Can I take the pony trap?'

'No,' he replied. 'I may need it.'

'But, Father, I cannot harvest much if I have to carry it home in a basket,' she protested.

'You'll manage somehow.'

Dortchen was not prepared to argue with him. 'Very well, Father,' she said, backing away. 'I'll do what I can.'

It was a long walk out to the market garden, and Dortchen was tired. It was a relief, nonetheless, to be away from the house. The streets were virtually empty, without the usual crowds of noisy soldiers bargaining for beer and sausages in the marketplace. Many of the barrows were closed down, and those that were open were tended by women. There was little to be bought. A few limp carrots or dirty potatoes, a few small fish, a freshly plucked chicken dangling by its feet.

The narrow, crooked streets of the Old Town gave way to the elegant squares of the New Town. Dortchen passed the grand residence of the Hassenpflugs just as the large blue door opened and two young men in shabby black coats and tall hats came out. The Grimm brothers.

Tears sprang to Dortchen's eyes and she hurried on, keeping her face averted. Her old jealousy of the pretty, clever Marie Hassenpflug stabbed her afresh. Wilhelm had time to visit the Hassenpflugs, did he, but no time to visit her? It was no consolation that Dortchen had warned Wilhelm many, many times not to come calling at her house. It was no consolation at all.

As she reached the market gardens, she saw that many of the trees were already turning red. It was going to be a hard winter. She unlocked the high gate and went into the garden. It was quiet and peaceful; the only sound was the twitter of birds. Dortchen looked about, wondering what the most urgent task was. She could not carry much back to the house. She decided to harvest the plums, which were beginning to fall.

'Dortchen.'

She looked up, her sudden colour betraying her. Wilhelm stood in the gateway, his hat in his hand.

'I saw you go past the Hassenpflugs with your basket and guessed you'd be here. Dortchen, you look so pale and sad. Is there bad news?'

Dortchen got unsteadily to her feet. She held out her hands and Wilhelm came to meet her, drawing her close, clasping his arms about her waist. 'Dortchen,' he whispered. 'What's wrong?'

She tried to tell him. 'Oh, Wilhelm, I'm so afraid . . .'

'For Rudolf? You've had no news, have you? If he was dead or injured, you would surely have heard.'

She shook her head. She was unable to find words for what she feared. Once again, she tried. 'My father . . .' But it was impossible to speak, and she fell silent.

Wilhelm tried to look into her face. She kept her gaze obstinately downwards. He lifted her chin and looked into her eyes. 'I do not like to see you so pale and wan. Smile, Dortchen.'

But she could not.

'What can I do?' he asked in distress.

'Kiss me,' she whispered.

So he did.

Dortchen and Wilhelm stood clasped together in the garden, the yellowing and reddening leaves all about them, the bruised scent of ripe plums filling the air.

'I knew it!'

An angry shout broke them apart. They turned, disoriented, their hands still woven together.

Herr Wild stood in the gateway, a heavy cudgel in his hand. His face was red, and his eyes bulged with rage.

'Sir,' Wilhelm said, 'you must know I wish to marry Dortchen.'

'I'll see you burn in hell first,' Herr Wild responded, stumping towards them. His cudgel was raised threateningly.

'Father, no!'

It was no use. Herr Wild caught Wilhelm a heavy blow across the shoulders. 'Seducer!' he roared. 'Libertine!'

'No, sir.' Wilhelm staggered but rallied himself. 'I assure you, sir—' Another blow caught him. 'Herr Wild, there is no need . . . sir!'

'Father,' Dortchen sobbed, 'leave him be.'

He struck her across the face with his spare hand and she fell to the ground. When Wilhelm rushed to help her up, Herr Wild caught him a vicious blow across the temple. Wilhelm almost fell, only just managing to save himself. He pulled Dortchen up and tried to shield her behind him.

Herr Wild was beside himself with rage, trying to beat Wilhelm with one hand and drag Dortchen away from him with the other. Foul words poured forth from his lips. 'Whore! Slut! Fornicator!'

'No, no,' Wilhelm said in great distress. 'Please, sir . . . If I could just explain . . . I love her.'

This last comment enraged Herr Wild more than ever. He hit Wilhelm so viciously that he was beaten down onto one knee.

'Go, go,' Dortchen cried. 'Wilhelm, please go. He'll hurt you. He's . . . he's not himself. Please, Wilhelm, go.'

'How can I go?' he cried. 'Dortchen, he'll hurt you.'

'No, no,' she lied. 'If you'll just go, I'll be fine. I'll . . . I'll talk to him. Please, Wilhelm, go.'

He lifted both arms, trying to protect his head from Herr Wild's flailing stick.

'Wilhelm, you're making it worse,' Dortchen cried. 'Please, please, go!'

Wilhelm got to his feet and seized the cudgel from Herr Wild, then flung it away into the garden. 'You'll not hurt her,' he cried.

'She's mine to do with as I wish,' Herr Wild shouted back. 'You have no right to tell me what I can and cannot do to her. Now, get out, else I'll have you charged!'

'Please, Wilhelm, just go,' Dortchen said.

He stood, fists clenched, his breath coming in wheezy gasps.

She gazed at him imploringly. 'Please.'

Wilhelm bent, picked up his hat, dusted it off and put it on his head. 'If you insist,' he said to Dortchen. Stiffly, he bowed to Herr Wild. 'I assure you my intentions are honourable, sir.'

Herr Wild gave a contemptuous snort. Wilhelm went out the gate. As he shut it behind him, he said, 'I shall call on you tomorrow, sir, so I can explain—'

'Come anywhere near my house or my daughter, and I'll sue you for an unprincipled seducer,' Herr Wild snapped.

Wilhelm's face was white, the bruises on his temple and cheek a livid red. He bowed to Herr Wild and then to Dortchen, and left.

'I knew you lied,' Herr Wild said. 'I knew you had an assignation with your lover.'

'No,' Dortchen said. 'He saw me pass by . . . He came to see if all was well.'

Her father struck her over the face again, as if lifting a hand to swat a fly. Dortchen fell at his feet, too sore and sick at heart to get up. All she could see was his boots, planted wide in the earth – and her sharp secateurs, glinting silver in the light. *I could pick them up and stab him in his black, evil heart*, she thought, *and we would all be free of him.*

But her hand did not reach for them. She knelt, waiting for her father's punishment.

'Get up,' he said. 'Get in the pony trap.'

She obeyed, picking up the secateurs. Something wet trickled down her cheek. She put up her hand and touched it – she was bleeding.

They drove home in silence. Her father tried to master his breathing, but it came harsh and quick from his chest. Together, they unbridled Trudi and put her in her stall, then pushed the pony trap into the shed. Dortchen followed three paces behind her father as they walked through the autumn garden and into the kitchen.

Old Marie was kneading bread. She looked up as they came in the kitchen. 'Bless me, my sweetling, what has happened to you?' she cried, seeing Dortchen's bruised and cut face. 'Are you hurt?' Hurriedly, she wiped her hands on her apron and came clucking forward, her fat arms held out to embrace Dortchen.

'Leave her be,' Herr Wild said. 'She's only got what she deserved. Dortchen, come.'

Numbly, she followed him down the hallway. She could hear Marianne screaming somewhere upstairs. Mia came clattering down the stairs at the sound of their footsteps. 'Dortchen, thank heavens you're home,' she called. 'The baby has the croup and I don't know—' Upon seeing her father, she fell silent and slowly backed away.

Herr Wild led Dortchen into his study and pointed at the floor. She fell to her knees.

'Pray to your Father, God Almighty,' he said.

She began to pray, a jumbled litany of half-remembered phrases and words. He sat in his chair, poured himself a large glass of quince brandy and watched her.

Then he got up and began to walk around her, so close that his long boots brushed against her breast. She recoiled. He chose a switch from the wall and flexed it in his hands, then whipped it through the air so it sang. Then he sat down again and hitched his chair forward so that his knees were set on either side of Dortchen's face.

'You disappoint me, Dortchen,' he said. 'Fornicating with your lover while your brother is missing and quite possibly dead.'

Dortchen looked up. 'No, Father, I swear it wasn't like that.'

He hit her hard across the face with the back of his hand. She ducked down, hiding her face in her hands, trying to protect her head. He put one heavy hand on the back of her neck, forcing her face even further down. 'Pray for deliverance from your sins,' he commanded.

Dortchen tried to lift her face, but he kept her head forced down. 'Oh, Father, deliver us from evil,' she gabbled. He struck her buttocks with the switch, cruelly hard, and she jerked forward involuntarily. Now her face was jammed into his groin.

'More,' he said. 'Don't stop.'

She kept praying, and he continued to strike at her buttocks, forcing her face lower and lower, till she could feel the hard pole of his erection next to her cheek, pressing against her through the woollen fabric of his trousers. His legs closed hard about her neck, holding her fast. He threw down the switch and seized her folded hands, pressing them against his erection. He began to move her hands up and down, crying, 'Pray, pray!'

Her mouth was pressed hard against the taut wool, his knees holding her head in a vice. She squirmed to get away but he was too strong, too insistent. 'Oh, God,' she whispered.

'Oh, God!' he cried. He convulsed. She felt everything beneath her hands change, his pelvis bucking and twisting, the cloth of his trousers dampening against her mouth.

He pushed her away so violently that she fell to the floor. 'You disgust me,' he said, standing and turning away from her. He poured himself a large glass of brandy and threw it down.

'You will never marry,' he told her. 'No one will want a little whore like you.'

She lay there, bewildered and frightened and ashamed.

'Go on, get up – get out of here,' he said. 'Don't you have work to do?'

She got up, wiping her hand across her mouth.

'Don't try to see him again,' he said. 'I'll know if you do.'

Dortchen went out of the study and down the hall. Mia was waiting for her. 'Dortchen, you're finished at last. The baby is sick, and Louise beside herself. Won't you come and help?' Mia's voice was cross and accusatory.

'Yes,' Dortchen said. 'I'm sorry.'

'Your face looks sore,' Mia said. 'Did he hit you?'

'Yes,' Dortchen said, and spoke no more.

PRAYING

October 1812

It was late when Dortchen was at last able to drag herself to her bed. She was so tired that her eiderdown enfolded her like magic. She slept at once, despite the pain in her bruised buttocks and face.

A creak on the stairs roused her. All was dark. The house was deathly still. Somebody fumbled at her door. Slowly, it swung open and candlelight pierced the darkness. Her heart pounding in sudden dreadful fear, Dortchen squeezed her eyes shut.

She heard her father's heavy footsteps, and could smell the reek of brandy and tobacco. He came and stood over her, breathing heavily. Then he sat on the edge of her bed. Putting the candle down on her clothes chest, he fumbled under the eiderdown. She felt his hand on the bare skin of her calf. Unable to help herself, she flinched away and cried out, then scrambled up and ran across the room.

'Marie, Marie!' she screamed.

Old Marie's door opened and the housekeeper looked out, her grey hair hanging in a long, skinny braid. 'Sweetling, what is it? What's wrong?'

Then she saw the dark shadow of Herr Wild by the bed, the flickering candle behind him making him seem faceless. He was dressed only in nightgown, nightcap and slippers. 'Sir,' she faltered. 'What's happened?'

'Nothing's wrong,' he answered, slurring the words. 'Dortchen . . . She was . . . having a nightmare. Go back to bed.'

'I beg your pardon, sir, but if Dortchen's having a nightmare I'd best settle her down, make her comfortable again.'

'No need. I'm here. I'll look after her.'

Old Marie looked from Herr Wild to Dortchen, who was standing barefoot and shivering in her nightgown in the doorway. Dortchen looked at her pleadingly. 'No need to worry yourself, sir. You go on back to bed – it's too cold to be standing about here in our nightgowns.'

'I was just . . . checking on her,' Herr Wild answered. He picked up his candle and came unsteadily towards them, the brandy fumes preceding him.

The candlelight fell full upon Dortchen, who shrank away. She was very conscious of her unfettered breasts beneath the thin cambric of her nightgown, her bare legs and buttocks, the loosened mass of her hair.

Her father stared at her, and Old Marie took a quick step forward. 'Goodnight, sir,' she said.

'Goodnight,' he slurred, then he stumbled as he passed, so that for a moment his bulk was pressed against Dortchen, trapping her in the doorway. 'Sorry,' he mumbled, then heaved himself away.

Dortchen watched as the candlelight flickered down the stairwell and away, then she flew to Old Marie. 'I'm sorry. I was so afraid. I didn't want him—'

'Shh,' Old Marie said, taking her arm and leading her back to bed. 'Don't say it. All is well. Back to bed now.' As Dortchen tried again to babble her relief and gratitude, Old Marie said, 'Shh, don't say a word.'

The next day, Old Marie was dismissed.

'Twenty-four years of service, sir . . .' she said numbly.

'We need you no longer,' Herr Wild said.

'But where am I to go? What am I to do?'

'I fail to see how that is my concern. The house is half-empty now, with most of our daughters gone and wed. What little work remains can be done by Dortchen and Mia. I bid you pack your bags and be gone. And, I warn you, I'll be counting the silver, so don't think to steal from me.'

'As if I would do such a thing,' she answered in a hurt tone.

'No need to be impertinent,' he replied. 'You may have till tomorrow to pack your things and make some plans.'

Old Marie turned to go. At the door, she turned back. 'What about the money you owe me, sir? It's been months since you last paid me.'

'We're at war, woman,' he answered irritably. 'No one has any coin.'

'I'll need the money I'm owed, sir,' she replied.

Herr Wild sighed. Dortchen, hiding outside the door with Mia, heard him unlock his desk drawer and draw out his cashbox. A few minutes later, they heard the clink of coins. 'That will have to do,' Herr Wild said. 'After all, have I not been feeding you for years, and at a time when food is more expensive than ever?'

Old Marie did not thank him. She came out and, seeing the two weeping girls, their hands pressed over their mouths, shut the door hastily. 'Go! Go!' she mouthed and shook her apron at them as if they were hens. The two girls fled down the hall and into the kitchen, with Old Marie following slowly behind.

'I'm so sorry,' Dortchen cried, as soon as the kitchen door was safely shut behind them all. 'This is all my fault.'

'No, no, sweetling,' Old Marie comforted her. 'It's no one's fault but that devil of a father of yours. Who can believe he'd turn me out into the street, after all my years of service? What shall I do? Where can I go?'

'To Lisette, of course,' Dortchen said. 'Or Hanne. Either of them would take you in the twinkling of an eye. Hanne needs your help more, but will not be able to afford to pay you much. Lisette has all the help she needs, but she'd give you a home without a second's thought.'

'Then I'll go to Hanne,' Old Marie said. 'I'd rather be where I'm of some use.'

'Oh, Marie!' Mia burst out into tears. 'I can't believe you're going. How are we to manage without you?'

'I'm right worried,' Old Marie admitted. 'I don't like to leave you, and that's the truth. I wish I could take you with me.'

'We wish that we could go too,' Dortchen said. A cold dreariness had dropped over her.

'We'll help you pack,' Mia said.

Old Marie snorted. 'What is there to take? I have nothing but the clothes on my back, my prayer and hymn books, and Mozart.'

'Oh, no,' Dortchen cried. 'Not Mozart too.' Fresh tears started to her eyes. She tried to gulp them back, not wanting to hurt Old Marie's feelings.

The old housekeeper understood, however, and chucked her under the chin. 'Bless you, my sweet, I'm sorry, but I need to take my bird. I reared him from a chick, I did, and he's spent every waking hour with me since. He'd not understand me leaving him.'

It was all too horrible to contemplate. Dortchen and Mia fled upstairs to their mother, who lay in her darkened bedroom with a damp cloth over her eyes.

'Girls, please, not so loud,' she moaned, as the sisters burst into her room.

'Mother! Father's sacked Old Marie,' Mia cried. 'You have to tell him not to.'

Her mother raised herself up on her pillows. 'Oh, no. But why?'

'He says he can't afford to feed her any more,' Mia said furiously.

Dortchen hung back, unable to tell her mother the true reason. She felt sick and frightened at the idea of not having Old Marie's comforting presence across the hallway any more.

'Oh, dear, whoever shall do the washing?' her mother said.

'Mother, you have to tell Father he's not to do it,' Mia insisted. 'We need Old Marie, we need her.'

'I can't be saying any such thing to your father,' Frau Wild replied. 'He gets so angry when his will is crossed. Dear me. We'll just need to make the best of things.' She lay down again, the cloth scrunched in her hand. 'I have a splitting headache. Dortchen, would you be a dear and get me a fresh cloth? This one is quite hot.'

'Louise can,' Dortchen said, in the hardest voice she had ever used towards her mother. 'Since she does nothing but lie around all day either.'

Old Marie left after lunch, declaring she would not stay another night in a house where she was not wanted. The girls walked her to the stagecoach, Dortchen holding Mozart's cage and Mia carrying the old housekeeper's small bag.

'A letter came for you this morning,' Old Marie told Dortchen in an undertone. 'I saw it when I took the post in to your father. He did not give it to you?'

Dortchen shook her head, heartsick.

'There was another letter in the same hand, addressed to your father,' Old Marie went on. 'I think he tossed it on the fire unopened, for his fireplace was full of half-burnt pages when I cleaned it out before we left.'

Dortchen said nothing.

'Have a care, my sweetling,' Old Marie said.

'Sweetling, sweetling,' Mozart chirped from under his cloth.

Tears welled up in Dortchen's eyes. She hugged Old Marie close.

'Now, now, no tears, not in the street,' Old Marie said. 'Come visit me at Hanne's, mind.'

Neither Dortchen nor Mia could stop crying. They kissed the old woman's rosy cheek one more time, then helped her clamber up into the coach and handed the starling's cage up to her. Both girls waved their sodden handkerchiefs till the stagecoach was gone from sight.

Then, lonely and bereft, they walked back to the shop. The kitchen seemed empty and cold, and far too silent. Dortchen and Mia sank down at the kitchen table and stared at each other.

'Everyone's going away,' Mia said. 'There's only you and me left.'

Dortchen shuddered.

'What's wrong?' Mia asked, her round face looking worried.

'Just a goose walking over my grave,' Dortchen lied.

That night, Dortchen could not lie down to sleep in her own familiar bed. She caught up her robe and slippers, and crept down to Mia's room.

'I can't sleep,' she whispered. 'Can I stay with you?'

'Mmm,' Mia mumbled. Dortchen lifted the bedclothes and crawled in beside her. She lay awake, tense and afraid, but the house was quiet. Slowly, she began to slip into sleep.

The passing of candlelight outside Mia's door and the betraying creak of the stairs roused her. She jerked awake. She heard heavy footsteps overhead. A moment's pause, then the steps began to creak again.

Mia's door was pushed open and her father looked in. Dortchen shut her eyes hastily as the candle was lifted high, its light wavering over the bed where the two girls lay together. There was a long pause, then the candlelight faded away and the door squeaked shut. Dortchen let out her breath. It was a long time before she slept.

The next day, at breakfast, Herr Wild said, 'Your mother is unwell. She needs looking after. I'm moving her into Gretchen's old bedroom so her moaning and tossing and turning at night will not disturb me any more. I'm a working man and need my rest.'

No one spoke.

He turned to Mia. 'You will sleep in her room on a pallet, in case she needs anything during the night.'

'Oh, but Father—' she protested.

He held up a hand. 'No arguments. Your mother needs to be cared for, and, Lord knows, you aren't much use for anything else in this house.'

Mia looked hurt. She had been trying hard to help Dortchen around the house and certainly did a great deal more than Louise.

As the day wheeled inexorably on towards darkness, panic began to rise in Dortchen's throat. She found more and more to do, scrubbing the kitchen table till it was spotless, wiping the pewter plates till she could see her own blurred reflection in them, shaking the rag rugs out the back door, and arranging all the jars in the pantry so that they were perfectly in line.

Mia went reluctantly to her new bed in her mother's room. Louise yawned and said, 'Rudolf told me Cassel was far gayer than Berlin. He was a terrible liar, that brother of yours.' She too went to bed. At last, Dortchen could find no further excuses, and she was so weary that her jaw was cracking with her yawns. Hoping that her father was asleep, she tiptoed up the stairs as quietly as she could, avoiding the steps that creaked.

She sat in her bed, the warming pan at her toes, and waited. Sure enough, she soon heard the creak of her father's footsteps, and the door cracked open with candlelight. Her father was an enormous, dark, shadowy beast in her doorway.

'You have sinned,' he whispered. 'Get down on your knees, girl, and pray.'

ALL-KINDS-OF-FUR

October 1812

Red-eyed and silent, Dortchen knelt before the kitchen fire.

It was cold and grey. She would have to clean out the hearth and light the fire again. She wondered dully how Old Marie had managed to keep the fire alight all night, so the hot coals were ready to be blown back into life in the morning. Raking out the cold ashes, Dortchen swept them up in her pan and emptied it into the bucket.

The wood basket was almost empty. Dortchen made the fire as best she could with the scraps of kindling that remained, shoving in a few crumpled handfuls of precious newspaper to help it catch. Her hands were so cold that she had trouble striking a spark from her flint. At last, the fire flickered into life and she put the kettle on to boil.

She took the bucket out to the ash hopper, then set to chopping up some more wood. Dortchen had never had to chop wood before. It had always been Rudolf's job, but since he had gone off to war, Old Marie had quietly added it to her chores. It was not long before Dortchen was sweating, despite the chill of the predawn air, and her hands were soon marred with blisters.

She carried the wood to the empty rack beside the fire, but dropped it all over the floor when she realised she had been so long that the kettle was boiling dry. Quickly, she seized a thick cloth, swung the kettle away and carried it, hissing and steaming, back to the water pump. When it was once again hanging over the fire, Dortchen picked up the scattered wood and stacked it in its rack, before hurriedly making some bread dough out of the meagre supplies, which she kneaded till her arms ached. She put the dough into the bread tins, took the whistling kettle off the fire and shoved the tins into the ashes. She hurriedly made tea, then filled her father's pewter jug of shaving water.

The sun was not even showing over the rooftops, but she felt exhausted. Dortchen had never before realised just how hard Old Marie had worked.

'You're late,' her father said as she carried in the tray. He stood in his shirtsleeves near the mirror, his watch in one hand, the razor in the other.

'I'm sorry,' she answered, not looking at him.

'Have you been lying in, you slug-a-bed?'

'No, Father.'

'Breakfast had best not be late.'

She nodded, put the tray down and made her escape.

The cow had to be milked, the chickens and geese fed, and poor Trudi watered. As Dortchen laboured from one job to another, her thoughts flitted about. One minute she was planning ways to escape; the next she was telling herself drearily that there was nowhere her father would not find her.

She longed for the comfort of Wilhelm's arms, yet she felt sick with shame that he might guess her secret. Dortchen felt as if it was branded upon her face for all to see. She was no longer the girl who had kissed Wilhelm beneath the linden blossoms. She wept as she raked the ashes from the fireplace, turning out hunks of blackened bread. She cut away the burnt edges, and her legs trembled as she took it to the breakfast table.

'Useless girl,' her father said, pushing his plate away. 'Katharina, do you not think your daughters should know how to make a loaf of bread? Useless, the lot of you.'

His wife and daughters looked down at their plates, and Frau Wild bit her lip. No one ate the bread.

After her father had gone into the shop, Dortchen took the breakfast plates and scraped the leftovers into the pig's bucket, tears burning her eyes. When Mia tried to comfort her, she pushed her away and went out to work in the garden. It was time to cut back the herbs in preparation for the first frosts. But even the smell of the crushed herbs and the humming of the bees could not comfort her. The tears overflowed and trickled down her face.

She heard her father's step on the brick path and froze. He stood over her for a moment but she did not look up. He snorted and went on his way, and Dortchen wiped away her tears with the muddy edge of her glove. In a few minutes she heard the *clip-clop-clip* of Trudi's hooves in the alleyway, and the rumble of the buggy's wheels.

A few minutes later, the gate slowly swung open. 'Dortchen?' Wilhelm called in a low voice. 'Are you there?'

Hastily, she scrubbed at her face with her sleeve. 'Yes,' she answered, her voice gruff.

He came through the gate, his hat held in one hand. His dark curls were all tousled, and his cravat was awry. 'I heard your father go out and came straight over. Oh, my little love, are you all right?'

She rose and stood quietly, her hands full of pennyroyal and rue. He came towards her quickly, then reached up to touch the bruise on her cheek. 'I cannot believe he would beat you so. The scoundrel!'

'You cannot be here. If he sees you, he will kill you.'

'I've tried and tried to see you,' Wilhelm said. 'I've come to the shop but he tells me to get out before he calls the constables and has me arrested. And once I came to the back but Old Marie told me it was best I went away, that your father was in a fine old temper.'

'Old Marie is gone,' Dortchen said. 'Father sacked her.'

'Oh, Dortchen, I'm so sorry.'

'You need to go,' she told him.

'Don't make me go,' he said. 'Your father's gone out – we need to seize our chance.'

'I have work to do.'

Wilhelm was puzzled. He tried to kiss her, but she could not bear to touch her soiled mouth to his. She turned her face away.

'Oh, Dortchen! What are we to do?' His face was troubled.

'There's nothing we can do. I must obey my father – you know that.' Without looking at him, she laid the bunch of herbs in her basket and bent to cut some more.

'Oh, Dortchen, I cannot bear it. Surely there is some way to change his mind?'

She bit her lip and turned away, slashing at the rue with her scythe.

'Is it because I am poor?' Wilhelm's voice was hard and angry.

'That's part of it.'

'Will he change his mind if I have an income?' Wilhelm asked. 'Because the fairy tale manuscript has gone to the printers. They are setting the proofs now, and it'll be available for sale in just a few weeks. Dortchen, if the book does well, will your father allow us to marry?'

'I don't know,' she answered at last, tying up the bundles of rue, the stink of it filling her nostrils.

'We have to have hope.' Wilhelm crouched and seized her hands. 'Please, my little love. I hate to see you so pale and wan. Did he hurt you again? I cannot bear the idea of him hurting you.'

Dortchen could not meet his eyes. When he tried to kiss her, she turned her face away again. So he kissed the curve of her jaw, the soft skin behind her earlobe. 'I want to keep you safe,' he murmured. 'I want to make sure no one ever hurts you again.'

Dortchen could not keep her arms from creeping about his neck. She leant her face against his chest, listening to his heart. He kept on kissing what little parts of her he could find, whispering to her. 'I know you should obey your father . . . but when he is so cruel to you . . . How can this be wrong, what we feel for each other? It feels so right, so beautiful . . . Surely he cannot keep us apart?'

'He can.' Her words were low and muffled.

'Shall we run away together, then? Surely there must be a way.'

'He'll find us, and then he'll kill you.' She spoke with utter certainty.

'No, no . . . Think of Hanne. She and Johann ran away, and he relented in the end.'

'It's not the same.'

'But why?'

She could not explain to him.

He turned her face up so he could look into her eyes, but she would not return his gaze. 'What is wrong, sweetling? Is it just your father?'

She laughed involuntarily, then she had to cover her face with her hands to stop herself from weeping. 'Yes,' she told him. 'It's just my father.'

'I'll talk to him, I'll reassure him. It'll be all right.' He drew her close, but she shook her head and moved away.

'He won't listen, Wilhelm. There's no point even trying.'

He was troubled. 'Don't lose hope. Dortchen, if the fairy tale book is going to be a success, it has to be as good as possible. I wanted to ask you . . . Do you remember that tale you told me on the hill near the Lion's Castle? About the girl who is sent out into the snow in a dress made of paper, to search for strawberries? And she finds three little men in the wood?'

Dortchen nodded.

'Will you tell it to me again? I couldn't write it down last time, but it's such a marvellous story, with the good girl who spits gold coins and the bad girl who coughs up toads . . . I just can't remember it all.'

Dortchen drew her hand across her eyes. She picked up her basket and headed towards the sanctuary of the dim, warm kitchen, away from the glare of daylight. 'Come in,' she said. 'I'll tell it to you again while I finish the herbs. You'll need to be quick, though, as my life won't be worth living if my father finds you here.'

'Can I borrow some paper and a quill?'

Dortchen nodded and drew down the little writing box in which her mother kept her accounting book and inkpot. She found some old paper and gave it to Wilhelm. As he sharpened the quill, she began to prepare small bunches of pennyroyal, hyssop, wormwood and rue to hang above the fire to dry.

'Listen out for my father,' she warned him. 'If he comes, you must fly as fast as you can.'

He nodded, though she could tell by his face that he hated the thought of such cowardice.

She sat down at the table, her hands in their heavy gloves working without thought. 'Once there was a man whose wife had died, and a woman whose husband had died,' she began. 'Each had a daughter. The girls knew each other, and one day they ended up together at the woman's house. She said to the man's daughter, "If you tell your father that I am interested in marrying him, I promise that you can bathe in milk every day and drink wine every day. My own daughter will have to drink water and wash in water."'

Like me, Dortchen thought. She paused, watching Wilhelm transcribe what she had said. His hands were stained with ink, his middle forefinger calloused where the quill rested. She remembered his hands on her body, and shuddered. He looked up enquiringly, and she went on, her voice thick.

'So the girl went home and told her father what the woman had said, and the man replied, "What should I do? Marriage can be a joy, but it can also be a torture."'

Wilhelm smiled, flashing his eyes up to hers, then back down to his page. Dortchen could not be still. She stood and moved over to the window to check that there was no sign of her father. She found one task after another to keep her hands busy, while the girl in the story went out into the snow in a frock made of paper to search for strawberries.

Wilhelm drew a new piece of paper towards him as Dortchen described how the girl was blessed by the three little men with the gift of spitting gold coins with every word.

'Let us hope you have the same gift,' Wilhelm said, sharpening a new quill with his penknife. 'It's such a wonderful story, it deserves to be in our collection. And maybe it will help make our fortune.'

Dortchen tried to smile.

She told the rest of the story, which ended with the wicked stepmother being rolled down a hill in a barrel studded with nails.

Wilhelm scattered sand over his pages. 'I'll write it up neatly tonight and send it to the publisher tomorrow,' he said. 'It'd be a shame not to include it.' He stood and stretched his arms over his head, shaking out his cramped hand.

Dortchen looked through the half-open door at the garden. There was still no sound of her father returning home. She dreaded hearing the rumble of the buggy's wheels and the sound of his heavy boots.

'I know another story,' she said. 'One I've never told you before.'

Wilhelm looked up in interest. 'Really? Will you tell me?'

She could not look at him. She busied herself grinding fallen acorns in the mortar, a job that never finished. 'Once upon a time, there was a king who was married to the most beautiful woman in the world, with hair of purest gold,' Dortchen said. 'Before the king's wife died, she asked that he would only marry someone who was as beautiful as herself, and who had hair as golden as her own. One day, the king looked at his daughter and saw that she was as beautiful as her mother, and her hair was as golden. He felt he must marry her, and told his daughter so.'

Dortchen's arms felt heavy. Her legs trembled, and her face and body were hot. Concentrating on grinding the acorns to a fine powder, she went on, though the words felt sharp in her throat. 'The wise princess said the king must first get her three dresses: one as golden as the sun, one as silver as the moon, and one as sparkling as the stars.'

Dortchen paused. Wilhelm's quill scratched across the parchment, pinning down her words with its sharp point. 'Then she asked her father for a coat made from all kinds of fur, from every kind of animal in the kingdom. A thousand animals were caught and flayed to make the coat, and the three dresses were made, golden as the sun, silver as the moon and sparkling as the stars. The king said they would be married the next day.'

Wilhelm frowned at his page, then looked up at her as she stopped speaking. Dortchen began to gabble the story as fast as she could, determined to get it out. 'During the night, she collected the gifts from her betrothed – a gold ring, a little gold spinning wheel and a little golden reel.'

'Wait,' Wilhelm said, his quill pausing. 'Who was her betrothed? Do you mean her father, the king?'

Dortchen paid him no mind, all her energies concentrated on forcing the story past her lips. 'She put the dresses in a nutshell, darkened her face with soot, put on the fur, and walked out into a big forest, where she fell asleep in a hollow tree. The next day, the king was hunting in the forest.'

'The king? Her father?' Wilhelm asked.

'Her betrothed,' Dortchen said, giving a little irritated shrug of her shoulders. She knew she was telling the story badly. 'His dogs found the girl in the coat of fur. She was caught and dragged home behind his cart. She was called All-Kinds-of-Fur.'

Wilhelm frowned. 'But did he not recognise her? If she was his betrothed . . .'

'She was all dirty,' Dortchen said. 'And disguised in the fur.'

She went on even faster, her hands grinding away at the mortar. 'She had to sleep in a sty without light under the staircase. She had to cook and clean and scrub all day and half the night. Before the king went to bed, she had to go and take off his boots, which he then threw at her head.'

Wilhelm looked up at her, startled. 'Why—?' he began, but Dortchen did not pause.

'Once there was a ball. All-Kinds-of-Fur wanted to see her betrothed and asked the cook for permission to go upstairs to look at the splendour. She washed off the soot, took off the coat of fur and put on the sun-dress.

'When she entered the ballroom, everybody stepped aside for this princess. The king danced with her. He thought the unknown princess looked like his betrothed and wanted to question her. But she curtsied and left. She changed her clothes and returned to the kitchen, where the cook asked her to make bread soup, and to take care to drop no hair in it. She made the bread soup and put in the gold ring that the king had given her.

'When the ball was over, the king had his bread soup. He thought it had never tasted so good, and then saw his engagement ring at the bottom. He wondered how it had got there and called the cook, who got angry with All-Kinds-of-Fur, threatening to beat her if she had dropped a hair in the soup.

'The king, however, praised the soup and was told that All-Kinds-of-Fur had made it. When she was questioned about her identity and her knowledge of the ring, she answered that she was only good for having boots thrown at her and knew nothing of the ring. Then she ran off.'

Wilhelm's quill was flying over the page. He dipped it in the inkpot and went on, doing his best to keep up with Dortchen's tumble of words.

'At the next ball, All-Kinds-of-Fur washed and dressed in her moon-dress. This time the king was convinced she was his betrothed, as nobody else in the world had such golden hair. But she disappeared, and back in the kitchen she put the golden spinning wheel in the bread soup. The king liked the soup even more, and was surprised to find the spinning wheel he had given his betrothed. First the cook and then All-Kinds-of-Fur were called, but the king got no better answer than the previous time.

'Hoping that his betrothed would turn up, the king arranged a third ball. This time All-Kinds-of-Fur put on her star-dress. During the ball, the king put the gold ring from his soup on her finger. But she disappeared and changed back into the coat of fur. In her rush, however, she forgot to blacken one finger. She made the bread soup and put the reel in it. When the king found it, he called for All-Kinds-of-Fur. The king saw her white finger, clasped it and found his ring. He then tore off the coat of fur and her golden hair fell down: she was his betrothed.'

Dortchen saw that the acorns were as ground as they could ever be. Her arms ached. She pushed the mortar away and raised her eyes to Wilhelm's face. He looked troubled, but there was none of the horrified comprehension that she both hoped for and dreaded.

'What happened then?' he asked.

Dortchen stretched out her arms and laid her head down. 'They were married.'

'It is the most extraordinary story,' Wilhelm said, cleaning the quill on a rag. 'It feels old, very old. It has a lot of mysteries in it, lots of oddities, but then so do all the best of the old stories. We had a similar tale in the manuscript we gave to Clemens. It too had a girl who goes secretly to a ball, and who reveals herself by hiding her ring in some food. This feels much more authentic, however, much more powerful and dark. It has echoes of *Vitae duorum Offarum* . . .'

Dortchen felt a chasm gaping between them. She could not understand a word he said, and it seemed he had not understood her either. She stood up abruptly. 'You need to go.'

He looked up at her, surprised by the sharpness of her tone. 'I wish I didn't have to, but I know your father will be home soon. And I need to get these stories off to the publisher as soon as possible, if they are to make it into the book.'

She did not answer.

'When can I see you again?' he asked, standing up.

'I don't know. My father . . .' She stood back to let him go through to the garden.

'We just have to hope he will change his mind,' Wilhelm said, pausing on the doorstep, 'once he sees the book is published and selling well.'

Dortchen tried to smile, but the muscles of her face seemed to have forgotten the movements. *He'll never change his mind.*

THE COLDEST WINTER

November 1812

A letter arrived from Rudolf. It was written on a mere scrap of paper, stained and tattered, his hand almost indecipherable. 'We are coming home,' it read. 'I cannot wait to shake off the dust of this accursed land. At first we thought Moscow was like something out of *A Thousand and One Nights*. It was so beautiful and strange, and we had conquered it. We were delirious with joy. But the city was eerily quiet, with hardly a soul to be seen. Everyone had fled. We made camp, worn half to death by the fighting and all the marching. In the dead of the night, they set fire to their own city, and us all sleeping within. The Emperor himself scarcely escaped with his life. I have never seen such a terrifying sight. My dreams are haunted by the roar of the fire, the howls of the burning dogs, the screams of the dying. Most of my battalion didn't escape. Those of us still alive are so weary we can scarcely walk. How we are to get home I cannot think.'

Another fragment came two weeks later.

'We have reached Borodino. The dead were never cleared away. They still lie there, their eyes staring at the sky, their skin so mottled with red and blue that it is as if they have painted their faces like cheap whores. The stink is indescribable. I went to the monastery where we had left our wounded. They have been left all this time with no kind of help. No food, no water, no medicines, not even any chamber pots. We are going to take them with us, though only the Devil knows how.'

When Dortchen and Lotte went to the market together, they heard other snippets of news from the mothers and sisters of other Hessian soldiers.

'My son says they are being harassed by Cossacks,' the fishmonger's wife told them, her eyes shadowed with fear. 'He says they swoop in on their horses and kill the slow ones, taking everything they own, right down to their underwear.'

'They've had to abandon all the guns,' the butcher said. 'My boy is heartbroken; he loves that gun like it was a woman. He says the horses simply haven't the strength to pull them any more.'

'It's begun to snow,' the miller's daughter said, tears making tracks through the white flour dust on her cheek. 'Oh, God, my brother wouldn't take his warm underthings. He said they'd be home before the end of summer.'

It grew cold in Cassel too. Dortchen's hands were red-raw with blisters from chopping wood. She and Mia pickled all the cabbages, and Herr Wild killed the pig. The screams as it died were horrendous.

'We have no food,' Rudolf wrote. 'We retreat the way we came. If we scrape away the snow, we find only black underneath where the Russians burnt the fields. The villages are deserted, with dead bodies still lying where they fell two months ago. I have seen soldiers carve a slice from a poor horse's rump while it staggers along, cramming it raw and bloody into their mouths. Another will do so a few paces along, and when the horse at last falls, we are all upon it, fighting for its heart and liver. A field with a few old cabbage stalks is a feast to us. We boil the stalks up with the stump of a tallow candle and a handful of gunpowder, then we must fight to stop others from stealing it.'

On 11th November, the newspapers reported that a disaster had befallen Napoléon's stepson, Prince Eugene. He and his men had tried to ford a river, but his heavy guns had been overturned by the swift current. Many men were swept away and drowned, while others froze to death overnight. He lost two and a half thousand men, all his heavy guns and artillery, plus the baggage trains that carried the food and ammunition for his men. All they could do was stumble on, while the Russians pursued them, bombarding the straggling troops and seizing the fallen as prisoners.

'They say Napoléon himself was almost taken,' Lotte told Dortchen as they stood together in the queue for flour. 'I heard that the Emperor now wears a bag with poison in it about his neck, so he can kill himself if the Russians get hold of him.'

In late November, Napoléon succeeded in building a bridge across the Berezina River, after tricking the Russians into thinking he planned to cross elsewhere. The Russians realised their mistake and came galloping back, determined to stop the French from escaping. A handful of men held the Russians off till the bulk of the French army was safe on the far bank. The bridge was burnt behind them, leaving the defending soldiers to be slaughtered by the Russians. Most of the soldiers left behind were Hessian.

The mood in Cassel was gloomy. Many shops were closed and shuttered, with wreaths hanging on their doors. The people in the streets were dressed mainly in black. Crowds stood outside the army barracks, begging for news of their loved ones. Women wept into black-bordered handkerchiefs. Louise went with Marianne, seeking word of Rudolf. She came home in the twilight, pale, red-eyed and silent. 'Too many dead,' she said listlessly to Dortchen. 'They told us it was best not to hope.'

Jakob and Wilhelm called on Herr Wild, seeking news of Rudolf. He shut the door in their faces.

Two weeks later, another letter came from Rudolf, scrawled on a shred of paper. 'It is so cold. I do not think I'll ever make it home. I'm so sorry.' It was undated and unsigned. There was no way of telling if it had been written before the fatal crossing of the Berezina.

The days passed, and terrible rumours reached the marketplace. Napoléon's army was nearly wiped out, dying from disease, starvation and the cold. Napoléon himself was dead. No, Napoléon was alive, but he had abandoned his army and driven home to Paris. There had been a coup, someone said. The Emperor was overthrown. No, no, someone else said, he has arrested the conspirators and still reigns.

In mid-December, the newspapers published the Emperor's official army bulletin. 'His Majesty's health has never been better,' it said. Very little was said about the health of his army.

Every day, Herr Wild drank in the gloom of his study. Every night, he crept through the dark house to his daughter's room. Dortchen would sit, huddled in her eiderdown, waiting for the creak of his footsteps, the piercing of candlelight through her keyhole, the dark loom of him in her doorway. It was better to wait than to be woken from sleep with his weight upon her, his hand on her mouth to keep her quiet.

It was the coldest winter Dortchen had ever known.

The River Fulda froze solid, and King Jérôme organised sleigh races from Aue Island to the bridge and back. Bells rang out merrily as the horses galloped along the ice, their hooves throwing up glittering shards of frost. One night he even held a ball on the ice. Couples in thick furs waltzed about an immense bonfire, while the musicians shivered as they plied their instruments with numb fingers. Mia went with Lotte and the Hassenpflug sisters. She came home with rosy cheeks and glowing eyes, describing the scene excitedly as she helped Dortchen serve supper.

Dortchen did not wish to go anywhere any more. She had drawn the boundaries of her life tight around her, like a small animal crouching in a hide. She especially hated going to church, where she would see Wilhelm and his worried eyes, and sense the curious glances of her old friends. She tried to make excuses not to go.

'I'm not surprised,' her father said. 'As steeped in sin as you are.'

THE YELLOW DRESS

December 1812

A week before Christmas, on a bright, frosty morning, a knock on the front door resounded through the house. Surprised, Dortchen went down the hall to answer it. As she passed the door to the shop, it swung open and her father filled the doorway. 'Don't you speak to him,' he warned her.

Her breath caught in her throat. Knees trembling, Dortchen opened the front door. Wilhelm stood there in a threadbare coat, his hat in his hand, snowflakes caught in his dark curls. 'I have a gift for you,' he said, and thrust out his other hand. A red leather book was clenched in his fingers. Dortchen took it and wonderingly opened it to the title page.

Children and Household Tales, she read silently. *From the Brothers Grimm.*

She raised her eyes to his. He smiled at her, his face glowing with joy and triumph. 'It's here,' he said simply.

'Dortchen, get inside,' Herr Wild said.

'Yes, Father,' she replied, slipping the book into the pocket of her apron. Wilhelm lifted two fingers to his mouth, kissed them, then held them out to her. Dortchen could not help a little smile. As she shut the door, he crossed his fingers, wishing for good luck.

Her father's face was livid with anger, and he had one fist raised.

'I did not speak to him,' Dortchen told him, passing quickly by, hunching her shoulders against the expected blow. He did not strike her, though his breath was harsh. As she reached the kitchen, she heard the shop door shut.

He had not seen Wilhelm give her the book. She hid it hurriedly and busied herself with salting and curing the bacon. Later that afternoon, when she was sure her father was busy, Dortchen sat down on a barrel in the pantry and looked through the little red leather book.

It was dedicated 'to Frau Elisabeth von Arnim, for the little Johannes Freimund'. Dortchen was hurt. What had Bettina von Arnim done to help Wilhelm and Jakob? She had not told them any stories, or helped write out any manuscripts, or made them soup and healing teas.

With jealousy a hot ache in her heart, Dortchen turned over the pages. First was the story of the Frog-King, which she had told Wilhelm. 'A tale from Hessen', the notes read. There was 'Cat and Mouse in Partnership', and then 'Mary's Child'. Both stories that Gretchen had told him. There was a long note about other stories of forbidden doors, but not a single word about who had told the Grimms this one.

She turned the pages faster. There was 'The Three Little Men in the Wood', and the one she had named 'Hänsel and Gretel'. There was 'Frau Holle' and, a few stories after it, 'The Singing Bone'. In rapid succession were the stories about Clever Elsie, and the wishing-table and the ass that farted gold, and the elves and the shoemaker. Towards the end of the book was the story about the girl who saved her sisters from the bloody chamber – and Dortchen's favourite, the story of the girl whose brothers were turned to swans.

'From Hessen', the notes read. But not a word about who had told the Grimms the tales.

Dortchen jumped up, clutching the book to her heart. Without changing her shoes or putting on her bonnet, she ran out into the garden and through the gateway, with nothing but her shawl to keep off the snow. She ran across the alleyway and up the three flights of stairs to the Grimms' apartment, and she banged on their door with her fist.

Wilhelm answered the door. 'Why, Dortchen,' he cried in pleasure, opening up his arms to her.

'Where are our names?' she cried. 'Why aren't we named in the book? We told you the tales. Our names should be there too!'

He was taken aback. 'Jakob thought it best,' he stammered. 'The tales belong to no one. They are a genuine expression of the spirit of the folk—'

'Rubbish,' Dortchen said.

He took a step away. 'But, Dortchen—'

She pointed to her mouth. 'I told you these tales. I told them. Does that mean nothing?'

'The tales came from many places, many people . . . We thought it best—'

'You! You thought nothing. You think nothing that Jakob does not think.' Dortchen slammed the book shut, then flung it open again. 'Look! All these pages of scholarly notes.'

She began to read out loud: 'In Müllenhoff, No. 8, the manikin is called Rümpentrumper. In Kletke's *Märchensaal*, No. 3, he is Hopfenhütel. In Zingerle, No. 36, and Kugerl, p. 278, Purzinigele.' She looked at him scathingly. 'You can list a whole lot of other names for Rumpelstiltskin, yet can't find room to add one line that says "told by Dortchen Wild". Four words – that's all it would take. Yet in this book, in all these thousands of words, you couldn't fit in another four.'

'Dortchen, I'm sorry. I didn't realise it mattered.'

'You're a fool,' she screamed. 'A weak, spineless fool, in thrall to your brother.' Vaguely, she was aware of Lotte and Jakob in the hallway, staring at her with shocked eyes. She did not care. She flung the book in Wilhelm's face and turned and fled.

He did not follow after her.

There was no goose to kill for Christmas supper.

Dortchen went to the marketplace, hoping to buy a chicken or a duck. Most of the stalls were shut, and the ones that were open were selling useless things, like silver snuffboxes, gold watches on chains or silken petticoats. She was able to buy only a few old turnips, and a ham hock. Dreading her father's anger, she trudged towards home.

A little girl ran past her, carrying the dangling body of a dead stork. 'They're falling from the sky,' she cried. 'Look, it's frozen to death, the poor thing.'

'Where?' Dortchen shouted after her.

'Down by the river,' the little girl called back.

Dortchen hurried down the road, then went carefully down the icy steps under the bridge. The frozen river showed black under its dusting of snow. Leafless trees shivered in the wind. She heard mournful cries and the slow flapping of wings. Storks were flying overhead, on their long journey from Russia to the south. She gazed up at them, remembering how her father used to bring her here at Christmas-time as a child, to feed the storks with a bag of old crusts. Tears stung her eyes, and she rubbed them with her gloved hands.

An ungainly body came crashing down from the sky, landing with a twisted neck out on the ice. Heedless of the possibility of the ice breaking beneath her weight, Dortchen ran to claim it, racing other children who had been lurking along the riverbank. She reached it just before a small boy, who attempted to wrest it from her.

'No, it's mine!' Dortchen cried, snatching it away. The boy kicked her in the shins but she hugged the stork close and limped away.

The bird was heavy in her arms, its head dangling down, and by the time she reached home her arms were aching. It felt wrong to pluck its long white feathers; the gaping pouch of its beak reproached her. But Dortchen turned her face away and persevered.

Church service that night was half-empty. Dortchen saw the Grimms, who all turned their faces from her. Dortchen did likewise. The Grimms lingered in the church afterwards, giving the Wild family time to walk home alone through the blowing snow. It was so cold that Dortchen's skull ached and she found it hard to breathe.

'What's wrong, Dortchen?' Mia whispered, slipping her mittened hand into her sister's. 'You look so sad.'

'I'm wondering where Rudolf is tonight,' Dortchen said. It was not entirely a lie.

'I think he must be dead,' Mia said miserably. 'It's been so long since we've had any word. Surely no one could survive a night like this?'

'Knowing Rudolf, he's probably singing by a fire somewhere, with a good bottle of wine and a fat roast goose,' Dortchen said, trying to sound cheerful.

'It doesn't feel like Christmas,' Mia said. 'We haven't a tree or anything.'

Dortchen hugged her close. 'It's still Christmas.'

It did feel strange to walk into the shadowy house without the mysterious smell of the pine forest rolling across them, and without the faint tinkle of the Christ child's bells. The parlour seemed cold and dark without any lights or decorations. A handful of small presents wrapped in brown paper and twine were set near the cold hearth.

Louise sat on the couch, bouncing Marianne on her knee. 'You Germans are very odd,' she said. 'Rudolf told me you were merry at Christmas-time. Is this what you call merry? Why can we not light a fire, at least?'

'Is it you who must pay for the firewood?' Herr Wild responded, lowering himself into his tall-backed chair.

'Mia, my sweet, will you hand out the presents?' Frau Wild clutched her shawl closer about her. 'I'm afraid the Christ child could not bring much this year . . .'

'You must make your confession first,' Herr Wild said, as Mia ran to the parcels. 'Kneel down.'

The sight of Mia kneeling at her father's feet made Dortchen feel cold and shaky. She had to turn her face away. Slowly and reluctantly, Mia admitted to having stolen sugar from the pantry, and to vanity and covetousness.

'You must try harder next year,' Herr Wild told her.

'Yes, Father.'

He turned to Dortchen. 'Your turn. Kneel and make your confession.'

In great confusion and anxiety, Dortchen slowly got down to her knees, keeping as far away from her father as she could. She could not speak, so Herr Wild listed her sins for her. Lust and fornication. Lying and deceit. Disobedience and dishonour. Dortchen kept her head bowed, hot waves of shame rolling through her.

At last it was over and she could get up and move to the window. She opened the curtain to look through the crack at the white square outside, the lamps hanging above the doors of the shops blurring orange through the falling snow.

Louise protested at her father-in-law's insistence that she, too, should confess. 'I am French, and we have left such foolish superstitions behind us,' she said airily.

'You are German now,' he told her. 'Get down on your knees.'

So Louise gave Marianne to Frau Wild and knelt down. 'Well, then,' she began. 'I confess to amazement at how poor and cold Cassel is, after all Rudolf told me. And to disappointment that he would leave me here all alone and go off to fight in this stupid war, and to some anger, too. But *mon ami* will soon be back with a mink coat for me, and we'll move back to Paris, where they know how to celebrate Christmas properly.' With a flounce of her skirts, she got up and took back her baby, shaking back her dark curls.

Herr Wild said nothing, though his eyes glinted with anger.

Dortchen took her package mechanically, expecting it to contain a lump of coal. It was soft, however, and rustled intriguingly. Drawing her brows together, Dortchen carefully untied the twine and unfolded the paper. Inside the package was a yellow silk dress, with tiny puffed sleeves and a low-cut bodice trimmed with golden beads. With trembling fingers she lifted it up. The beads rattled.

'Ooh, look,' Mia cried. 'So pretty!'

'Well, now I must confess to jealousy,' Louise said. 'Surely that must come from Paris? Why have you given it to Dortchen and not to me? I am your eldest son's wife.' She looked with dissatisfaction at her own parcel, which contained some knitting needles and unevenly dyed grey wool.

'Oh, I want a dress too!' Mia cried, throwing down her present of new leather gloves, which were plain but serviceable.

'Where would she wear such a thing?' said Frau Wild, a strange note in her voice. 'Is she to go to a ball at the palace?'

Herr Wild stood up. 'I don't understand what all the fuss is about. A customer could not pay his bill and offered me some used clothes instead. I saw the dress was about Dortchen's size and so accepted it. I want to hear no more about it. Are we not going to eat tonight? I'm hungry. Bring me my dinner.'

Dortchen folded the dress away in its brown paper and went to the kitchen. With a steady hand, she carved the stork and smothered it with gravy. She brought the meal to the dining room, put it down on the table and sat in her place, bowing her head as her father said grace. She did not look up as her father served the meal, nor did she respond when he said, in a disgusted voice, 'This is the toughest goose I have ever eaten!'

Later, she took the dress and thrust it to the bottom of her clothes chest. The very feel of the silk repulsed her.

NO USE WEEPING

January 1813

Three days after New Year's Eve, an emaciated figure staggered out of a snowstorm into the town of Cassel.

He was dressed in the ragged remains of a French soldier's uniform, with a woman's mink coat over the top. His feet were wrapped in bloody rags, and a red hand-knitted muffler was wound about his head. It was Rudolf.

He was the only man of the 8th Westphalian Infantry Corps to return from the Russian campaign. All the other Hessian soldiers were dead.

Two soldiers brought him to the apothecary's shop on a litter, their faces pale and sick.

Dortchen could not recognise her handsome brother in this gaunt stranger with the straggling ginger beard. They lowered him to the floor.

'Mia, we'll need hot water, a lot of it,' Herr Wild cried. 'Stoke up the fire, get the kettle on. Louise, stop screaming. Get the boiler on. You, bring my son into the kitchen. We will need to get him clean. Mia, get the hipbath from the scullery.'

Obediently, the two soldiers carried Rudolf into the kitchen and laid him down before the fire. Dortchen hurriedly dragged the rag rugs out of the way. Her brother was so filthy that she did not want him touching anything that could not be easily cleaned. Louise sobbed and would not go anywhere near him. Mia struggled to bring the hipbath out of the scullery, and the two soldiers went to help her. They set it on the paving stones near the fire, then Herr Wild tipped them and showed them out.

'Hot water,' he called from the stillroom. 'Hurry!'

The kettle was already on the fire, flames licking around its blackened base. Dortchen filled the biggest soup cauldron and hung it beside the kettle, and then rushed into the scullery to fill the boiler. Her hands were shaking so much that she had trouble lighting the fire beneath it.

Herr Wild was noisily clanking bottles together. He came from the stillroom into the kitchen with a great armload, which he piled onto the table. 'Dortchen, get him stripped. I need to see if he has any wounds.'

Dortchen knelt beside her brother and gently unwound the grimy red scarf and threw it in the bucket. There were dead white patches of skin on his face, and purplish bruises. Next, she unwound the rags that bound his hands. To her horror, a finger came away with the rags and fell to the floor. Dortchen gasped and leapt to her feet, backing away, her hand to her mouth.

Louise screamed and kept on screaming.

'Frostbite,' Herr Wild said. He opened a drawer and rummaged through until he found some tongs, then used them to pick up the severed finger. It was black at the tip, as if it had been burnt, shading to purple and orange and then a strange, waxy yellow. He dropped the finger into a bucket and pushed it away with his foot. 'You must be careful taking off his feet wrappings.'

Dortchen felt sick. She could not move.

Herr Wild glared at her. 'Do not just stand there. Do you want your brother to die? We must get him warm and clean, and see what other damage there is.'

She took a slow step towards her brother, and then another. Mia was crouched by the hearth, sobbing, while Louise was still screaming. Herr Wild took a quick step towards his daughter-in-law and slapped her hard across the face. She jerked and gulped and stopped screaming. 'Get out,' he said. 'You are only in our way. Mia, take Louise upstairs and tell your mother the news. Tell her to prepare herself. The loss of a finger may not be his worst injury.'

Still crying, Mia took Louise's hand and led her out of the kitchen. Herr Wild shut the door behind them. 'Dortchen, I need you to be strong. You're a sensible girl. I know you won't faint. You must help me, or else we'll be burying him tomorrow. Understand?'

'Yes, Father,' she answered, and she forced herself back to her brother's side. The stink of him was almost overwhelming.

'We must get him warm, but slowly,' Herr Wild said, kneeling beside his son's limp figure. 'Fill the bath but make sure the water is only lukewarm. Put some thyme or rosemary in it.'

Dortchen hurried to obey.

'He's shivering – he has a fever, by the looks of him.' Herr Wild gave Rudolf some willowbark and feverfew tincture, most of which ran out either side of his mouth. Gently, Herr Wild turned his head and lifted the matted ginger locks to examine the dead patches on his face. Most were on his forehead and cheekbones, above the edge of the muffler. There was also a nasty cut by his ear; its lips were suppurating with pus.

Dortchen's stomach lurched. She turned away, grabbing a bunch of dried rosemary to throw into the bathwater. The sharp scent steadied her and she concentrated on filling the bath.

Herr Wild gave Rudolf some laudanum to drink, lifting his head. Rudolf was only barely conscious, his bloodshot eyes glinting through mere slits of eyelids.

'Help me undress him,' Herr Wild said. 'Carefully, now.'

Rudolf was bundled in a long mink coat that was heavy with mud and filth. Carefully, Dortchen eased him out of it. Its lining was of rose-pink silk.

'He said he had found a fur coat for Louise,' she whispered. 'This must be it.'

'Probably saved his life,' Herr Wild said, busily cutting away the rags of Rudolf's uniform. 'We'll have to burn it all. Looks like he's infested with lice.'

As the tatters of his clothes were eased away, Dortchen saw that her brother's pale torso was covered in innumerable red spots, like angry fleabites. He shivered violently, then moved his hands weakly as if to try to warm himself.

'Typhus . . . ?' Herr Wild said to himself. 'Oh, merciful God, let it not be so.'

Cold spread through Dortchen. Typhus was one of the most dreaded of all diseases, capable of wiping out the entire population of Cassel. No one knew what caused it, but it was especially prevalent among slum-dwellers, seafarers and prisoners – anyone who lived in close proximity to others, in dirty, unhygienic conditions. She took a step back, her hand to her mouth.

'We must get him clean, and this place too,' Herr Wild said. 'Dortchen, be quick, help me get the rest of his clothes off.'

Trembling in every limb and sick to the pit of her stomach, Dortchen slowly unwound the filthy rags from her brother's feet. They were in terrible shape, bruised and swollen and filthy. Three toes on his right foot were black and dead, as were two toes on his left.

'He'll never walk straight again,' Herr Wild said. His voice was hoarse.

Looking up, Dortchen was horrified to see tears sliding down her father's face. She had never seen him weep before. He dashed them away with his forearm and blew his nose on his handkerchief.

'No use weeping,' he said to her fiercely, as if it were she who had shown such weakness.

Dortchen said nothing and began cutting her brother's trousers away. They were stiff with ordure. She used the tongs to drop them into the bucket.

'Dysentery,' Herr Wild said. 'Get a chamber pot handy, Dortchen – we're going to need it.'

She got one from the scullery, then gingerly took hold of her brother's ankles and helped her father lift him into the bath. He cried out in pain as he was immersed in the warm water and began to struggle weakly.

Herr Wild held him down. 'It's all right, my boy, you're home now, you're safe. We'll take care of you.' Rudolf gasped and relaxed a little.

Dortchen got some soap and began cautiously to wash his hair. 'Cut it all off and burn it,' Herr Wild instructed her, so she took the scissors and cut off the long, matted elflocks, flinging them into the bucket. Herr Wild was carefully washing Rudolf's feet. Despite his tender touch, three of the black toes fell away. Dortchen gasped and struggled with her tears.

'He's alive – that's what matters,' her father told her. 'And, my God, he'll stay alive too.'

Together, Dortchen and her father worked on Rudolf for hours, shaving his head and jaw, washing his skeletal body, and anointing the thousands of tiny red spots with goldenseal salve. They fed him healing teas and thin broth, bound his wounds with fresh bandages, and made up a pallet for him in the kitchen. He was too weak to sit on the chamber pot, so Dortchen wrapped his lower body in old linen towels. They had to be changed again and again as his bowels released a thin, bloody, foul-smelling liquid.

Unable to leave him for a moment, Dortchen called up to Mia and Louise to come and help her by lighting a bonfire in the garden to burn his rags. Red-eyed and pale-faced, they came downstairs, clutching each other's hands.

'How is he?' Louise asked. 'Will he . . . will he die?'

'Not if I can help it,' Herr Wild responded over his shoulder, as he went through to the stillroom.

Louise moved closer and bent to look at her husband's face. 'He smells,' she said, stepping back. 'Urgh!'

'Don't get too close – he has typhus,' Dortchen said, and rapidly Louise moved farther away, pressing both hands over her mouth. 'The bucket of rags is there,' Dortchen continued. 'Make sure it is all burnt. And that fur coat too.'

'My mink coat!' Louise cried. 'Urgh, look how filthy it is.'

'It has to be burnt,' Dortchen said, pressing a cool cloth against her brother's hot forehead.

'I've waited all my life for a fur coat,' Louise said with spirit. 'I'm not burning it. A good sponge down with vinegar and an airing, and it'll be good as new.'

She gathered it up into her arms and went into the scullery. Dortchen sighed. She was too exhausted to do battle with Louise. She looked up at Mia. 'Make the bonfire good and hot.'

'But it's snowing.'

'Use Father's brandy to help you get it going,' Dortchen answered, and she groaned as another gush of foul-smelling liquid poured out of her brother's body. Mia caught up the buckets and rushed outside. Soon a red glare struck through the frosty windows.

Darkness closed in on the shop, and Dortchen realised that the dull ache in her midsection was hunger. It had been a long time since she had last eaten. She was so weary that she could scarcely find the energy to rise, let alone start cooking. A knock came on the front door. Dortchen dragged herself to her feet and walked down the dark hallway.

Standing on the doorstep were Jakob, Wilhelm and Lotte, all well wrapped up against the snow. Wilhelm held a heavy cast-iron pot in one hand.

'We heard about Rudolf,' Jakob said, without any preamble. 'How is he?'

'Very sick,' Dortchen replied. A tremor ran over her and she put a hand on the door frame to support herself.

'We're so sorry,' Lotte said. Her thin face was tense with sympathy. 'Here. I made bread soup for you. I had no cream, so it's rather thin.'

'Thank you.' Dortchen reached out her hand for the pot, and Wilhelm caught it in his.

'I'm so sorry. Please, let us know if there's anything we can do.'

Dortchen nodded. 'I will. Thank you.' Gently, she withdrew her hand from his and took the soup from him. 'I have to go.'

As she made to shut the door, Jakob said, 'Will he live, Dortchen?'

Tears overcame her. Dumbly, she shrugged, shook her head and shut the door.

It was a long and horrible night.

Towards dawn, Rudolf's fever spiked and he grew restless and violent, punching Dortchen as she bent over him, and trying to scramble away from her. Nothing she could say would calm him.

'The Cossacks,' he screeched. 'To arms!'

Herr Wild tried to hold him down but Rudolf's strength was preternatural. He hurtled half-naked all around the kitchen, knocking over copper buckets with a great clatter, smashing bowls as he shouldered the dresser. He seized the broom and whacked at an invisible enemy, sending the roasting jack crashing to the floor. At last, exhaustion overwhelmed him and he sank trembling to the floor. 'So cold,' he moaned. 'So cold.'

Together, Dortchen and her father were able to help him back to his pallet and cover him with blankets, but he shivered and moaned and threw them off, starting up in terror. 'They come! The Cossacks are coming. Flee!'

He quietened again, and Dortchen cleaned up the mess and scrubbed the kitchen floor with rue water, throwing all his soiled linens into the fire that was smouldering under the boiler. At this rate, there would not be a sheet left in the entire house.

She sat in the rocking chair, meaning to rest for just a moment, but was so exhausted that she fell asleep. She woke a scant hour later, to find Rudolf leaning up on one hand, looking about with wondering eyes. 'Is it true? Am I home?'

'Yes,' she said. Quickly, she got up and brought him a cup of cool feverfew tea to sip.

'It seems impossible.'

Dortchen knelt beside him and gently rubbed some more salve into the spots on one arm, tenderly folding back the flowing sleeve of his nightgown. 'We're so glad to have you safe home,' she said.

'They're all dead.'

'We don't know that. Maybe some more will make it home.'

He shook his head. 'They're all dead.'

She did not want him to dwell on his ordeal, or on the death of his comrades, so she began to talk brightly. 'Soon you'll be well enough to see your little Marianne. She's crawling about now and getting into all sorts of trouble.'

He stared blankly at her, as if he did not know who she was speaking about, then said, in a strange dead voice, 'I thought Burl would make it. Our little drummer boy. All those months, all those miles, we marched together. But it was so cold. Every breath was torture. We could not lie down on the ground to sleep, knowing we'd not get up again. So we stood together under a tree, leaning on it, trying to rest. I swear I slept only a few minutes. Yet when I put my hand on his shoulder to wake him, he was dead. I tried to lay him out, but his feet were frozen fast to the snow.' Rudolf began to tremble uncontrollably. 'His feet . . . His legs just broke off at the ankles, Dortchen. They snapped like sticks. His feet . . . his feet are still there . . . stuck to the snow . . . Dortchen, his feet . . . He was only a boy . . .'

Dortchen hurried to soothe him, though she was so shaken that it was hard to move her own cold limbs. Terror overcame Rudolf again and she had to call for her father, as once again he was struggling around the room, flailing his arms and shrieking for help. Herr Wild held him down while Dortchen tried to get some more laudanum down his throat. Eventually, he calmed and slept again.

Dortchen's jaw throbbed where he had struck her the night before, and every muscle in her body ached. 'Get that worthless wife of his down here,' Herr Wild told her. 'You go and rest a few hours. Tell Katharina she must rouse herself and come too. She is his mother.'

Dortchen nodded gratefully. As she turned to go, her father reached out and gently cupped her face. 'You did well, Dortchen. I'm proud of you.'

The next Sunday, Louise came down the stairs dressed in her best day gown, with the black mink coat draped insolently over her shoulders.

'I thought I ordered that thing burnt,' Herr Wild said.

'I've given it a good clean,' she answered. 'I'll be the centre of attention at church today. Everyone will want to know about Rudolf. You wouldn't want me not to look my best, would you?'

'It'll be infested with lice,' he warned her.

'I wiped it down with rue water – nasty, stinking stuff,' she said. 'I had to use up a whole bottle of rose perfume to get rid of the smell.'

'On your own head be it,' Herr Wild said, and she smiled and twirled a few steps, the skirts of the mink coat flaring out behind her.

'Isn't it fine?' she asked. 'I'll be as warm as toast in that horrible draughty old church.'

Louise was indeed the centre of attention after the service. Everyone was eager to know how Rudolf was, and what had befallen him on the march home from Russia.

'He's too ill to have spoken of it,' Louise said, Marianne in her arms.

Dortchen, standing behind her with her hands shoved into the sleeves of her shabby coat, said nothing. She had heard many things in the last few nights. Rudolf's fever was always worse then, and so too was his ranting and raving. The burden of his words weighed heavily on her soul, however, and she could not have told anyone what he had revealed to her.

Rudolf had seen men murdered for an old potato, little girls raped in revenge for a burnt field, children captured and sold by the Cossacks as their rightful war booty, and injured men flung off carts and driven over in the desperate need to escape. He had even pushed a woman off a sinking bridge so that he might not drown with her. Her despairing face as she sank beneath the icy waters disturbed his dreams nearly every night, as did the young drummer boy who had frozen to death beside him. Rudolf had seen men burning to death in a cottage, and half-frozen soldiers rushing close to warm their hands at the blaze, uncaring of the screams of agony from within. All his dead comrades, all the atrocities he had witnessed, surfaced in his dreams. Dortchen was covered with bruises from Rudolf's attempts to fight the nightmare images away.

'What a lovely coat,' one woman said, fingering the thick pelt of Louise's sleeve.

'Isn't it?' Louise answered, lifting Marianne up against her shoulder so that she could show the woman the pink silk lining. 'My husband brought it home from Moscow for me.'

'What was Moscow like?' someone else asked.

'Like something out of *A Thousand and One Nights*,' Louise answered, smiling.

Dortchen turned away. She felt sick, her legs shaking so much that she was afraid they would fail to support her. Wilhelm saw her face and stepped closer, putting out a hand to support her elbow. 'Dortchen, are you well? You look so pale.'

She raised her eyes to his but did not speak.

'Come, sit for a moment,' he said, guiding her to a low stone bench nearby. 'I don't want you fainting.'

She sat.

'Are you still angry with me?' he said in a rush. 'I did not mean to offend you.'

Dortchen shook her head. She had forgotten about her rage and her jealousy, in the horror of Rudolf's return.

'It is just the way things are done,' he went on. 'So many of the stories are put together from different fragments, which came to us in different ways. We could not have named each source for each part of a story without making the book much too long. Already we are being criticised for the notes we did include.'

'It doesn't matter,' Dortchen said wearily.

'Dortchen . . .' He stepped closer, bending his head to scan her face. 'What is wrong, my little love? You seem so sad . . . so quiet . . . Is it just Rudolf?'

'Isn't that enough?' she answered. 'He's a cripple now, did you know? Half his toes are gone.'

'I'm so sorry,' he answered helplessly.

'I need to get back to him,' she said. 'Mia is sitting with him now, but she's only a girl.'

'You're not much more than a girl yourself,' he said, frowning.

Did he really think so? She felt immeasurably old.

Louise wore her mink coat all afternoon, saying it was the first time she had been truly warm since coming to this benighted country. Dortchen imagined she would even wear it to bed.

The next morning, Louise did not come down to breakfast. Dortchen went to check on her and found her lying in bed, pale and listless, the mink coat spread over her bed like a counterpane. 'I have such a headache,' she said. 'Can you take Marianne? She won't stop crying.'

When Dortchen lifted the little girl up, her skin was scorching hot. She cried out at Dortchen's touch.

'My head,' Louise whimpered. 'Make her stop!'

Dortchen laid the little girl down in her cradle, backed out of the room, shut the door and slid down till she was sitting on the floor, her knees hunched under her chin. It was a while before she found the strength to get up and go to tell her father the news.

For three days, Louise and her baby lay shivering and burning in their beds, without the strength even to lift their heads to drink the healing teas Dortchen made them. Louise would not let go of the fur coat, clutching it to her with desperate fingers, so Dortchen let her be. Marianne died before dawn on the fourth night, and her mother a day later. They were buried the next day in ground as cold and hard as iron.

Dortchen took all Louise's and Marianne's sheets and blankets, their clothes, their pillows – everything that had touched them – and threw them on a bonfire in the back garden. She used a shovel so she did not have to touch anything with her own skin. Last of all, she flung on the mink coat. It took a long time to burn and filled the air with a terrible stench. The acrid smoke brought tears to Dortchen's eyes but she would not allow herself to weep. She stood, leaning on the shovel, while the thick orange smoke spread a pall over the frosty garden.

When at last she went inside, she found Mia hunched over at the table, peeling turnips. Her face was white and she had dark shadows beneath her eyes.

'Go and rest, little love,' Dortchen said. 'I don't want you getting sick too.'

Mia looked up at her gratefully and pulled herself to her feet.

Dortchen went to make soup. *Two fewer mouths to feed*, she thought, then she was shocked at herself. She felt numb, as if she had lost the ability to feel.

After a while, she realised that Rudolf was awake and watching her. Although he was still pale and thin, his eyes did not have the strange wild light of fever, and his red spots had faded.

'Louise?' he asked. 'Marianne?'

Dortchen shook her head.

RED BLOOD, WHITE FEATHERS

January 1813

After Rudolf's return from the war, Dortchen's father only came to her at night in her dreams.

It was as if those few terrible months had never happened. Sometimes, in the daylight hours, Dortchen could almost convince herself it had all been a nightmare. Best of all, her father was so busy caring for his sick son that he no longer watched her so closely. Dortchen was able to go to market by herself, leaving Mia to empty the chamber pots and starch her father's cravats with the water in which the potatoes had been boiled.

One day she was crossing the Marktgasse when she heard Wilhelm's voice. 'Dortchen, wait.'

She turned in surprise, and saw Wilhelm waving at her from the apartment window. He lifted a finger to her, indicating he'd be just a moment, and she took shelter from the cold wind in a doorway, well out of sight of her father's shop. Soon Wilhelm was striding towards her.

'How is Rudolf?' he asked, taking off his hat as he came near her. The icy wind ruffled his curls.

'Better,' she answered. 'If only I could buy some good beef to make broth. But the cupboard is bare.'

'Ours too,' Wilhelm said. 'We're ready to start gnawing our shoes, like they say the soldiers on the Russian march did.'

'Father says King Jérôme is virtually bankrupt.' Dortchen began to walk again, not wanting anyone to see them in such close conversation, and Wilhelm took her basket and fell into step beside her.

'There's no "virtually" about it. Jakob says he spent sixty million francs last year, building the new wing at the palace, and buying jewels and dresses for his mistresses. He has even spent the army treasury on refurbishing the opera house. So while Hessian blood was being spilt at Borodino and Moscow, the King was spending the soldiers' pay on red velvet curtains and chandeliers. It's unforgivable.'

'He did not throw his usual New Year's Eve party,' Dortchen said. 'Surely that was out of respect for the fallen soldiers?'

'More likely he had no money left to pay for it,' Wilhelm said.

Dortchen nodded and showed him her thin purse. 'Neither have we.'

For a moment they walked in silence, then Wilhelm burst out, 'We have scarcely earned a single thaler for the book, Dortchen. Our publisher, Herr Reimer, refuses to send us any money, saying that sales are slow and times are hard.'

Dortchen saw how bitter his disappointment was and turned to him, her face full of sympathy. She would have liked to have touched him in comfort, but they were in the street, in full view of milkmaids and carriage drivers and market vendors, and she could not cause such a scandal. 'All those wonderful stories,' she said. 'I thought everyone would want to buy them.'

'We've not had a very good critical response, either,' Wilhelm said. 'I was hoping Herr von Goethe would write a review for me but he has not answered my letters. And they banned the book in Vienna, saying it's filled with superstition.'

'So?' Dortchen asked. 'The tales are old. They come from a time when everyone believed in spells and superstitions. How can they be so stupid?'

She thought of Old Marie, who was so devout and yet still so connected to the old ways, with all their fears and fables.

'One reviewer said . . .' Wilhelm took a deep breath. 'He said the book was filled with "the most pathetic and tasteless material imaginable". Those words are engraved on my heart.'

'But whatever do they mean?' Dortchen asked.

'They say it's immoral. They've singled out "Rapunzel" as one tale that must disgust, because she and the prince are not married and yet she bears him twins. "The Frog-King" is another. They don't like the way the princess takes the frog into her bed.'

'Oh!' Dortchen cried, then flushed crimson.

'I did not read it that way either,' Wilhelm said. 'I suppose I was naive.'

They had reached the end of the marketplace and stood at the parapet, looking across the snowy valley below. The river was frozen hard and the trees in Karlsaue Park were bare and black, but the sun shone on the golden dome of the orangery and faintly warmed their backs. Rooks circled overhead, calling mournfully. The bare twigs of the trees were filled with the dark tangle of their nests.

Dortchen wondered what it would be like to live so far above the ground, resting in nothing more than a twirl of twigs, shaken by every cold wind that blew. Were the rooks wild and free and fearless, or were they filled with terror and despair at the frailty of their own black wings?

'I must go,' she said, shaking with cold.

Wilhelm turned to her swiftly. 'Can't we walk by the river for a while? We've not seen the sun for so long.'

Dortchen hesitated.

Wilhelm caught her hand. 'I have not seen *you* in so long.'

She pulled her hand free. 'I can't. If my father should find out . . .'

He frowned. 'What are we to do? I can't go on like this, never seeing you.' He hesitated. 'I had given up trying to talk to him, he was so unreasonable, but surely now, with so much tragedy in your lives . . . Surely he cannot keep denying us our happiness?'

Dortchen shook her head.

'I wanted the book to sell,' Wilhelm burst out, at last. 'We cannot marry, we cannot make ourselves a life, unless I can earn some money. Oh, Dortchen, I'm so sorry.'

'Can you not rewrite the stories and make them more suitable for children?' she suggested.

'We didn't collect the tales in order that they be read to children,' Wilhelm said. 'We wanted to preserve the old tales and annotate them for scholars, so they could be studied and understood.'

'There are many more children in Germany than scholars,' Dortchen said.

Wilhelm smiled ruefully. 'True.'

'So why not write a book for children, in the hope you will get more sales?' she said.

'I would, but Jakob says—' He stopped abruptly. Dortchen went red. They stood side by side in silence, the cold wind cutting at their faces.

'I'm sorry I said all those things,' Dortchen said. 'I know how close you and Jakob are. I was angry. Things have been hard at home . . .'

'I know,' he answered, still not looking at her.

She did not speak.

'We're thinking of preparing a second volume,' he said. 'We've met a wonderful storyteller who knows many new tales. Her name is Dorothea, just like you. Dorothea Viehmann. She came to our door selling butter and eggs, and stayed to tell us stories. Perhaps a second volume would draw more attention to the first.'

'I hope so,' Dortchen replied.

'It's true some of the stories are rather rough around the edges,' Wilhelm said. 'Not everyone is a natural storyteller. I remember some of the stories Friederike Mannel sent us. They were just a long list of "and she said and then he said and then she said and then he said . . ." – it sounded just dreadful. I had to add a little detail, just to make it flow better.'

'Giving them a little bit of a polish surely wouldn't do any harm,' Dortchen said. 'Like cleaning the silver at home. Everything gets so black with tarnish after a while that it looks dull and ugly. But when I give it a good rub with some horsetail reeds, it comes up looking as pretty as anything. Surely it'd be the same with your stories?'

'That's a good way to look at it,' Wilhelm said. 'I'm not really changing the essence of the stories, just trying to bring back their natural beauty and shine.' He turned to her impulsively. 'Oh, Dortchen, do you know any more tales? The ones you've already told me are among the best in our collection. If we could have more of those beautiful old tales, full of magic and romance, I'm sure the second volume will sell better than the first.'

'I don't know . . . I'd need to think.'

'Tales that might appeal to children,' he prompted her. 'Funny ones.'

But the only story Dortchen could think of was sad.

'Will you tell it to me anyway?' Wilhelm said.

Dortchen's longing to be alone with Wilhelm, to have him watch her with his intent dark gaze, and listen closely to every word she spoke, was so strong that she felt herself weaken. 'Father mustn't know.'

He hesitated. A gentleman did not encourage a young woman to have clandestine meetings with him, even for so wholesome a reason as telling children's tales. Dortchen could see the struggle on his face.

'Where can we meet?' he asked at last.

'Not in the garden – it's too cold.' They were silent for a moment, thinking. Neither suggested the Grimms' apartment, or a friend's house. Both wanted to meet alone.

'In the stable, tomorrow morning,' she said at last. 'I can work while I talk.'

He nodded, tipped his hat to her and walked quickly away. Both knew they had been together far too long.

The next day, Wilhelm sat on a low barrel in the stable, his paper and inkpot on a larger barrel, writing down the story Dortchen told him as she fed and watered the animals.

'There was once a little child whose mother gave her a small bowl of milk and bread every day, and the child sat in the yard to eat it. When she began to eat, a toad came creeping out of a crevice in the wall, dipped its little head in the dish and ate with her. The child took great pleasure in this.

'One day, when the toad did not come at once, she cried, "Toad, Toad, come hither swiftly, come, thou tiny thing, thou shalt have thy crumbs of bread, thou shalt have thy milk." Then the toad came in haste and enjoyed its milk. It even showed gratitude, for it brought the child all kinds of pretty things from its hidden treasures – bright stones, pearls and golden playthings. The toad only drank the milk, however, and left the bread alone.'

Dortchen began to rake up the old straw. 'Then one day the child took its little spoon and struck the toad gently on its head, saying, "Eat the breadcrumbs as well, little thing." The mother, who was standing in the kitchen, heard the child talking to someone. When she saw that the little girl was striking a toad with her spoon, she ran out with a log of wood and killed the good little creature.'

'That's sad,' Wilhelm commented.

'I told you.'

'Is that the end?'

'No, it gets sadder yet.'

Wilhelm primed his quill with ink and waited expectantly. Dortchen leant on her rake. 'From that time forth, a change came over the child. As long as the toad had eaten with her, she had grown tall and strong, but now she lost her pretty rosy cheeks and wasted away. It was not long before the funeral bird began to cry in the night, and the red-breast began to collect little branches and leaves for a wreath. Soon afterwards the child lay on her funeral bier.'

'You're right, that is sadder.' Wilhelm blew on the page to help the ink dry. 'But somehow rather beautiful. Do you know another?'

'I thought last night of another tale I knew,' she said. She spoke truthfully, for she had lain awake half the night struggling with her desire to see Wilhelm and her fear that her father would find out.

'Can I come again tomorrow?' he asked eagerly.

She hesitated for a long moment, then nodded. Carefully, she opened the stable door into the alley, taking care not to make any noise. As Wilhelm went out, he caught her fingers and drew her close, bending his head to kiss her. Dortchen turned her face away so that he kissed her cheek and not her mouth.

'I'm sorry,' he said. 'You're right, we must be careful.'

Dortchen could not get away the next morning, for the shop was busy and her father wanted her help in the stillroom. The following day,

Dortchen went to the stable, hoping to see Wilhelm but trying not to hope. She found herself chore after chore to do and was just about to give up when she heard a soft knock on the stable door. She unbarred the door and let Wilhelm in. He took off his hat and bowed, and set his writing box on the barrel.

'I'm sorry I couldn't come yesterday,' she said, unable to look at him.

'I'm just glad you're here today,' he answered. She was very aware of his hands unpacking his quills and penknife, and the way his curls hung over his pale forehead. It was dim and gloomy in the stable, and rather cramped. They had no choice but to sit near each other. Dortchen took down a bridle from a hook, needing some kind of barrier between them, and began to clean it.

'It's rather long, the story I'm going to tell you,' she said.

'I don't mind. I have all the time in the world.'

'It's very beautiful, though. I think you'll like it.'

'I'm sure I shall – I've loved all your stories,' he said, dipping his quill in the inkpot.

'Once upon a time there was a man who was about to set forth on a long journey,' Dortchen began. 'He asked his three daughters what he should bring for them when he returned. The oldest one wanted pearls, the second one wanted diamonds, but the third one said, "Father dear, I would like a singing, springing lark." The father said that he should do his best, and then he set forth.

'Now, when the time came for him to return home, the man had bought pearls and diamonds, but he had searched in vain for a singing, springing lark. This made him sad, for his youngest daughter was his favourite. His path led him through a forest, in the middle of which there was a splendid castle. Near the castle was a great tree, and at the very top of the tree he saw a singing, springing lark.

'He began to climb the tree, but a lion jumped up and roared until the leaves on the trees trembled. "I will eat up anyone who tries to steal my singing, springing lark," the lion cried. The man was very sorry and promised not to take the lark, but the lion said, "Nothing can save you

361

unless you promise me whatever first meets you upon your arrival at home."

'Of course, it was his youngest daughter who first greeted him, and so she had to go to the castle in the forest and give herself to the lion. The lion was truly an enchanted prince. By day he was a lion, and all his people became lions with him, but by night they had their natural human form. So the girl stayed with the lion, remaining awake at night and sleeping by day.'

Dortchen found it hard to look at Wilhelm as she spoke this part of the tale. Her face grew hot. She bent all her attention to the bridle, aware of Wilhelm's eyes on her.

She went on with the story, and after a moment Wilhelm's pen began to follow her again. 'One day the prince came and said, "Tomorrow there's a feast at your father's house because your sister is getting married. If you would like to go, my lions will take you." The girl said yes, as she wanted to see her father.

'Later, when her second sister was to be married, the girl persuaded the lion to come with her. The lion, however, said that that would be too dangerous for him, for if a ray from a burning light were to fall on him there, he would be transformed into a dove and would have to fly with doves for seven years. "Oh, do come with me," she said. "I will protect you, and guard you from all light."

'But despite all her care, a thread of light touched the prince and he was transformed into a dove. The dove said to her, "For seven years I must fly about into the world. Every seven steps I will let fall a drop of red blood and a white feather. These will show you the way, and if you follow this trail you can redeem me." Then the dove flew out the door. She followed him, and every seven steps a drop of red blood and a little white feather fell down, showing her the way.

'When seven years were almost passed and the girl thought she must soon be reunited with her lover, the dove disappeared. The girl climbed up to the golden sun, followed the moon's silver path and called to the four winds, and at last she discovered her lover. He was once again a lion but was fighting to the death with a serpent, who was truly the daughter of a sorcerer. With the help of the wind, the girl was able to save her lover and return him to the shape of a man.

'But the sorcerer's daughter whisked him away, and the girl learnt they were soon to be married. Undaunted, she followed him and, with the help of gifts from the sun and the moon, was able to break the spell on him and win him back from the sorcerer's daughter.

'From that time on, they lived happily until they died,' Dortchen concluded, and she got up to hang the gleaming bridle on the wall. Her heart was twisting inside her. When she had been a little girl, 'The Singing, Springing Lark' had been her favourite story. She had vowed that she too would follow her one true love wherever it took her, even to the ends of the earth, following his drops of blood and his fallen feathers.

'That was the most beautiful story I have ever heard,' Wilhelm said. He wiped his quill clean, then got up and stretched. Dortchen stepped away, pressing her back into the wall. 'I like it much better than "*La Belle et la Bête*", which is a French tale that's rather similar. It does not have the girl's quest, though, or the celestial gifts. It is just the sort of tale I wanted.'

'I'm glad,' Dortchen said, in a low voice.

He took a step closer towards her, his eyes intent on her face. 'She was very brave, that girl.'

Dortchen could not reply or look him in the eye, so she dropped her gaze to his mouth.

He smiled and reached for her. 'Just one kiss,' he murmured, his breath brushing against her skin, making it tingle. 'I've been able to think of nothing else.'

She raised her face to his, unable to resist him. She had loved him for so long that it seemed impossible to stop. He kissed her, and Dortchen poured down before him like golden silk unravelling.

The sound of the door handle turning flung them apart. Dortchen paled and made an urgent movement. Wilhelm bounded over the rail and into the pigsty, pressing himself against the wall just as the door opened and Herr Wild came in. 'Dortchen, whatever are you doing out here for so long?' he demanded.

'I . . . I was mucking out the stable,' she said, taking the rake into her hand.

'You've not made much progress,' he said, his eyes narrow and suspicious. Dortchen could feel from the heat in her cheeks that she was blushing furiously. In the corner of her eye she saw Wilhelm's writing box, sitting half-packed on the barrel. She took a few quick steps forward, hiding it from her father's line of sight.

'I'm sorry. I'm . . . I'm not feeling well.'

Her father's expression changed. 'You're feverish? You do seem hot. Do your limbs ache, and your head?'

She nodded.

'May the Lord save us,' he cried. 'I had hoped you would be spared. You must come back to bed immediately.' He came forward and took her arm, and she tried not to flinch.

Meekly, she allowed him to lead her from the stable, closing the door behind her. She felt strange, giddy and light-headed, with a hot, melting sensation deep in her pelvis that unsettled her. She allowed herself to be put to bed, and drank the willowbark tincture her father gave her. But she could not rest. Her limbs twisted back and forth in the bed and she kept replaying the scene in the stable over and over in her head – the feel of Wilhelm's mouth on hers, the touch of his hands on her body, his body pressed so close to hers that every inch of her skin had been branded with its fire.

In the middle of the night Dortchen woke from a dream in which a man's body was looming over hers in the darkness, holding her down, forcing her. She was shaking, her breath panting, her skin sticky with sweat. Was it her father in the dream, or the man she had loved since she had first laid eyes on him?

Dortchen did not know. She did not dare sleep again, and lay with hot eyes till dawn.

THE BEAST WITHIN

January 1813

For three days Dortchen stayed inside, creeping from one task to another, so confused by all she was feeling and thinking that it was hard to frame a response to her mother's inconsequent conversation, or to remember how many cups of flour she had already put into a bowl. Then it was Sunday, and she knew she would have to go to church and see Wilhelm in the crowd. The thought frightened her, but her father felt her forehead and her pulse and pronounced her quite well.

As always, church was an ordeal. The sermon dragged on far too long, and afterwards the congregation stood about in the icy wind, exchanging meaningless pleasantries and wild rumours. Most of the talk was about the food shortages, and how any of them was to survive the winter.

'It makes me wish I had a magic porridge pot, like the one in that story you told me,' Mia said to Dortchen.

'I don't know that story,' Jakob said, turning from where he was talking to Louis and Marie Hassenpflug. Wilhelm turned too, and Dortchen's traitorous blush gave her away to all who stood near. She tried to regain her composure.

'I thought everyone knew that one.'

Wilhelm shook his head, his face grave. 'Won't you tell it to us?' he said.

'It's a simple enough tale,' Dortchen said. 'It's about a poor little girl who lived alone with her mother, and they no longer had anything to eat. The girl went into the forest, where she met an old woman who gave her a little pot. When she said, "Little pot, cook," it cooked sweet porridge, and when she said, "Little pot, stop," it stopped. The girl took the pot home to her mother, and they were freed from their poverty and hunger, eating sweet porridge as often as they chose.

'One time, when the girl had gone out, her mother said, "Little pot, cook." And it did cook, and she ate until she was full. Then she wanted the pot to stop cooking but she could not remember the right word. So it went on cooking, and the porridge rose up and poured over the side, filling the kitchen, and the hallway, and all the rooms. It kept on pouring till the street was full, and every house on it, as if it wanted to satisfy the hunger of the whole world. No one knew how to stop it.

'At last, the little girl came home and said, "Little pot, stop," and it stopped cooking, and anyone who wished to return to the town had to eat his way back.'

They all laughed. 'What I wouldn't give for a pot like that,' Lotte said. 'Though you'd get sick of porridge after a while.'

'I must write that down,' Wilhelm said. He bent a little closer to Dortchen. 'Could I . . . ?'

She shook her head, not looking at him.

'When?' he whispered. 'I must see you.'

The others were all laughing and talking about what kind of magic pot they would like. One that produced beef stew, Louis Hassenpflug said. No, a different meal every time, his sister said.

Dortchen stared straight ahead. 'Not at the house,' she whispered.

Wilhelm was silent for a moment, thinking. Lotte turned to him and asked him what he would want a magic pot to produce. He flashed a quick smile and said, 'Porridge at breakfast, soup at lunch, then roast goose at dinner,' which made everyone laugh again.

As the little group began to break up, ready for the walk home through the snowy streets, Wilhelm turned to Dortchen, bowed and doffed his hat, then said quickly, 'Meet me at the orangery on Friday afternoon.'

He did not need to tell her the time. They both knew the exact moment at which Herr Wild would close up his shop and walk to his church elders' meeting; the old man was as reliable as a clock.

She did not nod or smile, but her eyes flashed up to meet his before she turned away. It was not just Herr Wild who was watching her and Wilhelm, she knew. Many in the congregation had a long nose for scandal and shame.

The following Friday, Dortchen drew her coat close about her and made her way swiftly down the steep, icy steps to Aue Island. The park was deserted but for a lone man strolling by the frozen river, his dog trotting behind him.

Wilhelm was waiting for her by the entrance to the marble bath, his hands thrust into his coat pockets. 'You came. I wasn't at all sure you would.'

She nodded.

'Is all well? Were you suspected?'

She shook her head. 'I said I was unwell. Father thought I was feverish.'

He crooked a smile. 'I certainly was. Dortchen, I'm sorry. I seem to have no self-control where you are concerned . . . I shouldn't have kissed you.'

'I don't believe you were the only one doing the kissing,' she answered, not looking at him.

He grinned, and she could not help but smile too. 'Shall we walk? It's too cold to stand here.' He offered her his arm and she slipped her hand in the crook of his elbow, and they walked down a snowy path between tall evergreen hedges.

'I'm so glad . . . that we're talking again,' he said, finding his words with difficulty. 'And for the stories . . . and, yes,' he burst out, 'for the kiss. It's been a whole year, since that day in Hanne's summer house. A whole year of longing for you. Dortchen, what are we to do?'

But she did not want to talk about the future. It was too dark and unimaginable. She squeezed his arm. 'Tell me about the book. Have you had any better reviews?'

A shadow crossed his face and he shook his head. 'Even Arnim says he thinks the book would have been better with fewer annotations and some illustrations. He said his daughter loves some of the stories, especially the ones with rhymes, but that he cannot bring himself to read others to her.'

Dortchen thought about the maiden with no hands, and the girl disguising herself in the fur of flayed animals, and thought she understood why. 'Couldn't you add some more rhymes into the stories, then?'

'I'm not meant to change them,' he said. 'We decided we would only record what was told to us, so we could keep the stories as close as possible to the original – except that, of course, it's so hard to decide what the true original is. We heard so many different versions of the same story.'

'Well, that's to be expected,' Dortchen said. 'Each time I tell a story, I change it just a little. Like the little rhyme in the story about the brother and sister and the gingerbread house. That just came to me one day, so I said it, and Mia liked it so much that I kept it in.'

'I wonder if that's one of the rhymes that Arnim's daughter likes?'

'Of course it is! How many other rhymes are there?'

'How did it go again?' Wilhelm screwed up his face, trying to remember.

'Nibble, nibble, little mouse, who is nibbling at my house?' Dortchen said. 'Mia always loved that part. It would be easy enough to add another rhyme in answer to it.'

'Would it?' he said, teasingly.

'Of course.' In a high-pitched voice, she said, 'It's the wind so wild, the heavenly child.'

'Did you just make that up?'

'I did.'

'You're a natural born poet,' he teased.

Dortchen swatted him. 'Still, I don't see why you couldn't add a few more little rhymes like that to it,' she said. 'And some illustrations. You could take out the nastier stories, like that one about the murderous sausage. That's enough to give any child a nightmare.'

He smiled absently, his mind far away. 'Perhaps . . .' he said. 'Arnim told us that Clemens . . . Clemens himself said . . .' Muscles clenched in his jaw.

'What?' Dortchen asked, after he did not go on.

'Clemens said you can display children's clothing without it being all dirty, with the buttons torn off and the shirt hanging out of the pants.'

There was such hurt in Wilhelm's voice that Dortchen reached out both her hands and pressed his arm between them. 'He's just jealous. He wanted to collect old tales himself but was too lazy. You sent him all your stories and he lost them, remember.'

'I know, but . . .'

'Your book is wonderful. One day you'll be famous. Everyone will say to me, "Is it true you knew the famous Grimm brothers?" And I will fan myself and put on airs, saying, "Indeed, they lived right next door to me. I used to make them bread soup."'

Then Wilhelm said in a gruff voice, 'One day people will say to me, "Is it true your wife told you all those marvellous old stories?" And I'll say, "Yes, indeed, that's how we fell in love."'

There was a long silence. Dortchen was so choked with tears that she could not speak. They spilt down her cheeks, and Wilhelm put up his bare hand and wiped them away.

They had walked down the length of one of the pathways. The park stretched away on the other side, empty and white, the view framed in bare black branches. Nearby was a stand of old yew trees, their evergreen branches casting a deep shadow on the snow. Wilhelm drew her into the shade, and his mouth found hers. Soon her hands were at the back of his head, dragging it closer.

At last he lifted his mouth away. 'Dortchen, you're enough to drive a man mad. One day you will not let me kiss you, the next . . .' His voice was rough. He held her gently, kissing her eyelids, the soft, urgent pulse at the base of her throat. 'I love you,' he whispered.

Dortchen's knees buckled, her senses swam. Only Wilhelm's body kept her from swooning to the ground. She wanted him to love her, she wanted him to wipe away the past, she wanted to be lost to herself forever.

So she fell to her knees before him and put her hands to that hard male part of him, then pressed her mouth there. He cried out and clutched her head to him. 'Oh, God,' he groaned, as she freed him from his breeches. 'Oh, God.'

Dortchen said the words with him, 'Oh, God,' and opened her mouth to him. He arched his back, thrusting his hips forward, allowing her to fill her mouth with him. Then the next instant he pulled away. 'Dortchen, no,' he panted. 'We cannot.'

She followed him blindly, not understanding, seizing him with her hands, nuzzling her head into his groin, trying to take him into her mouth again. He stopped her, lifting her up and pulling her against him. 'We cannot . . . It's a sin . . . Dortchen, we must wait.'

Dortchen's head spun and her ears roared. Her body was both aching with lust and shaking with revulsion. 'A sin,' she said. 'Yes, a sin.'

She put her hands down and touched him again, and he groaned. Leaning against him, she worked him with her hands, then knelt once more, tasting him with lip and tongue. She was expecting him to groan and cry out like her father did, but he stopped her hands with both of his and raised her up, holding her away from him. His expression was not what she expected. He looked shocked.

'Dortchen, what are you doing? You must not . . . It's a sin.'

She gazed at him, confused.

'We must wait . . . We must be married first.'

Anger filled her. 'Marry?' she asked. 'How can we marry? You are the vassal of your brother and I . . . I am the vassal of my father.'

'But, Dortchen—'

'I cannot marry you. Not now, not ever. My father has forbidden it . . . and I . . . I . . .' She was unable to go on.

He spoke her name again and reached for her, but she struck out at him, then turned and ran away. Her long skirts tripped her but she scrambled up and ran on. The world was all grey and white and black and cold. She found a dark corner of ivy and stone, and pressed herself there, tearing at her hair and her face, wanting to hurt herself.

Wilhelm's face haunted her. She had tried to love him, to forget herself in him, but all she had done was reveal to him the wild side of herself, the beast within.

PART SIX

The Red Boundary Stone

CASSEL

The Electorate of Hessen-Cassel, September 1813–December 1814

They were both now free, so Roland said, 'Now I will go to my father and arrange for our wedding.'

'I'll stay here and wait for you,' said the girl. 'I'll transform myself into a red boundary stone so that no one will recognise me.'

So Roland set forth and the girl, in the shape of a red boundary stone, stood there and waited for her sweetheart. But when Roland arrived home, he was snared by another woman, who caused him to forget the girl. The poor girl waited there for a long time, but finally, when he failed to return, she grew sad and transformed herself into a flower, thinking, 'Someone will surely come this way and trample me down.'

From 'Sweetheart Roland', a tale told by Dortchen Wild to Wilhelm Grimm on 19th January 1812

THE FALL OF WESTPHALIA

September 1813

One warm autumn evening in late September, the gate to the Wilds' garden banged open and Lotte came hurrying down the path, the ribbons of her bonnet flapping behind her.

Dortchen and Mia were digging up angelica and sweet cicely roots, to hang and dry by the fire. 'Lotte,' Dortchen cried in surprise, straightening her aching back. 'What's wrong?'

Her immediate thought, on seeing Lotte's white, shocked face, was that something had happened to Wilhelm. She had not seen him since that awful day in the snowy park. He had spent the summer with his friends, the von Haxthausens, who lived on a grand estate near Paderborn. The last time Wilhelm had gone to visit them, his carriage had overturned twice on the potholed roads. Dortchen feared the same had happened again, and he had been injured. She could not ask, however. Even to think of Wilhelm brought a scalding rush of shame and humiliation upon her, so that she could scarcely breathe.

Lotte seized both her hands. 'Dortchen, have you not heard the news? The Russians are coming! They're only a few hours' march away. Oh, Dortchen, what are we to do?'

'The Russians are coming?' Dortchen repeated. Mia cried out and sank down onto a water barrel, her hands to her mouth.

'Yes, they've beaten the French and the Grand Army is fleeing,' Lotte said. 'Napoléon has no more men. The Russian army is marching right towards us now.'

Dortchen could not take it in. She leant against the wall, her head spinning.

She had been so busy all summer, in the house, the garden and the stillroom, that she had been only dimly aware of events in the outside world. The Russians and the Prussians had forged a new alliance, she knew, and had been fighting against the French for most of the year. Austria had joined them only a few weeks ago, after Napoléon had refused to sign a peace treaty that would have seen him lose all his mighty conquests there. There had been a battle at Dresden, but Napoléon had won.

What could Lotte mean when she said Napoléon had no more men? Surely Napoléon, the greatest military commander since Charlemagne himself, could not be losing the war? What did it mean for her family, for her country? How could the Russians possibly be here, at their very doorstep?

'Sit down,' Lotte said. 'You've gone white as a sheet.'

She guided Dortchen to sit on the back step, and Dortchen held her head in her hands while Lotte went into the scullery and pumped a mug of water for her. It was cool and refreshing, and helped Dortchen recover her senses. Mia was weeping, and Lotte passed her the cup and her own crumpled handkerchief.

'I don't understand,' Dortchen said. 'I thought Napoléon was winning.'

'He lost a major battle near Berlin a few weeks ago,' Lotte said, 'and has been retreating ever since. They say his troops fell into a wild panic at the sight of the Cossacks charging down upon them, and simply dropped their muskets and ran.'

'Cossacks!' Mia's blue eyes were rounder than ever. 'Dortchen, what will they do to us?'

'*Cossacks* are coming here? To Cassel?' Dortchen was on her feet at once, grasping the door frame to keep her balance as her vision swam. She had heard so many horror stories of the Cossacks.

'King Jérôme is fleeing,' Lotte said. 'He has ordered Jakob to pack up all the treasures at the palace. Jakob is in despair. Luckily, the King does not think much of books and so Jakob has been able to save some of the most precious.'

'The King is fleeing?'

'Yes, the whole court is trying to get away. The highway is jammed with coaches and carts. We can't get away, of course. Jakob says we must barricade ourselves in and hope for the best.'

'Wilhelm,' Dortchen whispered. 'Is he home? Is he here?'

Lotte nodded. Pity was on her face. 'Yes, he's here. He doesn't want to see you. Oh, Dortchen, I just wanted to make sure you were safe. I couldn't forgive myself if I didn't warn you and you were all hurt.' Tears were streaming down Lotte's face. She and Dortchen embraced, then Lotte ran out through the gate.

Dortchen locked it behind her, and then hurried to the outhouses, where she and Mia secured the stable door and dragged hay bales across it. They chased the chickens and geese into their coop and closed it up tight, then ran back to the house. 'Rudolf,' Dortchen called up the stairs. 'I need you.'

'I'll go up and tell Mother,' Mia said.

'Tell her to sew any jewels or coins she has into our petticoats,' Dortchen said. 'Help her.'

Dortchen ran into the shop, where her father was seated at his counter, writing in his logbook. He looked up, stern and unapproachable. Since Rudolf's return from Russia, her father had hardly looked at Dortchen or spoken to her. She was grateful for this, and did her best not to rouse his ire. So she slowed down, smoothed her muddy apron and said, 'I'm sorry to disturb you, Father. It's just . . . I've had news. The Russians are only a few hours' march away. The Emperor – Napoléon, I mean – he's been beaten in a great battle . . . King Jérôme is fleeing Cassel.'

Her father sat motionless for a moment, then turned and looked out the shop window. Dortchen followed his gaze. All was chaos out in the Marktgasse. People were running everywhere, and shop-owners were hastily banging down their shutters and wheeling away their barrows.

Herr Wild stood up. 'The drugs! The opium! Dortchen, shut the shop. I'll hide my cabinet.' He tossed her his heavy ring of keys, then rushed to the stillroom.

Dortchen hurried out through the shop door, clutching the keys close. Outside, all was in tumult. Carriages and carts jammed the street, with coachmen whipping horses forward. Anxious faces peered from the windows, shouting, 'Hurry, get a move on!' Two young men seized an old man and flung him down from his cart as if he were a sack of potatoes, beating his old, bony nag with their walking sticks so it lurched into an ungainly trot.

Mothers dragged their weeping children along by their hands. One young girl screamed in terror as her dropped basket of watercress was trampled by the fleeing crowds. A carriage driver locked wheels with the young men in the cart, who began to beat him with their walking sticks, trying to wrench the two vehicles apart.

Dortchen closed the heavy shutters across the windows and padlocked them. Someone jostled past her. 'Out of my way,' he shouted, pushing her so violently that she fell to her knees. It was a butcher's boy in a bloodstained apron, carrying a long stick strung with rabbit carcasses over his shoulder. Dortchen scrambled to her feet, shaken and bruised. The butcher's boy shoved past the little watercress seller, who caught hold of his arm. 'Help me, help me, please,' she sobbed.

He knocked her down, then, unable to make his way forward, threw down his stick of rabbit carcasses and bullied his way on board a cart filled with cages of chickens. A mangy dog darted forward and seized the leg of one of the rabbits, trying to drag it away. Dortchen grabbed the end of the stick and wrested it away from the starving dog, who ran off with one limp carcass hanging from its mouth. Dortchen helped the watercress seller to her feet, then pressed one of the rabbits into her arms and said, 'Go home, as fast as you can. Lock your door and don't answer for anyone.'

The little girl nodded and ran off, the limp rabbit clutched close to her chest like a strange doll. Dortchen dragged the stick of rabbits inside the shop and slammed the door. She locked and barred it, then stood against it, her heart pounding erratically. Three rabbits dangled from the stick in her hand – more fresh meat than the Wild family had seen in months.

She was busy skinning the rabbits when Rudolf limped into the kitchen. 'Dortchen, what's going on? Mia's crying something about Cossacks. Surely it can't be true?'

'The Russians are only a few kilometres away,' she said. 'Napoléon's army is fleeing. They'll be here soon.'

The colour drained from his face.

'The King has fled,' she told him. 'Perhaps they will pursue him and leave us alone.'

'The coward. Why won't he stand and fight?'

'Lotte says there are no soldiers left.'

Rudolf sat down abruptly. 'What are we to do?'

'Help me hide the valuables,' Dortchen said. 'Then we'll pack up some bags, in case we have to flee too. I managed to seize us some dead rabbits; I'll smoke them by the fire now, and I'll make some hard biscuits, so that we'll at least have some food.'

Rudolf made a face. 'Disgusting stuff, but I swear it saved my life – along with the muffler.'

Dortchen smiled faintly.

Frau Wild came fluttering downstairs in a panic, holding a few paltry trinkets. Mia was close behind her, with armfuls of petticoats. 'Are you sure?' Frau Wild asked. 'Better than burying them? What if they search us?'

'If we bury them, we have to leave them behind if we flee,' Dortchen said. 'Better carrying them on us, I think.'

She settled her mother in the rocking chair with her sewing basket, while she boiled up the rabbit bones for stock. Mia kneaded some simple biscuit dough. Herr Wild came in, bent under the weight of his large padlocked chest. 'Rudolf, help me bury this in the compost heap. I will not have my best drugs stolen by marauding foreigners.'

Rudolf obeyed, and then father and son set themselves to guard the shop with their old musket and flintlock pistol. 'It's one of the first places they'll break into,' Herr Wild said grimly. 'Soldiers are always in need of medicines.'

Mid-afternoon, they heard the sound of musket fire to the east, then the roar of cannon. Everyone stopped what they were doing and listened tensely.

'It sounds close,' Mia said, pressing close to Dortchen's side. Dortchen put an arm around her.

The fusillade continued for quite some time, then they heard more gunfire from the south. As darkness fell, the gunfire ceased, though every now and again a burst of cheering and shouting startled them. The family ate a simple dinner of rabbit and turnip stew at the kitchen table, then made up beds on the floor. No one wanted to be far from their escape route out the back.

Dortchen scarcely slept at all.

THE RUSSIAN INVASION

September 1813

The next day passed in much the same fashion, with intermittent gunfire and the occasional roar of cannon. Rudolf thought it was coming from the local troops defending the bridge over the Fulda, which entered Cassel only a few blocks from the Marktgasse. By sunset, Dortchen was feeling much easier. The gunfire was coming rarely now, and she hoped that any Cossacks had simply gone around Cassel to chase after King Jérôme and his treasure-laden baggage train.

All those hopes were dashed the following morning, when the dawn was shattered by the booming of cannon fire. It went on for hours without ceasing. Crouching by the shop window, Dortchen and Rudolf peered through the slits in the shutters. They saw a handful of French soldiers run past, tearing off their distinctive red and blue uniforms and throwing away their weapons. Then a long column of Russian soldiers marched past, wearing white breeches and green jackets with high red collars. They looked grim and determined. An officer rode at their head, heavy gold epaulettes on his shoulders.

'They don't look very wild,' Dortchen whispered to her brother, remembering his descriptions of long-haired Cossacks with matted beards and heavy bearskin coats galloping about on small, shaggy ponies, shooting down anyone that moved with their bows and arrows.

'They're not Cossacks,' Rudolf murmured back. 'That's the Russian infantry. Let us pray they're keeping the Cossacks outside the town gates, else the whole town will be sacked and burnt.'

Some time later a group of prisoners limped past, naked and shivering. Only their tall blue hats showed that they were French soldiers. 'The poor things,' Dortchen whispered. 'They must be freezing.'

Rudolf snorted. 'It's September. You should've tried being a Russian prisoner of war during the retreat. They made you march barefoot and naked through snowdrifts for hundreds of miles. If you fell, they'd shoot you. If you managed to stay upright, you'd lose your feet and your hands to frostbite. They were merciless.'

Dortchen shuddered, praying that the Russian officers would keep their troops in hand.

All day the long columns of green-clad soldiers marched through the town. They made no move to plunder any of the shops, though as twilight closed in, a few young men dressed in rough provincial clothes came swaggering through the Marktgasse, flaming torches in their hands. They shook the door of the apothecary's shop and Rudolf shoved the muzzle of his gun up against the glass. They laughed and went on their way. Later that night Dortchen smelt smoke and saw an orange glare over the rooftops, but the fire did not spread. Eventually they all slept, waiting to see what dawn would bring them.

The next morning, Russian soldiers marched through the town, issuing proclamations that were read in every square in perfect French and German. The town began to stir. Townspeople put their heads out of windows to listen, and a few brave souls opened up their shops to the Russians. One Russian officer came and knocked at Herr Wild's door.

'We mean you no harm,' he said, taking off his shako cap and bowing in a very smart military manner. 'We have wounded men and wish to buy supplies from you. We will pay, of course.' He hefted a small purse in his hand.

Rudolf hesitated, but his father called him a fool and unlocked the door. Rudolf could not bear to serve the Russians and went limping through to the kitchen, so Herr Wild called Dortchen to help, warning her with a grim look to be quiet and meek.

She came in with her eyes lowered and her hands folded tightly before her, hardly daring even to glance at the soldiers. One smiled at her and helped her lift down a heavy jar. Dortchen stepped away from him as fast as she could, taking refuge behind the safety of the counter.

'I hope you didn't have any trouble overnight,' the officer said to Herr Wild. He was tall, with strong eagle-like features and ice-blue eyes. 'We had guards posted but a mob of anarchists burnt a wool factory that was making uniforms for the French and broke off the nose and an arm from Napoléon's statue in front of the palace.'

'We had no trouble here,' Herr Wild replied.

'We envision no more upsets. Count Czernitcheff, our colonel, has taken charge of the treasury, such as it is, and established a provisional government. You are free of the tyranny of the French. The Kingdom of Westphalia is no more.'

Herr Wild grunted. 'Then what are we now? Part of Russia?'

'Not at all, sir,' the officer said. 'A settlement will be made with your former rulers – of that you can be sure.'

He paid and the soldiers went out, carrying their parcels. At the door, the officer turned and gave Dortchen a wintry smile, bowing from the waist. 'Thank you, Fraülein.'

Herr Wild turned to Dortchen. 'The Kurfürst may return?' His voice broke. He cleared his throat and turned away, but not before Dortchen saw that there were tears in her father's eyes.

A few days later, just when the people of Cassel were daring to go about their normal business again, a wild rumour swept the town: the French were coming back! King Jérôme had gathered an army!

Dortchen thought it was just another wild surmise, until the Russians quickly packed up and disappeared into the hills. Everyone was stunned. For good measure, the Wilds bolted and shuttered their shop again, and Frau Wild hastily sewed her jewellery back into the hem of her petticoat.

On 7th October, Dortchen and Mia watched in bewilderment as the

French army rode back into Cassel, without a single shot being fired. They arrested a few people who had helped the Russian provisional government, and they hanged the young men who had defaced Napoléon's statue, but otherwise the Russian invasion might never have happened. Ten days later, King Jérôme rode into town on his white prancing charger, dressed in full regimentals, waving at the quiet, subdued crowds that had been rounded up and ordered to cheer for him.

That night, every shop and house was ordered to hang lanterns above their front steps and to set lamps in every window so that the whole town was illuminated in celebration of the King's return. Once, Dortchen and Mia would have begged to be allowed out to witness such a pretty sight. That warm October night, however, Dortchen and Mia lit all the lanterns, as instructed, and then locked and shuttered the house and retreated to the safety of the kitchen, where they sat, quietly sewing, with their mother and brother.

Dortchen felt a kind of bewildered exhaustion, as if she had been battered in a storm. She no longer hoped for the war to end; it would never end, she now believed. Peace was nothing but an empty dream.

Only a few days later, rumours once again began to circulate. Napoléon himself was only a few hundred kilometres away, and was determined to crush the Allied army once and for all. A great battle was being fought, the largest ever seen. After church that Sunday, everyone huddled in the porch. Charlotte Ramus told Dortchen that a peddler had told their housekeeper that he had seen the sky to the east glowing a lurid orange, and lit with constant white flashes, like lightning.

'If the rumours are true, there'll be many casualties,' Herr Wild said to Rudolf. 'We might have a chance to make back some of our losses. We must be prepared.'

He called his wife and daughters to him, and obediently they hurried home and began cutting old linen into strips to roll for bandages. Herr Wild and Rudolf looked over their stocks and prepared a list of the herbs and flowers they would need. Herr Wild came to the kitchen with the list in his hand.

'Dortchen, you must go to the forest and gather me some wood betony. Then come home by the meadows and get me yarrow, adder's tongue and toad flax.'

Dortchen nodded; these herbs were used to restrain violent bleeding.

'Mia, you will go to the garden. I need thyme, feverfew, lemon balm and woundwort.'

'Yes, Father,' the girls chorused, though Mia's eyes flew to Dortchen's in distress. It had never been her job to work in the gardens, and she was not at all sure that she could identify all these plants. Dortchen reassured her with her eyes.

The two girls took their baskets and scissors and walked to the garden outside the town walls. Dortchen showed Mia the plants she was to gather, then walked on towards the palace. It was a long time since she had been to the forest, and she lifted her face to the sun, breathing deeply.

Dortchen was making her way through the royal park when she saw a lone French soldier galloping up the hill towards the palace. His horse was flecked with foam and breathing heavily, and the soldier himself was begrimed with smoke and blood. Dortchen crept as close as she dared to the road, wondering what news he bore.

The beleaguered horse shied at the rustle she made in the leaves and reared, then collapsed to its knees. The rider fell heavily. Dortchen ran out and knelt beside him. He was dazed, blood trickling from a cut near his hairline. He grabbed at Dortchen with his grimy hands.

'Disaster,' he gasped. 'I must tell the King. The Emperor is defeated.'

'What has happened?'

'We fought all day, for hours and hours, but there were too many of them.' He gave a sharp crack of laughter. 'Three times as many men as we had. We fought valiantly for our emperor and might still have won the day if some fool corporal had not . . .' His voice broke. 'He blew up the bridge too early – with all our men still on it. And the rearguard is still in Leipzig. All is lost. I must . . . I must tell the King.'

He struggled to get up, and Dortchen helped him to stand. Together, they tried to coax the horse to its feet, but the exhausted animal collapsed onto its side. The soldier began to stumble towards the palace but swayed and almost fell. Dortchen ran to support him.

'The King must flee,' he told her. 'The Emperor is on the run, and so is all that's left of his army. There's no hope. We can't hold them off. The Cossacks are rampaging through the countryside, killing anyone in French uniform.'

A shout rang out from the guard's sentry box, and the guard ran forward.

'He's hurt,' Dortchen said. 'His horse has fallen down the road. He has news for the King.'

After delivering the injured soldier into the guard's hands, Dortchen walked rapidly away, her heart skittering with panic.

'Wait,' the soldier cried, and she turned, desperately afraid.

'You must flee too,' he said to her. 'Westphalia is no more. The Empire is no more! All hell has broken loose.'

Dortchen nodded, then ran back to collect her basket.

Flee? she thought. *Where can we flee to? There is nowhere to go.*

UNKIND

November 1813

'I can't believe how much they eat,' Dortchen said to Lotte, as they stood in the queue at the butcher's. 'Our winter stores are gone already.'

'I can't believe how noisy they are,' Lotte answered. 'They sing and dance half the night, and keep calling for more vodka.'

'I guess we shouldn't complain,' Dortchen said. 'At least we're still alive.'

'Just hungry,' Lotte said sadly.

The girls were silent for a moment. It had been almost a month since the catastrophic defeat of the French at Leipzig, and the Russians had once again occupied Cassel. They spent their days and nights drinking and carousing and flirting with the town's prettiest girls, but they did not loot and rape and murder, as everyone had feared. The dreaded Cossacks had gone chasing after the retreating French army, hoping to catch the Emperor. Life in Cassel was eerily normal, the only difference being the colour of the soldiers' uniforms and the language in which they cursed.

The Austrians had tried to stop Napoléon's withdrawal from Germany by engaging him at Hanau, but the Emperor had won the battle and secured his army's line of retreat. Now all the talk was of whether the Austrians, the Prussians and the Russians would pursue Napoléon all the way to Paris.

'Surely not,' Rudolf said. 'The French would die rather than surrender their emperor. Surely they will just draw up another treaty?'

Dortchen was not so sure. The Russian tsar and the Austrian emperor and the Prussian king had been humiliated most publicly. They would seek revenge, she felt. They would want to crush Napoléon and regain their honour.

Both the Wilds and the Grimms had a houseful of Russians. Seven were crammed into the Grimms' small third-floor apartment with Jakob, Wilhelm and Lotte, while fourteen had taken up residence in Herr Wild's house. Dortchen and Mia had given up their bedrooms and slept together on pallets on the kitchen floor. Rudolf slept in the hallway outside to make sure that no lusty Russian soldier decided to visit them during the night.

'The poor boys hate it,' Lotte said. 'It's so hard for them to work with all the noise. It sounds like elephants dancing, the way the Russians crash about.'

'Is Wilhelm still working on the fairy tale book?' Dortchen asked, after a long moment. It was hard for her to say his name without pain.

Lotte nodded, looking at her sideways. 'Yes. He's hoping to put out another volume.'

There was an awful, awkward silence, then Lotte said in a rush, 'Dortchen, you need to know, Wilhelm's in love . . . Well, I'm not sure he's in love, because he doesn't seem anything like as sick and miserable as when he was in love with you, but . . . Oh, I think she's in love with him. She writes all the time, and Wilhelm won't read her letters out loud, the way he usually does.'

'That's good. I'm glad. Who . . . who is she?'

'Jenny von Droste-Hülshoff.'

'Noble?'

'And Catholic. There's no hope, really. She's the niece of Werner von Haxthausen – you know, Wilhelm's friend who lives on that grand estate near Paderborn. Wilhelm spent the summer there.'

Dortchen nodded.

'Her family would never agree to any match, though.' Lotte's voice was filled with resentment. 'They are noble and wealthy, while we're scratching to keep ourselves alive. Wilhelm says she's sent him some beautiful tales. There's one about twelve princesses who wear their dancing shoes to shreds every night. Wilhelm says it's among the finest stories he's ever heard.'

'No wonder he's in love with her.' Dortchen spoke lightly, easily, yet Lotte winced and looked at her askance.

'Oh, Dortchen, you're unkind,' she murmured.

'Am I?' Dortchen could not bear to stand in the queue any longer. Abandoning all hope of a meal that night, she walked away, ignoring Lotte's cries.

RETURN OF THE PRINCE

November 1813

On Sunday, 21st November, Dortchen went into her mother's bedroom and sat down on the bed beside her.

'Mother, I have wonderful news,' she said in a low voice.

Frau Wild rolled towards her, pressing a hand to her left breast. She was very pale. 'What is it, Dortchen?'

'The Kurfürst is to return to Cassel. He will ride into town this afternoon.'

'The prince? The dear prince is to return?'

'Yes, Mother. I wondered . . . Surely you would like to get up and come with Mia and me to see the royal family ride in? You have not got out of bed for days.'

'I feel so weak. But I would like to see him. Will you help me?'

Dortchen helped her mother sit up and brought her some clothes. They hung on her bony frame. Frau Wild was cold, so Dortchen brought her a few extra shawls to wrap about her shoulders. Frau Wild's hand kept returning to press against her chest.

They went downstairs slowly, calling to Mia to join them. Rudolf came too, limping along with the help of a wooden walking stick. Herr Wild closed the shop and walked with his family to the Königsplatz, his wife leaning heavily on his arm, her scarves and shawls fluttering behind her.

The Königsplatz was crowded with people from all walks of life; many were clutching bunches of late-blooming wildflowers, blue speedwell, ragwort, honeysuckle and bindweed. Soldiers in Hessian green kept the road clear. It seemed so strange to see the once familiar uniform again, after so many years of the French blue, white and red. A cheer rose from far down the road. Everyone caught their breath and craned their necks to see.

At last, the triumphant procession reached the Königsplatz. Banners and scarves waved wildly, and the people of Cassel cheered and shouted. For once, the Kurfürst was not wearing shabby old hunting clothes but was regally attired in red velvet and ermine, medals draped on his shoulder. His hair was powdered and caught back in a queue, a style that made him seem both hopelessly antiquated and yet somehow regal. His wife, Princess Wilhelmine, sat beside him in the open carriage, ramrod-straight, waving a white-gloved hand. Sitting opposite them were Crown Prince Wilhelm and his wife, Princess Augusta of Austria. All were grandly dressed, sparkling with diamonds. All looked stern and unforgiving.

Another carriage carried the royal grandchildren, one boy and two girls, who were much more animated, bouncing up and down and squealing with delight as they were showered with wildflowers. A governess did her best to keep them from falling out.

As the carriages rolled through the Königsplatz, the jubilation of the crowd overflowed. Everyone surged forward, breaking through the line of soldiers. The mob surrounded the Kurfürst's carriage, cheering, shouting, weeping. When he leant out, touching as many hands as possible, he was lifted up and carried on the shoulders of his subjects. The soldiers grew agitated and would have fired on the crowd, but the Kurfürst only smiled, rather stiffly, and bade them put him back in his carriage. The crowd obeyed and the soldiers lowered their muskets.

Next came the carriages of the court, filled with ladies-of-honour and dignitaries. Dortchen spied Aunt Zimmer, who looked much thinner and much older, waving her lace handkerchief enthusiastically. The next minute she saw Jakob, Wilhelm and Lotte, who were racing alongside the carriage, waving and calling endearments and blowing kisses. Dortchen had forgotten that their beloved aunt would be returning with the Kurfürst's court. She was surprised to find herself in tears.

Wiping her eyes, she looked up to see Wilhelm standing still, gazing at her. As their eyes met, he flushed, hunched one shoulder and turned away. Dortchen's tears overflowed.

Cassel's joy at the return of the Kurfürst was soon dimmed. Wilhelm I insisted that everything must return to the way it had been before the French occupation. All the liberties they had enjoyed under the *Code Napoléon* were taken away again. Dortchen worried most about the poor serfs. They had been freed from servitude but now were slaves once more.

The Kurfürst was furious at the state of the treasury, laid waste by the Merry King's extravagance. Taxes were raised at once, and the shopkeepers, merchants and artisans howled in protest, Herr Wild as loudly as any of them. The big-spending Russians had all marched on Paris, leaving Cassel feeling strangely quiet and empty.

It would be another long, hard, lean winter.

Dortchen saw Jakob and Wilhelm only at church, when they raised their hats to the Wild family in the chilliest way imaginable. She saw Lotte more often, for it was the job of the girls of the family to haunt the markets, begging, borrowing and bartering for food to keep their families from starving. For some reason, Lotte seemed to have forgiven Dortchen for whatever had come between her and Wilhelm. Perhaps she sensed Dortchen's heartfelt misery and despair.

Life was harder than ever for the Grimms. Jakob had lost his job as royal librarian with the fleeing of the Westphalian court, and at first it seemed as if the Kurfürst would not be very forgiving of those who had been employed by the French. Karl Grimm had lost his job at the bank, along with all of his savings, and was back living in the small third-floor apartment with his brothers.

In December, Jakob was offered a job as secretary to Count Keller, the diplomat sent to negotiate the peace terms for Hessen-Cassel. Count Keller and his entourage would follow in the tail of the Allied army as it pushed the French back towards Paris. It would mean being away from Cassel for months.

Both Karl and Ludwig decided they wished to join the Hessian army and help defeat the French, but the cost of uniforms and weapons was prohibitive. Wilhelm, in particular, chafed against the confines of the Grimms' poverty. He started a literary journal called *Old German Miscellany*, which had met with a scathing attack from a leading critic.

'It's made him very downhearted,' Lotte said. 'I've never known him to be so miserable. Karl and Ludwig are miserable too, because they want to go and fight against Napoléon, and Jakob's miserable because he hates having to leave home. I thought everything would be fine once the French were thrown out of Cassel, but in fact things are worse.'

Dortchen gave Lotte some calendula and lemon balm tea, hoping that might help her brothers. Her own brother was just as morose. The coming of the cold winter months made Rudolf's frost-scarred feet and hands ache, and brought back nightmares of the retreat from Russia.

Just before Christmas, Gretchen and her husband came back to Cassel with their four small children. They hosted a grand Christmas party at their townhouse. Gretchen tried to persuade Dortchen to borrow a party dress, but she did not want her arms and bosom to be bare, or to feel silk against her skin. She wore an old woollen dress of her mother's, with long sleeves and a high neck, and shook her head whenever anyone asked her to dance.

'What a pious old bore you've grown into,' Gretchen said in disgust.

'Leave her be,' Herr Schmerfeld said. 'It's refreshing to see such a modest young woman.'

Gretchen pouted her red lips, fluttered her feathered fan across the bare expanse of her bosom and rustled away.

Herr Schmerfeld looked down at Dortchen. 'Is all well with you?' he asked.

'Of course,' she answered, then looked away.

Good news soon came for the Grimms. With the help of his Aunt

Zimmer, Wilhelm at last was granted a position as secretary to the royal library. The job only paid a hundred thalers a year, most of which went immediately on outfitting Karl and Ludwig in their soldiers' kit, but it did at least settle two of the brothers' immediate futures – and it gave Wilhelm a new sense of purpose.

Each morning, Dortchen would kneel on her bed and watch as Wilhelm went out the side door and down the alley, dressed like an old grandee in a frockcoat and knee-breeches, his dark curls tied back in a neat pigtail, a tricorn hat on his head. Once he turned and looked up at her window, and she ducked down, red-hot with embarrassment and shame. It had been a year since they had last spoken.

In early February, Napoléon won a series of brilliantly executed victories against the Allied armies. Over the course of six days, he fought four major battles, his army of only thirty thousand men outmanoeuvring a force of one hundred and twenty thousand.

'He's a genius,' Rudolf said, shaking his head over the newspaper. 'Will he never give up?'

'Surely he cannot win against such odds?' Dortchen said, reading the paper over his shoulder.

'A normal man, no, but this is Napoléon,' Rudolf said. 'I've seen him on the battlefield. He could rouse even the most exhausted and war-weary trooper. His men would gladly give up their lives for him and the glory he brings.'

It was not enough, however. Despite his victories and the steep losses suffered by the Allied troops, Napoléon's army was simply too small and too exhausted. Step by step, they fell back, and at the end of March the Allied forces tramped into Paris.

On 6th April, the Emperor abdicated.

The news was greeted with joy in Cassel. The Marktgasse was full of people cheering and singing and dancing arm in arm. Everyone wore white cockades pinned to their hats, or white ribbons in their hair, to celebrate the restoration of the monarchy in France.

Dortchen did not dance; she disliked anyone putting their hands upon her. She stood on the steps of her father's shop, watching. She could not help feeling sorrow mixed in with the joy. It had been twenty-five years since the Declaration of the Rights of Man and the Citizen in France – twenty-five years of constant war and struggle and strife. The world had been remade. It would not be easy to turn back to the way things were before.

But we're at peace now, she told herself. *That's all that matters.*

On the far side of the square, she saw Wilhelm and Lotte dancing arm in arm. As if sensing her eyes upon him, Wilhelm looked up. At once he flushed and looked away, and Dortchen felt all the old hurt and shame. She bent her head to hide her face.

It seemed there was to be no peace between her and Wilhelm.

IN THE VALLEY OF THE SHADOW

April 1814

A few weeks later, Lotte came to tell Dortchen that the Grimms were moving away from the Marktgasse.

'We can't afford the rent,' she said, sitting down in the rocking chair by the fire.

'Oh, Lotte,' Dortchen said, the kettle in her hand. Tears pricked her eyes.

'I know. I simply can't imagine not living next door to you. Not that I see you much any more.'

Dortchen gestured helplessly with the kettle.

Lotte shrugged. 'I know, I know. Work, work, work – that's all we ever do. At least my life is a little easier now that I only have Wilhelm to look after, and he's out half the day anyway. We don't need so many rooms now, with the boys all gone off to fight and Jakob away in Paris.'

'Have you heard from him?' Dortchen asked, hanging the kettle above the fire and bringing over her basket of darning. Lotte reached for a needle and thread too. She was no more able to sit idle than Dortchen.

'Indeed, yes. You know Jakob – he never puts his pen down. He makes me so cross, though. All he writes about are the old books and manuscripts he's found, when I want to hear about the new French king. I heard he's a miserable old fellow in a wheelchair, too sick even to go to Paris. I wonder whether they'll have a grand coronation for him.'

'I wonder whether he'll call himself Louis the Seventeenth or Louis the Eighteenth,' Dortchen said. 'I mean, his nephew, the poor little Dauphin who died in prison, never ruled.'

'In the eyes of the Bourbons, he was king regardless of whether he sat on a throne or lived in a prison. Poor boy. I heard they made him spit on portraits of his mother and call her nasty names.'

The kettle boiled and Dortchen made them peppermint tea with honey.

'Where will you move to?' she asked, clasping her hot cup between her hands.

'Wilhelm has found us an apartment in the New Town, near Wilhelmshöhe Gate,' Lotte said. 'It'll be much quieter, he says, and we'll be able to walk in the royal park.'

'That's so far away,' Dortchen said in dismay.

'I'll be able to visit you in your garden,' Lotte said comfortingly.

Are you moving because of me? Dortchen wanted to ask, but she did not dare. Any answer would hurt. If Lotte said yes, it meant that Wilhelm still had feelings for her, even if they were ones of anger, resentment and hurt. If Lotte said no, it would mean he did not care. Dortchen closed her eyes, bending her head to breathe in the fragrant steam. Why could she not stop caring for him? She had tried and tried, but the stump of her love refused to wither and die.

On the day the cart came for all the Grimms' belongings, Dortchen crouched on her bed, watching from above. The washing line that ran between her bedroom and Lotte's was heavy with flapping eiderdowns, so she could see only glimpses of Lotte and Wilhelm as they piled boxes onto the cart. They both looked worn and anxious.

Dortchen wished that she could help them somehow. If only the fairy tale book had sold better. If only her father had let them be married. If only . . .

In a way, it was easier not having Wilhelm living next door. Dortchen could walk down the alleyway between the two houses without listening for his distinctive cough, and she could go to the market without being afraid of bumping into him. Church was no longer an ordeal, with his thin, upright form sitting only a few pews away, never turning to smile at her like he used to do.

Yet Dortchen still found the months after he had moved away more grey and empty than ever before. Spring turned to summer, and she worked from sunrise to midnight in the house, the garden and the stillroom. There was never a moment's rest in which to think of him, yet he was always present in her thoughts, like a bruise that refused to heal.

Late in June, Dortchen heard that Jakob had returned from Paris, bringing with him some of the treasures that had been stolen by the French. He was home only a few weeks; in August he once more set forth, this time to Vienna, where the great powers were meeting to decide the future of Europe. The social standing of the Grimms was much improved by Jakob's work at the Vienna Congress. After church on Sundays, many people would hail Dortchen and ask for news of him, expecting her to be well informed. She could only smile and shake her head, and offer whatever stale titbits she had gleaned from others.

Then something happened that drove all thoughts of Wilhelm or the peace negotiations out of Dortchen's mind. She took her mother a bowl of chicken broth and found her sitting up in bed, her nightgown unbuttoned to her belly button, her husband's shaving mirror in one hand. Dortchen had come in so swiftly that Frau Wild had time to do no more than cry out and try to hide her uncovered breast. It was red, swollen and misshapen, with a great sunburst of yellow pus near the twisted, deformed nipple.

Dortchen stared at it in horror. 'Mother,' she whispered.

Frau Wild laid down the mirror and buttoned her nightgown with shaking fingers. 'Dortchen, you should knock,' she reproved.

'Mother, what . . . what's wrong with you?'

'It's nothing,' her mother replied. 'A lump that has burst. It'll get better now.'

'Let me look.' Dortchen moved quickly to her mother's side. 'How long has it been there?'

Frau Wild laid her hand protectively over her breast. 'There's no need to gawk at me. I've felt it growing for a while, but now that it's burst all will be well.'

'It doesn't look well, not at all.' Catching her mother's hands, Dortchen drew them away and folded back the collar of the nightgown. She gazed down at the red-lipped, yellow-hearted tumour growing from the side of her mother's slack breast. 'How long?' When her mother hunched her shoulders, she asked, 'Why didn't you tell me?'

'You do so much . . . You work so hard.'

'But, Mother—' Dortchen felt the familiar choke of impotence in her throat. She buttoned her mother up again. 'I'll make you a poultice of trefoil and adder's tongue, but I think we must call the doctor.'

'Fiddlesticks,' her mother said sharply. 'Doctors will see you into an early grave. Some nice tea is all I need.'

Normally, Dortchen was inclined to agree, but she had never seen anything like that terrible seeping tumour. She hurried to tell her father, who, after examining his wife, agreed that the doctor must be called.

The beautiful summer morning was sucked into a dark funnel of fear and grief and horror. The doctor was dour and very sure. 'A few months, no more. I can operate if you like. I doubt it'll do any good.'

'What, cut off my breast?' Frau Wild cried. 'Absolutely not.'

'It's the only chance,' he responded, 'though I think it's far too late. If I'd been called a year ago . . .'

Dortchen could not sleep for the guilt that tore at her. She had always thought her mother was malingering, pretending to be ill so she could lie in bed and have her supper brought to her on a tray. At times, Dortchen's anger and resentment had been so sharp that she had deliberately given her mother the thinnest part of the soup, or not sweetened her healing tea with honey. *What agony my poor mother has endured*, she now thought, *and all without uttering a sound. What a dreadful, unloving daughter I am.*

The doctor and Dortchen's father decided to operate. Frau Wild was not to be told, to spare her the fear that would overcome her. A day the following week was decided upon, and Dortchen was told to cut up old sheets for swabs. Herr Wild gave his wife a double dose of laudanum, so she was drowsy when the doctor came, rubbing his red hands together, his assistant bearing a bag filled with knives and saws. Dortchen was ordered to help hold her mother down.

The scream she gave when the doctor first cut around the tumour was heart-wrenching. Choking back sobs, Dortchen held her mother's thrashing shoulder as the doctor hacked away at her breast. Blood and pus poured down. Dortchen shoved piles of linen beneath her. They turned a sodden red in an instant. The doctor chopped away the last lump of flesh, leaving a raw hole where her mother's breast had been.

He poured brandy onto the wound, deftly bound a wad of old cloth to it with bandages wound about her thin torso, and then set leeches to feed all around. 'They'll soon suck the poison out,' he said with satisfaction. Within half an hour he was gone, having shared half a bottle of quince brandy with Herr Wild first.

Dortchen sat by her mother's bed, holding her limp hand and staring at the leeches with revulsion. Her mother lay with her blue eyelids shut, as silent and still now as she had been convulsed with agony previously.

The excision of Frau Wild's breast did not help. She lingered for another few weeks, dying quietly in her bed while Dortchen slept on a pallet beside her.

Nothing could comfort Dortchen, not even the arrival of all her sisters and their families for the funeral. Even Röse came, plump and pregnant, with two little girls clinging shyly to her hands and her elderly husband beaming with pride. The old house was once again filled with children's laughter and the running of small feet, but Dortchen's grief was in no way eased. She felt as if she were walking in the valley of the shadow of death, and no longer knew the way back to the land of the living.

HEAD OF THE HOUSEHOLD

September 1814

After his wife's death, Herr Wild once again began to drink alone in his study. The brandy inflamed his temper. Once again, he struck out at his daughters and quarrelled with his son.

It was harvest time, and Dortchen was kept busy in the big garden, picking the fruit before it fell and rotted on the ground. Mia stayed at home, doing the housework on her own. Many evenings Dortchen came home, hot and sunburnt, her arms and hands scratched and stained with juice, to find Mia silently weeping as she peeled the vegetables for their supper, a new bruise on her arm or face.

One evening Dortchen came home to find the kitchen empty. The soup was bubbling wildly. She put her baskets of fruit down on the table, took the soup off the fire and walked through the house, dread tightening about her heart. Then she heard a sobbing gasp from her father's study, at the end of the hall. 'Please, no, Father,' Mia's voice said.

Dortchen crept down the hall and put one eye to the crack of the door. Mia knelt at her father's feet, her face in her hands as he prayed over her head. The look on her father's face turned Dortchen to stone. She could not take a step, nor scarcely breathe. She swayed, then put up a hand to save herself. The door creaked a little wider.

Her father looked up and saw her. With his eyes on hers, he bent and put his hand on Mia's head, pushing her face down so it was pressed against his thigh. 'Pray,' he commanded. Mia obeyed, her voice trembling.

Dortchen stepped away. She felt so faint that she had to lean against the wall, her face bent into the crook of her arm. She was gagging. At last, she heard her father's voice, saying, 'Go on, get out of here. Haven't you work to do, you lazy slut?' Then her sister's slow footsteps approached her.

Dortchen managed to straighten. She turned and put out her hand to Mia as her sister came out of the study. Slowly, they made their way together down the hall.

That evening, Rudolf and Herr Wild had a terrible argument. Rudolf was angry that his father was drinking away the shop's profits and leaving all the work to him.

The following morning, Mia flinched when her father came near her, knocking over a bottle of quince brandy on the dresser. It shattered on the floor. She dropped to her knees, trying to clean up the shards of broken glass. Herr Wild slapped her across the head. 'Fool girl!'

Mia cried out. She had cut her hand on the broken bottle. Blood welled up and flooded down her wrist. Dortchen ran to her aid, but Herr Wild shoved her away so violently that she hit the wall and fell. Mia wept, rocking back and forth, holding up her bleeding hand.

'Stupid fool,' Herr Wild said. 'Get up, and clean up that mess.' When Mia shrank away from him, he slapped her again. It sounded like a gunshot.

Rudolf came limping in as fast as he could. 'What are you doing? Leave her be. Can't you see she's hurt?'

'Don't tell me what to do,' the old man roared. 'I'm the head of this household, and I'll do what I think best.'

'Beating up a young girl is not the best choice, in any circumstance.' Rudolf helped Mia to her feet and gave her his handkerchief to wrap around her hand.

'Beat the child at the first sign of wilfulness and you will be the master of the child forever,' Herr Wild said.

'Like you did with Dortchen? She was the sweetest, merriest little girl in the world, and now look at her.' Rudolf glanced at Dortchen, who was still cowering against the wall. 'I can't remember the last time she smiled or made a joke. How can you think that is the best thing for your daughter?'

'Dortchen is quiet and obedient, like a daughter should be,' Herr Wild replied.

The argument continued but Dortchen did not stay to listen. She ran out the back door and through the garden to the stable, where she sank down on a bale of hay and wept. So Rudolf had thought her a sweet, merry child? And now she was nothing but a sour, miserable old maid.

When at last she had calmed enough to creep back into the house, she found Rudolf up in his bedroom, throwing clothes into a travelling bag. 'I will not stay here a minute longer,' he said. 'Father is intolerable. I will go back to Berlin and get work as an apothecary there.'

Mia was sitting on the bed, sobbing. 'Don't go, Rudolf, please don't go.'

'Will you take Mia with you?' Dortchen asked.

Rudolf stopped and looked at her.

'Please,' Dortchen said.

Mia looked up hopefully. 'Can I?'

Rudolf shook his head. 'I wish that I could. I'd take you both with me. But I have no right, nor, I'm sorry to say, enough money. I'll barely be able to afford to feed myself.'

'It's too late for me,' Dortchen said. For a moment she could not speak, but then she found the courage to go on, her voice uneven. 'But I'm afraid for Mia. Father's anger, his . . .' She could not frame the words that sprang to mind. *Needs. Hunger. Lust.* 'She would be better away from here.'

'I'm sorry,' Rudolf said.

'She could keep house for you while you work. There's nothing strange about a sister looking after her brother. And she will save money for you, by bargaining in the markets and washing your clothes.'

'I would!' Mia cried.

'I suppose I could do with some help,' he said. 'But, Dortchen, what about you?'

'He'll pursue us if we all go. It'll be harder to slip away. I can cover for you – make sure he doesn't realise till you are well away.'

'But, Dortchen—' Mia protested.

'You'll need to leave straight away,' Dortchen said. 'Before Father finds out. Mia, I'll help you pack.'

Hurriedly, the two sisters threw a few necessities into a bag. Mia had very little to take. Some spare underclothes, her Sunday best, her pincushion and thimble, her prayer book. Then, tiptoeing, Rudolf and his sisters went down the back stairs. As they crept through the kitchen, they could hear Herr Wild clinking bottles in the study. At the gate into the alleyway, they hugged and kissed each other goodbye.

'I'll write to let you know where we are,' Rudolf said.

'But Father will—'

'I'll write to Lotte,' he said. 'She can slip you the letter.'

Mia was weeping. 'Dortchen, come with us. Please.'

Dortchen wanted to go so badly that it felt as if every muscle in her body was straining to escape. But she was sure her father would pursue them; he would find her and drag her back, and Mia too. She shook her head. 'Go, little love,' she said. 'I'll be fine.'

Her composure almost broke as the gate swung shut behind them. She turned and looked back at the house. It towered against the grey September sky, all its windows staring and blank. Most of its rooms were empty now. There was only Dortchen and her father left.

GO TO HELL

October 1814

Dortchen would not tell her father where Rudolf and Mia had gone, even though he beat her and threw words as hard as stones. Later that night, when he came drunk and stumbling to her bedroom door, she showed him the carving knife she had brought from the kitchen.

'I will kill you if you touch me again,' she said, sitting up fully dressed in a chair. 'And then you will go to hell.'

Her father reeled back, aghast. He blundered out, almost falling down the stairs. Dortchen set her chair under the door handle, put the knife under her pillow and lay down. It was a long time before she was able to sleep.

The next day she made up a potent tisane of skullcap, chamomile, valerian and hops. She stirred it round and round with her long spoon, chanting under her breath, 'Make him sleep, make him sleep, make him sleep.' She liked the sound and rhythm of the words, so she repeated them twelve times before pouring the mixture into his quince brandy. As she had hoped, it made him sleep heavily.

Herr Wild slept late into the next day, and Dortchen opened the shop herself, serving anyone who came as well as she knew how. To any query, she answered, 'I'm sorry, my father is unwell. I'll go and ask him, if you like.' Then she would go through to the stillroom, wait a few minutes,

403

then come back, saying, 'Father says a tisane of marigold flowers and chase-devil will do you the world of good.'

Eventually, he woke and came lurching into the shop, shouting at her to bring him some ale. She brought him willowbark tincture and wood betony tea. When he dashed it from her hand, smashing it to the ground, she went silently to get the broom.

When she returned, he seized it from her and beat her over the shoulder with it, but she fought him and, to the surprise of them both, managed to wrest it from him. She had grown strong with all the hard work of the house and garden, and he was soft and flabby now. 'If you strike me, I shall strike you back,' she warned him.

Herr Wild did not know what to do with her. So he drank and slept and snored, then drank some more, and Dortchen ran the house and the shop alone.

HER MASTER

October 1814

One evening in late October, Dortchen was struggling to carry two large and heavy baskets of apples home along Wilhelmshöhe Alley when someone tried to take one of the baskets from her hand.

She looked up, instinctively tightening her grip on the handle. It was Wilhelm.

Dortchen relinquished the basket, her heart beating so fast that it hurt the bones of her chest. She was very conscious of her dirty apron, and her shabby black gown and bonnet.

'You should not be carrying such heavy baskets.' His voice was disapproving.

'How else am I to get the apples home from the garden?'

'Couldn't you load them into your buggy?'

'The Russians took our horse,' she replied.

'Oh,' he said. 'I didn't know.'

'They ate all our chickens too,' she said. 'I'm hoping to barter some of our apples for a hen.'

'It's been a hard year,' he said.

'Yes.'

The church bells tolled eight times. Dortchen's step quickened. It was long past suppertime. Her father would be angry.

'You should not be out so late alone,' he said, as if reading her thoughts.

'I did not realise the time. I was busy trying to collect as many apples as possible. Twilight crept up on me, and then it's such a long way home.'

'You shouldn't have to walk so far, carrying such heavy baskets.'

She gestured with her free hand. 'There's no one else to do it.'

They walked on together, both stiff and self-conscious. It was the first time they had spoken in almost two years. Dortchen remembered how she had fallen on her knees before him, how she had sought to swallow him whole. Shame scalded her. She gripped the handle of her basket tightly and looked away, hiding her face behind the brim of her bonnet.

'I was sorry to hear about your mother,' Wilhelm said after a while. 'She was always very kind.'

Dortchen nodded, her eyes stinging with tears. Another long silence stretched between them. She hurried into speech. 'Is there any news from Jakob? How do the peace talks go?'

'A lot of talking and not much else, by all accounts,' he replied. 'Matters are not helped by the British being distracted by the war in America. Did you hear they have burnt down Washington?'

'No, really? So they've won?'

'I don't think it's that simple. I think it's much like the war in the Peninsula – a battle won, a battle lost, and another ending in stalemate.'

She nodded. It was dark in the narrow streets between the houses. Lanterns were being kindled in a few windows, shining out in golden squares across the cobblestones.

A carriage clopped past them, a linkboy hurrying before it, his lantern bobbing up and down. Overhead, stars swarmed in the gap between the gabled roofs. Wilhelm was silent, staring away from her.

'You . . . you must miss Jakob very much,' she ventured, unable to bear the tension between them.

'Yes.'

Again the silence stretched long, then Wilhelm burst out, 'He's not just my brother, Dortchen. He's my dearest friend, my partner in everything. I know you think that I'm under his thumb, that I'm *in thrall* to him.' The intensity with which Wilhelm repeated her long-ago words showed her how much he had brooded upon them. 'But you don't understand. Family is everything to us. It's all that we have. We've been apart so rarely, and we have so little else . . .'

'I do understand,' she said. Her breath came short. 'He's more like your twin than your older brother.'

'Yes.'

'I'm sorry I spoke so to you. I'm sorry. I can't explain. My father . . .' She was unable to say more, but he waited courteously for her to go on. Somehow, in the darkness, she found the words. 'He made me think . . . wrongly about things. He's not a good man. He has to shape everyone to his will. Even if it means breaking them. I couldn't . . . I can't . . .'

She could speak no more, and tears ran down her cheeks.

Wilhelm heard the catch of her breath and turned towards her, his hand on her arm. When he saw her face, he put down his basket so he could wipe away her tears. 'Please don't cry, Dortchen.'

The tears came faster. Wilhelm bent his head to kiss her. Dortchen dropped her basket, and apples tumbled into the gutter. She rose up on her toes, wound her arms about his neck and kissed him with all her heart. It was a single magical moment, in the starlit darkness, the smell of bruised apples about them.

'I've tried so hard to cut you out of my heart,' Wilhelm said, when at last they fell apart. His voice was low and angry. 'Yet every time I see you, I feel it all again.'

She tried to master her voice. 'You think it's any easier for me?'

'I suppose not.'

They picked up the apples and walked on in silence. They turned a corner and came down the road into the wide square of the Marktgasse. Dortchen looked fearfully at her father's shop but it was dark and quiet. Together, they turned into the dark alley leading to the garden.

'What are we to do?' he asked. 'We can't marry without your father's permission, even if I were to find some way of earning enough to support a wife. We can't see each other without . . .' He cleared his throat.

'Without falling into temptation,' Dortchen finished for him, using her father's words.

'Yes. It hurts too much to see you, Dortchen. I'm afraid . . . I'm afraid I'll fall into sin.'

Dortchen did not want to talk about sin. She took a deep, ragged breath. 'Can't we just be friends?'

'I wish we could. But, believe me, none of my friends . . . rouse me like you do.'

They stood close together in the darkness, the baskets of apples at their feet.

Dortchen's cheeks were hot. 'I . . . I'm sorry,' she said at last. 'I never meant to hurt you.'

'I know.' His finger traced a soft path down her throat and into the cleft of her breasts. 'I've missed you,' he murmured. 'You torment my dreams.'

She shut her eyes and lifted her face. His kiss was gentle. Very slowly, his hand slid down and cupped her breast. Her breath caught, and he shifted her closer, so that she rested in the crook of his arm.

She drew her mouth away. 'If the war would only end . . .' she whispered.

'Maybe, if I work on the fairy tales, make them better . . .'

They kissed.

'Maybe Father will relent . . . ?'

'We don't need much money, surely? Just enough to eat . . .'

'And buy quills and ink and paper.'

He smiled, and kissed her again.

'We wouldn't have to move away,' she continued. 'We could live with Jakob still. I don't take up much more room than a mouse; surely he wouldn't mind a little mouse in his house?'

He answered her with a kiss of growing passion and urgency.

'I'd so hate for him to be lonely,' she said, when she could speak again.

'I have a job now. Perhaps the prince will make me his librarian. It has a much better salary. And the second volume of tales will be published soon. Maybe they will sell—'

'Once the war is over, everyone will want to read beautiful stories of courage and triumph . . .'

'And love . . .' He deepened the kiss.

'Surely . . .'

'Yes.' He tasted tears on her cheeks. 'Don't cry, Dortchen, I can't bear it.'

'I can't help it,' she sobbed. 'Oh, Wilhelm, you don't know . . . You don't realise . . . If you only knew—'

'What?'

But she couldn't tell him. He kissed her again but she turned her face away. 'Wilhelm . . . whatever happens, I want you to know I truly love you.'

They clung together in the shadows, then Dortchen drew away. 'I have to go. If my father knew I was here . . .' She shuddered at the thought.

'Don't let him hurt you,' he said. 'I wish . . .'

She shook her head, picked up the baskets of apples and went through the gate. *Once upon a time, when wishing was still of use . . .*

Her father was waiting for her in the kitchen, his stick swinging in his hand. She had no time to run for safety, no time to find some way to protect herself. He set himself to prove that he was still her master. She could do nothing but fall before him. She thought this time he might kill her.

Afterwards, she wished that he had.

AN EARLY GRAVE

November 1814

He seemed to want to drink himself into an early grave. Perhaps it was the only way that he might forget what he had done.

He began to find it hard to climb the stairs. He made Dortchen come to him in his study. His feet and legs were so swollen that he could not pull his boots on. He began to wear his carpet slippers even in the daytime. Often he did not shave. He would wear his frockcoat over his nightgown and shuffle about the house, shouting at Dortchen to bring him more brandy.

When he was asleep, she would make more of the sleeping tincture, stirring it around and around. 'Make him sleep, make him sleep, make him sleep, make him sleep,' she chanted under her breath. She worried he would notice how empty the jars of skullcap, chamomile, and valerian were, but now he only went into the stillroom to search for brandy and laudanum. He noticed little else.

She did her best but there was never enough time. Each day was a long ordeal, and each night a misery. Fear and hopelessness were her chains.

His face was red. His eyes sank into puffy eyelids. Soon his hands were so swollen that his wedding ring cut deep into his flesh. Dortchen had to try to get it off with soapy water. It hurt him so much that he slapped her across the face, sending suds flying. He wheezed when he walked. When

Dortchen emptied his chamber pot, she saw that his urine was a strange, dark colour. It smelt bad. He smelt bad.

Autumn passed. At least there was less work in the garden in the winter. She kept herself busy pickling cabbage and bottling plums, sometimes working long past midnight by the light of a sputtering candle. He rarely came to the kitchen. If she went to bed, he might hear her footsteps and call to her. It was better to sleep on the floor by the kitchen fire. She lay on the old rag rugs, rubbing bits of fabric between her fingers.

Nightmares haunted her.

He got sicker. The brandy no longer seemed to work. He was angry, but weak, panting, thrashing about, unable to catch her. Dortchen polished all the jars in the stillroom, turning them so the labels were perfectly aligned. She would not clean the study. He lay there on his couch, calling for her, banging on the floor with his stick. She brought him soup and took away his chamber pot.

Once, finding him sleeping, slack-jawed, with saliva creeping down his silvered jowls, she imagined putting the cushion over his face. Her hands clenched by her side. When she stirred the tisane, muttering, 'Make him sleep, make him sleep,' she imagined saying, 'Make him die, make him die.' It would be easy enough. A handful of crushed nightshade. A few monkshood flowers. Some white baneberries. No one would suspect her. Everyone knew he was sick. But she could not do it. He was her father.

It snowed one night, and he was restless, crying out, unable to breathe. The only way he could sleep was sitting up. His face was now so swollen that she could scarcely recognise him at all.

She called the doctor. Dropsy, he said. He prescribed some medicine. Dortchen had to measure it all out herself. It came from the locked cupboard, the one where the most dangerous drugs were kept. Her father felt her taking the keys from his pocket. He struck out, making her ears ring. When she brought the medicine, he would not drink it. He thought she meant to poison him. So she sent a note to Gretchen, asking her to come and help nurse him.

Reluctantly, Gretchen came. When she tried to give him the medicine, he struck it from her hand. It spilt all over her silk dress. 'Well, that's the last time I do that,' Gretchen said.

'Rudolf,' her father said. 'Get Rudolf.'

So Dortchen wrote to her brother and told him to come home, giving Gretchen the letter to post. She dared not leave him even to walk to the post office.

The week before Christmas was long and lonely. He was much worse. He could not eat. His swollen belly pained him. His lungs were wet, his breathing ragged.

Rudolf and Mia came home. It was such a relief to have them back that Dortchen could scarcely speak, her body shaking with tears. Mia flew into her arms, crying, 'But you're so thin and pale. Have you been sick too?'

'I'm fine,' she answered. 'Everything's fine.'

'It won't be long now,' Rudolf said, after he had examined their father. 'Why didn't you write sooner, Dortchen? We would have come if we'd known.'

She shrugged.

'Well, we're home now,' Mia said. 'And you're to do nothing, Dortchen. Sit and rest.'

Dortchen could not. It felt too strange. She went to the garden and cut holly branches and hung them over the mantelpiece, and brought snowy fir branches home from the forest. When Mia decorated them with gilded fir cones and angels, she almost managed a smile.

Her father died on Christmas Day. Dortchen sat beside him in her black gown, listening to his breath rasp in and out, ever more slowly. When at last it stopped altogether, it took her a while to notice.

She stood up abruptly, casting her handkerchief over his awful, congested face. She backed away from him, then turned and ran out of the room, almost knocking Rudolf over on her way. She grabbed her bonnet and coat from the hook in the kitchen, and ran through the snowy garden, tying the ribbons under her chin. Mia called after her, but, once she began running, Dortchen did not stop. She ran out the gate and down the alley and along the Marktgasse. People stopped to stare. 'Is everything all right, love?' the saddler's wife called. Dortchen shook her head and ran on.

Soon a stitch in her side slowed her. She ran and walked, ran and walked. At last she was free of the town. She went into the winter-bare, snow-frosted woods. She went to the linden grove. There at last she could dance. There at last she could laugh out loud in her relief and her gladness. There at last she could cry.

Wilhelm found her in the alley outside the shop's garden. 'Our time will come,' he said, kissing her. 'Love works magic.'

Dortchen no longer believed in magic. And she certainly no longer believed in love.

PART SEVEN

The Singing, Springing Lark

CASSEL

The German Confederation of Nations, 1819–1825

The poor girl who had wandered so far took courage and said, 'I will continue on as far as the wind blows and as long as the cock crows, till I find him.' She went on a long, long way, until at last she came to the castle where her sweetheart and the false princess were living together. A feast was soon to be held, to celebrate their wedding. She said, 'God will help me still,' and opened the little chest that the sun had given her. Inside was a dress as brilliant as the sun itself. She took it out and put it on, then went up into the castle, where everyone, even the bride herself, looked at her. The bride liked the dress so well that she asked if it was for sale.

'Not for money or property,' answered the girl, 'but for flesh and blood.'

The bride asked what she meant. She said, 'Let me sleep one night in the chamber where the prince sleeps.'

At last the bride consented, but told her page to give the prince a sleeping-potion.

That night, when the prince was asleep, the girl was led into his room. She sat down on the bed and said, 'I have followed you for seven years. I have been to the sun and the moon and the four winds and have asked about you, and I have helped you against the dragon. Will you then forget me?'

From 'The Singing, Springing Lark', a tale told by Dortchen Wild to Wilhelm Grimm on 7th January 1813

IMPOSSIBLE DREAMS

August 1819

'I am so hideous,' Gretchen said, turning sideways so she could see the size of her extended stomach in the mirror.

'Hideous is the last word anyone would use about you,' Dortchen said. 'You're quite beautiful.'

'I look like the side of a barn.'

'You're about to have a baby,' Dortchen said. 'You have to expect to be a little bigger than usual.'

'A little bigger? I'm enormous. I look like I'm about to give birth to an elephant. I *feel* like I'm about to give birth to an elephant.'

Dortchen came to stand beside her, looking into the mirror. She looked thin and plain and serious next to her elder sister. Her hair was screwed into a knot at the back of her head, while Gretchen's hung in tight ringlets on either side of her face. Her sister wore a blue silk dress with puffed sleeves, a high waist and a deeply ruffled hem, with pearls about her neck and both plump wrists. Dortchen wore a shabby black gown, although five years had passed since the death of their parents. She had no money to pay for a new dress.

'I wish I didn't feel so unwell,' Gretchen said, returning to her chaise longue, where she lay down and ate another meringue. Her ankles were grossly swollen above her embroidered silk slippers. The sight gave

Dortchen a sharp twinge of memory. She turned away, trying to steady her breathing.

'Dortchen, be a dear and tell the governess to take the children to the park. I cannot bear their noise.'

The sound of distant childish laughter barely penetrated the elegant panelled doors, but Dortchen did not protest. She went as directed to the schoolroom, where two little girls in ruffled white frocks sat drawing at a table. Four sturdy boys lay on the floor, playing with tin soldiers. A stern-faced young woman sat darning stockings by the window. Like Dortchen, she was dressed in a plain black dress, though hers was rather less faded.

'Ida, I'm sorry, but Frau Schmerfeld has asked that you take the children to the park. She needs to rest.'

Ida looked at the great basket of mending still to be done and sighed. 'Very well,' she said, rising to her feet. 'Ottilie and Sophie, get your bonnets and gloves, please. Adolf, Karl, Julius and Friedrich, get your coats.'

'But it's so hot,' Julius complained, sitting up. He was wearing a pair of tight blue high-waisted trousers that buttoned over his jacket. The older two were dressed in similar outfits, with floppy lace collars. All looked most uncomfortable. 'Please, Ida, don't make us put coats on as well.'

'You can't go out without your coats,' she said. 'But, if you like, we can take your model ships and sail them in the pond.'

Julius whooped with joy and ran off to find his boat. Friedrich, an angelic looking two-year-old with a head of pale golden curls, lifted his arms to Dortchen. 'Uppy, Aunty Dortchy.' Dortchen lifted him up, and he clamped both legs about her hip. 'Come park.'

'I'm sorry, sweetling, I can't today. Your mother's sick and needs me to look after her.'

He frowned. 'Mama always sick.'

'She'll be well again soon,' Dortchen said. She tried to pass him over to Ida but he clamped his legs harder, clinging to her with both chubby arms and burying his face in her neck. She cuddled him close. 'How about we go downstairs? You can give your Mama a kiss goodbye.'

He nodded his curly head. Dortchen said teasingly, 'Why don't you walk with me? You're too big to carry all the way now. And I'd like to have such a handsome gentleman escort me.'

Friedrich consented to be set down on his sturdy legs and walked alongside Dortchen, holding her hand. He was dressed in a frilly white dress and bib. His curls hung down to his shoulders.

Dortchen brought him into the drawing room, where her sister was flicking through a fashion periodical. 'You've been such an age,' Gretchen began, then she saw her son. 'Oh, hello, Friedrich. Aren't you going to the park?'

Friedrich ran towards her and climbed up on the chaise longue. 'I'm such a handsome gentleman,' he told her proudly.

'Is that so? Don't you know that vanity is a deadly sin? Dortchen, bring me my embroidery scissors.'

Her heart sinking, Dortchen did as she was told. Gretchen took her son's curls in one hand and chopped them off with the scissors. They fell to the floor in pale gold circles.

Friedrich watched them in interest, then shook his shorn head. 'Not so hot,' he said approvingly. He saw the plate of meringues and seized one.

'Manners,' Gretchen said, taking it from his hand. 'What do you say?'

His face had fallen, but he looked at her hopefully and said, 'Please?'

She gave him the meringue, saying, 'Go and eat it outside, I don't want your sticky hands ruining my silk.' As the little boy ran to join his brothers in the front hall, she said, 'Would you sweep up the mess, Dortchen?'

Dortchen knelt down to pick up the fallen curls. 'Do you want to keep one, as a memento?' she asked, holding them out to her sister.

'Good heavens, no. If I kept every tooth or lock of my children's hair, I'd have to move to a larger house. Not that I'd mind, I must admit. Really, with six children and another on the way, you'd think Ferdy would buy us something a little more spacious. We're all on top of each other here.'

As Dortchen sprinkled some lavender water on a handkerchief for her sister, she wondered how Gretchen could speak so. The Schmerfelds lived in one of the biggest and grandest houses in Cassel. Built on an elegant square in the new French quarter, it had nearly a dozen bedrooms, not counting the servants' quarters in the attic. It had a pleasant sunny garden to the rear, in which white roses grew inside neat green hedges, and a long ballroom with gilded chandeliers. Gretchen had her own dressing room, and a bathroom with a huge enamel bath that took the housemaids a dozen buckets of hot water to fill. She even had a separate room for her chamber pot, which was hidden under a cushioned seat in an ornately carved chair. Dortchen could not understand how her sister could live in such a beautiful house and still not be happy.

She's getting close to term, Dortchen reminded herself. *She must be so hot and uncomfortable.*

Certainly Gretchen was looking hot in the face, and her fingers were so swollen that Dortchen had to ease off her rings with some soapy water. This caused another frisson of memory. Dortchen pushed it away determinedly. She never thought of the past at all now, if she could help it.

The last five years had not been easy for anyone. In early 1815, Napoléon had escaped from Elba, the tiny island on which he had been imprisoned after his abdication. He had marched on Paris, gathering men with every mile. The French king, Louis XVIII, had fled, and Napoléon had been carried into the Tuileries Palace on the shoulders of a cheering crowd. Soon Europe was at war again.

As long lines of soldiers once again marched through the German landscape, the sunset skies were as red as fire from horizon to horizon, as if the very gates of hell had been flung open. The newspapers said the vivid sunsets were the result of an erupting volcano in Java, which had killed thousands of people. Dortchen could only think the fiery evening skies a portent of evil.

In mid-June, the French army had been defeated by the British and the Prussians at the small village of Waterloo, in Belgium, at the cost of many thousands of men. Napoléon surrendered and was sent to the most isolated island in the world, the tiny rock of St Helena, in the South Atlantic Ocean.

Dortchen had been most relieved but was also filled with compassion. *How must Napoléon feel?* she wondered. *To have ruled the world, and now be alone, exiled, living in a hut on a rock. What anguish he must feel.*

The following year of 1816 was called the Year Without a Summer. The eruption of the volcano in Java the previous year had filled the world's atmosphere with ash. The sky was leaden and grey every day, and streaked with blood red every evening. Dortchen would hang out the clean white sheets in the morning and bring them in that afternoon grey and speckled with black.

The harvest had failed and food prices had soared. Famine soon followed. Starving families came to Cassel from the country, begging on street corners. Soon there were riots in front of bakeries and angry rampages through the markets. Granaries were looted and set on fire, and shops were robbed. Rudolf slept in the apothecary's shop, his battered old musket beside him.

The next winter was the hardest Dortchen had ever known. They lived on thin soup and bread made from acorns, and saved every thaler they could to prevent their shop from falling into bankruptcy.

Life was even harder for the Grimm family. Jakob had returned from the Vienna Congress jobless once more, and so had applied for the position of second librarian at the royal palace – the job Wilhelm had been hoping to receive. Lotte said Wilhelm did not mind; he was just so glad to have his brother home.

The two elder brothers were once again supporting the whole family. Ludwig and Karl had returned to Cassel after the war, and Ferdinand constantly wrote begging letters from Berlin, where he was employed by Jakob and Wilhelm's publisher for a pittance.

Lotte, standing with Dortchen in the long queue for meat, said that she dreamt every night of food, and woke in the morning to find nothing to eat but a stale heel of bread that had to be divided between them all.

'And it's so cold. Last night, Ludwig chopped up the chairs and threw them on the fire just so we wouldn't freeze. But now we have nothing to sit on.'

'We have some old stools in the attic. Come and borrow them,' Dortchen said, huddling her icy hands into her sleeves.

'Ludwig will probably burn them too. He hates the cold. It means his fingers are so stiff that he cannot draw.'

And Wilhelm will not be able to write, Dortchen thought, her heart pierced with pity. She did not say the words out loud, though, and Lotte was always careful not to mention his name.

The passing of time had not made Dortchen's heartache any easier to bear. She and Wilhelm took care never to be alone, though they were polite enough to each other when they met. They never spoke of the past, or their promises to each other. It was hard enough to keep body and soul together through these cold, lean years without weakening themselves with impossible dreams.

Rudolf suspected how Dortchen felt about Wilhelm; he had even once offered to scrape together a dowry for her. Dortchen knew that he needed a horse and buggy, however, so that he could make house visits. Horses were very expensive in the aftermath of the war. She had shaken her head and told him to keep his thalers for more important things.

'I'm sure the girls would help,' he had told her. 'I know times are hard, but Gretchen's husband seems to have come out of the war richer than ever, and you know Lisette wants to see you happy.'

'Too much has happened between me and Wilhelm,' she said. 'It's all dead between us.'

Rudolf had looked troubled but did not press her. Afterwards, Dortchen wept by herself in the scullery, afraid that she had spoken the truth.

In 1817 Mia had married a stout Englishman who cared nothing for her lack of dowry. She moved with him to Ziegenhain, leaving Dortchen to keep house for her brother. Dortchen was kept busy in the garden and stillroom, and Rudolf was quietly grateful for her help. It was not just Rudolf who needed her. Dortchen's sisters were always having babies, so Aunty Dortchen was in great demand, to support the new mother and look after the older children. Sometimes she joked that she had no sooner unpacked her bag from one trip away when a letter would arrive from another sister, begging her to come at once.

In 1818 the von Haxthausens had visited Cassel, returning a few months later with their nieces, Jenny and Annette von Droste-Hülshoff. Everyone thought this meant that the family approved of a match between Wilhelm and Jenny. Although she was rich and he was poor, the family were generally good-hearted, and by all accounts Jenny pined with love for him.

Dortchen went to the Grimms' apartment with her sister Gretchen to meet the family one hot summer's afternoon. She could think of no excuse to stay away but sat at the back of the room, her head bent over Friedrich's curly mop. Jenny was a sweet-faced young woman, and clearly in love with Wilhelm.

It was like a stab in the heart, seeing how her face lit up at the sight of him, and Dortchen had to turn away, her vision obscured by a mist of tears. She went blindly out to the garden and pinched off dead flower heads with her fingers, Friedrich hanging on to her hand. Lotte came out to join her, looking anxious, but Dortchen had recovered her composure and teased her about how she would soon have a sister-in-law, and a pretty, fashionable one too.

Lotte caught her hand. 'He does not love her, Dortchen.'

'Well, if he doesn't, he's a fool,' she returned. 'Anyone can see she is smitten with him, and you must admit it'd be an excellent match.'

'Do you really not care?' Lotte asked, searching her face with troubled eyes.

Dortchen turned away, saying lightly over her shoulder, 'Oh, you're thinking of that silly crush I had on Wilhelm all those years ago? I grew out of that long ago, my dear.'

Lotte stepped back. 'I'm sorry, I thought . . .'

Dortchen smiled. 'Do you think he'll make an offer?'

'Maybe he should,' Lotte replied, and went back inside.

Dortchen blotted away tears with the edge of her glove.

As the weeks passed, she had tried to steel herself for an announcement of a betrothal. None came. At the end of the summer, the von Haxthausens took their nieces home and did not come visiting again. Dortchen could not help being glad.

She had not seen so much of Wilhelm and Lotte after that. Dortchen told herself it was for the best. As another year wheeled past, she had kept herself busy helping her brother and sisters, and told herself she was happy being of use.

* * *

'I have such dreadful heartburn,' Gretchen said, pressing her hand to the top of her distended belly. 'And my feet hurt.'

Dortchen ordered some ginger tea for her, then eased off her slippers so she could rub her sister's feet. Gretchen remained fretful, though, and did not want Dortchen to go. 'It's unkind of you,' she told Dortchen, who was packing up her basket. 'I'm all alone here and have nothing to do. Why can't Rudolf make his own supper? Stay and play cards with me.'

'I'm sorry, but I need to go,' Dortchen said. 'Poor Rudolf has had a long day in the shop, and I have to cook him supper. Besides, I want to be home before dark. The streets are dangerous right now.'

'Why?' Gretchen demanded.

'People are harassing the Jews, throwing stones at their houses and at the synagogue, and beating them up in the street. They say there have been full-blown riots against the Jews in Frankfurt and Leipzig, and it's only going to get worse.'

'Well, what do they expect, when they charge such exorbitant interest rates?' Gretchen replied.

'People knew what the rates were when they borrowed the money.'

'Yes, but it was a famine. People had to borrow money to feed their families. Now they face bankruptcy just trying to pay the interest.'

Dortchen thought it was not quite as simple as that, but she did not want to argue with her sister when she was so close to term. 'I'll come back and visit you tomorrow,' she said, then kissed Gretchen's powdered cheek. She put on her bonnet and gloves, and walked quickly through the streets, which were crowded with angry men and women. They were milling about Jewish homes and businesses, shouting, 'Hep! Hep!'

Somewhere glass smashed. The crowd surged forward. 'Hep! Hep!' they shouted. 'Down with the Jews!'

Dortchen kept her head low and quickened her pace, a drab figure in black among the gathering shadows.

A SHEATH OF ICE

August 1819

Later that evening, a servant brought a message for Dortchen, begging her to come to see Gretchen at once. Although it was already dark, Dortchen put on her bonnet and gloves and hurried through the streets to the French quarter, wondering what could be wrong. She carried some ginger tea in her basket, in case it was indigestion again.

Frau Claweson, the housekeeper, opened the door to her, her round face worried and upset. 'Oh, Fraülein, thank heavens you're here. Frau Schmerfeld has been taken mighty poorly. We've called for the doctor but he's out at a house call and hasn't come yet.'

'Is it the baby? It's not coming already, is it?'

'I don't rightly know. Maybe.' Frau Claweson stood back to let Dortchen in.

To her surprise, Wilhelm was sitting in the front hall, his hat in his hands. He rose at the sight of her, colour coming to his pale cheeks.

She greeted him in some confusion. 'What are you doing here, Wilhelm?'

'I've come to ask Herr Schmerfeld for some advice,' he answered. 'About money, you know. He said I should come by tonight but he's not home yet.'

'I'm sure he'll be back any moment,' Frau Claweson said over her shoulder as she bustled back to the kitchen. 'We've sent for him.'

'Gretchen's feeling unwell,' Dortchen said. 'I hope it's not the baby coming early – she's not due for another few weeks.'

'Perhaps I had better go,' Wilhelm said.

'I'm sure there's no need,' she answered. 'The heat is making her fretful.'

'Surely she does not call on you at all hours of the day?' Wilhelm glanced at the clock.

'I don't mind,' she answered, walking towards the stairs.

'You didn't walk here, did you?' he asked. 'The town's all in uproar. It's not safe in the streets.'

'The Jews simply want the Kurfürst to allow them the same freedoms they had under King Jérôme,' Dortchen said. 'You can't blame them.'

'No. God bless the Kurfürst, but he is rather old-fashioned,' Wilhelm said. 'The Jews are not the only ones who want a new constitution along the lines of Napoléon's code. Even Jakob thinks the Kurfürst should make some changes, and you know he hated the code for throwing out all our legal traditions.'

'I do know,' she answered, smiling. 'But I must go up. Gretchen wants me.'

'You're too good,' he told her.

She shook her head and began to mount the stairs.

'Will you wait for me, Dortchen? I'll walk you home.'

'You only live around the corner. There's no need to walk me all the way back to the Marktgasse.'

'I'd like to. Please.'

Dortchen shook her head and went on up the stairs, not looking back.

To her dismay, Gretchen was clearly in distress. Her face was drenched in perspiration, her ringlets hanging limply. She walked up and down, clutching her belly. 'It hurts,' she panted. 'Oh, Dortchen, I think the baby's coming early. Why isn't the doctor here?'

Dortchen soothed her as best she could. Suddenly Gretchen gasped. Her blue silk dress was stained dark from pelvis to hem. 'My waters have broken. Oh, God!'

'No!' Dortchen did not know what to do. She had never assisted at a birth. She rang the bell. 'We need to get you to bed.'

'The doctor still hasn't arrived,' Gretchen said irritably. 'How can I give birth without the doctor?'

But give birth Gretchen did. It was quick, and bloody, and terrifying.

For Dortchen, time folded together like a black silk fan. She saw a door opening, and the loom of her father's shadow. *On your knees, for you have sinned.* His thick fingers thrust inside her. The joints of her jaw cracked apart. Darkness swallowed light. Panic swallowed breath.

Gretchen was screaming but Dortchen could not help her. She had to get away. She ran to the door and threw it open. The housekeeper was outside, the doctor beside her. Dortchen pushed past them and ran down the stairs. She was scarcely aware of where she was. She needed air. She looked from side to side, sobbing for breath.

'Dortchen!'

She hardly heard the voice. She ran down the corridor, looking for the door to the garden. Out she ran, into the warm, scented darkness. The step tripped her and she fell heavily, bruising her knees on the gravel.

'Dortchen!' The voice came from behind her. She looked up. Then Wilhelm's arms were around her. He lifted her up and helped her to a stone seat nearby. 'What is it? What's wrong? Is it Gretchen?'

'My father . . .'

'What?'

'My father!' Sobs shook her and she clutched at his coat. Memories passed over her like the shadows of thunderclouds. She was shuddering so hard that her teeth chattered.

Wilhelm held her close, his hand smoothing her hair. 'What is it? What's wrong?'

Dortchen couldn't control her tongue any more than she could control her skin and her nerves. 'He . . . oh . . . he . . .'

'Who? Your father?'

'Yes. He . . . he . . .' She could not breathe.

Wilhelm soothed her as if she were a child. 'There, there. It's all right. Put your head down. Just breathe.' He pressed the back of her head, trying to make her put her face down between her knees.

But Dortchen could not bear it, and she shrieked and struck out at him blindly. She struggled away, and ran, and fell. Wilhelm tried to help her up but she cowered away, scarcely able to gulp enough air to sob.

'What is it? What's wrong? I don't understand.'

'He . . . he . . .' Dortchen crouched in the darkness, her arms over her head, her chest heaving.

'Your father?' Wilhelm crouched down beside her.

She leant away from him with all her strength. 'Yes, he . . . he made me—'

'He made you do what?' Wilhem's voice was sharp.

She could not say the words. She could only struggle to catch her breath.

'Dortchen, Dortchen, darling Dortchen.' His voice was ragged. 'Are you trying to say . . . Do you mean . . .' He could not say the words either.

She remembered how she had tried to tell him once before, and how he had written down her words. 'The king looked at his daughter,' she said. 'Her hair was as golden. He . . . he wanted . . .' She could not go on.

'Oh, God,' Wilhelm said. 'No.'

Dortchen could not breathe. Her lungs were on fire. 'He wanted her,' she said. 'He took her.'

'Oh, my lovely girl,' Wilhelm said. 'Oh, God.'

'Don't say that!' Her words were as quick and cruel as a striking snake.

Wilhelm's breath was uneven as her own.

'I can't believe it,' he said. 'Please tell me it's not true.'

Dortchen was silent. Slowly, her head drooped. Sobs struggled in her chest. Wilhelm tried to draw her close but she pushed him away. He eased himself away, leaving space between them.

They sat there in the darkness, in silence, for a very long time. Gradually, her sobs quietened. She forgot how she had shrieked at him, and hit out at him, and felt only hurt that he did not seek to comfort her.

'Is it true?' he asked.

She nodded, then, realising he could not see her in the darkness, whispered, 'Yes.'

'That's why . . . that's why you turned so cold . . . and so strange?'

'Yes.'

'Why didn't you tell me? I could've done something. I could've helped.'

She did not answer.

He got to his feet. 'I don't know what to say. It's so hard to believe.' He walked away, the gravel crunching under his boots. Then he walked back, paused, and walked away again. She sat still, exhausted. Eventually, he came back and put down his hand for her. She let him draw her up from the ground, let him sit her down on the seat, let him sit beside her, playing nervously with her fingers. She was numb.

'How long?' he asked.

She shrugged.

They sat in silence. There was no moon. The stars were bright, innumerable. The air smelt of roses.

'I don't know what to do,' he confessed to her. 'I feel I should seize a sword, strike your father dead . . .'

'He's already dead.'

'Yes. But, Dortchen, you're alive . . . you're still alive.'

'I feel dead in my heart.'

'No. Don't say that. Please.'

She did not answer.

'So much makes sense now. A horrible kind of sense.'

'I shouldn't have told you. It doesn't matter. It was all so long ago.'

'Dortchen . . .'

She stood up. 'I need to go. Gretchen needs me.' She walked away as quickly as she could. Her limbs felt all wrong. Too long. Too heavy. Her head was light. Drunk.

She went back inside the house. The lamplight hurt her eyes. She could hear distant sounds. A high-pitched wailing. She followed the noise.

Gretchen was limp, lying in her bed. The sheets were stained with red. The doctor was trying to stop the flow of blood from between her legs. The housekeeper was holding a tiny bundle, jiggling it up and down. The bundle was screaming.

As Dortchen came in on unsteady feet, Frau Claweson thrust the bundle at her. It was a tiny, blue scrap of a thing, all screaming mouth and scrunched up eyes. Dortchen sank onto a chair by the bed, holding the baby up against her shoulder. It nuzzled into her, quietening.

Gretchen turned a waxen face towards her. 'Why, Dortchen,' she said. 'Have you come? We need to go home to Father and Mother.'

Dortchen did not know what to say. She took her sister's hand. Gretchen closed her eyes. Her hand was limp, and she did not respond when Dortchen squeezed it.

'She's lost too much blood,' the doctor said. 'I'm very sorry.'

Dortchen did not understand.

In her arms, the little blue thing wailed again. Dortchen gave it a knuckle to suck. The little blue thing concentrated all its energy on devouring it. The feel of its mouth on her knuckle cracked the sheath of ice encasing Dortchen's heart. She felt it splinter with a sharp, physical pain.

Dortchen began to weep, and could not stop. She rocked the little girl in her arms, her tears dampening the soft tuft of flaxen hair upon the baby's tiny skull. The doctor shook his head and drew the sheet up to cover Gretchen's face.

'I'll look after her for you,' Dortchen told her dead sister. 'I'll make up for it all, I promise.'

GOLDEN LEAF

August 1819

Dortchen tried to forget her confession in the dark.

Surely Wilhelm would not believe her.

If he did, how repulsed he must be.

How horrified.

How disgusted.

Whenever she thought about it, shame wracked her. She tried to pretend it had never happened.

Dortchen was well practised at such self-deceptions.

And Berthe took up all her time. Berthe – it meant 'bright'. Such a big name for such a tiny scrap of a thing. Yet, like a lighthouse's searching ray, Berthe lit up the darkness.

Dortchen did not go back to the shop after Berthe's birth. There was too much to do. The baby screamed for milk that no one could provide. Dortchen sent a servant running to find a goat, and set another to make some pap from boiled water and a little rice flour so at least the baby had something to suck on. She had to wash and dress her dead sister, hang a cloth over her mirror, and take turns in sitting vigil beside her. Gretchen's children were all distraught with grief and shock, and Herr Schmerfeld was struggling with his own sorrow.

'You are too good to us,' the grieving Herr Schmerfeld said, as she helped him prepare for the funeral.

'Nonsense,' she answered, turning away.

After a few days, he ordered a bedroom to be made ready for Dortchen, with a door that led through to the nursery. It was clean and white and had no memories. Dortchen sat on the bed and looked about her. There was a dressing table with a large mirror, and an array of silver brushes and combs and silver-topped crystal jars.

A maid came in and curtsied. 'Would you like a bath, Fraülein? I've got water boiling ready for you.'

Dortchen nodded. She had barely had time to wash her face or brush her hair in days. She sat, watching, as two footmen carried in a hipbath and set it down by the fire, followed by two maids with jugs of hot water and fresh white towels. She sat in the bath till the water was cold.

That night, at supper, Herr Schmerfeld said to her, 'I do hope you like your room.'

'Yes, sir,' she answered.

'So you will stay a while? To help with Berthe?'

'Yes, sir. If you don't mind, sir.'

'Mind? I don't know what we'd do without you,' he answered, and indicated that the footman should serve her some more roast beef.

As Dortchen ate, relishing each mouthful, Herr Schmerfeld continued talking. 'No doubt you have some belongings you would like to bring from your brother's shop. My carriage is at your disposal, whenever you need it.'

'But, sir—'

'Nonsense,' he said. 'The sooner you get there, the sooner you can be home with us.'

Rudolf had not seen her since the funeral, and was full of anxious questions about the children and the baby. 'It's so hard to believe she's gone,' he kept saying. 'So you will stay, to help look after the baby?' he asked at last.

Dortchen nodded. 'I promised her.'

'I will miss your help in the garden and the stillroom,' Rudolf said.

'I'm sorry,' she said. 'It won't be forever. Just till Berthe is a little older.'

He nodded and tried to smile.

It was dark when she bade Rudolf goodbye. It was a great relief to have the carriage waiting for her, and not have to face the long walk back to the New Town.

She was troubled, though, by how tired Rudolf had looked. He was lonely, she thought. That evening, Dortchen was even quieter than usual at supper. Herr Schmerfeld noticed, and asked her if all was well. Dortchen found the courage to confess her worry to him.

'Well, that's no problem at all,' Herr Schmerfeld said. 'Rudolf must come here and take his supper with us. The children would love to see their uncle more often. And I know you have always loved your garden. Why don't you go there each day and spend an hour or two, and then bring Rudolf back with you in the carriage for supper?'

'But . . . Berthe—'

'She sleeps in the afternoon. She'll not miss you.'

'But what if she wakes?'

'Ida can look after her for an hour, or Frau Claweson. I don't want you getting sick. A break will do you good.'

Dortchen bit her lip. 'If you think it'll be all right . . .'

'Of course it'll be all right. You can bring us back some flowers, or fresh vegetables for our supper, and I'll think I'm getting a very good bargain for the use of my carriage.'

So Dortchen went each day, riding in the carriage like a fine lady, to walk in the garden and gather baskets of herbs and flowers, to watch the butterflies dance above the blossoms, and to work in the stillroom, making the teas and candied flowers and herbal tinctures that she so loved. Rudolf came back with her each evening for supper. He and Herr Schmerfeld would talk of business and politics and bank rates, while Dortchen quietly sewed little white dresses for the growing Berthe.

She found it strangely restful to allow Herr Schmerfeld to manage such things for her.

Days whirled by. Months.

Gradually, the little household settled down into a new routine. The children stopped waking in the night and crying out for their mother. The housekeeper began to consult Dortchen on the best dishes to tempt her master's appetite.

Berthe fascinated her aunt. The funny little expressions she pulled. The way she sucked her fists. The way she nestled into Dortchen's shoulder, sleepy and content, ready for bed.

In early December, Berthe surprised her by managing to roll over onto her stomach. The little girl screamed in terror. Laughing, Dortchen lifted her up and comforted her. 'I had best not lay you down on the bed any more,' she told her. 'Soon you'll be crawling.'

Dortchen discovered Herr Schmerfeld's library. She had never had much time for reading before. It was a wonderful luxury to curl up in a big chair by the fire, a book in her lap, and as many candles as she liked to light the page. There were so many books in the library that Dortchen hardly knew where to start.

She took down a volume of Herr von Goethe, remembering how she had struggled to read one of his books as a girl, stealing candle stubs and trying to decipher the tiny words by the frail light. Somehow, it was much easier to read now.

One night Herr Schmerfeld came into the library and found her there. Dortchen started up. 'I'm sorry, sir. I'll go.'

'No need to go,' he replied, smiling kindly. 'Unless you would prefer to read alone?'

She hesitated, not wanting to leave the warmth and comfort of the library, but not wanting to intrude either. He sat down, opened his book and began reading. After a while, he turned a page. She sat down too and picked up her own book. She did not read. She was too aware of the soft sound of his breathing, but gradually she relaxed and returned to her own book.

After that, they shared the quiet of the library many times, and Herr Schmerfeld began to pick out books that he thought she might enjoy. In this way, Dortchen discovered the English writers Jane Austen and Sir Walter Scott, and the Romantic poets, and Madame de Staël. She also read old legends and myths, and books of history. A whole new world was unfurling before her.

A few days before Christmas, Wilhelm came to visit. She had not seen him since the dreadful night of Gretchen's death. When his name was announced, she sat still and silent, with Berthe in her arms. Herr Schmerfeld looked up from his accounts. 'You do not have to see him, if you do not wish,' he said.

The thought of seeing Wilhelm made her anxious. He knew her darkest secret, the thing she had kept hidden from everyone. It would have been so easy to deny him, to tell Herr Schmerfeld to send him away. Then Dortchen could have pretended her secret was still locked away.

She looked down at Berthe's sleeping face, so trusting, so innocent, and sighed. 'No. I'll see him.' She laid Berthe down in her crib and went down the stairs to the front hall.

Wilhelm was still muffled in his coat and scarf. Snow lay white on his shoulders. Dortchen found it hard to look at him. She looked at his boots instead, snow melting into puddles on the tiles.

'I've brought you a gift,' he said. 'Dortchen—'

She made a swift gesture. *Stop! Don't speak!*

He showed her a leather-bound book. 'It's the new edition of the fairy tales. I've . . . rewritten the tales.'

She looked at him questioningly, twisting her hands together. His dark eyes were grave, intent on her face.

'I've thought very hard about what you said to me that day in the park, Dortchen. How the beauty of the tales could be obscured over time, like old silver blackened by tarnish. Perhaps it was not enough to simply gather the old tales, to stop them being forgotten. Perhaps it was also my job to restore them to their beauty and mystery and wonder. To do that, I had to find the essential truth of each story, the truth hidden under the tarnish of time.'

She nodded.

Wilhelm chose his next words carefully. 'The whole reason for telling the fairy tales is to awaken the heart. To help people *believe* that misfortune can be overcome and evil conquered. If the fairy tales are to do their work, they must shine.'

Her eyes were fixed on his face. Her breathing was painful.

'I've tried to make them shine,' he said. He passed her the book. It fell open to a page towards the end. A golden, heart-shaped leaf had been inserted to mark the story there. A linden leaf.

She lifted the leaf so she could see the title. 'All-Kinds-of-Fur,' she read. Her hand slammed the book shut.

'I rewrote it for you,' he said. 'In the tale you told me, it seems as if the king, her father, is the same as the king, her betrothed. It's as if she cannot escape him, no matter how she runs or hides. I don't think that's the truth of the tale. I think she escapes him and, by her own cleverness and bravery, is able to find love and happiness.'

Slowly, Dortchen clasped the book to her breast.

'I know you'll find it hard,' he said. 'But I hope you read it and see what I've done.'

Still she was unable to speak.

He examined her face closely, frowning and stern. 'I can't give you much. I haven't the money for jewels, or silks and satins, or for a fine horse and carriage in which to drive you around.' There was a faint trace of bitterness in his voice. 'There was only one thing I could do for you, and that was to make your story as beautiful and true and good as I could.'

Dortchen stepped forward and kissed him on the cheek.

'Thank you,' she said.

After Wilhelm had left, Dortchen went up to her room and sat on the edge of her bed, looking down at the book in her hands. After a long time, she opened it to the page marked by the golden linden leaf, and she read the story.

The changes Wilhelm had made were small, but profound. Much of the violence had been softened. Instead of a great many animals being caught and flayed to make the girl's coat of fur, only a small piece of their hide was taken. Instead of the girl being dragged behind the cart, she was put on it gently and taken to the king's castle. The reference to the king throwing boots at her head was taken out, as was the mention of her being naked under her coat of fur.

Hidden in the text was a small salute to Dortchen. He had described the princess as a 'Wild deer', capitalising the *W* in a subtle reference to her name. She smiled through her tears and read on.

Most importantly, the new version of the tale made it clear that the king in whose house the princess had taken shelter was not her father. The three gifts that she hid in his soup aroused only curiosity, not recognition. The story's ending was one of joy, not of submission and fear.

Dortchen laid the linden leaf back in the book and closed it, hugging it to her chest. Tears ran freely down her cheeks.

He had given her a great gift.

BLINDMAN'S BLUFF

January 1820

The new edition of the fairy tales became Dortchen's greatest treasure. She often drew it out at night, to read the stories again and to twirl the golden leaf between her fingers.

'All-Kinds-of-Fur' was not the only story changed. The murderous queen in 'Little Snow-White' was now her stepmother, not her mother, and Snow-White was woken when the servant helping to carry her glass coffin stumbled, instead of striking her across the face. Rapunzel no longer complained about her dress being too tight, and a spinning wheel had been introduced into 'Rumpelstiltskin', for the miller's daughter to spin the straw into gold. The miller's daughter also came up with a string of funny and ludicrous names, such as Beastrib and Muttoncalf, before guessing the dwarf's real name. In addition, Wilhelm had added Dortchen's rhyme about 'the wind so wild, the heavenly child' into 'Hänsel and Gretel', which pleased Dortchen a great deal.

The book was beautifully illustrated by Ludwig Grimm, and the scholarly notes had been left out. Dortchen thought it a great improvement.

Wilhelm came to visit her often. His excuse was that he was studying children's games, so he came to watch the Schmerfeld children and listen to their play. He and Dortchen would sit together in the garden, Berthe on her lap, while the older children played. The girls chanted rhymes as they skipped, while the boys built kites from sticks and paper and string.

'How are you, Dortchen?' he asked one day, as he came to sit beside her. The children were playing blind man's bluff on the lawn, their laughter filling the air.

'Busy as a mouse in childbirth,' she answered.

He laughed. 'I always wish I had quill and ink when I'm with you, Dortchen. The things you say. I always want to put them in a story.'

She smiled. 'I'm sorry. It comes from spending so much time with Old Marie. She was full of old country sayings and superstitions.'

'How is Old Marie?'

'She's living with Mia now, in Ziegenhain. I saw her when I was there last year.' Dortchen's face clouded. She had not wanted to see the old housekeeper, who knew too much. It had been an ordeal for Dortchen to subject herself to Old Marie's scrutiny, still trying to pretend that all was well.

'What else did Old Marie used to say?'

'When she tucked us up at night, she'd say, "Sweet dreams for sour pickles."' Dortchen paused for a moment, feeling sad, then went on. 'And when somebody was a bit odd, she'd say, "He's got a mill turning in his head." She used to say that about you and Jakob all the time.'

Wilhelm laughed ruefully. 'What about you? Did you think I had a mill turning in my head?'

'Of course,' she teased.

'Well, you need to tell Old Marie that this poor old mill-head has just been awarded an honorary doctorate from the University of Marburg.'

'Really? That's wonderful.' Her hands flew out towards him, then clasped each other and returned to her lap. 'Well, congratulations, Herr Doctor Grimm.'

'Thank you. I must admit, it's pleasing. We may not have made a lot of money with our fairy tale collection, but we've certainly earned ourselves a reputation of sorts. Jakob is quite delighted, for all that he pretends he doesn't care.'

'I'm glad,' she answered.

He rose and bowed to her. 'I must get back and write down those sayings of yours before I forget them. Goodbye, Dortchen.' He used the formal form of farewell, and she repeated it in her own goodbye.

Dortchen watched his tall, slim figure walk away from her with a strange tight feeling about her heart. She was the one who had told Wilhelm that it was too late for them, and that they must put away any hopes of being together. She was the one who had pushed him away when he tried to help her, and held him at arm's length when he tried to come closer.

Yet a part of her was still filled with longing. It was hard to see Wilhelm and not want to brush that errant lock of hair away from his eyes, or rest her head against his shoulder. Seeing him brought such a turmoil of desire, grief, hurt and yearning that Dortchen often thought it was easier not to see him at all.

She told herself that she did not want him, or anyone else, to touch her. Love hurt. Love harmed.

One day Herr Schmerfeld asked her, in his tactful way, 'I see Herr Grimm has been here again?'

'I hope you don't mind,' she said anxiously. 'We grew up next door to each other, you know. We are very old friends. He likes to talk to me about his work.'

'Is that all, do you think?' he asked after a moment.

She understood his meaning. 'Oh, yes,' she said firmly.

'I'm glad,' he answered.

This distressed and worried her. Dortchen was careful to keep a polite distance from Herr Schmerfeld after that, only talking to him about the children and commonplaces. She took books up to her room to read, rather than sitting by the fire in the library. Herr Schmerfeld understood her reticence and was polite in return, though once or twice she noticed him watching her with sadness in his eyes.

In May, on her twenty-seventh birthday, Herr Schmerfeld said to her, 'Dortchen, your time of mourning is long over and yet you are still wearing your blacks. I was thinking you might like to choose some of Gretchen's dresses as your own. It is time I gave away all her things, and I'd like you to have first choice.'

Dortchen shook her head emphatically. She could not live in her sister's house, caring for her sister's children, and wear her sister's clothes. It would not be seemly. Besides, all Gretchen's gowns were so indecorous.

'I cannot make you change your mind?'

Dortchen shook her head again.

Herr Schmerfeld sighed. 'Would you let me buy you some new clothes, then? I don't like to see you going about in that shabby old gown. It reflects badly on me. People will think I use you harshly.'

She was filled with dismay at that, and said that he might buy her some cheap material so she could make some new gowns.

'I would like to make you an allowance, too,' he said. 'So you can buy books, if you want, or new ribbons.'

She started to protest but he said firmly, 'No, Dortchen, this is something I must do if you are to stay under my roof. It is only right.'

Dortchen reluctantly agreed. She was surprised at how much pleasure she took in shopping for cloth, and looking through fashion plates with Ottilie and Sophie, deciding what dresses to make.

Another year passed quietly.

WRITTEN IN THE STARS

August 1820

The summer was damp and rainy, but one evening the sky cleared. Dortchen was sewing in the nursery, with Berthe playing at her feet, while the governess taught the older girls their letters.

A maid came for Dortchen. 'Herr Grimm is here to see you, Fräulein.'

Dortchen went downstairs, smoothing her dress with hands that trembled slightly.

Wilhelm was waiting for her in the hallway. 'It's a beautiful evening, and I've not left my desk in days. I wondered if you'd like to walk with me?'

She hesitated.

'I thought we could walk in the park,' he continued. 'All the lamps will be lit; it'll be pretty.'

Dortchen nodded and went to find her pelisse and bonnet. When she came back, she saw that Herr Schmerfeld was talking with Wilhelm in the hall. 'I'm just going for a walk,' she said. 'I hope you don't mind.'

He raised his brows. 'My dear Dortchen, you are free to do as you wish,' he answered, but Dortchen sensed he was not pleased.

Wilhelm and Dortchen walked in silence, her hand in the crook of his arm. Everything seemed washed clean, the sky a translucent green shell, the half-moon bright over the hills.

'You must be a great help to Herr Schmerfeld,' he said at last. 'It cannot be easy, being a widower with seven young children. All the servants in the world cannot replace a mother. A loving aunt can come close, though.'

'Perhaps,' she said. 'I certainly love the children as if they were my own. Especially little Berthe. She was given into my arms as Gretchen died. I . . .' She hesitated, then went on in a low voice. 'I could not help her. Gretchen, I mean. I ran from her. You know. You were there. I feel I must take extra care of her little one, to make it up to her.'

'You couldn't have saved her,' Wilhelm said gently.

'I know. But I can love her baby that much harder for her.'

'What about the father?' Wilhelm said after a moment.

'Herr Schmerfeld?'

'I think . . . I think he has a very high regard for you.'

She was silent.

'Some people think he should marry you,' Wilhelm said, not looking at her. 'It's not entirely regular, you living in his house and caring for his children, when he's an unmarried man.'

'What of the housekeeper and the maids?' Dortchen said, letting go of his arm. 'I am not without a chaperone.'

'Nonetheless.'

Her chest felt tight. She walked on and he followed. A tumult of emotion filled her. She tried to hold it down.

'I'm afraid he thinks sometimes of marrying me,' she confessed at last. 'But he has said nothing.'

'What would you say, if he did ask you?'

She shook her head dumbly.

He took hold of her shoulders and turned her to face him. 'What of me? Have you forgotten me?' He spoke in a light, teasing way but his gaze was intense.

'No,' she whispered, looking away.

He took a deep breath, nodded, then let her go.

They had come to the end of the park. She looked up at the starry sky. 'Look, I can see Cassiopeia.'

'It's shaped like a *W* – for "Wild",' he said.

'And "Wilhelm".'

'Both our names, written in the stars.'

He had made no attempt to step closer to her but still she drew away. There was a spark between them that made her uneasy. 'I had better go home,' she said.

As they turned back, Wilhelm tucked her hand in the crook of his arm again. 'Your fingers are chilled through.'

'Herr Schmerfeld calls me "Frog" because I'm as cold,' she told him.

For some reason, that made him cheerful. 'Poor man,' he said.

Dortchen sneaked a look at him and caught his gaze. She blushed and looked away. Unexpectedly, he covered his eyes with his hand and pretended to be blind. 'I cannot see a thing. I do hope you're not leading me astray.'

She could not help but laugh. She had to take his hand to stop him from blundering about. His grip was strong and sure.

'You had better open your eyes now – we're almost home.'

His step slowed. He pretended to grope about and found her shoulder and her arm. 'Don't let me fall.'

'Please, open your eyes,' she begged. 'People will see.'

'What does it matter, if I can't see them?'

'Here's Herr Schmerfeld's house. You have to open your eyes now because I'm going in and you'll have to find your own way home.'

He did not open his eyes. His hand slid down her arm, then lightly traced the curve of her waist. He leant close to her, breathing in the scent of her skin and her hair. 'I don't want to open my eyes,' he whispered. 'They say the other senses are heightened when you're blind.'

Dortchen stood very still. A curious sensation had taken hold of her. On the one hand, she did not like his closeness. It made her feel vulnerable and afraid. On the other hand, his touch was so gentle, and his playfulness had delighted her. It was the first time that anyone had come so close to her in a long time.

His eyes still shut, he pressed his body to hers, bending his head so that

444

his mouth was only inches from hers. If she had lifted her face, they would be kissing. She dared not. Nothing had changed.

'I've rung the bell now,' she said, suiting her actions to her words. 'You can't stay any longer.'

He let her go, opening his eyes. 'Dortchen,' he said, softly, pleadingly.

'I have to go,' she said, and was glad when the door to the house opened and she could whisk inside.

In November 1820, Wilhelm was offered a job as tutor to the young prince, the Kurfürst's eldest grandson. He gave his first lesson on a raw, wild day, and came, windblown, to have tea with Dortchen afterwards.

'Tell me about the prince.' Dortchen sat opposite him.

'He had all kinds of books, still all beautifully wrapped, and not one of them opened. The whole time I taught him he did nothing but play with his hair. One of the courtiers tells me he reads nothing but the genealogical tables. I'm not sure I can teach him much.'

Wilhelm looked unusually elegant that day, with a new cutaway coat of midnight blue over long, narrow trousers of a soft biscuit hue and a blue satin waistcoat. His white cravat was tied in a soft bow.

'But what an honour. You must be pleased to be so marked with the Kurfürst's notice.'

'I'm not so sure. The Kurfürst is old and ill now, and he doesn't get on with his son, who has a mistress, you know, and a whole brood of illegitimate children. I think being in favour with the princess means being out of favour with the prince. And he will be Kurfürst when his father dies.'

'Will it be a problem for you?' Dortchen asked, clasping her hands together.

'I hope not. But what could I do? I'm glad of the extra money, though I wish it were more.' He paused for a moment, as if about to add something, then stood up. 'Why don't we take a walk? I'm sure you've been cooped up all day with the children. Some fresh air would do you some good.'

'Very well,' Dortchen said, a warm glow filling her.

It was still rough and wild outside. The wind buffeted Dortchen and made her skirts swing. She had to hold on to her bonnet with one hand. Wilhelm strode along quickly, his hand drawing Dortchen in close to his side to protect her from the wind. A carriage clopped past, sending up a spray of icy water, but Wilhelm swung Dortchen round so she was not splashed. She felt breathless and giddy.

They came to the end of the street and crossed the road so that they could stand on the clifftop, looking out over Aue Island. It lay below them, the golden dome of the orangery the only colour in a world of grey clouds and black trees. Rooks soared high, riding the winds, calling to each other in mournful voices. The wind was so cold that Dortchen felt her toes and fingers go numb. It was as if they were alone at the top of the world.

'Although I am not sure that I can teach the prince much,' Wilhelm said, 'I'm glad to be earning some more money. We are much more comfortable now, with both Jakob and I working at the library, and Ludwig beginning to earn some money with his art.'

'You're looking very fine in your new clothes, Herr Doctor,' she teased.

He coloured. 'I could not go to the palace to teach the prince in a coat with frayed sleeves, and shoes with holes in them.'

'No, of course not.'

'The new edition of the book brought in four hundred thalers, and it looks as if it might be selling well enough that another edition will be needed soon.'

'That's wonderful!'

He grinned at her. 'I cannot deny that it makes me happy. It's been eight years since we first published it, and at last we seem to be reaping some rewards for all that hard work.'

'I'm glad,' she said, pressing his arm.

'I wonder . . . I mean, what I want to know . . .' He turned to face her, taking both her gloved hands.

She felt a sudden squeezing of her chest.

'Dortchen, things have changed these past few years. I'm earning an income now, and I'm not dependent on Jakob to support me as well as the rest of the family. The war is over. Your father can no longer forbid us from marrying. Dortchen, I—'

She began speaking rapidly. 'Wilhelm, Berthe is still just a little baby. I promised Gretchen on her deathbed that I would look after her. I cannot leave her, not yet. It wouldn't be right. And it's not just Berthe, it's the other children too. It's a terrible thing to lose your mother, you know that. What would you have done without your Aunt Zimmer? The children need me. I can't let them be brought up by housemaids and governesses—'

'I understand, Dortchen, really, I do. It's your loving heart and your wish to always do good that I love most about you. And I understand . . . I know you've been hurt. I know you find it hard to trust now.'

Dortchen pulled her hands away and turned, hunching her shoulder. She could not believe he would speak of it.

He grasped her shoulders and pulled her back to face him. 'Dortchen, I need to know if there's any hope for me. Please.'

She gazed up into his thin face, his dark eyes intent on hers, the wind playing havoc with his curls. Her heart gave a treacherous lurch. She reached up and cupped his cheek.

'Wilhelm, so much has changed. I . . . I'm afraid . . . I'm afraid of so many things. That I'll hurt you. That you'll hurt me.' He started to speak but she laid a finger on his lips. 'I need to try to make amends somehow. I need . . .' Her voice changed, growing stronger. 'I need to atone for my sins.'

'What sins?' he burst out. 'Whatever happened, it was not your fault.'

She stepped away from him, hugging her arms about her. She was shaking. 'I have to try to do what's right. They're only little children. They've lost their mother . . . they'll never know a mother's love . . . Can't you see? Don't you understand?'

He turned away from her, not speaking.

'I just need time,' she said desperately. 'Please.'

In one quick movement, Wilhelm was beside her, spinning her to face him. His mouth came down on hers. He bent her over his arm, his lips hard and demanding, his hand gripping the back of her neck. Dortchen clung to him, her senses reeling, her traitorous body flaring with heat.

At last, he drew his mouth away. 'How much time?'

She could not answer. She could not breathe.

'Dortchen, how much time?'

When she did not answer, he kissed her again, roughly. When at last he let her go, she swayed and he had to steady her with both hands. She laid her head on his chest, listening to the rapid beat of his heart. He raised her face and kissed her again, so gently that it brought tears to her eyes.

'Dortchen, when?'

'I don't know,' she whispered. 'I want . . . Oh, Wilhelm, I do want you.'

'Please don't make me wait too long,' he said.

She bit her lip. They walked back towards Herr Schmerfeld's house in silence. As they turned into the street, lined with old plane trees, she took his hand and pressed it to her lips. 'I'm so sorry,' she whispered.

His eyes softened. He squeezed her hand. Slowly, she drew her hand out of his and walked up the steps and into the house.

A HIGH REGARD

February 1821

As time passed, the nightmares and flashes of panic that had plagued Dortchen began to come more rarely. She took joy in small things. A robin singing in the bare thorn tree. Berthe's first babble of words. Jakob writing her name in the family Bible as if she truly were one of the Grimms.

In February 1821, Wilhelm turned thirty-five. Dortchen made a damson plum cake and took it to the Grimms' small apartment, which was crowded and merry with family and friends.

'I made it for you with my own hands,' she told him.

'It smells delicious,' Wilhelm said, taking the cake from her. 'What's in it that smells so good?'

'Cinnamon and nutmeg and damson plum jam,' Dortchen told him. 'Isn't it wonderful to be able to get ingredients again?'

'I haven't eaten cinnamon in an age. Thank you, Dortchen.' He drew her close to kiss her on the cheek.

The cake was a great success, and after supper everyone sang songs and told silly riddles. Then Wilhelm opened up a great pile of presents. 'Look, Dortchen, Karl has brought me a whole pile of new cravats,' Wilhelm cried, showing her the package. 'And Lotte embroidered me some handkerchiefs.'

'A true sign of love,' Dortchen said. 'I know how much she hates embroidering.'

'And Ws are hard,' Lotte complained. 'Why couldn't his name begin with a nice easy I, or an L?'

The Hassenpflugs had brought him a book of poems, and the Ramus sisters a beautiful set of quills, enough to last him several months. Wilhelm thanked them, then drew a small package towards him. It was covered in stamps and addressed in a bold, flamboyant hand.

'Something else from Fraülein von Schwertzell?' Lotte asked, perched on the arm of Wilhelm's chair.

He nodded as he opened the package. Inside was a small grey stone, scribbled all over with strange markings. Wilhelm examined it closely, then glanced at the letter. 'It's another of the runic stones her family found on their estate. She tells me I must come again and examine them more closely. She cannot hold off other scholars any longer. Jakob, did I tell you that Professor Rommel has already been? He is convinced they are magical symbols, inscribed by a pagan priest, but I am not so sure.'

Jakob came to examine the stone, and soon he and Wilhelm were deep in an arcane and incomprehensible conversation. Dortchen pulled Lotte to sit beside her on the couch.

'Who's this Fraülein von Schwertzell?' she asked, trying to sound casual.

'She's the sister of an old university friend of Wilhelm's,' Lotte said in an undertone. 'They're a grand noble family that live in a big old castle on their estate at Willingshausen, two days' ride from here. She writes to Wilhelm all the time, sending him stories or legends, or these strange stones. Ludwig and I think she has a *tendré* for him.'

'What is the stone?' Dortchen asked. 'Is it really magic?'

'The family found these ancient mounds on their land, with burial urns and such things, and these stones with strange inscriptions on them. She sent one to Wilhelm and asked him to come and visit, to help them dig for buried treasure. He stayed there some weeks and was very intrigued by it all. It inspired him to write a book on the history of runes, partly to set that Professor Rommel straight. Wilhelm thinks they are just random markings on the stones, and not an alphabet at all.'

'Is she . . . is she pretty?' Dortchen whispered.

Lotte gave her a hug. 'Nowhere near as pretty as you.'

The Hassenpflugs would not let Jakob and Wilhelm talk about runic alphabets all afternoon. Jeannette sat down at the fortepiano and tinkled a tune, and Marie grabbed Wilhelm's hands and made him dance with her. Lotte danced with Louis, and the Ramus sisters danced with Jakob and Ludwig. The room was so small that everyone kept bumping into each other, but there was much laughter and teasing.

Dortchen sat on the couch, her feet tucked up underneath her to give everyone else more room. There were not enough men for all the girls to dance. As soon as another song started, however, Wilhelm came and took her hand. He lifted Dortchen to her feet, and she let him put his hand on her waist and turn her about the room, his shoulder strong and square under her fingers.

Afterwards, she could scarcely breathe and would not dance again. 'I'm tired,' she told Jakob. 'I've been up half the night with Friedrich, who's been sick.' She lay on the couch and drew her coat over her, watching the twirling couples till her vision was obscured by tears. She shut her eyes and pretended to sleep.

Sometime later, when everyone was out in the hall saying their goodbyes, she felt a warm, strong hand slip up the sleeve of her coat and find her hand, which was crossed upon her breast. She smiled without opening her eyes, and murmured Wilhelm's name.

'How did you know it was me?' he whispered.

'I would know your hand even when there were ten thousand hands,' she whispered back. He bent and kissed her.

The next morning, Lotte came to tell Dortchen that the Kurfürst had died in the night. Dortchen had to dig out her blacks again, and put black armbands on the sleeves of all the boys. The funeral procession was a sombre affair, with twelve horses in hooded black caparisons with black plumes on their heads pulling along the funeral hearse with the Kurfürst's coat of arms on the door.

His son, Wilhelm II, promptly moved into the palace with his mistress and her brood of illegitimate children. His wife, Princess Augusta, set up a rival court at Schöenfeld Castle, encouraging artists, musicians and writers to visit her there. Jakob, Wilhelm, Ludwig and Lotte were all frequent guests, as were Louis Hassenpflug and his sisters. Dortchen even went once or twice, with Herr Schmerfeld, and was amazed and impressed by the ease and grace with which Wilhelm moved in such grand circles.

Napoléon died in May. Dortchen could not help feeling a pang of grief. He had been like a comet, beautiful in his dreadfulness. He had changed the world – for the better, many would argue. Certainly people everywhere were jostling for the rights he had once granted them with such a high hand.

A few weeks later it was Dortchen's twenty-eighth birthday. Wilhelm gave her a belt buckle of amethysts that must have cost him a month's wages. Dortchen wore it everywhere.

Spring turned into summer. Wilhelm spent a lot of time visiting his friend Fritz von Schwertzell at Willingshausen, working on the book of runes, which he hoped would be published later that year. Dortchen went to help Hanne after the birth of her fifth child, and stayed for three weeks. In October Rudolf married his childhood sweetheart, Sandrine Landré, in the garden. Dortchen made herself a new red striped dress. It was wonderful to be out of mourning again.

Then, in November, Herr Schmerfeld asked Dortchen to marry him.

'You know I have a very high regard for you,' he said, standing before the fire in the library. Dortchen was sitting in a chair, a novel in her hands. 'The children all love you. I cannot think of anyone who I would rather have presiding over my family and my home.'

When she did not answer, he said, with a faint colour in his carefully shaved cheeks, 'It would be most suitable.'

Dortchen could only shake her head. 'I'm sorry,' she said.

'It's been a surprise. You need time to think it over.'

She got to her feet, dropping the novel, and went out of the room in a rush. In the sanctuary of her bedroom, she sat on her bed and pressed her hands over her eyes. He was a kind man. She loved his children. She had found peace in his beautiful house. If she married him, she would have everything a young woman could want. Money. Status. Comfort. Affection. It would indeed be most suitable.

Dortchen opened her copy of the fairy tales and took out the faded linden leaf. She twirled it in her fingers. She got up and paced the room. Again and again she picked up the linden leaf and put it down again. At last, at dusk, she put on her bonnet and coat and gloves and walked around to the Grimms' apartment. It was cold and windy, reminding her of the night she and Wilhelm had walked to the lookout, when he had asked her not to make him wait too long. It had already been a year.

The thought of marrying Wilhelm filled Dortchen with dread. He would want to touch her. He would want to probe her mouth with his tongue. He would want to thrust his . . . his thing between her legs. Horror shook her.

Yet she loved him. She wanted him to love her. She daydreamed of a little house with a garden. She would cook for him, and darn his stockings, and he would read his stories to her. She sometimes imagined having a baby of her own. It always had Wilhelm's curls and grave, dark eyes. Now and again, at night, she imagined Wilhelm kissing her, his hand stroking the curve of her waist, cupping her breast, sliding down between her legs. A little bud of warmth would open inside her. At those times she would think, *Yes, I'll marry him.*

Then she would wake from a nightmare, a dark shape lurching over her, holding her down. No matter how she struggled, she could not save herself. She woke in such a sweat of terror and revulsion that she comforted herself by saying, 'You're safe. No one will ever touch you again.'

Dortchen reached the Grimms' apartment and knocked. Her hand felt so weak that she could scarcely make a sound. Jakob opened the door for her. He was surprised to see her. 'Is something wrong?'

'No. I'm fine.' She tried to smile.

'Wilhelm will be glad to see you. Come in.'

Jakob led her into the study, where Wilhelm was working away with his quill, a great pile of books and manuscripts around him. Dortchen noticed a line of small pebbles laid out before him, each covered in indecipherable squiggles. He rose at the sight of her, opening and shutting his ink-stained fingers and arching his back. 'Dortchen, what a lovely surprise. Would you like to stay for supper? Lotte's out with the Hassenpflugs but she'll be home soon.'

'No. Tea's fine. I need to get back.' She went with him into the kitchen, where he busied himself putting the kettle on the stove.

He gazed at her keenly. 'What's wrong? You look troubled.'

She sat at the table and laid her head on her arms. 'It's nothing. I'll tell you when the trees are blooming.'

He did not press her, making her tea and telling her about the book on runes that he was writing, and how he was correcting proofs for the third edition of the fairy tale book. 'I'm mainly working on the notes now,' he told her. 'I'm examining the key motifs, trying to trace where they came from, and looking at different versions of the same story.'

Dortchen listened quietly. He asked her again to stay for supper, but she stood and said, 'I must get back. Supper is a handful with so many children.'

'I'll walk you home,' he answered, and got his coat.

They walked in silence, her hand in the crook of his arm. He let her be, then, when they reached the end of her road, drew her under the shelter of a tree. 'Dortchen, what is it?'

'Herr Schmerfeld wants to marry me,' she whispered.

He stiffened. 'He said so?'

She nodded.

'What did you say?'

'I said no.'

He was silent for a moment. 'I don't think you should stay there, Dortchen. It's not . . . seemly.'

Her throat closed over. This was what she had been afraid of.

'Berthe is still only a baby,' she whispered. 'Barely two years old. She won't let anyone else button her shoes for her, or put her to bed. She will only drink her milk if I make it for her. I can't leave her, Wilhelm.'

'But you cannot stay with her forever,' he answered. 'You must leave her sometime. We only live a few streets away. You could see her every day.'

'It wouldn't be the same.'

'No, I guess not. After all, I see you nearly every day and that's not enough for me.'

'Don't be angry.'

'Has he tried to touch you?' he demanded. 'Did he kiss you?'

Dortchen shook her head.

'He doesn't love you,' Wilhelm said. 'He couldn't love you and not want to kiss you.'

'He's a good man.'

'I don't like it,' Wilhelm said. 'I don't want you staying there any more, Dortchen. He'll try to woo you. He'll wear you down with quiet persistence. He's that kind of man. They say he's ruthless in business, that he always gets what he wants. Dortchen, don't go back. Come home with me. I know the apartment's very small, but we can make room for you. You don't take up much more room than a mouse.'

She could not smile at the old joke. He tried to kiss her but she turned her face away. 'I'm sorry. I can't. Not now.'

He straightened his back. 'I see. Very well.'

In silence he walked her down the dark, windy street, a yard of space between them.

DOG IN A MANGER

December 1821

Late that year, the Grimms were given notice to leave their apartment at Wilhelmshöhe Gate.

The prince no longer needed a tutor, and the Grimms were struggling to manage on their lowly earnings. They moved to a small, dark, noisy apartment above a blacksmith's shop in the Old Town. It was almost an hour's walk away from Herr Schmerfeld's house, and somehow Wilhelm rarely found the time to walk the distance.

Dortchen could call the carriage any time she wanted, and, hearing Wilhelm was sick again, she did drop around with some soup when she could. Seven young children were enough to keep her busy, though, particularly Berthe, who seemed determined to explore the whole world.

Berthe had begun to talk in pretty, broken sentences. 'What's that?' was her favourite phrase. She wanted to do everything herself, then would throw herself on the ground in a storm of tears when she couldn't. Dortchen would pick the little girl up and rock her on her lap, till at last she quietened and put her thumb in her mouth. Then she would show Berthe how to button her own boot, or tie her own sash, and watch lovingly as the little girl struggled to master the task.

Winter wheeled into spring, and then spring into summer, with each week bringing a fresh delight as Berthe discovered something new.

Lotte and Louis Hassenpflug announced their engagement and were married in July 1822. Dortchen made Lotte her myrtle wreath, and wept through the whole ceremony. Herr Schmerfeld gave her his handkerchief, which was soon quite sodden and crumpled. Wilhelm could never bear to see anyone cry. He came to Dortchen and put his arm about her for the first time in months.

She could not help stiffening under his touch. His arm fell away. He turned and walked off, and did not look back.

That night, Dortchen wept so much that her pillow was damp. It seemed the world was moving along without her. She was like a girl turned to stone, unable to break the spell upon her.

The rest of the year was swallowed up by scarlet fever. Sophie, the second-eldest Schmerfeld daughter, caught the disease in late July, and Dortchen fought for weeks to save her life. Each day was a nightmare of pain and fever for the little girl, and Dortchen nursed her alone, sick with terror that the other children might catch it too. At last Sophie recovered, but Dortchen was so thin and worn out that she fell sick too, and it was spring before she began to recover her strength.

The year of 1823 passed in much the same pattern. Friedrich was breeched on his sixth birthday, and Dortchen cried to see the little boy out of his skirts. He was very proud of himself, though, and swaggered about in his new breeches in such a comical manner that Dortchen had to laugh. Ottilie, the eldest daughter, turned thirteen, and Dortchen began to teach her how to cook and what herbs to use for healing. Berthe was three and a half, and full of mischief and laughter. She still would not let anyone but Dortchen warm her milk for her.

Wilhelm was often away. He had been angry and disappointed when the new Kurfürst had appointed his old rival, Professor Rommel, to the position of court archivist, for which Wilhelm had also applied. To make matters worse, the Kurfürst had ennobled the professor, who then insisted on everyone addressing him as 'von Rommel'. Wilhelm decided to pursue his research into runes in even greater depth, to prove Rommel wrong, and so he spent many long weeks at the Willingshausen estate. He was also working on a book of German heroic tales; as he told Dortchen, the von Schwertzell family had an old library filled with books that were invaluable to him.

Dortchen suffered agonies of jealousy in silence.

In the summer of 1824, the von Schwertzell family decided to visit Cassel for a few weeks.

'I don't know where they can possibly stay,' Lotte declared, lying on a chaise longue in her white-and-gold drawing room, a saucer and cup resting comfortably on her burgeoning stomach. 'I would have them here – Louis says they are very well connected – but I'm not fit to be seen in public.'

'You look perfectly gorgeous,' Dortchen said, smiling at her friend. Pregnancy suited Lotte. Her sallow cheeks had filled out, and her dark curly hair was more lustrous than ever. She wore a lovely gown of dark red with a low-cut bodice and full sleeves, with a spangled shawl draped about her shoulders.

Lotte smiled at her. 'Thank you. I must admit, I'm enjoying being pregnant much more than I'd imagined I would. Louis is in transports of delight. He is sure it's going to be a boy. I do think it's bad timing for the von Schwertzells to want to come right now, when I cannot hold a ball for them or even show them around the palace.'

Dortchen gave a peal of laughter.

'What is it?' Lotte asked in surprise.

'You just sound so grown-up, talking of giving balls.'

'Well, I am grown-up now, Dortchen, and so are you. Isn't it time you were thinking of settling down too?'

An uncomfortable silence stretched out.

'I know you love your nieces and nephews, but you shouldn't be wasting your life looking after them,' Lotte said. 'The eldest girl is fourteen now – that's old enough to help with the care of the young ones. The baby's learning her letters and numbers and will soon be going to school. Dortchen, you're thirty-one years old. It's long past the time when you should have been married and be thinking of a family of your own.'

Dortchen plaited together the fringe of her shawl.

'Wilhelm won't wait for you forever, you know,' Lotte said.

Dortchen stood up. 'He lives with two of his brothers, in a few tiny rooms above a blacksmith's shop. There's no room there for me, and Wilhelm will never move away from Jakob. You accuse me of always putting my family ahead of Wilhelm, but hasn't Wilhelm always put his family ahead of me?'

Lotte blushed. There was enough truth in Dortchen's words to sting. She began to speak angrily, but Dortchen was pulling on her bonnet and gloves. 'I'm doing my best, Lotte, I really am. But my best is never enough for anyone.'

Dashing tears away, she ran out of the room, leaving Lotte staring in dismay after her.

Wilhelmine von Schwertzell was not pretty. That was a small comfort to Dortchen.

She was, however, extremely fashionable in a way that spoke of easy money and trips to Paris. A tall, lean woman, she was dressed in a pink dress with a narrow waist and full skirt, embroidered most lavishly with black velvet ribbon. Her sleeves were puffed from shoulder to elbow, and then were skintight to her wrist, with a dozen tiny black velvet buttons. The same buttons ran down her back. Wilhelmine could not have got dressed without the help of a maid.

On her head was the largest hat Dortchen had ever seen, decorated with enormous pink bows. It made Dortchen's simple poke bonnet look countrified. Fraülein von Schwertzell also carried a pink silk parasol, with an ebony handle and black velvet ribbons. It struck envy into the heart of every woman in the Schlosspark.

She noticed Dortchen was watching her, and smiled. 'How do you do, Frau Schmerfeld?' As she spoke, she cast a sharp glance over Dortchen's gown; it was obvious that it was home-made.

'I am well, thank you,' Dortchen replied quietly. 'But I'm afraid you are mistaken. I am not Herr Schmerfeld's wife. I am his sister-in-law.'

Fraülein von Schwertzell raised both perfectly plucked eyebrows. 'Indeed? I am so sorry. Is not that little girl yours?'

Dortchen looked down at Berthe, who was hopping along beside her, clinging to her hand. The whole family had come to the royal park to join the Grimms and the Hassenpflugs in showing the von Schwertzells the famous palace and its gardens. Herr Schmerfeld walked ahead, with Jakob and Wilhelm, while the rest of his children ran on, shouting with excitement as they explored the narrow paths through the shrubbery. Above them, Wilhelmshöhe Palace stood on its hill, a fluttering flag showing that the Kurfürst was in residence.

'No, I am not married,' she replied. 'She is my niece. My sister died giving birth to her, and I have cared for her ever since.'

'So you live with Herr Schmerfeld?' Fraülein von Schwertzell found this deliciously shocking.

'Yes, I do.' Dortchen wanted to defend herself against any salacious implication but could not find the words. 'I care for the children.'

'I see.'

'They were all so young when my sister died,' Dortchen explained.

Fraülein von Schwertzell looked bored. She twirled her parasol.

'Are you enjoying your stay in Cassel?' Dortchen asked.

'Oh, yes, indeed. I had heard that Wilhelmshöhe Palace was the Versailles of Germany. That, of course, is a gross exaggeration, but it is a pleasant little place and the park is quite pretty, though it's rather wild, with all those woods so close about. I am used to more formal gardens, I suppose.'

'The garden behind the palace is laid out in a formal pattern,' Dortchen said. 'And the water cascades are wonderful.'

'Ah, yes, they run down from the famous Herkules statue, don't they? Wilhelm!' she called. He turned and came to her side. 'Wilhelm, will you take me to view Herkules? I have heard it is the absolute epitome of masculine beauty, magnified a thousand times. Now, that is something I must take a very close look at.'

As she spoke, Fraülein von Schwertzell laid a hand on Wilhelm's arm and fluttered her lashes at him in a most exaggerated manner.

Wilhelm laughed. 'I'm afraid you can't get too close, Wilhelmine. Look, that is him up there, at the very top of the mountain.' He pointed.

The path had led them out onto the flat lawn behind the palace. Beyond the formal gardens lay a small lake with a tiny temple on its shores. Far above them, on the peak of the hill, stood the Octagon, a large stone structure that looked rather like a palace itself. A narrow pyramid soared from its centre, with the statue of Herkules perched at its tip. Artificial water cascades fell in steps from the base of the Octagon all the way down the steep slope to the lake. It was a most dramatic sight.

'Good heavens,' Fraülein von Schwertzell said, clutching at Wilhelm's arm. 'How extraordinary.'

'The statue is a copy of Benvenuto Cellini's famous sculpture,' he told her. 'You can climb up there, of course, but it is a long way and very steep, and even when you get there you cannot see him easily, since the Octagon and the pyramid are both so high.'

'Could we not drive up there? That is why carriages were invented.'

'Of course, if one is lucky enough to have a carriage.'

'Then we shall do so. Tomorrow, perhaps. Tell me, Wilhelm, is it true that he is quite naked?'

'Oh, yes,' Wilhelm answered.

'Then I shall bring my opera glasses.'

Wilhelm laughed again.

Dortchen listened in silence. She did not at all like the way Fraülein von Schwertzell called Wilhelm by his first name in such a familiar way, or how she clutched at his arm. She did not like the way she made Wilhelm laugh. Dortchen could not remember the last time she had heard Wilhelm laugh like that.

'Perhaps we could have a picnic up there,' Fraülein von Schwertzell went on. 'I will tell the cook to pack us some champagne.'

'I finish in the library at one, but am quite free after that,' he said.

'Then I shall pick you up in my carriage,' Fraülein von Schwertzell said. 'And then you must accompany me to the concert at the palace in the evening. They are playing Gluck, I believe. I last heard *Iphigénie* in

Paris. I'm interested to see how your local musicians measure up.'

'I believe they are very fine,' Wilhelm replied. 'Though the Kurfürst is not much interested in music.'

'I've heard the only thing he's interested in is his mistress,' Fraülein von Schwertzell said. 'Is it true she's the daughter of a blacksmith?'

'Her father was a goldsmith,' Dortchen said. 'A very respectable profession.'

Fraülein von Schwertzell ignored her. She leant in close to Wilhelm. 'Will we see her at the palace? I believe she's quite the beauty, in a vulgar sort of way.'

Wilhelm hesitated. Like many Hessians, he had been shocked by the way the Kurfürst had separated from his wife, Princess Augusta, so that he could live openly with his mistress and her children. Wilhelm and his brothers had shown their displeasure by attending Princess Augusta's salons, avoiding social events held by the Kurfürst. He, in return, had not increased the brothers' salaries or promoted them, despite their growing reputations as scholars.

'I believe the countess is in retirement at present,' Wilhelm said.

Fraülein von Schwertzell screeched with laughter. 'Oh, is she in an *interesting condition* again? She breeds like a rabbit! How many is it now?'

Wilhelm did not answer. Dortchen knew he disliked such talk, and she was pleased that Fraülein von Schwertzell did not seem to understand that. *She will offend him*, Dortchen thought, *and he will not be comfortable in her company. There's no need to fear.*

Fraülein von Schwertzell, however, had gone on in her bold, forthright way, saying, 'Well, I'm sorry I won't have a chance to see her, but there is plenty else to do in Cassel, I'm sure. I'm thinking of organising a party to sail down the river. I'd have musicians to play for us. I know how you love music, Wilhelm.'

'I do, indeed,' he agreed. 'But you'll never convince Jakob to join us. He doesn't like either boats or music.'

'Ah, never mind. I'm sure your younger brother will join us, and my brother and sister too. You will need to help me gather together a party.'

'I'm sure Dortchen would like to come. She loves music too.' He turned to her, trying to draw her into the conversation.

'How nice.' Fraülein von Schwertzell showed her teeth in a smile. 'Then, of course, we'd be happy if you would join us, Fraülein.'

Dortchen murmured something and made her escape. She felt unhappier than she had in a long time. She could not understand herself. If it hurt so much to see Wilhelm talking and laughing with another woman, why had she not married him when she had the chance? She was like the dog in the fable by Aesop who lay in the manger, not eating the hay himself but stopping the horse from doing so.

She called to Ottilie and gave Berthe into her care. The two sisters went off happily to look at the little temple near the lake, and Dortchen went alone into the shade of the shrubbery. Her head ached abominably and her eyes were hot. She was afraid she might weep. Down the path she walked, to the lake at the base of the palace, watching the swans as they glided past.

The scent of linden blossoms hung heavy on the air. Dortchen made a sharp, jerking movement, as if to walk away. But she hesitated, then turned and went down the long, winding path, past the tangle of briar roses and into the secret grove of linden trees. She picked a blossom and held it to her nose, inhaling deeply. Then she sat on the grass, the blossom cupped in her hand, leant her head back against the tree and closed her eyes. All she could hear was the soft sough of the wind in the leaves, and the humming of innumerable bees as they gathered the nectar from the creamy-white flowers.

It had been twelve years since she and Wilhelm had lain together on this grass under the linden trees. Twelve years. She was an old maid, the thing all girls dreaded most. What was wrong with her, that she could not take happiness when it was offered? Was she misshapen somehow, in her soul? Had she been broken and healed all awry, like a bone that had not been properly set? She had loved Wilhelm with all her heart, yet she had pushed him away.

Tears dampened her eyes.

A lark began to sing in the tree above her. Dortchen opened her eyes and looked up. It was such a small, plain, grey thing, yet its song was so full of joy. She could see its breast swell, its thin throat tremble. It lifted its wings, as if seeking to draw more air into its lungs. Song-notes were flung into the air, like golden coins thrown by a generous hand. All the lark's strength was poured into its music, all its joy.

Dortchen took a deep breath, so deep that she felt her lungs expand and the muscles of her chest crack. She wanted to live like the lark did, filled with rapture. She stood up, looking up at the bird through the sunlit leaves. It flung its wings wide and soared away into the sky. She wanted to fly with it.

When Dortchen came out of the linden grove, the blossom still in her hand, it was in her mind to find Wilhelm, to try to tell him what was in her heart. But he was nowhere to be found; nor was Fraülein von Schwertzell.

She sat with the others on the hillside, looking down over the palace, trying not to reveal how eagerly she was awaiting his return. A quarter of an hour passed excruciatingly slowly. The children played among the trees, then went down to the lake to race little boats they had made of leaves and sticks. Dortchen crushed the flower in her hand and thrust it into her pocket.

'Fraülein von Schwertzell has clearly set her cap at Wilhelm,' Marie Hassenpflug said to Lotte. 'By the looks of it, she's caught him.'

'She obviously has a *tendré* for him,' Jeannette agreed. 'But he's as poor as a church mouse. I'm surprised her family will countenance the match.'

'Her younger sister married a one-armed artist,' Lotte said. 'He lost his right arm at the Battle of Leipzig, taught himself to draw with his left hand, then quit the army to make his way as a painter. Wilhelm at least has both hands.'

Jeannette shook her head in amazement at the von Schwertzells' eccentric ways. 'He'd be a fool not to marry her. She's rich and well connected.'

'And they have a very fine library,' Lotte added with a giggle. 'Wilhelm would care more about that than how much money the family has. You know he's not at all worldly.'

Dortchen could bear it no longer. She rose and said, 'I must call those children away from the lake. Berthe will fall in if she's not careful.'

She was conscious of the eyes of all the young women on her back as she walked away. She heard Jeannette say, 'Do you think she's upset? I always thought she had a *tendré* for Wilhelm herself.'

'She and Wilhelm are just old friends,' Lotte lied, and Dortchen quickened her step.

As she passed the men, sitting on the grass together and talking about politics, Jakob rose and came to walk by her side. She tried to smile and greet him with her usual warmth, but failed.

'I'm afraid Wilhelm means to marry that woman,' he said. 'I will be very sorry if he does.'

Dortchen could not speak. She stared at the lake, trying to will the tears back into her eyes.

'He will move away and live with her in Willingshausen. She does not understand the importance of his work. She will expect him to dance attendance on her, and go to picnics and parties and balls and such things.' There was scorn in his voice. 'He will be her pensioner, dependent upon her. Better that he be poor and lonely.'

'But if he loves her?' Her voice broke, and she pressed the heel of her hand to one eye, then the other.

'He does not love her. I'm sure of it. She amuses him and shocks him . . . but that will wear off quickly, and then it'll be too late. He'll be bound to her his whole life, and deeply unhappy.'

'I cannot bear it!'

'Do you still love him?' His words were quiet, but hard with determination. She nodded.

'Then you must fight for him.'

Her hands rose and fell. 'It's not so simple.'

'Yes, it is. Anything worth having is worth fighting for.'

She was silent. He waited, his hands gripped together behind his back, scowling at the lake. 'You don't think it's too late?' she asked at last.

'It might be. I don't know. I think he loved you truly. But he is hurt and angry. I don't know what went wrong between you, but it cut him to the quick.'

'I'm sorry.'

He passed her his handkerchief, and she turned away to wipe her eyes and blow her nose, hoping that no one on the hill was observing them too closely.

'I don't know how,' she said to Jakob.

Unexpectedly, he smiled. 'I'm afraid I cannot help you. I know nothing about the affairs of the heart. But it seems to me that if you were able to make him love you once, then surely you can do so again.'

She shook her head. 'He hasn't forgiven me.'

Jakob looked grave. 'Have you asked him to?'

Berthe came running across the grass towards them, holding up her arms so Dortchen would pick her up. Jakob bowed his head, then went to show the boys how to skip pebbles across the water. Dortchen went down to the water, pretending to wash Berthe's grubby hands but in fact giving herself time to compose herself before she returned to the party of friends sitting under the tree.

Wilhelm and Fraülein von Schwertzell returned ten minutes later. She was limping, and leaning heavily on his arm. She had twisted her ankle at the Devil's Bridge, he explained. Everyone looked knowing. Fraülein von Schwertzell looked smug.

That night, Dortchen sat on her bed, so weighed down with misery that she felt all her bones had been filled with lead. She did not know what to do. She opened the book of fairy tales and read again the tale of the singing, springing lark. She remembered how he had kissed her after she had told it. They had come so close to consummating their love there and then, up against the stable wall.

She laid down the crushed linden leaf to mark the page, then got into bed. It took a long time for Dortchen to sleep. When at last oblivion claimed her, she dreamt her father lay on her, weighing her down, panting in her ear. She could smell his foetid breath. She woke with a strangled cry, then wept hopelessly. She would never be free of him.

Dawn came at last. She rose, dressed and went down to breakfast. Herr Schmerfeld was reading the newspaper.

'Excuse me, sir, would you be able to spare me for a few days? Mia has written, asking me to visit her and help her with the baby.'

'Of course,' he answered, laying down his paper. 'I'll order the carriage brought round to you. You'll take Berthe, of course.'

Dortchen took a deep breath. 'There's no need. Ottilie can help look after her. She's old enough now to be trusted.'

Herr Schmerfeld was surprised but nodded in agreement. 'Of course. It'll do her good to have some responsibility.'

An hour later, Dortchen's carriage clip-clopped down the road. As it turned onto Wilhelmshöhe Alley, the carriage passed Fraülein von Schwertzell and Wilhelm, sitting close together in an open landau pulled by two beautiful grey horses. Wilhelm was laughing, and Fraülein von Schwertzell was pulling a ludicrous face. Fraülein von Schwertzell, Dortchen had discovered, was a gifted mimic who felt no shyness in mocking those of her acquaintance.

Dortchen sat back and pulled down the little leather curtain.

BY THE LIGHT OF THE NEW MOON

June 1824

Mia lived in a small half-timbered house surrounded by a profusion of flowers in the hamlet of Ziegenhain. Built on the River Schwalm in a dip between two low forested mountains, the village had an old church and a pretty fortified castle with a moat, and was surrounded by kilometres of thick beech forest.

Even though it was dark when the carriage at last trundled up outside the front gate, Dortchen could smell roses and mignonette and evening-scented stock. Golden lantern-light glowed through the mullioned windows. She climbed down wearily.

'Dortchen!' Mia opened the door, surprise and pleasure written all over her round face. 'Whatever are you doing here?'

'I've come to stay a few nights. You said the baby was unsettled. I thought I'd come and help.'

'Well, you are welcome.' Mia embraced her, then looked into the carriage. 'But where is Berthe?'

'I've left her at home. Ottilie has been set to watch her.'

'And a very good idea too. Come in, you must be half-rattled to death.'

'The roads have certainly not improved,' Dortchen said, following her sister inside. She looked around the narrow hall, with its red-brick floor and heavy oaken rafters. The whitewashed walls between the crooked supporting beams were decorated with vivid oils of flowers and trees, painted by Mia herself.

'Come into the parlour.' Mia opened a low door and stood back to let Dortchen pass by.

It was a small room with a low ceiling, but cosy and warm, with a fire glowing in the hearth. A tabby cat purred on a cushion, and big jugs of flowers were set on the mantelpiece and table. It was just the sort of room that Dortchen had always imagined for herself and Wilhelm. She had to breathe deeply to stop her misery from overwhelming her.

Mia's husband, Herr Robert, sat at the table, glueing together a model ship, while Old Marie was sitting in a rocking chair, knitting. Aged in her late seventies, her face was as wrinkled as a winter apple. Her hair under the lace cap was white, and her eyes were clouded. A cradle sat beside her.

'Dortchen, welcome,' Herr Robert cried, in a strong English accent. 'What a lovely surprise.'

'I do hope you don't mind. I . . . I needed a break.'

'Of course we don't mind. Those children must run you ragged. Come in and sit down.'

First, Dortchen went to greet Old Marie, bending over the old lady, who put up two frail hands to pat her back. 'It's lovely to see you, Marie.'

'And you, my sweetling.' As Dortchen straightened, Old Marie put both hands on her cheeks so she could examine her face closely. Evidently, she did not like what she saw, for she frowned and squeezed Dortchen's cheeks. 'It's good you've come to stay with us. You need some fresh country air and some good country cooking, by the looks of you.'

'It's such a lovely surprise,' Mia said. 'I expected you to send me the recipe for your colic tonic, not come all this way.'

'I wanted to see my new little niece,' Dortchen said, bending over the cradle in the corner to drop a gentle kiss on the soft little face of Mia's baby, turned into her pillow in sleep. 'They grow up so fast, and I do love them when they're so tiny and sweet.'

'She's not so sweet when she's awake,' Mia said.

'Screams all the time,' Old Marie confirmed. 'A fine set of lungs, she has, for such a little mite.'

'I've brought the ingredients for my colic tincture.' Dortchen indicated her basket, which she had put down on the table. 'I'll make up some for her before I go to bed.'

'What do you put in it?' Old Marie asked in lively interest. 'I've tried fennel tea and chamomile tea, for both mother and child, and nothing seems to work.'

'I use both of those, plus some ginger and lemon balm and blackthorn.'

'Ah.' Old Marie committed the ingredients to memory. 'Lemon balm, of course. I'll come and watch you make it, so I know how much of everything I need.'

She began painfully to lift herself out of her chair, but Mia soothed her, saying, 'Sit, be still. We'll have some tea first and hear all Dortchen's news.'

She bustled out to fetch the tea, and Dortchen sat wearily by the fire. Old Marie rocked and knitted and watched her with a small frown between her eyes. They drank tea and exchanged news. Dortchen let her sister do most of the talking. Soon the baby woke and began to scream. Mia rushed to pick her up, and Dortchen found the strength to get up, go to the kitchen and set the water to boil on the fire. Old Marie limped after her, leaning heavily on an old polished stick.

It was warm and shadowy in the kitchen, and Dortchen breathed in the familiar scent of herbs hung up to dry above the mantelpiece. Old Marie came to help her unpack her basket, and they worked side by side, just as they had done when Dortchen was a girl. The old woman peppered her with questions about the Schmerfeld children and their father, and Rudolf and his new wife.

'And how is Lotte?' Old Marie asked, as Dortchen measured out spoonfuls of ground ginger.

'She is married, as you know, and big with child.'

'I never thought she'd marry that Louis Hassenpflug.' Old Marie sniffed.

'She seems happy.'

'And what of you, sweetling? Are you happy?' Old Marie took Dortchen's hand, peering at her face anxiously.

Dortchen could not lie any longer. Not to Old Marie. She shook her head. 'No. No, I'm not.' Tears burnt her eyes.

'But why, sweetling? Tell me.'

Dortchen sat down and hid her face in her arms. She felt Old Marie lower herself into the chair beside her and pat her shoulder. The tears came pouring out, and, brokenly, so did words.

She told Old Marie everything. How her father had mistreated her, and how hard she had tried to forget. How she had watched Gretchen die and promised her to watch over her little girl. How Wilhelm had wanted to marry her, and how she had asked him to wait. How she felt as if she was standing still, frozen, unable to move onward, while the rest of the world left her behind. How she was afraid Wilhelm had forgotten her. And she told Old Marie about the nightmares.

All of this Dortchen said into the dark hollow of her arms, unable to lift her eyes and see Old Marie's expression. The old woman was uncharacteristically silent. Was she repulsed by Dortchen's tale? Did she blame Dortchen for being so weak?

At last Dortchen sat up. Old Marie dried her eyes with the corner of her apron.

'My poor sweetling. Men can be beasts. I always feared for you in that house. But I could not think my fears had any grounding. Your father was such a godly man. Always going to church. It just goes to tell.'

Dortchen sighed.

'But not all men are beasts, you know,' Old Marie went on. 'There are good, kind men, just as there are bad men. I always thought Wilhelm Grimm was a good man.'

'He is.'

'Then why are you afraid of him?'

'I don't know.'

The baby's screams could be heard echoing down the hall. Old Marie began to measure out the dried leaves and flowers, looking to Dortchen for guidance. Mechanically, Dortchen helped her.

'Is it fear of the heart, or of the body?' Old Marie asked at last.

'Both, I think,' Dortchen admitted.

'You can't protect your heart from hurt – that's part of living,' Old Marie said. 'No matter how hard you try to guard against it, something will slip past and make you love it.'

Dortchen nodded. She had discovered this for herself.

'And the love between a man and a wife is a beautiful thing, Dortchen. I'd be sorry if you were never to know that.'

They worked together in silence a while longer.

'I want to trust him,' Dortchen said. 'I want to love him. But every time I decide to risk myself, something happens to stop me. He . . . Father . . . comes to me again in a dream, or a flash of memory . . . It's like he's there in the room with me, holding me back.'

'It feels to me like you're being haunted,' Old Marie said decisively. 'Whether it's his spirit not willing to let you go, or just the memory of him, I can't tell. But you need to banish him. Tell him to begone.'

'I wish it were that easy.' Dortchen managed a smile.

'It's times like this I wish my grandmam was still here with us,' Old Marie said. 'She knew many an old trick for driving away haunts. I will think on it. But don't you fret, now. There'll be a way to drive that old nasty away, don't you worry.'

Very late on the night of the next new moon, Dortchen went by herself through the dark sleeping streets of Cassel to the graveyard in which her parents were buried. First, she took a handful of dirt from her father's grave and put it in a small wooden box. Then she went to the elder tree that grew nearby and broke off a flowering twig. 'Thank you, Lady Tree,' she said, bobbing a little curtsey, as Old Marie had warned her always to do.

Dortchen then walked out of town, towards the royal palace. It was frightening, being out alone so late. She was wearing a black dress and a black hooded cloak, which she wore drawn down over her face so that no one might recognise her. The moon was so thin that the stars seemed very bright. Bats flittered past, and somewhere an owl hooted.

She reached the last crossroads before the forest. One road ran back towards the town, the other towards the palace, and the road that crossed it led into the forest on one side and the open countryside on the other.

Dortchen took the elder branch out of her pocket. Breaking it into four pieces, she chanted the spell Old Marie had taught her: '*Break the root, break the hex, break me free from this evil vex.*' She then cast one part of the twig in each of the four directions. Only then did she take out the box of grave dirt. She threw the soil as hard as she could over her left shoulder, shouting, 'Begone!'

The dirt scattered in the wind and was blown away.

Without looking back over her shoulder, Dortchen walked rapidly home again. She let herself in with her key and ran lightly up the stairs to her room. She pulled back the curtains and opened wide the casements, letting in the soft evening air and the faint light of the moon. She breathed in deeply, then lit her fire and set a silver basin of water to warm before it. Into the water she dropped a handful each of speedwell, eyebright, self-heal, lemon balm, chase-devil, toadflax and foxglove. A sweet smell filled her room. She kindled two white candles and set them on the mantelpiece, one on either side of the mirror.

Then Dortchen stripped off her clothes in front of the flames, and let down her hair till it hung in flaxen waves down her bare back. She stood and looked at her face in the mirror, then, with shaking hands, she read out the second spell Old Marie had told her.

'*He that cast his curse on me*
Let him suffer his own curse.
Let these candles be his candles.
Let this burning be his burning.
Let the pain he caused me
Fall upon him instead.'

Then, slowly and thoroughly, Dortchen washed herself with the herb-sweet water, not missing a single inch of her skin. Between her toes, under her arms, behind her ears and up between her legs. Dortchen took her time, imagining herself washed clean inside as well as out. She dressed herself in a white nightgown, then she flung the water out the window and into the garden. She climbed into bed, made up earlier that evening with fresh white sheets, and watched the two candles burn themselves out. By the time the flames were guttering, Dortchen was asleep.

She slept dreamlessly all night, and woke in the fresh, bright dawn feeling like a woman reborn.

CORNFLOWERS

June 1824

Dortchen opened the chest in the garret of the shop that was now Rudolf's.

Her hands were dusty, and she rubbed them clean on her handkerchief before kneeling and rummaging through the chest. She found her doll, Wilhelmina, which Wilhelm had lowered to her from the window on a string. She had always hoped to have a daughter of her own one day, to whom she could give the doll. She put it aside and dug deeper. She found her old prayer book and opened it to find the squashed brown cornflower that she had hidden there so many years before. There was only the faintest trace of blue left in its dried petals. Dortchen hid it in her bodice. A cornflower worn next to the heart brought love, Old Marie had always said. New love or lost love. Dortchen could only hope it was true.

Then Dortchen searched right at the very bottom of the chest, till she found the yellow silk dress her father had once given her. Carefully, she folded it and wrapped it in brown paper and twine.

Then she drove through the narrow, crooked streets, which were cool even in the heat of the summer day, until she reached the premises of Madame Fleury, the most fashionable dressmaker in town.

'It is of the silk most luxurious, it's true,' Madame Fleury said, as she examined the dress. 'And the beading is exquisite. It is, however, very much out of fashion.'

'I thought that a seamstress of great skill would be able to remodel the dress,' Dortchen said. 'Drop the waist, add some flounces.'

Madame Fleury stroked the silk. 'Perhaps.'

'I'd be willing to sell it to you and put the money towards another dress,' Dortchen said. She drew out her purse, heavy with the money she had saved from her allowance. 'I need it quickly, though.'

'When?'

'For a pleasure cruise this Saturday night,' Dortchen said.

'Do you have a colour in mind, a style?'

'Cornflower blue,' Dortchen said.

As she stood before the mirror a few days later, Dortchen had to admit that Madame Fleury had worked a miracle. The dress was the most beautiful she had ever seen.

Made of pale-blue silk, with a low-cut square bodice and a cone-shaped skirt, it was embroidered with stylised cornflowers about the bodice and hem. The short sleeves were extravagantly puffed and ruffled. The dress made Dortchen's eyes seem very blue.

She made sure the dried flower was safely nestled in her bodice, then carefully pinned a small bunch of cornflowers at her breast. Only then did she go to join Herr Schmerfeld downstairs. He rose at the sight of her. 'You look beautiful,' he said. She thanked him, and they walked out to the carriage together. As they rode towards the river, he cleared his throat and said, 'Dortchen, you know that my regard for you has not wavered. If you should ever wish it, I—'

She shook her head. 'I'm sorry. I cannot.'

He regarded her closely. 'There is someone else?'

She nodded.

'Then I wish the both of you the very best.' He turned and looked out the window.

The steamboat that the von Schwertzells had hired for the river cruise was long and white, and hung with coloured paper lanterns from bow to stern. Already it was crowded with people. A quartet of musicians played on a small stage at one end of the deck, while waiters circulated with glasses of champagne. Dortchen accepted one and took a curious sip. She had never tasted champagne before.

Fraülein von Schwertzell was easy to spot, since she was wearing an extraordinary gown of orange stripes, with enormous puffed sleeves. Dortchen thought she looked rather like a bumblebee. Wilhelm stood beside her, elegant and austere in black, but with a snowy-white cravat and waistcoat. Dortchen took a deep breath, gathered up all her courage and walked to him. She said his name softly, and he turned.

His face stiffened, his pupils dilating. He did not say a word, but he could not take his eyes from her. Dortchen heard his breath shorten.

She smiled. 'What a beautiful evening it is. Do you know, I have lived in Cassel all my life and never sailed on the river before. I am looking forward to it.'

He stammered something.

Fraülein von Schwertzell turned. Her smile died on her lips. She looked Dortchen up and down, noting every detail of her dress. Dortchen smiled at her. The consternation on the other woman's face gave Dortchen a jolt of fresh courage.

They said all that was polite, while Wilhelm continued to stare at Dortchen. He did not notice when Fraülein von Schwertzell pressed close to his side, taking his arm in a proprietary manner.

Dortchen said to him, 'Do you like my new dress? It reminds me of that day you told me about Novalis and the blue flower. Do you remember? In the garden.'

'Of course. You were cutting cornflowers. We had tea in the summer house.'

'I've been reading Novalis lately. I always loved what you told me about him. How we should try to see the ordinary as extraordinary.'

'Gracious, what a serious topic for a summer's evening,' Fraülein von Schwertzell interrupted.

'"To see the ordinary as extraordinary, the familiar as strange, the mundane as sacred, the finite as infinite,"' Wilhelm quoted.

'Yes, that's it.' Dortchen took another deep breath. It was very hard to speak in this way to Wilhelm with Fraülein von Schwertzell hanging on to his arm, but there was no other way. 'My favourite quote, though, is the one you told me the day my father died. You said that love was the "Amen" of the universe. Do you remember?'

'A long time ago now,' he answered coolly.

She nodded. 'Yes. Far too long.'

Fraülein von Schwertzell looked from one to the other, her eyes narrowing. 'Wilhelm, I love this song! Let's dance.'

He bowed and offered her his arm, and they moved towards the dance floor. Dortchen watched them go, her heart sinking. Then Wilhelm turned and looked at her. She smiled. Involuntarily, he smiled back.

Dortchen felt a little bubble of warmth inside her. She moved away to join Herr Schmerfeld and some other friends. She was merry and light-hearted, making them all laugh. When Herr Schmerfeld asked her to dance, she rested her white-gloved hand on his arm and let him lead her to the dance floor. She could not help her heart accelerating as he put his arm about her, but she breathed deeply and forced herself to relax, and soon her twinge of uneasiness had passed. *It'll take time*, she told herself. *I can't expect never to be afraid again.*

Old Marie had warned her that she could not expect the charm to work completely; she might have to repeat it a few times. Perhaps many times. Dortchen was prepared to do it as many times as was needed.

Later, she danced with Wilhelm. Once again, she found it hard to breathe, her heart racing in her chest. It was not fear that caused it to pound so, however, but longing and desire and hope. His arm was strong about her back, and she could feel the imprint of his hand on her waist, burning through the thin layers of silk. If she looked up, if she raised herself on her toes ever so slightly, his mouth would be only a breath away from hers. She concentrated instead on the buttons of his coat.

They did not speak at all, but when the music came to an end, Wilhelm released her reluctantly. She looked up at him.

His eyes were fixed on her face. 'You can dance now, without fear?' he asked.

She nodded. 'I . . . I am trying to learn how to be brave.'

His lips flexed and she knew he wanted to kiss her. God only knew, Dortchen wanted him to. They stared at each other till the scrape of the bow over the violin made them realise they were standing still in the centre of the dance floor. Without speaking, Wilhelm held out his hand and she put hers into it. They began to dance again.

'I need to tell you how sorry I am,' she said to his shirtfront. 'I never meant to hurt you. I cannot explain—'

'You don't need to explain,' he said. 'I understand. I mean, I tried to understand.'

'I . . . Wilhelm, please forgive me. I don't know . . . I don't know if you can ever love me again. The way you used to. It's been so long, and so much has happened, and I . . .' For a little while she couldn't speak. 'I just want you to know that I have never changed,' she managed at last. 'I have loved you for as long as I have known you, and I think I always will. I . . . I want you to be happy. Even if you marry that horrible woman!'

The last words were unplanned and came out in a rush. He repressed a little smile and drew her closer. They danced on in silence.

At last, he bent his head and whispered, 'Dortchen, I don't know what to say. I've tried and tried to dig you out of my heart. But just the sight of you is enough to stir me to the very depths of my being. You shake it all up, everything I determine to do, and turn it all topsy-turvy. I hate you for the power you have over me.'

'I hate you too. For all the same reasons. If I didn't love you so much, I'd marry Herr Schmerfeld and have a very comfortable life, thank you very much!' This was not going as she had planned.

He laughed. 'Dortchen,' he whispered.

She raised her face and looked him in the eyes, and everything else faded away. He drew her so close that there was not a finger's breadth of space between them from thigh to breast. She could feel that he desired her. She leant closer, loving the way his breath shortened and his pupils flared.

'I don't think you'll marry that horrible woman,' she said.

He quirked his mouth ruefully. 'But I could have such a comfortable life,' he complained.

She smiled and pressed even closer. He twirled her about. 'Little witch.'

They could not dance again without causing a scandal, and much offence to their hostess, so when the music finished Wilhelm bowed and left her. Dortchen went to stand at the rail. Her cheeks were hot and her body thrummed. She drank some more champagne. The boat glided along the dark water, reflections of the coloured lights dancing on the ripples. It passed under the arched bridge, and away from the town. The stars were bright overhead, the trees black against the luminous sky.

Wilhelm found her there some time later, looking up at the sky. 'The music sounds beautiful on the river, doesn't it?' he said.

'Yes. Somehow so much more ethereal.'

'Have I told you that we are moving house again? Jakob insists we must have a larger place. He has found us the most beautiful apartment near Bellevue Palace, overlooking the park and the river. I'll be living near you again.'

'I'm so glad. I know you hated living above the blacksmith.'

'It was so noisy and smoky and hot. On Bellevuestrasse, I'll hear nothing but birdsong.'

'Will it not be very expensive?'

He nodded. 'Yes, but the fairy tale book has begun to do much better. They brought out an English translation, you know, beautifully illustrated, with stories picked just for children. It has been a surprise bestseller. We earned nothing from it, of course, but it has attracted a lot of attention to us, and some new sales of our edition.'

'I wish that you would bring out a children's edition here,' Dortchen said. 'With beautiful pictures that the little ones can look at. I read to Berthe and Friedrich every night from the book you gave me, but some of the stories are not really suitable for them, and they get cross when I won't read a tale to them. And Friedrich, in particular, loves a book to be illustrated.'

'I have been thinking of doing a small edition,' Wilhelm said slowly.

He put up his hand and touched her wrist. 'Dortchen, would you help me choose what stories should go in it? You'd know better than I what tales little children would love.'

'Well, that's easy. "Hänsel and Gretel", and "Aschenputtel", and "Little Snow-White", and "Little Thorn-Rose", and "The Frog-King", and "Rumpelstiltskin", and . . .'

'Wilhelm!' an imperious voice called. 'I want you! Come and be introduced to the Baron von Berlepsch.'

Wilhelm was annoyed to be interrupted, Dortchen could tell. She smiled at him. 'Perhaps I could come and have supper at your new apartment. We can look at the book, and I'll tell you which are the ones the children love the most.'

'I'd like that. When can you come?'

'Just as soon as you want me,' she answered.

He bowed and turned to go. She put her hand on his wrist, stopping him. When he turned back to her, she offered him a cornflower from her bouquet. 'A bachelor's button,' she whispered.

He kissed it and put it in his buttonhole, before going to Fräulein von Schwertzell's side. Their hostess was not at all happy. Wilhelm did not seem to care. His gaze returned to Dortchen many times. She hid her smile and turned away, not wanting anyone to see her glowing face.

EPILOGUE

The True Bride

CASSEL

The German Confederation of Nations, December 1824

When she began her song, and it reached Roland's ears, he jumped up and shouted, 'I know that voice. That is the true bride. I do not want anyone else.' Everything he had forgotten, and which had vanished from his mind, had suddenly come home again to his heart.

From 'Sweetheart Roland', a tale told by Dortchen Wild to Wilhelm Grimm on 19th January 1812

'It is ten years today since my father died,' Dortchen said, basting the goose on the roasting spit.

It was Christmas Day, and she was standing in the kitchen of the Grimm brothers' apartment on the Bellevuestrasse, an apron tied over her red striped dress. Wilhelm was in his shirtsleeves, mixing wine and brandy and spices together for mulled wine. It was a lovely room, with a high, arched ceiling and windows that looked out over the low blue hills in the far distance.

'It seems impossible to believe,' he said, taking a quick sip, then adding more cinnamon and honey. He lifted the spoon for Dortchen to taste, then kissed the flavour from her lips.

'So many wasted years.' She could not help feeling a little melancholy.

'Not wasted.' He put his arms about her, pressing his lips to the back of her neck. 'You looked after Gretchen's children for her, and fulfilled your promise to her. And I wrote some beautiful books. Perhaps I wouldn't have spent so much time working and writing if you had married me when I wanted you to.'

She sighed. It had been six months since they had found their way back to each other, and in that time both had been gentle and wary, afraid of hurting and being hurt again.

'I have a gift for you.' He led her out of the kitchen and into the drawing room, where the resinous scent of a small Christmas tree filled the air.

'But it's not time for gift-giving yet.'

'I want to give it to you before the hordes arrive.' He bent and retrieved a small paper-wrapped present from under the tree and pressed it into her hands.

Dortchen sat and looked up at him in curious anticipation, then laughed and ripped open the paper. Inside was a small leather-bound book. She lifted the cover and read the title page: '*Kindermärchen*'. Tales for children. Eagerly, she looked through it. There were all her favourite tales, beautifully illustrated by Ludwig.

'Oh, it's a treasure,' she cried, jumping up to embrace Wilhelm. He hugged her close.

'They have done a print run of one thousand five hundred copies, almost twice as many as the first edition,' he said, 'and our publisher has already received so many orders he thinks we'll need to reprint soon.'

'That is such wonderful news! At last.' She flung her arms about his neck and he kissed her passionately. Then they heard the key in the lock. Wilhelm and Dortchen broke apart guiltily as Jakob and Ludwig came in, each carrying a heavy load of firewood. They dumped them down by the fire, then shook the snow off their hats and unwound their scarves. She went and put the book in her basket, while the brothers greeted each other cheerfully.

Wilhelm came and caught her hand, saying in a low voice, 'Dortchen, can you leave the goose for a while? I want to walk in the woods with you, before everyone gets here. It's a beautiful evening.'

'It'll be another few hours before the goose will be ready,' she answered. 'I'd love to.'

Both wrapped up warmly, for the snow was thick on the ground outside and twilight was closing in. Outside, the sky was the colour of pale-blue glass, with one star hanging over the distant hills. Dortchen turned to the left, thinking they would walk in Karlsaue Park, but Wilhelm seized her hand and pulled her to the right.

'Where are we going?' she asked.

'I thought we'd go to the Schlosspark,' he said. He hailed a carriage and lifted her into it, then climbed in himself, smiling at her surprised face. As the carriage jerked forward, she lurched into his arms. He drew her even closer and lowered his mouth to hers. By the time they reached the Schlosspark, Dortchen's hair was half unpinned and she had to button up her bodice again.

'I wish that drive was twice as long,' Wilhelm said, straightening his cravat.

Hand in hand, they ran along the frozen lake. The palace glowed with light on the hill above them. Dortchen could hear violin music and distant laughter. She knew where they were going. Laughing, she led the way past the briar hedge and into the linden grove. She spun and held out her hands. Wilhelm bowed, then took her in his arms. They waltzed about, knocking snow from the branches in a freezing shower. Their dance slowed as he drew her closer, lifting her face so he could kiss her.

'Dortchen Wild, will you marry me?' he asked.

Her pulse leapt, and her breath shortened. 'Wilhelm Grimm, I shall,' she answered. 'With all my heart.'

Their kiss was full of sweetness.

'We must marry as soon as we can,' he said, when at last he lifted his mouth away from hers. 'I don't want to wait any longer. It's been far too long already.'

'Tomorrow?' she laughed.

'I will need to ask the Kurfürst for permission,' he said. 'But I'm sure there'll be no difficulty.'

'Perhaps in the spring, so we can marry in the garden,' she said. 'Wilhelm, my brother has told me that he will give me a dowry. His shop is doing so well now, and Herr Schmerfeld has given him such good investment advice that Rudolf feels he can afford to look after me.'

'That is good news!' He hesitated. 'Dortchen, once you said that you would not mind if we still lived with Jakob once we were married. Do you still feel that way?'

'Of course,' she said firmly. 'Ludwig too, if he wants. I'll keep house for you all.'

He kissed her fervently. His nose was cold but his lips were warm and flavoured with honey and cinnamon. 'We'll have babies of our own,' he said. 'I know how much you love babies.'

'A little boy that looks just like you.'

'A little girl with your beautiful blue eyes.'

'We'll love them and look after them, and never, ever hurt them.'

'Never,' he promised her.

'I was afraid this day would never come,' she whispered.

He cupped her face in his hands. 'I told you love works magic.'

AFTERWORD

I first read about Dortchen Wild in Valerie Paradiž's wonderful book *Clever Maids: The Secret History of the Grimm Fairy Tales*. Until I read this book, I had always thought, like most people, that the Grimm brothers travelled about Germany collecting their tales from old peasants. It was a revelation to know that more than half of the tales were actually contributed by educated, middle-class young ladies of their acquaintance. I was also enchanted to know that Wilhelm had married one of the key storytellers, the girl who had grown up next door to him.

Millions of words have been written by, or about, the Grimm brothers. Thanks to their own letters and diaries, and the writings of people who knew them, we know what they wore, ate, read and thought on nearly every day of their lives.

Dortchen Wild, however, was virtually silent. Few of her writings remain: a childhood memoir she dictated to her daughter when she was an old lady, and a few letters, including one she wrote to Lotte when she was twelve confessing her crush on Lotte's handsome elder brother Wilhelm. Otherwise, all I had to help me imagine her life were her stories.

This one young woman told the Grimm brothers almost a quarter of all the tales in their first collection of fairy stories, when she was just nineteen years old. Stories told to Wilhelm by Dortchen include 'Rumpelstiltskin',

'Hänsel and Gretel', 'The Frog-King', 'Six Swans', 'The Elves and the Shoemaker', 'Sweetheart Roland' (about a girl whose betrothed forgets her) and 'The Singing Bone' (about a murdered boy whose bones are used to make a mouthpiece for a flute that then sings to accuse his murderers). She also told a very gruesome version of 'Bluebeard' called 'Fitcher's Bird', the primary difference being that the heroine saves herself and her sisters, and a very beautiful version of 'Beauty and the Beast' called 'The Singing, Springing Lark'. A key tale of hers was 'All-Kinds-of-Fur', about a princess whose father wants to marry her.

While researching Dortchen's stories, I read a study by a psychologist about the therapeutic use of fairy tales to help victims of abuse. The psychologist had noticed the key differences between the first version of 'All-Kinds-of-Fur', which was written down by Wilhelm Grimm and rushed to the printers in October 1812, and the later, edited version of the story, published in the 1819 edition. Victims of abuse who read the 1812 version always identified strongly with the girl in that tale, and thought that the king she married in the end was in fact her father. The later version very carefully made it clear that the father-king and the bridegroom-king were different men. The first story was identified as a tale of incest fulfilled. The second was a tale of incest diverted.

Later, I read a book by the eminent fairy tale scholar Jack Zipes in which he speculated that the reason Wilhelm Grimm changed that particular story, and other incest tales in the collection such as 'The Maiden With No Hands', was that he himself had been abused as a child. But why, then, would he have included them in the first place, I wondered. It occurred to me that perhaps it was Dortchen, his future wife, who had been abused, and that Wilhelm, once he realised this, had changed the story as a kind of gift to her. He certainly included a veiled reference to her as a 'Wild deer' in the final version of 'All-Kinds-of-Fur'.

Speculating about the possibility of this hidden aspect of Dortchen's life helped me find a potential solution to a few other problems that had been puzzling me – primarily the long gap between the beginning of her romance with Wilhelm, in 1812, and their eventual marriage, in May 1825. By then, he was thirty-nine and she was almost thirty-two. It's known that Herr Wild did not like the Grimm brothers, and had declared that Dortchen would be the one to stay home and care for him and his wife till their deaths. However, he died in 1815, and Wilhelm and Dortchen were not married for another ten years.

Of course, Wilhelm, Dortchen and their families had to struggle against their poverty and the hardships caused by the end of the Napoleonic Wars, which were followed by famine and widespread political turmoil. Dortchen was also busy caring for her nieces and nephews after her sister Gretchen's death, at a time when such family duty was widely expected. However, many other impoverished lovers managed to marry and be happy, despite the times, including Dortchen's own sisters.

Many scholars think that Wilhelm was a confirmed bachelor, happy in his quiet life of scholarship with Jakob. Wilhelm's diaries are filled with yearning, however. In September 1819, for example, he wrote: 'I read aloud to Auguste Canitz [Herr Schmerfeld's sister]. While I was reading Dortchen came and put a flower that she had been wearing on her bosom on the book. Perhaps that was by mistake.'

I wondered what else might have kept them apart, and speculated that if Dortchen had indeed suffered abuse at the hands of her father, she may have had difficulty in trusting again. And so I built this novel by listening to the story within the stories that Dortchen told.

In his autobiography, Wilhelm later wrote: 'I have never ceased to thank God for the blessing and happiness of this marriage. I had known my wife ever since she was a child, and my mother loved her like one of her own, without ever guessing that one day she would be.'

SOURCES OF THE GRIMMS' STORIES

The Grimm brothers never formally acknowledged the tellers of the fairy tales they collected for their first volume of *Kinder-und-Hausmärchen*, generally saying only 'a story from Hesse' or 'a tale from the Main River', and so on.

However, Wilhelm did scribble notes in the margins of his copy of the first edition of the tales. Sometimes, it was simply a name: Dortchen; Gretchen; Marie; Frederike. More rarely, it included a date and the place in which he had heard the tale. For example, this is how we know that Dortchen Wild told him three extraordinary tales – 'The Singing Bone', 'Six Swans' and 'Sweetheart Roland' – on 19th January 1812, in her sister Hanne's summer house in Nentershausen (which was fifty-four kilometres from Cassel, and would have been a day's journey for Wilhelm in a hired carriage, along terrible roads).

For many years, it was believed that the 'Marie' who told Wilhelm some of the most famous and beautiful of the tales was the Wild family's housekeeper, Marie Müller, or 'Old Marie'. Marie lived with the Wilds up until 1812, the year of the publication of the first volume.

It was Herman Grimm, Wilhelm and Dortchen's son, who had helped identify Old Marie as a key source of stories. He wrote in 1895:

Dortchen also got her trove from another source. Above the Wilds' nursery in the apothecary building, with its many hallways, stairways, floors and rear additions, through all of which I poked through myself as a child, was the realm of 'Old Marie' . . . One feels immediately that Dortchen and Gretchen only recounted what had been impressed upon them by Old Marie.

Most early biographies of the Grimm brothers do not hesitate to credit Old Marie with telling such tales as 'Little Red Riding Hood', 'Sleeping Beauty', 'The Maiden With No Hands' and 'The Robber Bridegroom'.

However, in 1980, a German scholar called Heinz Rölleke reissued the 1857 edition of the *Kinder-und-Hausmärchen* – the final and definitive version – with a new appendix in which he listed all the contributors and their tales. He removed Marie Müller's name and replaced it with Marie Hassenpflug, Lotte Grimm's sister-in-law. Rölleke had examined the Grimm brothers' diaries and realised that, on many occasions, the brothers had been visiting the Hassenpflug household on the date on which those tales had been transcribed. Since the Hassenpflugs were of French descent, this also explained why so many of the stories told by the mysterious 'Marie' were versions of Charles Perrault's well-known French tales.

Most Grimm scholars now agree with Rölleke's conclusions, and Old Marie is no longer credited as a key storyteller. Indeed, some go so far as to say that she never existed at all, and was invented to allow the Grimms to pretend that they had collected stories from old peasant women instead of young, well-educated, middle-class ladies.

However, I am inclined to believe some, if not all, of Herman Grimm's recollections of what his mother had told him. Someone told Dortchen a great many stories, and it seems unlikely to have been her mother, who only contributed two tales to the collection, both of them short and rather silly.

So I have allowed Old Marie a place in this story, both as a warm and loving servant and as a teller of stories, spells and old superstitions. She tells Wilhelm two stories. The first, 'Little Snow-White', is now usually credited to Marie Hassenpflug. However, it is known that Jakob first sent a version of this tale to Karl von Savigny in 1808, a year before the Grimms met the Hassenpflugs. It is entirely possible, then, that it was Old Marie who told the tale.

The second, 'The Maiden With No Hands', is thought to have been told by Marie Hassenpflug on 10th March 1811. However, I have given this terrible, heartbreaking story to Old Marie to tell, primarily for dramatic reasons, but also because it does not have a French source and is unlike any other stories told by the young, elegant and well-brought-up Marie Hassenpflug. Rölleke himself has admitted that Old Marie may have been the source of some of the stories.

Another small liberty I have taken with known historical fact is allowing Dortchen to visit the Marburg storyteller in the poorhouse and transcribe two tales from her: 'Aschenputtel' and 'The Golden Bird'. It is not known who transcribed these tales, although it was said to have been done with the help of the warden's wife.

ACKNOWLEDGEMENTS

Writing *The Wild Girl* was intense, challenging and, at times, very difficult. The story worked its way into my dreams and gave me terrible nightmares. The opening scene with Dortchen dancing by herself in a snowy, twilit forest, with ravens flying over, was inspired by one of these dreams. Some of the darker scenes later in the book also came to me in my sleeping moments, and I had to force myself to write them as a form of exorcism, to rid myself of Dortchen's terrors.

Luckily for me, I have a very loving and supportive family, and they allowed me the space and time I needed to brood over this story and find its shape and rhythm. Particular thanks need to be said to my long-suffering husband, Greg, and my children, Ben, Tim and Ella, for letting me go to Germany on my own to research this book, and for many burnt offerings in the place of dinner. I also need to thank my sister, Belinda, who gave me many books on German history, helped me with my shaky attempts at translation and let me talk about the book at any given opportunity.

To my wonderful, tirelessly working agents – Tara Wynne at Curtis Brown Australia and Robert Kirby at United Agents in the UK – and to the fabulous team at Allison & Busby – Susie Dunlop, Lesley Crooks, Sara Magness, Chiara Priorelli and Sophie Robinson – I cannot thank you enough. Thank you also to Christina Griffiths, for designing the gorgeous cover.

Most of the excerpts from the tales told by Dortchen Wild to Wilhelm Grimm were translated from the German by me, so any mistakes are all mine. At all times, I tried to draw upon the earliest known versions of the tales – those recorded in the 1808, 1810 and 1812 manuscripts – since these were closest to the original oral source. I am also grateful to the excellent fairy tale website at the University of Pittsburgh, found at *www.pitt.edu/~dash/grimm.html* and run by the American folklorist and writer D.L. Ashliman, which contains many variants of the tales, including links to the German originals.

I also need to thank Dr Cay Dollerup, the Danish fairy tale scholar, who wrote the definitive research on 'Allerleirauh' or 'All-Kinds-of-Fur' in *A Case Study of Editorial Filters in Folktales: A Discussion of the 'Allerleirauh' Tales in Grimm*, which examined in great depth the first version of the tale, told by Dortchen Wild to Wilhelm Grimm on 19th October 1812, only a few days before the typesetting of the first volume of *Kinder-und-Hausmärchen*. He was also kind enough to answer numerous questions via email, as did Professor Jack Zipes and Professor Ruth B. Bottigheimer.

To write this book, I had to read many books and articles – and many, many fairy tales! I cannot list them all here but I must mention a few that were utterly invaluable to me: *Fairy Tales: A New History* by Ruth B. Bottigheimer; *Grimms' Bad Girls and Bold Boys: The Moral and Social Vision of the Tales* by Ruth B. Bottigheimer; *One Fairy Story Too Many: The Brothers Grimm and their Tales*, by John M. Ellis; *The Reception of Grimms' Fairy Tales: Responses, Reactions, Revisions*, edited by Donald Haase; *The Brothers Grimm: Two Lives, One Legacy* by Donald R. Hettinga; *The Brothers Grimm* by Ruth Michaelis-Jena; *The Owl, the Raven and the Dove: The Religious Meaning of the Grimms' Magic Fairy Tales* by G. Ronald Murphy; *The Brothers Grimm and Folktale*, edited by James M. McGlathery; *Clever Maids: The Secret History of the Grimm Fairy Tales*, by Valerie Paradiž; *Paths Through the Forest: A Biography of the Brothers Grimm*, by Murray B. Peppard; 'Why Not "Old Marie" . . . or Someone Very Much Like Her? A Reassessment of the Question about the Grimms' Contributors from a Social Historical Perspective' in *When Women Held the Dragon's Tongue and other Essays in Historical Anthropology* by Hermann Rebel; *Brüder Grimm Kinder-und-Hausmärchen: Die handschriftliche Urfassung von 1810* with commentary by Heinz Rölleke; *The Hard Facts of the Grimms' Fairy Tales* by Maria Tatar; *The Brothers Grimm: From Enchanted Forests to the Modern World* by Jack Zipes; and *Brothers Grimm: The Complete Fairy Tales*, translated and annotated by Jack Zipes.

Finally, I need to thank my German translator, Barbara Barkhausen, who helped me greatly with my research, and, last but definitely not least, Irmgard Peters – a direct descendant of Rudolf Wild – who translated Dortchen's memoir and Wilhelm's diaries for me, plus gave me many small details of family oral history passed down through the generations, including the fact that Rudolf had ginger whiskers.